AUTHOR'S NOTE

I wrote *Her Second Husband* for women my age (i.e. those over fifty) and for those who don't know they're beautiful. You are! Here's to staying young at heart, forever . . .

HER SECOND HUSBAND

An unputdownable psychological thriller
with a breathtaking twist

JANE E. JAMES

Joffe Books, London
www.joffebooks.com

First published in Great Britain in 2023

Cover art by Nick Castle

ISBN: 978-1-80405-919-7

THEN

Eyes as blue and warm as the water. Hair white as the froth on the incoming tide. A setting sun creates a soft golden halo around his handsome, movie-star face.

Except this man is no angel. Not with that devilish, teasing smile and those sharklike teeth. He's dressed in his trademark middle-aged, middle-class, creased ivory linen shirt and trousers, and his bare feet, pedicured to perfection, pause on the wet sand when he recognises my shadow approaching. Do I imagine it, or does his still-muscular, tanned chest, covered in a fine layer of silver hair, puff up like a silverback gorilla when he sees me? He has every right to look annoyed, but his surprise gives me an advantage I intend to use.

A calming hum of insects is in the air around us and further away in the distance towards the promenade the laughter of loved-up holidaymakers can be heard, clinking glasses of iced ouzo, and rolling pitted olives around in their mouths, red faces recovering from a day in the sun while being charmed by dark-haired, olive-skinned waiters who look like gods.

The smell of tobacco and something else . . . marijuana, I think, wafts over, curling itself around us. The smoke sticks to our clothes like sweat. But he acts all cool. Pulling a crumpled packet of cigars out of a back pocket he puts one to his mouth and lights it. Closing his lazily suggestive eyes, he inhales, absorbing its substance as if it were a woman's scent. This makes me hate him all over again. Marcus the lover. Marcus the womaniser. Marcus the liar.

His eyes are cloudy with drink, and he's unsteady on his feet — swaying as if to a slow dance, only this time there's no woman in his arms. His fingers tremble slightly as he inhales a second time, and I watch him gaze distractedly across at the Albanian coastline, sprinkled with darkened ruins in the distance. Tossing the lit cigar into the tremulous waters of the Ionian Sea, he swipes a hand across his stubbled face that's as scratchy as the sand beneath our feet. Like a battling gladiator with bloodshot, weary eyes, he waits.

We don't speak. Our eyes do the talking. He mocks me still, I can tell. Dares to goad me in that superior way of his. He doesn't take me seriously. Not yet. Doesn't believe I'm brave enough. He thinks I won't fight back. But I'm not the coward he takes me for.

Well, well, it's come to this, has it? he seems to say, grinning like the narcissist he is.

Your fault. All your fault, my eyes blaze.

When he unexpectedly loses his footing and puts out a hand to stop himself from falling into the water that swirls around his feet as it closes in on the shoreline, I watch his panicked eyes shoot sideways. Something inside me changes. *Now I have him,* I think. And to his credit, we both realise at that moment how vulnerable alcohol has made him, because for the first time I see a delicious hint of doubt in his eyes.

Neither of us wastes a second. As he lunges forward, intent on saving himself from the surging tidal wave that has appeared out of nowhere to wrap around his lower half, I push him in the chest and feel the palm of my hand connect with his still-strong-for-an-old-man ribcage. Once again, he stumbles, and the water rises higher above his chest as the seafloor disappears from under him. Arms flailing, he fights back at me and the clear dark blue water that until tonight

2

has been his friend, but in his drunken state he is slower than I. Fear is in his eyes as they lock with mine, for the last time. Guilt consumes me, but the desire to hurt him as he has hurt me is more powerful than anything. This man, who doesn't care about anything but his own happiness and to hell with anyone else, does not deserve my pity. On a good day — and this *isn't* a good day — I think even Marcus would agree with me.

We can sort this out like adults. There's no need for . . .

His darkened eyes, no longer twinkling but filled with shock and disbelief, plead for help. He's used to being easily forgiven. Men like him take so much for granted. But the hate he must see etched on my face doesn't give him any hope whatsoever.

Did you really think you'd get away with it? Without being punished? My eyes burn into his, letting him know that this time he doesn't get to win. This time, there is no forgiveness.

He's not as angry as I thought he would be, and I sense that he somehow always knew this day would come, that it was his destiny to suffer at the hands of someone who has every reason to hate him. He seems almost accepting of his situation. For someone who's able to get other people, women especially, to do as he wants, he doesn't try to argue his case. *What's wrong with him?* Instead, he nods solemnly as if giving me permission to do my worst. But that's not what I want. Nor how I imagined it. I'm the one in control. Not him. He doesn't get to tell me what to do. Now or ever.

If I hesitate, I'm not aware of it. While Marcus is still present and very much alive, I'm going over in my mind how I'll remember this moment in the future, knowing that it will be important when I'm lying awake years from now, torturing myself with the truth. If only I can make him go away, then I can make the pain stop. Hurt and humiliation are all I think about. It consumes me. Night and day.

Panic gets the better of him at last, and I realise the bravery was a bluff on his part. The bastard thought I wouldn't go through with it. I've never seen him look frightened before and the feeling of power this gives me over him is better than if I were to cut out his lying tongue with a knife, afterwards plunging the blade into his cold, uncaring heart.

But I don't have a knife, so I push him again, more forcibly, as if the first was just for practice. This time I use both hands against his chest. He goes down without a fight. *Is he that drunk?* I imagine I hear him chuckle, but I know that to be impossible. Even Marcus, with his passion for adventure and danger, is not that crazy. His smell, a heady mix of sex, sweat, cigar smoke and aftershave, mixes with saltwater and seaweed as he sinks beneath the strong current of the incoming tide. He comes up only once, eyes bulging, wet hair covering one eye, sucking in deep breaths but choking and spluttering on the water at the same time.

Closing my eyes — *I told him I never wanted to see him again, and I meant it* — I put a firm hand on his head and push harder as if I were a school bully giving a smaller, weaker kid a dunking in the swimming pool. The water, cold suddenly, is up to my own chest by now. *Should I be worried?* For one terrifying moment, I imagine Marcus taking me down with him. How apt, he would think, if that were to happen. But he's disappeared beneath the waves.

Just as I think it's over, that he's gone and can never hurt me or anyone else again, a hand reaches up through the water, palm splayed open, fingers clawing, a last cry for help. My heart is in my mouth as I watch. *Should I try to save him?* But then I see the glimpse of gold on his finger, and something inside me dies as I watch it twinkle in the dying rays of the sun.

When it's over . . . when the grasping hand with the band of gold on its ring finger has sunk beneath the froth of the waves and I can't see him anymore, I realise that the blood has been pumping through my veins so hard my heart is hammering louder than the sound of the ocean. Where he'd once stood towering over me, basking in his masculinity, the waves crash down, then fade away again, leaving nothing of him behind. Not a trace.

4

There are no spoils of the sea to suggest either one of us was ever here. So, I slink away, like one of the silent, furtive creatures that rush to escape the sea at night, and my guilty footsteps join their tracks in the sand as I make my escape.

CHAPTER 1

It's him. I'm sure of it. But it can't be. Can it? I mean, it looks like him, even if the picture is blurred, but I know this to be impossible. Either I'm mad or drunk, but knowing I'm neither, since it's only nine o'clock in the morning, I decide I must be hallucinating. Depression can do terrible things to a person, even one as ordinary as me. No-nonsense Linda, that's me, according to my family and friends — who I rarely see anything of these days. Not that I blame them. I mean, who wants to be around a lonely, menopausal woman with brain fog.

Dammit, if only the picture weren't so fuzzy. Then I'd know for sure.

After losing most of my life savings, I'm ashamed to admit I'm surviving on benefits for the first time in my life, and with only a zero-hour contract at the fish-and-chip shop across the road to top it up — the owner of which also happens to be the landlord of my grubby one-bedroom, first-floor flat — I'm not made of money. But I could kick myself for not splashing out on an upgrade to the premium-rate membership, because at least then I'd be able to see an unobstructed photograph of the man and get to read his full bio instead of the anonymous one-hundred-word intro that everyone's obliged to write when they sign up to *Welcome Back*, an online dating site for the over-fifties. Except, it isn't really a dating site, if you can believe the PR, more of an opportunity for *people like me* to reconnect with others.

The familiar words *Hallo, mooi vrou* had me choking on my buttered toast the minute I saw them, because it's a language I instantly recognised: Afrikaans. Marcus was born in British Columbia, moving to South Africa when he was eight, so of course it struck a chord with me. Returning to English, his opening statement continued — *My day lit up the moment I saw your profile. I feel as if I know you already. I bet, like me, you love the good things in life, cocktails on the beach and fine dining. I can see you now, with the sea breeze in your hair, gazing at a magnificent sunset. But what's a sunset without a beautiful woman like you?*

'Corny as hell,' my best friend Gail would've snorted, poking me with one elbow and suppressing a giggle, should she have come across this mystery man's intro, and I would've duly nudged her back and agreed while secretly thinking the words meant something. To me, at least. I might not be used to the good things in life, and I've never felt comfortable eating in fine-dining restaurants, but the words smack of Marcus all the same, which is why I can't get them out of my head.

Making up my mind to upgrade my account right this very minute so I can make a rational decision about the man in the photo — who may or may not be Marcus — I fetch my credit card from my bag, slip off my bulky, bobbled dressing gown so it falls onto the floor of the cramped windowless kitchen, and sit back down at the small table where my old, heavyweight laptop is open like a big unfriendly yawn.

I'm meant to be going to another of those awful women's self-help groups where everyone except me stands up and tells their story, but whoever decided ten in the morning was a suitable time to bare your soul should be shot. At that time of the day, I'm barely functioning. If it weren't for coming across the Marcus look-alike, I'd still be walking around with my eyes half shut. Although I'm not actively looking for a relationship — and I'm really not, unlike others who strenuously deny the same thing only to end up living with someone after five minutes of knowing them — I do log on too often sometimes.

I tell myself it's a harmless enough activity and helps pass the time, if nothing else. You've a lot of time on your hands when you're cut off from your loved ones like me.

All I want from *Welcome Back* is to connect with friends of a similar age. There's nothing wrong with wanting a bit of companionship, is there? And that doesn't mean having to meet up in person. Online is fine. Preferably, I'd like to get to know those who've been through a similar experience to me, but I suppose there's fat chance of that happening.

Unlike the mystery man, whose intro smacks of passion and adventure — *just like Marcus*, my profile, which took several attempts until I was happy with it, doesn't give much away:

My name is Linda. I'm fifty-seven years young, and I love animals, dogs especially. I enjoy travel, although I hate flying, but haven't done any of that in a while. I feel the cold a lot, so I'm definitely a warm-weather person. People say I look ten years younger than I am, but I don't feel it. Lol. I'm also quite shy, more of a listener than a talker.

Writing that intro proved difficult, as I'm a private person. Not one for airing my dirty laundry in public, unlike the youngsters today on social media. Oh, my lord, some of the things they say!

I assume that's why my profile hasn't attracted any messages . . . until now. But until I sign up to the premium-rate service, and I'm doing it as fast as I can — *Where are my bloody glasses?* — I won't be able to open the big green tick that tells me this man messaged at 2.05 a.m. this morning. He must be a night owl, again like Marcus, to be awake at that time, which I ponder as I wait for the link to be sent to my email address, the same one I've had for years: lindadelamere@ gmail.com. I never got around to getting an email address in my married name of Bouchard, which never suited me anyway. Marcus was much more glamorous than me, and he could carry it off, whereas I felt uncomfortable with it.

The link duly arrives in my inbox. I've never worked in an office or had a professional career, so I'm not a fast typist, more of a one-fat-finger puncher. Not sure if that's a real term for how oldies like me type, but it'll do, "does what it says on the tin" and all that, which is one of my favourite sayings. Along with "it is what it is." Age makes clichés out of all of us, I find, but not in a good way. As I click on the link to access my upgraded account my fingers nervously tremble as if I were a young girl on a first date. But first I must pretend to have an online chat with "Heavenly Helen", who talks me through how everything works.

'Piss off, Helen,' I hiss uncharitably. She's only trying to help. But as I wait, I wonder if she's actually called Helen or if she's a woman at all. She might be one of those bots you hear about. At last, Helen ditches me for someone else, and I'm free to "click" or "swipe" or whatever it is they call it these days when you send decent, hardworking people to the recycling bin just because you don't like the way they look or the colour of their hair, or they're a bit uninteresting until you get to know them better, like me. These people deserve more of a chance than that, I decide, and so I make up my mind that I won't be binning anybody unless they're rude or nasty. *But first things first — where is he?*

One click on the big green tick he's awarded me — which I can't help feeling a tiny bit flattered about, although I hope to God this doesn't make me sound vain, as I'd hate to be thought of that way — and the message he's sent me is finally revealed, albeit incredibly slowly. Nerves get the better of me, and I realise I've curled my hands into fists, nails digging into my palms, as I watch it open.

Lovely Linda. Your profile is so like somebody I used to know and miss still. I would love to talk to you some more if you are willing to give an old man a chance. How about we meet up sometime? Best wishes, Tony Fortin.

My eyes swipe right, as they're supposed to, and zoom in on Tony's face. Now that the blurring has been removed from the photo, I recognise him at once.

My vision blurs. I feel myself go weak all over. The darkness is back. I can't breathe.

Nothing feels safe anymore.

How is this possible?

If I'm not careful, I'll end up having another panic attack. Remembering what I've been taught, I attempt to talk myself down from the threat.

Breathe, Linda. That's it. Stay calm. Focus on your breathing. Nothing is going to happen to you. It's all in your mind.

'Bollocks.' There's nothing wrong with my mind, for a change. Far from it. And the man I'm staring at is *not* Tony Fortin.

But I'm being ridiculous. 'Wishful thinking,' my younger daughter Abby would say. And she'd be right for once.

And yet . . . another peek at the laughing blue eyes, sun-damaged skin, and familiar lazy smile causes my stomach to lurch until I think I'm going to throw up on my laptop.

It's Marcus.

And if it isn't . . . then he's got a lost twin somewhere. Everything right down to the way he's holding his head, slightly angled to the left because that was his better side, screams of my husband. He was always vain, and I see nothing has changed.

But it can't be him. No matter how much I might want it to be. Because my husband is dead. Has been for the last eight months, ever since he went into the dangerous waters at Barbati Beach in north Corfu — where we'd been holidaying in Greece — and never came out.

They never found his body.

But if this is Marcus, why would he get in touch through a dating app? Why not go straight to the police or approach me in person? If he did somehow survive that night, does he mean to come back just to punish me?

CHAPTER 2

'Am I being daft? What do you think?' I bite my nails, a nasty new habit of mine, as I test my theory out on my best friend.

'Of course, you're being daft.' Gail sniggers down the phone, refusing to take me seriously. 'Nothing new there.'

I can tell by the way she pauses every so often, as if she's not really listening, that she's smoking. Every month she gives it up, along with drink and men, but starts up again by day three. Right now, I wish I could put my hand down the phone and steal that fag right off her.

'But it looks so much like him, Gail.'

'As do a million others. We all have a double out there somewhere.'

I groan, not wanting to go down that route with her again. Gail, who is usually a sensible, hard-nosed, practical woman, has this thing about each of us having a doppelganger living a different life on another planet. Sometimes I wish I could also believe this.

But not today. Definitely not today.

'Besides,' she continues, 'even if it was Marcus, who it most definitely is not, why wouldn't he just turn up on the doorstep and say, "Hey, babe, I'm back. Now get your kit off because I'm dying for a shag"? Get it? *Dying* . . .'

'Yes, I get it,' I say, trying to keep the annoyance out of my voice. Gail always has to see the funny side of everything, whereas I . . . well, let's just say we're quite different. Opposites, in fact, which is why I suppose we've remained friends so long, since our schooldays, actually, when she rescued me from a good kicking from an older, bigger girl. Claire Mullins.

'Look,' she says, attempting to take charge, 'you've been on those tablets for a while now, and they're clearly not doing you any good except making you more doolally than usual. Seeing things and shit, like today. You should think about coming off them.'

'I will. Just not yet. I still need them.' I squirm at how pathetic I sound. Thank God she can't see the face I'm pulling. She'd pee her postmenopausal thong. She's right though. I should come off the tablets. According to my doctor, one person in a hundred suffers from serious serotonin side effects and, whilst my symptoms are considered more moderate, I am one of them. It's known as mild serotonin syndrome. I've been prescribed sertraline, which when paired with tramadol often leaves me feeling confused and can even lead me to hallucinate if I over-medicate, which I've been known to do on occasion. Not that I'd admit that to my doctor, Gail, or anyone else.

'I know, babe. You're depressed, which is only natural. You've been through a lot, and you're missing him like mad, so nobody's going to blame you for not wanting to accept the truth that he's never coming back.'

Obviously, I can't tell Gail about the night Marcus went into the water. That secret will have to accompany me to my grave, but the desire to spill the beans grows stronger every day. She's my best friend and I should be able to trust her. I'm about to bring up the subject when I realise Gail isn't done with me yet.

'I think you should definitely stay off that dating website for a while an' all. Not that I don't think you shouldn't be putting yourself out there, but if you respond to that message you could end up making yourself ill . . .' She trailed off.

'Again. You were going to say ill *again*,' I point out without being churlish about it. Everyone knows how close I came to ending it in those first weeks after I lost Marcus. It's a wonder I wasn't sectioned. Even *I'm* surprised I made it through that dark time.

'Speaking of husbands . . .' Gail is quick to change the subject. 'I saw Jim the other night in the Cosy Club. Out for a drink, he was, wearing a shirt and tie, of all things.'

I imagine Gail rolling her eyes, and I get why. Jim, my ex, has never worn a tie in his life, except on our wedding day. Being in a pub is also out of the ordinary for stay-at-home Jim.

'Was he with one of the girls?' I ask, hoping for a snippet of information about Abby or Rosie. I miss them both so much, but I'm not allowed to ask after them as a rule, as Gail gets all snippy about it. 'Putting her on the spot,' she calls it. But they're my children, not hers, even if she has been like an aunt to them. Of course, I don't say this. You don't get away with such things with Gail, who is formidable even as a best friend. Never mind protective aunt.

'Well, he was with *a* girl, if you must know. Just not either of the ones you're thinking of.' Gail spoils it all by saying, and I feel myself clam up again, relieved that I didn't give myself away earlier. The way she tells it, as if it brings her pleasure to hurt me like this, is not new. But I put it down as usual to her insensitivity. She's always been like a clumsy Labrador. Never worrying about the impact her behaviour has on others.

'Oh,' I state simply, not wanting to pry but itching to know more. Jim was my husband for twenty-eight years. Of course, I'm interested in his life.

'Don't be like that,' Gail snaps.

'I wasn't. I'm not . . .'

'I know you better than that, Linda Delamere — or Bouchard or whatever it is you're calling yourself these days,' she says, not unkindly, 'but Jim deserves to be happy.'

'After what I put him through, you mean.' I press my lips firmly together and end up sounding meaner than I intended. There's silence at the other end of the line. Gail knows when to shut up.

'What was she like?' I whisper, unable to stop myself.

'Nice, respectable, a family type of person, I'd say,' she responds absently, as if her busy mind has already moved on to something else. Gail can't stay in the same place for long, physically, or mentally. She's incredibly impatient and always on the move.

I'm still stuck in the same place though, imagining my ex with this nice, respectable, family type of woman. I don't know how Gail can make that assumption about somebody she's only seen once, but deciding it wouldn't be wise to point this out, I change the subject.

'So, you don't think there's anything I should worry about?' I persist with the Marcus theory.

Instead of the reassurance I was hoping for, I hear the echo of a door slamming, followed by footsteps on gravel and the shriek of a squeaking gate. These are sounds I'm familiar with. Gail must have parked up that sports car of hers, no doubt taking up two parking bays in the process and is on her way to her riverboat, *The Grand Dame,* which is moored on mahogany-brown water beside a pub that serves organic cider and beer-battered halloumi fries. I wonder where she's been all night. Obviously, she's spent it elsewhere, not on the boat. I imagine her pixie-cut, flame-red hair flattened by an unknown pillow, mascara-smudged eyes, and a lacy 34E bra shoved in one skinny-jean pocket.

'What was that you were saying, babe?' She checks back in with me just as I'm about to give up, dizzy with envy, and end the call.

'About Marcus. You don't think I should do anything. Tell anyone.'

'God no. They'd put you in a straitjacket and throw away the key if you did that.'

Sighing, I say my goodbyes, pretending that I'm okay, a necessary pastime for any grieving person, and wish her luck for tomorrow's job interview, the one she's forgotten about, all the while wanting to scream, *It's not fair. I hate this. I just want the pain to end. I can't do it anymore.* But if I did that, Gail would call the police, my doctor, her doctor, Jim, the ambulance service, Ray from behind the bar at the Cosy Club, whom she's slept with four times and can't decide if she wants to do so again — and anybody else she could think of.

As soon as I've hung up, I wonder if Gail's right. A lot of what she said made sense. Perhaps the antidepressants are to blame, and I should stay off the *Welcome Back* website for a while.

But as far as Marcus is concerned it's much more complicated than Gail will ever know. The more I think about that night, the easier it is to convince myself I'm responsible for hurting Marcus. There was an argument. I remember that part, and the jealousy and anger I felt towards him. But did I push him? Have I been beating myself up all these months for nothing when it was an accident, plain and simple, as the verdict at the inquest had concluded? If only I could get my memory back, then I'd know for sure. I've thought about seeing a hypnotist, but I'm terrified of what I'd discover. How can I live with myself if it turns out I let my husband die, or worse still, that I'm responsible for his death?

My doctor has told me to expect to experience a wide range of emotions, including self-blame and guilt. Both I have in abundance, although not for the reasons she thinks. If she knew what I might be guilty of, then perhaps they would put me in a straitjacket, just as Gail said.

CHAPTER 3

I'm fifteen minutes late due to the upset with the dating website and then my conversation with Gail. But I've managed the head-down-so-nobody-notices-me walk to the community centre despite the downpour of miserable November rain and can sink into my plastic seat without causing too much disruption.

Luckily, somebody is already up talking, which lets me off the hook, as I hate being in the spotlight. Stashing my sopping wet anorak and cheap faux leather bag under the chair, I hear snippets of what the woman is saying, and words like *forgiveness, evidence-based, myths of grief, tools to cope, confusion, participating in your own recovery* and *action steps* wash over me without comforting me, although I do recognise the familiar, kind tone of her voice.

Her name is Sue, and she's a grief recovery specialist who lost her husband five years ago to skin cancer and went on to train in the subject because she wanted to help others. All very commendable, I'm sure, but so far, I haven't felt myself engage with the process despite this being my third group meeting. If I could afford to go private, I would, but as it is these sessions are being funded by Victim Support, so I can hardly not turn up when there are other people desperate for a place on the course. As I explained to Sue last week, and she is such a lovely, caring woman that I find myself wanting to please her, I can't get my head around the fact that writing a letter to a dead loved one is meant to take all the pain away.

She's explained to me that it's not so simple as that, because there are a lot of steps to be taken first, including participation in group discussions, something I've grown to fear as much as my annual flu vaccination, which usually gives me a three-day migraine.

Today, when she's finished talking, she's bound to ask me again to share my story with the group. It's not that I don't want to. I've practised reading my testimonial aloud to myself. But doing it in front of six other people, mostly strangers except for Sue, makes me feel physically sick. I honestly don't know where my daughters Abby and Rosie get their confidence from, doing presentations at work and such, but it's not from me, or Jim.

I'm only here because I know it's good for me, but not in the way Sue means. If I'm among people then I can't be obsessing over the website and the man who looks just like Marcus. Despite Gail's warning, I'm tempted to send a reply saying, 'Yes, please. As soon as flipping possible' to his suggestion of meeting up. Because I'm dying — oh God, there's that word again, making me sound all flippant like Gail — to find out if it's really him even though Gail says it can't be. Logically, I know she's right.

But on an emotional level, my heart is telling me something entirely different. Nobody knows Marcus like I do. His ways. His smile. That look that lets you know how pleased he is with himself. Everything about that profile picture, the intro, and the style of writing has my husband's name all over it.

After Sue has finished talking, we break for a cup of tea and a Hobnob. I greedily gobble three, hoping no one notices. I'm starving and can't remember the last time I ate anything that I was able to keep down. Also, I'm nervous. Terrified, even. Because, of course, Sue nabs me as soon as she gets the chance and asks me again if I'll stand up and share my story with the group. This time she isn't taking no for an answer, explaining that it's essential for my recovery and that nobody will judge me or be alarmed if I break down in tears.

'Crying is allowed and openly encouraged,' she says forcibly, noticing, I think, the biscuit crumbs around my mouth and, staying true to her word, not judging me for it.

I want to tell her that where I come from crying is frowned upon. Jim and I grew up on the same council estate in Stamford and had similar life experiences. Neither of us did well at school. I left without any O Levels, called GCSEs these days. Once I had Rosie, and then Abby, I held down a succession of low-paid, part-time jobs, while Jim's carpentry business unexpectedly flourished, giving us a comfortable lifestyle and affording us the chance to buy our own doer-upper, which Jim worked on for eight years, giving up his evenings and weekends so we could have the home we (meaning I) had always dreamed of.

Despite owning outright the large four-bedroom house in the sought-after area of Victoria Road, now worth half a million, we were still the same people deep down. Jim never talked about his emotions, not even when his dad passed away. According to him, bad mental health was something other people suffered from. I wasn't as bad as Jim and was open to new ways of thinking, for my daughters' sake if nothing else, but by then it was too late for me, or so I thought. Until I met Marcus and my life changed.

Holding my crumpled bag against my waist for comfort, as if it were a child, I smile nervously at the expectant faces around me, some old, some young, some better dressed than others. Six strangers and Sue. My new family, I'm told. All smiling kindly, encouraging me with expressive eyes and nods of the head. All willing me to do well. Although I don't know these women, their being there suddenly brings tears to my eyes because they're offering me the sympathy and understanding I need and that I don't get from my daughters.

'My name is Linda Delamere. Bouchard, actually.'

My words come out high-pitched and different to how I normally sound. Posh-sounding, except I'm not. Abby would accuse me of putting on a fake voice to impress, and she'd be right. But thinking about my daughters won't get the baby a new dress, I decide as flippantly as if I were Gail.

'And I'm a widow.'

This time, my words come out flat sounding, as if they aren't particularly important. I might as well be ordering a fry-up in a greasy café, the kind Jim used to take me to all those years ago when we were hard up for money.

Unexpectedly, everybody in the room gets to their feet and claps. I'm shocked at first and take a step backwards, not understanding, but then it dawns on me what they're doing. In their eyes I've broken through the wall, finally admitting to myself and others that my husband is dead and isn't coming back, that I'm alone forever.

But as I stand there, I can't help but think: *what if they're wrong?* What if Marcus is alive, as I suspect he is? What would they think of me then? And if they knew the truth about what I may have done to him, they'd put me in the stocks. But then I decide, if Marcus *is* alive, what's to stop me talking about him? Because if he's not dead, then all the pain and hurt of the last eight months will have been for nothing. It'll all vanish as if it were never there, and I'll no longer be a widow. Or guilty. My visits to this group will cease, and I won't be one of them anymore. That thought brings a shaky smile to my face, and I look at these women differently, with pity this time because it is I and not they who should be offering sympathy.

'It's been eight months,' I say carefully as if I were practising lines in a play, wondering if Marcus might suddenly poke his head around the door and come in, shaking his head as if everything has been a joke. *Don't look at me like that, Lindy*, he'd laugh, crushing me in a big bear hug before glancing around at the other women, wanting them to love him too.

Marcus always was a great actor. He'd have loved being a widower. Would have made a much better go at the role than me. Would have played to this audience as if it were his last, making them all fall for him. The following week, he'd be inundated with invites to dinner and drinks, somebody would knit him a scarf, another widow would make him a cake, and he'd tell her it was the nicest thing he ever tasted. That was Marcus for you.

Reminding myself that this is no soap opera nor the *Marcus Bouchard Show*, I get another attack of nerves as it hits me again that Marcus is probably dead after all. Every time I remember I've lost him, it gets harder. Waking up in the morning always comes with the numbing realisation that he's gone. I imagine every woman here feels the same. Even the one with hairy legs, big moles and thinning hair knows what it's like to love and desire someone. Nobody should be fooled by the way people look, least of all plain old dumpy me.

'It's what us widows do, isn't it?' I admit, breathing in and out deeply and visibly so they'll understand what I'm doing. 'Prepare for our next anxiety attack.' I inhale another deep breath that I can feel shuddering all the way down to my toes.

'But as I was saying, it's only been eight months since I lost my husband.' I wonder if it matters to these women how long it's been, as we're all in the same boat. I hold my breath, anticipating that somebody might object and say that eight months is nothing compared to the three they're going through. I know I'm waffling. I always do when I'm nervous. Like now. At the thought of talking about my personal circumstances. About Marcus and me. As if we were still a "we". For some reason unknown to myself, I attach a little "ha" to that inner thought, only I do it aloud as if it were genuinely worthy of a laugh. But of course, it isn't.

It's difficult to talk about what happened, and I don't want to sound competitive about my widowhood, but I can't imagine anyone else feeling as grief-stricken as I do. It's not that I want to be the queen bee of the mourning club, but there was only ever one Marcus. Yet I've been warned the group is open to anyone who's suffered a loss of any kind. Not just those who have lost their soulmate. For all I know, I could be opening my heart to somebody who's grieving for their dog. Don't get me wrong. I love dogs, but it isn't the same. Believe me. Although I wouldn't dream of saying so, as some people object to everything these days.

When did life get so politically correct? I wonder. Having lived abroad for the last three and a half years, I hadn't noticed all this seriousness creeping up on us Brits. But now I'm back in the good old United Kingdom, it's become more apparent. Madness, really, when you think about it. Something to do with millennials and snowflakes, I'm told, but I don't even pretend to understand what that means.

My daughters would, of course. Rosie is the elder, although you wouldn't think so to listen to her. Abby's an old bossy boots. I don't know where she gets it from. Not me or Jim for sure. It's more like Gail's influence.

But there's no point thinking about them when they won't even see me. I don't blame them, not after how I behaved, but I'm a *widow*, for God's sake, and it wouldn't hurt to show a little sympathy. I'm still their mother. Even if I did walk out on them to live a new and exciting life that didn't include them. I thought they'd be pleased for me that I was finally going to follow my dream and see something of the world — to live rather than simply exist, as I'd always encouraged them to do — but I was wasting my time. All they could see was how much I was hurting Jim — except I wasn't, not really — and them by abandoning them. But if you can't leave your children when they're grown up, when can you?

Sighing heavily, I sit down on the plastic chair, the blue one I've come to think of as mine because I always make a beeline for it, and bow my head, unable to go on. One woman with dreadlocks and large hands with brown age spots pats me on the back, drawing soothing circles on my jumper while Sue passes me a tissue, even though I'm dry-eyed, before resuming her place in the middle of us to fill in the awkward silence. I don't know what happens after that, because all I can think about is the blue chair that matches Marcus's eyes, wishing I were back at my flat so I could open my laptop and stare at his picture again.

CHAPTER 4

Throwing off my soaked-to-the-skin charity shop anorak and hanging it on the only hook in the entire flat, I reach for the laptop that is as chunky as a child's waist. Taking it into the living room, where at least there's a window and a view of sorts staring across at the grey concrete wall of the fish-and-chip shop opposite where I also happen to work, I plop myself down on the hard two-seater sofa with its ugly marigold checked cover. Opening the screen, I check on the laptop battery to see it is at sixty-one percent, the same age Marcus would have been if he'd lived. I haven't been able to get the website or Marcus out of my head all day. His voice. Those words. That picture. Following me around Stamford.

I keep telling myself that not wallowing in grief was the main reason I signed up to the *Welcome Back* website in the first place, but I'm starting to regret it. The search history on my browser confirms that I've read up all I can on widowhood and loss, and apart from feeling hopeful for all of five minutes before returning to my usual morbid, "*life is over, there's no point in going on alone*" state of mind. That's before I discovered reaching out to like-minded people was a step in the right direction. I wasn't meant to use it as a dating site as such, because lord knows I wasn't anywhere near ready for that. Probably never will be.

Right from the start, I could tell that the site was aimed at getting people from older age groups to reconnect with each other. Judging by the abundance of grey hair and watery eyes, which popped up when I first logged on, I realised most of the regulars were older than me: and I couldn't make up my mind if that was a good or bad thing. I'd been concerned that I wouldn't be on the same wavelength as a seventy-year-old pensioner. But then I reminded myself that we were all in the same boat, and I shouldn't be ageist. It's not as if I were a spring chicken, although fifty-seven isn't exactly old either. Try telling that to the younger people today who write you off as soon as you hit fifty. Sad really. But then again, I remember being one of those young people once, who made up their minds that anyone over thirty, and then forty, was ancient. Laughable now.

The site is easier to negotiate than most, due to its target age group who, like me, aren't all that good with computers, but I get by when I have to, and I do have to. The benefits I'm entitled to wouldn't keep a dog, which is why I make a little bit extra in the chippy, and good old George, who's also my landlord, pays me in cash so it doesn't go through the books, which means I don't have to declare it.

Abby, who works as an office manager in the unemployment office in town, would be furious if she knew about this arrangement and would insist that I pay back every penny or risk being thrown in prison. She doesn't know how close to the truth she is when she says things like that. I only have to think back to that last night on the beach, and what I may or may not have done, to know how lucky I am to have my freedom.

Although only twenty-three, Abby is notoriously harsh, brutal at times, but once again she doesn't get that from Jim or me. We're both as soft as a baby's bottom. That much we do have in common. The whole family fears Abby. Even our eldest daughter, Rosie, who's twenty-five but goes along with everything her sister wants because it makes for an easier life. She's so like Jim in that respect.

Abby's due to get married soon although I'm not allowed to attend. She's made that abundantly clear. It's her soon-to-be husband I feel sorry for. He sounds nice enough, according to Gail, but my daughter is high-maintenance so I'm not sure how he'll cope. They're both ambitious, though, so there's a chance they can make it work. For her sake, I hope so. Abby has never been rejected in her life. I think the experience would kill her.

When a light comes on in the chippy across the road where I spend Friday, Saturday, and Monday nights out back, cutting the bad bits out of potatoes, afterwards serving behind the counter, I know I ought to feel guilty, because it's my job to open up, but, as usual, I don't feel anything. None of the right emotions come to me at any of the right times. George uses a machine for chipping the potatoes, but he doesn't like to serve chips with black bits, hence where I come in. The poor old boy's a widower himself and is understanding of my situation, although not so much that he'll continue to tolerate my absences. I wonder what he'll say when he realises I'm not going to turn up tonight. Again. He'll no doubt call around later and pound on the door, claiming to be worried about me, but really, he'll be narked about customers having to put up with black bits in their chips.

Until now, I've been pretending that I'm going to go to work tonight as usual and forget all about the laptop, the website, and Marcus, but I've known, all along, in the back of my mind, that I've been lying to myself all day.

Rather than go home after the meeting this morning, I went to the primary school where Rosie works as a teacher and hung around in the rain, opposite, hoping to catch sight of her at breaktime in the playground but either she wasn't in today or she was avoiding the rain.

After that, I went to sit on the wall outside the dole office — is it still called that these days? I'm not sure. I was luckier with my younger daughter, as I did manage to catch a glimpse of her. She was stomping (Abby never walks) across one of the charming, cobbled back streets that Stamford town is renowned for, into an up-and-coming Turkish restaurant, talking on the phone and peering out occasionally from under a navy and burgundy umbrella. Pausing to avoid the splash of a four-by-four's tyres in the puddles, I saw her flick her perfectly straightened, platinum blonde hair in annoyance as a drop of rain landed on it.

All the time I was watching her, she didn't see me. But does anyone really see a widow? Aren't we invisible? Death does that to people. Nobody wants to be around us in case our bad luck and misery rubs off on them. People hate to be reminded of their own mortality.

Luckily, I didn't bump into any of the old crowd on my travels today, not even when I took my usual seat on the bench dedicated to "Dearest Ivy, who liked to sit here and watch the world go by" in the water meadow, where I come every day to feed the ducks, swans too if they'll let me. I bring stale bread with me even though a heated person with a middle-class twang once told me off for feeding them that, saying it was bad for them.

When I told the do-gooder, 'I don't see the ducks complaining,' she stomped off, exactly as Abby would have done, promising me that no good would come of it. After that, I looked for this person every day but never saw her again. All I can conclude from that is she wasn't the duck warrior she made herself out to be and I felt disappointed, almost let down.

A few weeks ago — *has it been that long?* — I spotted Sadie and Rachel in the park. They were pushing grandchildren in buggies and were dressed up like yummy mummies, all leather boots, wax jackets, and designer scarves, even though they'd long since given up that crown. I never had that much in common with them, as both women had attended grammar school, and had office jobs. Yet Gail and I would spend time with them, together as a foursome and with our appropriate other halves. Jim and me, Gail and Adam, Sadie and Charles, Rachel and John. But the group started falling apart when Adam left Gail for another woman, and then of course I walked out on Jim, and nothing was the same after that.

I know that they saw me that day and felt them recoil in horror, drawing closer together, almost touching, as they took in the old woman feeding the birds, with unwashed, un-straightened hair, creased mum jeans, peeling trainers, and who no doubt stank of lard, as I'd just come from a shift in the chippy. Neither acknowledged me, for which I was grateful. What would I have said? *Oh, hi ladies, aren't you pleased to see me, so you can point out how right you were and how wrong I was. Because you can't gain happiness by hurting others, isn't that right?*

Bitterness is like bile. It sticks in your throat and makes you want to be sick, over yourself and everybody else. So, I hid my head in my hands that day and let them pass by without apportioning any guilt, because they hadn't done anything wrong. Unlike me.

I'd spent today, like most others, drifting from one familiar place to another, reliving mine and Jim's childhoods and the early years of our family life by visiting the church where we got married and our first house in Blackfriars Street where Rosie was born. You'd think I wouldn't want to see any of these places again because that part of my life is over, but it brings me comfort. As much as I'd hurt Jim, Rosie and Abby, those years had felt safe.

CHAPTER 5

As I open the laptop, I catch a glimpse of my reflection in the smudged screen, which is alive with my fingerprints and DNA. I'm only fifty-seven, I could still have decades left to live, but look ten years younger. I wasn't lying when I included that in my online profile. It's not like I say it to be vain or big headed, but enough people have said so for me to think it's true.

Before Marcus died, or *went away*, I'd always taken care of myself, moisturising my skin every day, watching my weight and drinking plenty of water. Eating healthily has gone down the drain the last eight months though and some days I forget to eat at all. Losing weight is the only positive thing to come out of widowhood. Not that I was fat before, but I've always been a generous size fourteen with a pear-shaped figure. Solid thighs and a small bust. That's me. Being tall for a woman, at five foot nine, I'm able to carry it off.

Marcus was tall too and, at six foot one, he said we made a striking couple. He reckoned we were an inspiration to the younger generation, us being so much in love and young and attractive for our ages. I wouldn't have gone quite as far as that, and blushed every time he said it, but what woman could argue with those words. Not me. But then again, nobody ever argued with Marcus. Everybody loved him — abroad, that is. He wasn't so highly regarded in the UK. Certainly not by my family.

Marcus was the only one to call me Lindy, as if I were a tiny young thing and not a goliath of an older woman. He had a way with women that made you feel special. I'd only known him a few hours before I found myself falling for him. He had deep navy-blue eyes that reminded me of the Ionian Sea in the Greek island of Kefalonia where we first met. His smile came out of nowhere, appearing like a late sun in the grooves of his sun weathered face. The untameable silvery white hair he kept hidden under his straw Panama only served to make him more attractive. A regular silver fox, that's what he was.

The trouble was he loved women just as much as they loved him. But he was no womaniser, believing in honesty, equality, and a meeting of the minds, or at least that's what he professed. At the time of bumping into him, quite literally, I'd lived a full life. Or so I'd thought. I'd been married to Jim for twenty-eight years, albeit separated for the last six months, and had two daughters by him. We'd loved, lost, cried, and laughed together but I'd never given myself over to Jim, completely and utterly in the way that a woman can, as I had with Marcus. I'm not one for reading or writing, preferring soaps or reality TV shows, but there was something about Marcus Bouchard that made me want to write poetry. A fact that made my cheeks burn redder than the sunsets we drank to.

We married a year later on a beach in Bali after Marcus managed to talk Jim into agreeing to grant me a no-blame divorce. Jim would have said and done anything to make me happy and was even open to us being friends after my marrying Marcus, but the girls objected and turned him against the idea. Despite everything, I miss Jim. He was a loyal and dependable husband. A good man. Good father. Too good for me, as it turned out.

There were no friends at mine and Marcus's wedding. No guests and no witnesses. Just the celebrant and ourselves. It was a barefoot ceremony on the beach, and we waited for the sun to rise before exchanging our vows. Marcus wore a white linen shirt open at the neck, with friendship bracelets dangling from his wrists. By then he was as brown as a bear. I wore a white maxi dress with a yellow pashmina purchased at the eco hotel we were staying at. I remember that it only cost me two pounds. I even wore matching yellow flowers in my hair, which I'd grown long for the first time in my life. 'My sun-kissed blonde,' Marcus called me.

There were no photos. Marcus didn't believe in capturing moments with a camera when you could live them instead, and he was right, of course. He was right about so many things including being in the present and marvelling at our own bodies. Like in that silly movie, *Shirley Valentine*, he taught me to love the skin I lived in; never giving a thought to my wrinkles, saggy boobs and stretch marks. He opened my eyes in so many ways that I'll always be grateful to him. Every woman should love as I did. If only once in her life.

It was a perfect day and so unlike my first wedding to Jim. That had been a full-blown church affair with one hundred guests, many of them unwanted, in attendance. Jim had worn a tight blue suit and was hungover from his stag do. Like me, Jim rarely drank so he spent most of our wedding night throwing up in the hotel bathroom and apologising for it. It wasn't as if our first night together was completely ruined, as we'd already had sex. I was no virgin bride, but Jim was my first and only lover.

I was indifferent to sex in those days even though Jim wasn't demanding and didn't expect anything from me other than the odd peck on the cheek or a hug when things weren't going so well. He went to work and came home. He took turns changing the girl's nappies and getting them off to sleep at night when I was exhausted from motherhood. He was an excellent provider and we rarely argued. In many ways we were the perfect couple. And yet, I grew to resent him for not being what I wanted. Of course, I never told him that. I'm not cruel and I never deliberately set out to hurt him. Deep down, I always knew the fault lay with me. But it was years before I realised I wasn't in love with Jim and never had been.

Feeling like I was missing out on life, I craved passion and adventure, and was desperate for freedom from the daily grind that I felt was suffocating me. Thinking back now, to the woman I was then, I sound like a spoiled brat. Somebody who had everything they'd ever dreamed of but who wasn't satisfied; always wanting more.

Picking at a piece of ragged skin around my fingernail, another new habit to me, I think back to my wedding day with Marcus, still so fresh in my mind. Marcus did something completely unexpected, surprising even the celebrant. He'd taken out a piece of paper from his trouser pocket and read it aloud, never taking his eyes off me. I have the words still, locked in our box of memories that I cannot take out without crumbling into a ball on the floor and sobbing my eyes out. I don't have to see them to know the words off by heart.

'There are ten reasons why I, Marcus Bouchard, love you . . .'

Before I could listen to another word I was already crying. Black streaks of mascara rolled down my cheeks and I could hardly breathe as he took my hand and smiled at me with laughing eyes. In that moment I was a queen, a princess, a sea mermaid with golden hair. I was Juliet, Boadicea, Mary Queen of Scots and all the revered women of history I'd learned about at school. How could I, somebody as boring as me, Linda Delamere, then fifty-five years old with a pear-shaped figure and a big bum, inspire such words in a man?

'The first reason is this. With you I can be myself.' He stated with tears in his eyes. 'Two, I love the way you look at me. Three, you make me feel like I'm the only person in the world. Four, you know me better than I know myself. Five, you love Abba as much as I do.'

The celebrant and I both laughed at this point and the three-piece band we'd hired to play our favourite songs spontaneously broke into *I Do, I Do, I Do, I Do, I Do.*

It was a magical moment that no bride could ever forget. We both felt ridiculously silly, of course. Or at least I did. At our age, we should have known better than to make such a fuss, but I can't pretend I didn't enjoy the attention. Who wouldn't? Silencing the band with a majestic wave of his hand, Marcus settled back into romantic suitor mode, and I held my breath waiting to see what he would come out with next. Marcus had that effect on everyone, not just me. Wherever we went, whether he was ordering a drink in a bar, hiring a car, booking a hotel room, or bartering with beach vendors trying to sell us something. The list was endless.

'Six, you make me smile when no one else can.' He'd added dramatically, as if he were Henry VIII, swooning over my hand. 'Seven, because when you laugh, I laugh. Eight, I can always be honest with you. Nine, you make me a better person. And ten, you make me feel less alone.'

It hurts so much. Remembering that day is like a pain I've never experienced. Far worse than childbirth and labour pains — twenty-two hours of them in first-born Rosie's case. I desperately want my children with me in moments like this. I'd even settle for Jim if he could visit, but the girls have made it clear I'm not welcome in their lives. They will protect their father from me at all costs, even though Jim doesn't need looking after and never has.

I can't just leave and then expect to come back and pick up where I left off, that's what people say, but that's exactly what I crave. Does that make me a bad person? I suppose it does, but I've never seen myself that way before. I've never set out to hurt anyone in my life. Ever. I can't even bring myself to squash a spider. I don't have it in me.

Except, I do, because when I think back to that night on the beach . . . but that wasn't the real me. I was drunk, a little bit stoned. Was I angry? I was furious. I wanted to kill Marcus for humiliating me by flirting openly with that woman at the bar, so perhaps I did hurt him. My memory of what happened remains a blur. I could have pushed him, couldn't I? Or did he run into the water to escape me? Either way, I'm to blame.

But the real Linda puts other people first. That's why I don't tell Abby and Rosie the truth about how I really am because I want to spare them. I will never say to them the words I'm feeling. Like, 'I don't want to wake up in the morning or find myself alone anymore. Having my loneliness thrown back in my face when I'm suffering the most is killing me.'

On that depressing thought, and knowing I've got nothing whatsoever to lose, I press the "respond to message" button and quickly, for me, type in the words, "*Hi, Tony, Thanks for getting in touch. I'd love to meet up and find out more about you. Are you local? When and where do you suggest we meet? I look forward to hearing from you soon, Linda.*" And then, before I can change my mind, I add a kiss and hit SEND.

CHAPTER 6

Clutching Marcus's passport in my hand, I trace the shape of his face with a newly polished, pink-tipped fingernail. Every time I see this photograph more creases seem to appear on his face. When I'd first caught a glimpse of it, on our wedding day, I thought he looked typically happy and carefree. Impossibly handsome and distinguished, like a learned professor. Now I wonder if I saw only what I wanted to as there are hard lines around his eyes and a grimace at the edge of his mouth that make me wonder, *Did I really know Marcus?*

During those first nightmarish days and nights after Marcus went into the water, grief protected me, people were kind. Even the Greek police. But it wasn't long before the authorities insisted that I take the impossibly difficult steps to formalise what had happened. My inability to cope was met with frustration. I tried to explain that I was a woman alone in a country that was not my own. I didn't speak the language and had no idea what to do or who to notify. Turns out I didn't know much about my husband either because I couldn't find any other paperwork for him, except the passport, which had been left in the hotel safe with a wallet that contained very little money. Marcus didn't own a credit card, preferring to use cash. But I had no idea where he got his income from, except for a small retirement fund, and to this day I don't know whether he had a bank account or savings. Mostly, we used my divorce settlement to fund our travelling. I never minded, as we were a team.

Thank God for Gail, that's all I can say. One teary phone call from me and she dropped everything to fly over. I couldn't have got through any of it without her. She instantly took charge and when she wasn't sending off for birth certificates and registering Marcus's death and dealing with the police and the hotel staff, she drank cocktails on the beach and worked on her tan. I never minded as I was so grateful to her. She was the best friend ever and I was lucky to have her. So, I tried not to mind when she ended up having a fling with the guy on the beach who hired out sun loungers, while I was beside myself with grief, holed up in the hotel swallowing down sedatives like they were going out of fashion.

We never did trace Marcus's birth certificate, but that didn't prevent the authorities from listing him as "presumed dead". According to the international register, the only Marcus Bouchard traceable to South Africa or British Columbia had died at the age of eighteen in a boat accident, raising the investigative police's suspicions. There was a lot of talk at the time, repeated to me in stilted English by a police translator, that my husband might not have been who he said he was, but I never believed them. Marcus had a mother living in Devon, England, and we'd planned to visit her on our return to the UK. I have her address still. Gail agreed with me, claiming cock-ups like that happened all the time abroad.

The passport photograph is a perfect match to the man known as Tony Fortin on the Welcome Back website. I never doubted it would be. What wife wouldn't know their own husband? I could always spot Marcus in a crowd. The way he stood, head held high, a bounce in his step accompanied by the willingness to shake hands with anybody he met. The smile that never faded, came across as so genuine. The laughter in his eyes. That raucous belly laughter when something rude tickled him. The morning cough from too many cigars. The way he chewed his lip when he was concerned. *What was it you worried about, Marcus?*

A quick glance at the clock tells me it's nearly seven. The thought of what I'm about to do fills me with a sickening amount of dread and excitement. Today, for once, hasn't been spent roaming Stamford's cobbled streets searching for my past, or whiling the time away in a succession of coffee shops and cold, empty churches where I habitually light candles for the people I've lost. Mum. Dad. Marcus. Instead, I've treated myself to a pampering session, something I haven't done in months. Now that I've been exfoliated, plucked, shaved, and moisturised to within an inch of my life, the old body feels better for it. My toe and fingernails have been painted in matching colours and I've curled my hair, so it falls in trendy blonde waves. A dash of natural makeup later and I'm dressed in a denim maxi dress with suede boots from the charity shop on the high street. This, teamed with a cord jacket and a leopard print scarf means I look half-decent for once.

I'm gathering my bag, getting ready to leave, remembering to slip in a lip gloss so I can touch up my makeup later, when a knock on the door causes me to freeze. I never get visitors except for my landlord, but it's not my night on at the chippy, so it can't be George. Besides, he's forgiven me already, sort of, for letting him down the other night, and I've made up for it since, having promised to do the next three nights on the run. He'd wanted me to do this evening's shift as well but that was easy to say no to. Tonight, I have plans.

When I open the door a beautiful, perfumed blonde with perfectly straightened hair and swollen, tearful eyes, falls into my arms and my flat. Her tears dampen my own face as she clings to me.

'Abby. Oh, Abby. What is it? What's wrong?'

She trembles in my arms, unable to speak. Like any mother, I think the worst.

'What's happened, love? What is it?'

'It's Josh,' she finally sobs, a giant shudder passing through her nine-stone body.

I pull her inside and shut the door. Then I take her by the hand and tug her into the small living room, pushing her onto the uncomfortable sofa that I've just vacated. Abby is crying so hard she can barely breathe.

'Is he all right?' I ask gently, worried something has happened to him. My thoughts automatically go to *his* poor mother.

'The wedding is off,' she says hysterically, furiously wiping tears from her face.

Realising that Abby is mad as hell rather than grief-stricken, my heart rate decreases, and my panic levels subside. Thank God the lad is all right. For a minute there I thought he'd been involved in an accident, or worse. But judging by Abby's shrunken, hard-as-nails eyes, she already thinks the worst that could happen has happened. That's youth for you, I suppose, so I don't judge her too harshly.

'What happened, Abby? Has he done something?' There's no space for me on the sofa so I sink to my knees and put a reassuring hand on her arm.

'You mean is there someone else? Typical of you to think that.' Abby shrugs me off. More forcibly than is needed. 'He's not like that.' She snivels, looking around expectantly for a magical tissue to appear, which I dutifully supply. 'But it's over anyway.'

'You can't be that over him that you still want to defend him,' I point out reasonably and this earns me an Abby eyeroll.

'He's insisting we wait five years before we have a baby, saying we are still too young and should see something of the world first.'

Although I completely agree with Josh and as a result, he goes up in my estimation, I do not say so. But I am gobsmacked by my daughter's admission, because to date she's never demonstrated a maternal bone in her Boden-clad body.

'You want a baby?' I asked, trying to keep my voice neutral.

'You think that's funny.' She sulks, tearing the tissue into small pieces and leaving a snotty trail on the orange laminate floor.

'No. Not at all,' I recover quickly. 'I'm surprised that's all because, well, you've never shown any interest before. You always said babies were boring, expensive, time-consuming, and not for you.'

'Just because you failed at it doesn't mean I'm going to,' she spits.

I don't react to the injustice of this as we both know full well, I was a bloody good mum to her and Rosie — until recently that is. So, I say instead—

'I think you'll be a brilliant mum, Abby. As you are in everything you do.'

Slightly mollified by my words, she inches along the sofa and allows me to perch on the edge closer to her than she would normally. Pursing her lips, she confides, 'I told him we were incompatible, both wanting different things and that it would never work, that we should call the wedding off. And do you know what he said, Mum? He said *fine*. Just like that, *fine*. That's how little he thinks of me.'

She's sobbing again now, and I dutifully pat her on the back, instinctively knowing she won't want me to engulf her in a full-blown hug. She's not ready for that yet.

'But aren't you the one who wanted to call it off, not him?'

'Yes. *Duh*.' She pulls an unattractive face. Although more beautiful than her elder sister, Abby is the uglier sibling when she cries. Usually, she works herself into such a state we have to put her to bed with a cup of sweet tea and draw the curtains, blocking out what light there is so as not to give her a headache on top of everything else.

'But I never expected him to go along with it. I only said it, so he'd do what I wanted.'

I nearly smile, thinking how wonderful it is to know Josh has some balls. Used to winning over her father her entire life, and to some extent, me, Abby has finally found someone who is going to stand up to her. Of course, I don't say any of this. I simply advise her to speak to Josh again to come to a compromise as it is essential for any marriage.

I get another Princess Abby eyeroll for that but at least she doesn't have another dig at me. *Is Abby finally growing up?*, I wonder. The fact that she's here at all is a miracle, but her timing couldn't be more out. On that note, I make the fatal mistake of glancing at the clock on the mantelpiece, and she stiffens at once. I should have known better than to give myself away. The girl is all-knowing, and my heart is in my mouth as I watch her eyeing me warily, trying to fathom out what's going on with me, why I'm all dolled up and preoccupied with the time. For somebody her age, she's so perceptive, yet has no conception of how she hurts others with her outspokenness.

'Have you got something better to do than console your daughter whose life is over?' she enquires coldly, getting to her feet and deliberately jutting out her chin at the clock.

It takes a lot of patience for me not to retaliate, but today is not the day to remind her of a few home truths. Not when she's like this, obviously upset and feeling hurt, despite the bitterness coming out of her mouth. Scrambling to my feet, I struggle to produce an explanation that won't be an outright lie, so I remain guiltily silent.

'I should have known.' Abby raises her voice in mock triumph. 'You're going to see a man. Meet up with a man.'

'It's not how it sounds, Abby. Not what you think.' I stumble on my words feeling like a schoolgirl receiving a grilling from my parents for stopping out late. Back in the day that would have meant a slipper against the backside and cuddles and milky tea afterwards.

'This is so typical of you.' Abby jerks at the zip on her jacket, not once making eye contact with me.

'What is, Abby?' I swallow down my anxiety knowing full well I could be screwing up the only chance I have to make up with my daughter but knowing there is little I can do about it. I can't put this other thing off. Not even for her.

'You. Running off to meet a man instead of being there for your family when you're needed.'

This is an old record, one we both keep on turning. And once again Abby is muttering 'Simply unbelievable' under her breath but nonetheless loud enough for me to hear.

'I was there for you throughout your childhood, Abby, and I stopped loving your father. What did you want me to do? Ask yourself what you'd have done in my place. If it were Josh . . .'

'Don't make this about me,' she shrieks hysterically no doubt believing all the waffle she's coming out with due to her heightened senses. 'It's you. You're to blame for everything. And I hate you and I never want to see you again.'

'Yes, I know. You told me so two weeks ago, remember, when I texted you to see how you were,' I point out unnecessarily, hoping it might clip her wings, and forgetting for a minute that my youngest daughter cannot be tamed.

'Well, I mean it this time. I never want to see you again and I'll make sure Rosie feels the same too.' She spits, storming towards the door.

'Please don't do that, love.' I say following her, all bravado gone from me now. 'Let's sit down for a minute and calm ourselves down.'

'No. I'm going.' She declares, even though she makes no effort to escape through the door. 'I wouldn't want to come between you and your love life. How many men do you need, Mum? Can't you be on your own for five minutes?'

Even though I know she only says this to hurt me, my hackles rise immediately. I'm not such a pushover as her dad.

'I was alone in my marriage, Abby. All twenty-eight years of it. I know you find that hard to believe but it's true.'

'Bullshit,' she yells, loud enough for the downstairs tenant to hear. 'Well, are you going to ask me to leave or are you going to stay here and do what mothers are supposed to do?'

I can tell by the challenge in her watery blue eyes that are so like mine that she expects me to do as she wants. Nothing surprises her more when I fold my arms, meet her gaze, woman to woman, and say determinedly—

'I'm going to ask you to leave.'

'Fine. Just fine.' She mutters tearfully, doing up the zip on a puffer jacket that would have paid my rent for a month, and then barging past me, she slams out of the flat. I hear the clip clop of her high-heeled boots bouncing down each of the thirteen concrete steps that lead up to flat number thirteen and then I wait a full five minutes more, torn between fear of being late for my date and not wanting to bump into Abby outside, before letting myself out.

CHAPTER 7

The pub stinks of pickled eggs, beer and sweat. In that order. Disturbingly not as gross a smell as it should be. It somehow reminds me of my dad. Over by the pool table two young men wearing torn jeans that hang comically around their arses, exposing brightly coloured designer pants, lazily shoot balls at each other, never exchanging a word.

The older clientele is propped up on their elbows at the bar and are on first-name terms with the bartender, who doesn't seem that friendly to me. Every so often they turn to look at me as if figuring out what I'm doing here. A woman on her own. Middle-aged at that. I could ask myself the same thing. But I stare back, not once blinking until it is them who look away. The one wearing a faded All Nations rugby top, shrunken in the wash and exposing plenty of bum cleavage, winks at me. Sensing he's being friendly rather than flirtatious, I smile weakly in his direction before focusing on the drink in my hand.

I hate the fact they've probably guessed that I'm here to meet someone, *a blind date at her age. What a joke*, they must think. And I begin to wonder why Marcus thought this old man's pub would be a desirable choice for our meeting. The Marcus I knew wouldn't be seen dead in a place like this.

Realising this makes me anxious and I worry for the hundredth time since arriving that I've got it wrong, that Marcus is dead, and the man I'm about to meet is an imposter or someone who happens to look a lot like my husband. But that would be one coincidence too many. Peering at my watch, I see he's late. By eleven minutes. My body squirms and my insides threaten to abandon me.

Sipping my tonic water, I glance casually around the pub as if I'm not in the slightest bit bothered by the barman whose greedy eyes follow me, put out that I'm taking up space at a sought-after corner table without spending any real money or even asking for a refill. As my eyes roam, they land on posters advertising quiz nights on Thursdays and dominos on Fridays. It's the sort of place my dad would have frequented were he still alive but not one he would have taken my mum to. A good honest working man's refuge that sells excellent beer is how I'd describe it, with its live sport on big screens and L-shaped bar.

I continue to get the feeling that something isn't right. Why would Marcus ask me to come here? As Gail had already implied, surely, he would just turn up at the flat to see me. I can't be that hard to track down. Unless it's so he can remain hidden and unseen. I imagine there must be some sort of secret that is preventing him from telling the authorities that he's alive. Perhaps his life is in danger. Someone could be after him for money. Marcus played a heavy hand at cards and enjoyed winning. He never could hide his delight when he took hundreds of pounds from people who could ill afford to lose so much.

My phone is on the sticky table in front of me, but it remains silent, so I don't give up. Not yet. I've already shredded one soggy drinks coaster, leaving a pile of wet cardboard behind, and I'm about to attack another when the bleep finally comes through, making me spill my drink. Luckily, it's not red wine but I'm still annoyed. It might only be a charity shop dress, faded in places, with the belt missing, but it's dressed up for me. I had to improvise with another belt, otherwise it would have hung off me, due to my having lost so much weight in the last few months. Marcus wouldn't recognise me.

'*Sorry can't make it. Something came up. I'll text you later.*' The text comes with a kiss and the word Tony, which alone makes me huff and puff into my drink. *Tony, my eye.*

I'm so mad, I could spit in the barman's eye. What right does this stranger, *if he is a stranger*, have to stand me up? I still can't decide if I want it to be Marcus or a random person that looks like him. Either way has unpleasant outcomes attached. The whole thing is making me sick with worry. Sitting bolt upright in my chair, I feel my body tense with anger. Then, quickly knocking back the remainder of my tonic water as if it were a whiskey chaser, I get to my feet, attracting all eyes at the bar. I haven't been this angry since that night on the beach when I caught Marcus flirting with that underdressed trollop from the hotel.

'I'm sure she can light her own cigarettes, she's not disabled.' I'd surprised them with my curtness, having crept up on them at the beach bar without their noticing. Marcus looked at me in bewilderment, because I was no longer his lovely Lindy, more like a jealous fishwife. The woman had the grace to blush, not so Marcus, who simply pulled up a chair, greeted me with a wet kiss, partially on the mouth and partially on the cheek, and ordered me a drink. When he said the words 'Tonic water, please,' I was having none of it and insisted on a double gin and tonic. It wouldn't be my last of the night. Marcus may have looked surprised, as I didn't usually drink much, hardly ever at all, but he didn't react.

She, the floozy, wore dangly gold earrings that bounced off her bare shoulders, which were on display in one of those awful cold-shoulder tops that I despise so much, and which Marcus knew I hated, so it felt like a double insult to find him talking to her in one. She had massive boobs, unlike my own smaller, no-need-for-underwire bosom, which made me feel insignificant beside her. Her skin was ravaged by the sun but had noticeably few wrinkles. Another reason for me to dislike her.

Ignoring me, she laughed at everything my husband said, right down to when he told her how much he liked crab meat, even the brown bits. I couldn't see anything remotely funny in that statement and I told her so. Marcus, finally twigging what was up, sighed and drew the drinks to a close. Then, putting an arm around my shoulders, he was about to escort me to our room, no doubt thinking I'd had enough to drink for one night. But I hadn't. Nor was I going to be marched away from an uncomfortable scene as if I were a toddler who couldn't control her temper. So, I stormed off to the beach, our beach until tonight, hoping he'd follow me and not go back to Lilo Lil as I'd christened her in my head. Luckily, or unluckily in his case, he pursued me.

He tried to talk me around but I was having none of it because my pride was hurt. Also, I didn't like who I was. I'd never wanted to be the jealous sort of wife who tried to control her husband and yet there I was for all to see. Marcus didn't know what to do with me. I'd never behaved like that with Jim, I remember thinking at the time, horrified by what I'd become, but then again Jim had never given me reason to act that way. And that's what I told Marcus. Soon, he was as mad as I was, demanding to know why we were talking about Jim.

'But then again, when are we not talking about Jim?' he'd accused sarcastically.

I remember it as if it were yesterday. Because I slapped him. Hard. I've regretted it ever since, of course. And the words. The last words I ever spoke to my husband went like this—

'Yes, well, Jim was a gentleman. Unlike you. And he would never have humiliated me the way you just did. I hate to say this, Marcus, but he's twice the man you are.'

How could I? I didn't mean a word of it. Honestly, I didn't but it was too late once I'd said it. Marcus tried to push past me then. Muttering something about 'bloody hysterical women' which really got my goat and so I grabbed hold of him, tearing a button from his shirt in the process which I looked for later but never found. It's still on the beach somewhere, like a bad penny, and I'm sure it will turn up one day if only to point an accusing finger at me.

I remember refusing to let go and pushing him harder when he resisted because I wasn't finished with him yet. Hours later I woke up on the beach, dehydrated and hungover, with no Marcus in sight. I went back to my room then, only to find our bed empty, so I sat at the dressing table staring at my ugly, tear-stained face in the mirror, waiting for him to come back. I wasn't worried at first, except for panicking at the thought of him waking up in Lilo Lil's bed and not mine, but I was sure he'd crawl home eventually, tail between his legs, wanting to make up with me. Only I never saw him again after that night.

Out on the street, away from prying eyes, I take out my phone and impatiently type '*What happened to you?*' Luckily, predictive texting is on, so I make no spelling mistakes. My fingers shake at the thought of what I'm doing. *'I need to see you. Tell me where you are, and I'll come to you.'* I break all the laws of dating by being needy and clingy, and no doubt showing my cards too soon, but this is no ordinary man I'm chasing. This is my dead husband I'm arranging a date with. *Bloody hell, Linda,* I think, *what the hell am I doing?*

CHAPTER 8

'Jim, it's me.'

I'm back at the flat, pacing up and down its confined grey space, wanting answers. I've heard nothing back from Tony Fortin alias my dead husband and so I do what I always do when I'm in a predicament, turn to my ex-husband — good old, reliable Jim, who is completely ignorant of the fact that he was the cause of the last ever argument I had with Marcus. After such a prolonged absence from his life, a lesser man would have come back with a cutting response, such as 'Who is this?' but he doesn't.

When he answers straightaway, not a trace of bitterness to his tone, I feel a sense of overwhelming relief knowing some people don't change. I try not to remember that this used to be one of my main complaints I had about Jim when we were married.

'Hello, me.'

He's trying to be playful, and I want to tell him that it doesn't suit him. But what do I know of Jim these days. According to Gail, he's moved on, and about time too, she reckons, and has taken to wearing ties as well as dating other women. Not *other* women, I remind myself, realising that I no longer have any claims on my former husband. Slowly it dawns on me that I am now the *other woman*. It doesn't go down well with me. A fact I hate to admit.

In the background, I can hear laughter echoing from the hand-built kitchen that houses the big family table that we all used to sit around every day. Before I can ask if the girls are there, I hear Jim closing the door, shutting out the sound in case we are overheard. He knows how Abby and Rosie feel about me — well Abby mostly but whatever road she goes down, Rosie is sure to follow. I'm meant to leave him alone to heal, but if he's got a new woman then this must mean he has healed. In which case, surely, it's safe to call. It's not as if I've ever promised the girls that I wouldn't. Jim and I are both adults, and as such, there's no reason we can't be friendly . . .

I panic momentarily, worried in case the other woman is there with him now. Sitting at what I still think of as *my* table, eating off my sage green John Lewis dinner service. Is she even now enjoying a family meal with my daughters? Consoling Abby's tears when her own mum wouldn't? Has the new woman replaced me in more ways than just being Jim's girlfriend? As if that weren't bad enough, I'm horrified I might have intruded on their evening, hating the thought of this unknown woman secretly judging me to be a crazy, obsessive ex, who doesn't know when to let go. I'm about to chicken out and hang up when—

'Are you all right, Linda?'

He sounds like he cares. But there's a hesitancy to his voice too. My heart sinks when I realise he thinks I'm after more money. He must know I'm broke, and that Marcus spent all our, *my*, money but Jim had been more than fair about my divorce settlement considering the circumstances. That's why I've never asked for another penny. I know he had to re-mortgage the house at a time in his life when he'd hoped to be able to retire, so he could pay me my share. Poor Jim. No chance of that now. And with Abby and Rosie living at home rent-free and not contributing to the household, or doing their share of the housework, it can't be easy.

I want him to be happy, but I still can't bear the thought of another woman, Jim's woman, living in *my* house. Walking from room to room, moving a cushion there, a vase here, smoothing the bedspread or hoovering the hall carpet that I spent three whole days choosing.

'I'm fine,' I say, wiping a tear from my cheek.

I'm far from fine and we both know it.

'How are you?' I ask, secretly hoping he'll tell me that nothing has changed, he still loves me, and desperately wants me back. But of course, he doesn't. Because that wouldn't be true and nor do I want my first husband back. Not really. But I do sometimes miss my old comfortable life. The one I gave up so easily. Tossed aside, in fact, as if it were worth nothing.

'Good. All good,' Jim tells me.

'How's work?'

Now we're on familiar ground, Jim goes on to tell me about his day. How many jobs he's quoted for this week and the house in Great Casterton he's helping to refurbish for a mate.

'But I'm not doing it for mates' rates,' he jokes, fooling no one, not even himself.

Where once he would have told me the name of the friend, he now doesn't. It shouldn't feel like a big deal, but it does. Until the separation, Jim had been one hundred per cent mine in every aspect of my life. Throughout the divorce and then my marrying Marcus, I still felt connected to him. After Marcus died, I even dared to think we might get back together. At one stage it felt like that would be the most natural thing to happen and I thought Jim felt the same.

But it turns out I was wrong. Jim, being Jim, was just being kind and even now doesn't want to rub his new relationship in my face. I'm guessing that's why he doesn't mention her. I don't begrudge him his happiness and, just because I never loved him, not properly the way a wife is meant to, doesn't mean he can't find someone who will. He deserves to experience true love . . . but it still feels like I'm being dumped. *Oh God, Linda, you really are turning out to be the crazy, obsessive ex who doesn't know when to let go.*

'So, are you going to tell me what's wrong?' Jim finally asks.

He knows me so well. Better than anyone else. Even Marcus didn't get me like Jim does. It's only when you've been married for years, grown up together in fact, and had babies together that you truly know someone, warts and all. A value I never cherished until now.

'Can we talk?'

'Isn't that what we *are* doing?'

'I mean in person.' I say, crossing my fingers and wincing at how desperate I sound. 'I don't think I can tell you this over the phone.'

'Is there something I should worry about, Linda? Anything I ought to know?'

There it is again, the cautious tone. Just as he knows me inside and out, I can read him. He's hiding something. I don't press him on this, because obviously he's trying to protect me from finding out about the other woman, or he knows that I know and is worried I'm going to cause trouble. Either way I'm not in the right head space to hear about this other woman, nor how she's so bloody good for him and getting on well with the girls. I really couldn't bear it. I don't even want to know her name although in my head, I think of her as a Sarah. A soft, feminine name for someone Gail described as being a respectable family type of person, not spoiled or demanding like me. Of course, Gail hadn't dared to say the last bit aloud, knowing better than that, but I could tell it's what she meant. It's natural that Jim would go for the opposite of me, after what I put him through, and I don't blame him.

'It's not anything to do with you or the girls, or money or anything, if that's what you're thinking,' I add quickly, hoping to dispel his fears. Self-respect is all I have left in my miserable life and I won't give it up no matter what. Neither Jim nor my daughters will ever hear me beg.

'Okay. When?'

'Now?' I offer, hopefully.

I hear a drawn-out sigh. Then, silence for a few seconds.

'It's already nine o'clock and I've got . . .'

I don't wait for him to tell me he's got people, people being *her*, and possibly my daughters too, waiting in the kitchen for him.

'It's all right, Jim, I understand. I hadn't realised how late it was and of course you're busy . . .'

I'm about to put the phone down when I hear him say—

'No. It's not that. It's just,' another sigh, 'give me fifteen minutes, okay.'

'Okay,' I agree, hanging up quickly in case he changes his mind.

CHAPTER 9

I add a sly shot of out-of-date Baileys to my coffee but don't put any in Jim's. He's never been much of a drinker, unlike Marcus, and is not impressed by drunks. He's also not a fan of overemotional women, so I force myself to keep it together for his sake, not wanting to make him feel uncomfortable. When we were married I used to think we were similar, in that neither of us had a romantic bone in our bodies. It would be years later, and take meeting Marcus, before I realised that wasn't true.

Our hands clash when I pass Jim his coffee in a mug with only one slight chip in it. I make sure to give him the better of the two ugly white mugs that I inherited when I took possession of this flat. He no longer takes sugar as it's not good for him and I wonder whose influence that is. Jim is careful to avoid eye contact. His eyes sweep the small living room and I sense his disapproval of my circumstances. I offer him the hard-backed ugly marigold one-person sofa, but he refuses and says he prefers to stand. I can't help thinking how good he looks. Not tired, old, and exhausted like me. If I didn't know better, I'd suspect him of working out.

Jim is around the same height as me, a fact that never bothered him, like it would a lot of egotistical men. He never minded if I wore high heels when we went out together although these days, I'm more inclined to something comfier. His hair is sandy coloured but peppered with grey at the edges, and his pale skin has never seen much of the sun due to his working mostly indoors and a dislike of foreign holidays. His hands are small and freckly, and, in all honesty, I never liked them very much. They felt pale and limp and there were times towards the end of our marriage when I couldn't bear his touch. The same went with kissing. I'm ashamed to admit that I used to turn my head away to deflect his attempts to kiss me. When Marcus first slid a sexy tongue into my mouth, I didn't know what to do with myself. That was when "sexy Lindy" was born. Unlike the me of now, she wasn't at all inhibited and knew how to have fun under the sheets.

Having such thoughts makes my cheeks burn and I turn away from Jim in embarrassment, lest he knows what I'm thinking, and, since he hasn't accepted my offer of the only chair, I sink down into it instead.

'Thank you so much for coming, Jim. I know it's late and I'm sorry to . . .'

'I've already told you it's okay. Not a problem.'

He seems sincere enough, but I can't shake off the desire to apologise some more but then I ask myself what exactly I am trying to say sorry for, getting him to drop everything so he can visit his ex-wife late at night just to listen to her ramble on about her troubles or for treating him the way I did three and a half years ago. Both, I suspect.

'Thanks,' I say instead, meaning it.

'What's up then? You said you couldn't talk about it on the phone.' He shifts, sounding slightly impatient now.

Of course, he's in a hurry to get back, *to her*, and I figure he didn't really want a coffee at all, thinking it would only prolong his visit. I feel embarrassed when I realise that's why he refused to sit down. He's made it clear his visit is going to be short, even if he has shrugged off his jacket. So, I'll just have to be grateful for whatever time he does give me.

'It's about Marcus,' I clear my throat and swallow what feels like a giant marble. 'I can't be sure, in fact, I'm not at all, because it would be madness to think it, but I believe he may have come back. From the dead.'

Jim's grassy green eyes bulge at that and when he chokes on his coffee, I fight off the threat of hysterical laughter. If I give into it, I might drown in it.

'I know it sounds crazy, but—'

'It *is* crazy, Linda. Whatever makes you think that? Has something happened?'

Odd that Jim's slurping of his coffee is no longer an irritant. When we were together it used to put my back up until I wanted to scream. Funny how married couples get hung up on the trivial things. Flaws like that mean nothing in the big scheme of things but you only understand that once you've experienced real fear and grief. When your heart has been broken and ripped apart you see everything differently. You can't not.

'I need to show you something.' I'm back to my bossy self, the way I always was around Jim, as I open the laptop and gesture him to come over.

'Look. See.' I point at the photograph of Marcus on the Welcome Back website. My eyes flick between Marcus and Jim, waiting for him to clock it. 'Well?' I demand.

'It certainly looks like Marcus.' He concedes, frowning.

'Well, whoever he is, he's been in touch.'

'With you?' His kind eyes widen.

'Of course, who else, the pope?' I almost laugh at that and so does he but then we both remember what we're doing here, that this is a serious matter.

'And?' He's growing more curious, leaning in for a better look. He smells of anti-dandruff shampoo, the same one he's used for years, and freshly sawn wood.

'He asked to meet.'

'Tell me you didn't, Linda.'

I nod, taking in how worried he appears. He does still care a little then, like one would an ex who used to be a big part of your life. Not in a romantic way, of course, but neither of us can forget the life we created together, good, and bad. Not when we have two grown-up daughters to show for it.

'I went to meet him tonight at a pub in town, but he didn't show up and then I got this text,' I rummage in my bag for my phone and show him the text Marcus AKA Tony Fortin sent me and my response, making Jim's pale eyebrows climb higher up his head.

'You know that it can't really be Marcus, don't you?' Jim warns solemnly, staring too long into my eyes as if searching for signs of madness.

'That's what Gail said.' Sighing, I take another gulp of my coffee, realising for the first time that I too slurp, yet Jim never once brought it to my attention during our marriage as I did his faults. He really is the better person. Not for the first time I remind myself that the grass isn't always greener on the other side, and you never know what you have until it's gone. Old wives' tales still mean something even in this modern-day age. 'But it's the spitting image of him. You've got to agree. And look at the language, he uses, it's South African.'

'Hmm.' Jim is mulling things over in his head, and that's a good sign. It means he's not dismissing the idea, not immediately anyway. He always was a thinker who would wait things out rather than jump right in, whereas I'm the opposite, impatient as hell and demanding instant answers.

'You do realise that if it isn't Marcus, and it most probably isn't although I do agree this is all a bit bizarre, you have no idea who this man is. He could be up to no good, making you think that Marcus is still alive.'

'Oh God, Jim. I hadn't thought of that.' What Jim's said has truly panicked me. As usual, I didn't think about what I might have been getting into. I should have listened to Gail.

'You should have listened to Gail,' Jim is saying in unison, proving once again that we think alike. 'We don't know anything about this Tony . . .'

'Fortin. Tony Fortin. And before you ask, I've already looked him up online, but couldn't find any profile on social media that fitted his age. Now that really is suspicious.' I share this information boastfully as if I'm already halfway there to convincing Jim.

'Or he might not be into social media. A man of his age. There are plenty of us who aren't.'

I'd forgotten for the moment that Jim has never been on Facebook or Twitter in his life and most likely still hasn't heard of Snapchat or TikTok. They're just things the girls talk about over dinner without his really listening.

'But if it isn't Marcus, and you've got to admit that they are complete doppelgangers, then why is he interested in me?'

'Perhaps he saw your profile and liked what he saw.' Jim half-smiles when he says this, and I feel myself almost blushing again. Validation from my ex, however small, is a welcome ego boost. But we both know it means nothing. Especially since he has a new girlfriend and, knowing Jim from old, I know for sure he is a one-woman man. No doubt about it. Gail was always one for reminding me that a lot of women would kill for someone like Jim. I couldn't see it back then, but I can appreciate his good points now in a way that would have been impossible before. What's that saying? Familiarity breeds contempt. Too bloody right it does, and it happens to the best of us, despite our good intentions.

'Or Marcus has been searching for me and now that he's found me, he wants to meet up so he can explain what really happened that night. He might want to warn me about something.' I don't really know where I'm going with this as the thought terrifies me. Once again, the very real fear that Marcus has come back to punish me, grips me. Jim must see this in my eyes because he looks worried. His pale, sun-starved face is whiter than ever.

'If you want my advice, Linda, and presumably you do, otherwise, you wouldn't have invited me here, I think you should drop this thing, whatever it is, right now. We know what happened the night Marcus died. Best not drag the whole thing up again. Otherwise, you could end up being hurt all over again.'

I sit up straighter in my chair and try not to feel aggrieved by his response. 'I know you mean well, Jim. But I can't just forget about it. This is my husband we're talking about.' I ignore the very real look of hurt on Jim's face when I say this. 'I'd never forgive myself if he needed my help. I can't get over the feeling that he's somehow in hiding and that he might be in danger.'

'So, what are you going to do about it?' Knowing me as well he does, and that he's on a hiding to nothing, Jim changes tack.

'I intend to find him.'

'And how exactly do you plan on doing that?' Jim finishes his coffee in one massive swallow and turns to put his mug on the table, evidently ready to leave.

'I'm going to track down his mother and find out all I can from her.' The idea hadn't occurred to me until just this minute, but I won't let on to Jim. He's more likely to give me credit if he thinks I've given this matter some thought and not reacted hastily.

'She's still alive?' Jim appears stumped by this and when I consider Marcus's age, I can understand why. Jim and I are younger and have lost both sets of our parents.

'Yes, and I have her address. She lives in Devon.'

'Are you sure about this, Linda? I mean you didn't know Marcus that well, not really. We don't know anything about his past.'

I ignore Jim's passive-aggressive jibe about my husband because he's not too far out, if I'm honest. Not that I'll admit as much to my ex.

'I don't want to see you get any more hurt.' Jim shrugs on his cord jacket. It's the same one he's had for years. Brown with patches on the elbows. I used to tell him it made him look like a geography teacher, but year on year he refused to send it to the charity shop. I can't help wondering if his new woman will insist on smartening him up a bit. He's more likely to do it for someone new while the honeymoon period is in full swing.

'That means a lot to me. Really it does.' I fight the overwhelming desire to fling myself in his arms and cry into his shoulder until I'm as red-eyed as Abby was earlier. Poor Abby, I haven't even asked Jim how she's faring, but then again, he'd be reluctant to talk about her to me, knowing how his daughter feels. It's probably best I don't.

Jim nods as if he too feels nostalgic for how things used to be and then, pausing as his hand reaches for the doorknob, he turns back to me and grins. Suddenly I'm reminded of the boy from two doors down, Jim Delamere, who used to walk me home from school every day, no matter what, in case I got picked on by one of the older girls. Funny that, between them, Gail and Jim have protected me from harm for most of my life.

But I never needed rescuing. Not really.

Before I lost Marcus, I'd always seen myself as someone who had it together. As uncomplicated as they come. I wasn't co-dependent or reliant on anyone for my happiness. I knew who I was and faced the world realistically, knowing there were good and bad people in it, and one had to kindly reject the toxic ones. But since divorcing Jim, I've often wondered if I'm one of the bad, toxic people who leaves a trail of damage behind them.

'You know,' Jim says, interrupting my thoughts, 'I've always wanted to go to Devon, and I think I'm due a holiday, so what do you say to a road trip this weekend?' Jim gives me a familiar wink.

'Really?' I can't believe my luck. I still can't bring myself to throw myself into Jim's arms, knowing it wouldn't be appropriate, but I do go over and enthusiastically rub his arm. 'Thank you. You've no idea how much that means to me. I'm so glad we can still be friends.' I know I don't deserve Jim's kindness or support, but I'll take it all the same.

Girlfriend or no girlfriend. He was mine first.

CHAPTER 10

I must've fallen asleep watching *Eastenders* on catch up, my favourite of all the soaps because when my eyes flutter open, I have no idea what's happening. I adjust to the sounds gathering around me and become aware of how dark and cold the room is. Stretching and yawning, I pull my dressing gown around me and secure the threadbare belt around my shrinking waistline.

My feet hit the cool laminate floor and I quickly find my slippers and slip them on. Wondering what woke me, I switch on the table lamp, scramble for the remote and punch the off button for the TV.

That's when I hear it. A sound so subtle at first, it's barely distinguishable. Like a gentle scrape. Making up my mind that I must have imagined it, I'm about to go through to the bedroom and fall into my crumpled, unmade bed when I hear it again. The creak of a door opening, or closing, followed by a tentative footstep that doesn't want to be heard.

My body is on high alert as I listen out for the sound again, terrified that somebody has broken into my flat. I feel my heart whack against my ribcage as adrenalin pumps around my veins. Fight or flight, that's all a body knows when it's in danger. But in a flat this size, there's nowhere to hide or escape to. I'd have to flee right past where that noise came from. If there *is* an intruder inside, I'm trapped.

It suddenly hits me why I'm so cold. There's a draught coming from under the living room door as if the front door had been left open. It's always cold out in the corridor due to the concrete steps and single glazed entrance door at the bottom of the staircase that's shared between me and the downstairs flat. Has the tenant left the door open? Is that what's causing the draught and the chilly air? But that wouldn't account for the creaking door and the footsteps that sounded as if they came from directly inside my flat.

'Hello. Is anybody there?' My voice comes out as a nervous croak. I can't think of anything better to say other than the obvious, which I've seen performed by many actors on TV, in the type of scary movie where victims get picked off one by one. 'Hello?' I try to inject some confidence into my voice, to scare whoever it is away.

That's when I see a shadow flit across the bottom of the door. 'Oh, my God.' I stumble back, putting some distance between it and me. Now I know for certain that someone is in my flat. But who? And what do they want from me?

'Marcus? Is that you?' I whisper tearfully, feeling scared for my life. Has my worst fear been realised? Has Marcus come back to punish me?

'Marcus, it's me, Linda. If that's you, you'd better say so.' I've never peed myself before, though I am susceptible to the odd leak or two, but I feel a surge of urine escape into my pants. I've no time to feel shame because I unexpectedly experience a "fuck fear" moment, the kind Marcus used to coax within me, and as a result, impulsively thrust open the door.

The front door to my flat stands wide open. As I rush to slam it, not knowing if I'm trapping the intruder in with me, I hear a smothered thudding from the other side of the door and recognise it as the sound of someone descending the concrete corridor steps. Seconds later, I hear the slam of the external door that exits onto the street below. Quickly turning the key in the door, I lean against it, staying there in case that person should come back and try to force entry.

My hallway is barely four feet by four feet and has three doors going off it, one to the kitchen, one to the living room and one to the ensuite bedroom. The doors have paint brush marks on them. A fact that would have rubbed Jim up the wrong way when he saw them. He hates sloppy work. Switching on the main light, hating its bright orange glow, I'm disgusted by the dead flies in the bottom of the glass shade. Then, I go into the living room and using all my strength, drag out the hard impractical marigold sofa and push it in front of the door. Assessing it with the full weight of my body, I sigh with relief when I realise nobody is going to be able to push it away from the door. Nobody living that is.

Next, I hole up in the bedroom, making sure to keep all the doors in the flat open and every single light fitting on, deciding I'll worry about the electric bill another time. Once in bed, I rub my hands together to get warm and dig my toes further down in the bed, wrapping the duvet around them. With each inhale and exhale as I practice my meditation techniques, white puffs of air escape from my mouth, reminding me of the white foam that sometimes tops sea waves. Of course, I can't think about the sea, without conjuring up memories of Marcus. Is he alive? Has he really come back? Did he break in to alert me to something or was his presence something more sinister than that? If it was him, does he mean to hurt me?

Deciding it could have been anybody, a regular opportunist burglar, or one of those hooded youths that hang around the fish shop trying their hand at scaring me, I wonder if I should call the police? But, after what happened in Greece, when I was extensively questioned and cross-examined by the police about Marcus's disappearance, I've been terrified that I could be implicated in his death so it's natural for me to want to avoid them. Then again, if Marcus *is* alive, and responsible for the break-in, the police wouldn't be able to make the connection. I'm still trying to decide what to do when my phone beeps loudly, making me jump out of my skin. Swiping it off the bedside table, I glance at the screen and feel my heart freeze. It's him. Tony Fortin. AKA Marcus.

'Hi, Linda. Sorry to text so late. I expect you're all cosied up in bed in your flat by now.'

My heart is in my mouth as I read this. I never once mentioned to him that I live in a flat. How can he know this? Unless he's been watching me. He has to be the one who broke in. I'm one hundred per cent convinced of that now. My Marcus. Alive. Here. In my flat. Just a few feet away from me. But why? Just to frighten me? To punish me for trying to kill him? Is that what I did? I wish I could remember. That night is so fuzzy in my head.

'Sorry about earlier too. Something came up and I couldn't get back to you. My loss, I know. I have a lot going on in my life currently and I don't want to overcomplicate things, so I think it's best we don't meet up just yet. Please don't think I'm giving you the cold shoulder. Nothing could be further from the truth. Speak soon. Tony x.'

There's no way his texting isn't connected to the break-in. That would be too much of a coincidence and as I've said before, I'm not a believer. How odd that minutes after someone has broken into my flat, I get a text from the man I believe might be my dead husband. If there was nothing fishy about it, why text me now and not earlier? He's had all night to do so. Does he mean to frighten me? Is that what this is about? Or is he trying to tell me something I'm too stupid to work out? The only other connection I can think of, apart from mentioning my flat, is his reference to "cold shoulder" as memories of Lilo Lil and that awful revealing top she had on come back to haunt me. That was the night Marcus went into the sea and didn't come out again. I don't text back immediately but when I do, I keep it simple, not wanting to give too much away.

'That's a shame as I'd really like to meet you in person. I under-stand how complicated life can be sometimes, but it helps to talk. Please

get in touch soon.' I take a big breath before typing, '*By the way, how do you know I live in a flat?*'

When I don't receive a reply, I'm tempted to call Jim, to run things past him in the hope he'll be able to make sense of it all, but another glance at my phone reveals it's almost 3 a.m. and I'm not going to bother the poor man again tonight or risk disturbing him while he's in bed with another woman. I don't know when I started to think of Jim as "the poor man" either. Was it before, during or after our divorce? Jim is as resilient as they come. He's never been one for drama or romantic gestures. He copes, calmly and quietly with whatever is thrown at him without causing a fuss. Where once I would have looked down on him for these personality traits, thinking him boring, I now admire him. He's always been my rock, yet I never appreciated his strengths. Then again, I was always one for taking what I had for granted, at least that's what Gail would say. I realise now that she'd be right.

It might be too late to contact Jim, but I don't have the same reservations where my best friend is concerned, so I punch in a long elaborate text to Gail, filling her in on all the details, including the blind date that was a no-show, Jim's visit, the break-in, and Tony Fortin's latest text message. I wait but don't receive any response from her either which surprises me. It's not like Gail to ignore a text, no matter the time. I try not to feel hurt by this. She could be asleep with her phone switched off although that's unlikely as Gail lives for her iPhone, always trading up to the latest version and boring me to death with all the latest gadgets it boasts.

Feeling abandoned by everybody, which is exactly what I'd done to my family three and a half years ago, I ask myself why I'm texting Gail when I know I should be dialling 999 but I'm too scared to do so. I've been bloody broken into for Christ's sake. My miserable grey flat, which boasts no attractive features, is, or was, meant to be my personal space, but it no longer feels safe, making me long for home in a way I've never done before. My old bed with Jim in it always felt like the most secure place in the world.

But I can't phone the police because if the break-in has anything at all to do with Marcus, then I, like him, have too much to hide and can't afford to involve them. The more I think about it, the more I decide against telling Jim about the intruder because my ex, being who he is, will want me to do the right thing and call the police. He can be persistent when he wants to be, and I don't fancy putting myself in that position or risk alienating him. Later, when I finally get to speak to Gail, I'll play things down with her too, letting her think I had a nightmare and imagined the whole incident. The last thing I want is for her to mention it to Jim.

CHAPTER 11

It's Saturday. The day we've planned to set off on our trip to Devon — and Jim, being the early bird he is, was outside pipping the horn at 8 a.m., while I was still pulling on my clothes. Hadn't even finished my first cup of tea of the day. On coming outside, weighed down by a hastily packed hold-all, hair still wet from the shower, I'm surprised but amused to see a vintage pale-blue Volkswagen camper van dominating the road.

'Bloody hell, Jim. When did you get a campervan?'

'It's been a project of mine these last twelve months or so,' Jim boasts proudly as I hop in next to him, throwing my bag into the rear and putting on my safety belt.

Jim runs an appreciative hand over the shiny steering wheel. 'You know how I love a refurb.'

'Did you do all this yourself?' I ask in amazement, taking in the lovingly refurbished vintage interior, complete with cream leather and oak-veneered tops. 'Christ, it's got everything,' I gasp, twisting around for a better look, 'Even a kitchen sink.' And it really does have everything — a pull-out bed, table, fridge, cooker etc.

'Not ideal weather for its first road trip, still . . .'

'Where are you planning on going in it?'

'I thought France and Spain. Take a few months off in the summer, see a bit of the world.'

To say I'm gobsmacked is putting it mildly. I find myself seething inwardly as Jim puts the camper van into gear and pulls off. For years, he refused to go anywhere other than Hunstanton in Norfolk for our summer holidays. Always the same caravan site, same caravan even. Lodge number twenty-three, I remember as if it were yesterday. Jim hated flying, didn't like foreign food — or foreigners come to that, although he wouldn't admit to that now — and it used to drive me crazy. For the girls' sake I'd pretend to like the dirty grey Atlantic Sea, windy beaches, warm beer and hard-as-nails ice cream. Not to mention those awful entertainment shows in the clubhouse. Jim, shandy in hand, would roar with laughter at the sexist comedians, while I'd feign excuses and take the children back to the caravan for an early night, tucking them into their bunkbeds so I could have some time alone.

When my phone rings, it's a welcome diversion, because it's not my business anymore how Jim has changed and become more adventurous, although it does still hurt realising that he wouldn't change for me, but is quite willing to do so now, for the new girlfriend.

'Hi, Gail. Are you okay? I've tried texting and ringing a few times.'

'Been busy that's all,' Gail replies, exhaling what I know to be cigarette smoke. She sounds hungover which isn't unusual for her on a Saturday morning.

'Me too,' I say grinning, and sharing a smile with Jim. 'You'll never guess where I am.'

'Mount bloody Everest? No, I know, bungee jumping in Ibiza, anything's possible with you.'

Her laughter is intended to be friendly, but I narrow my eyes anyway. I haven't always been irresponsible. For twenty-eight years I was a doting mother and industrious housewife.

'No. On the way to Devon. With Jim.'

I expect her to come back with an OMG or WTF but I get nothing.

'Gail, are you still there?'

'Yes, I'm here,' she says finally, 'which is where you should be. Don't tell me you're on a mad hunt to find your not-so-dead husband's mother to see if you can dig up any secrets?'

'You've got it in one,' I laugh nervously, convinced that she's pissed off.

'You know, Linda, this is so typical of you.'

'What is?' my voice is as small as a sparrow's.

'For one thing, it's bloody selfish of you to involve Jim, after all you've put him through and another, well you could have asked me. I would have come with you.'

Remembering how incredibly supportive Gail had been when I lost Marcus and how she hopped on the next flight to Greece to help me out, I feel guilty. Shit. Why hadn't I asked Gail instead of involving poor Jim? *Because, Linda, you got swept away by Jim's invitation and was grateful at last to be on good terms with him, knowing it means you are halfway to being forgiven. And if Jim forgives you, then the girls will too.*

'I know how you feel about . . .' I slide my eyes at Jim, not wanting him to know he is the subject of our discussion because that would be plain embarrassing, 'but we're cool.'

I realise I'm talking to myself as Gail has hung up on me. Jim raises his eyebrows in a knowing fashion.

He laughs. 'Gail being Gail.'

'Nothing changes, does it?' I offer helplessly, hating the fact he must know the row was about him.

'Everything changes, Linda. Everything.'

He's not looking at me when he says this, instead concentrating on joining the A43, and I don't like to admit how much Jim's thirst for change makes me feel uncomfortable. I hate the idea of some other woman being the source of that newfound eagerness. I don't want Jim for myself, not really — although I do miss "us" as we once were — but I still feel hurt. So, I have words with myself and try to be happy for him. If anyone deserves a second chance, it's Jim.

When his phone goes off, he answers through Bluetooth. The fact that he's able to find his way around this scary technological world reminds me once again of how much Jim has moved on. I wouldn't have a clue how to set something like that up in my car. *If I had a car.* At first, I wonder if it's Gail, calling him up to tear him off a strip, but no—

'Hello, love,' he says. 'Is everything okay?'

Oh God. I don't know where to look. It must be Jim's new woman. I wonder if she knows he's with me. I'd better keep silent, I don't want to get him into trouble or make him regret helping me out.

'Oh, that's nice. I'm glad you and your sister are spending the day together. I'm sorry about lunch, but I had other plans.'

My heart settles in my chest as I realise Jim is talking to one of our daughters. Which one, I can't tell yet. But when Jim coughs uncomfortably and shifts around in his seat, signs of a guilty husband that I remember from old, I'm guessing it's Abby and that she's giving him a tough time for being with me.

'I know, love, I know. Yes, you did warn me, but everything's fine. And no, she didn't make me, I offered.'

When Jim hangs up, we're equally as embarrassed as each other. My cheeks certainly feel hot to the touch.

'Looks like we're both in the doghouse,' I grin, breaking the ice.

'Scooby dooby doo,' he howls suddenly, and I laugh at his impression of the cartoon dog our girls grew up watching. They loved the show as much as we had as kids when it was first aired. They could never get enough of their dad fooling around, playing the adorable but clumsy Great Dane. I, on the other hand, had seen it enough times to no longer be impressed.

'You've even got your own Mystery Machine.' I point out.

And then we're both doing the "Scooby dooby doo" howl and I laugh until I think I'm going to piss my pants. Smiling back at Jim, I can't ever remember it being this good between us. We both seem different somehow. The same but not the same in an odd sort of way. It's as if we were newer versions of ourselves. Improved models.

CHAPTER 12

Jim might have done an excellent job on the exterior and interior of the campervan, which is as good as new, but he's not so hot at the mechanics side of things. So far, we've broken down three times and had the AA out twice. They offered to tow us to the nearest garage for repairs to be arranged, but Jim refused as he's insistent he can get it going again.

The fault has something to do with the starter motor, which means if Jim hits it with an iron bar for long enough, there's a good chance of it starting up again. What Jim didn't tell me before setting out is that he already knew about the issue but was confident in the iron bar technique, which he'd purposefully brought along for the trip.

All of this means we've lost four hours and we're barely at Bristol which means we've still got at least another three hours to go. It gets dark at 4 p.m. in November and it's raining heavily, with no sign of letting up. Even if we do make good time, we won't reach Clovelly, the small fishing village in North Devon where Marcus's mum lives until dark.

I am desperate to pee and, for once, starving hungry, but until Jim gets the campervan going again, I'm having to wait in the passenger seat, staring at the rain drizzling down the windows. I watch him repeatedly bash the engine, all the while sheltering under a bit of tarpaulin he managed to find in the boot. Neither of us thought to bring any food or drink with us, hoping to stop at service stations on the way for snacks and refreshments. This means I'm parched but reluctant to say anything. The trouble with being a non-fee-paying passenger is that you're obliged to remain grateful, no matter the circumstances. I'm not sure how long I can keep it up though. We haven't even joined the M5 yet, with Jim deciding to opt for quieter roads like the A429, which again is adding to our journey time. Clovelly seems further away now than when we first set off. But of course, I don't say so.

The driver's door opens and Jim leaps athletically into his seat. *When did he get so trim?* Rain runs down his nose and clings to his eyelashes. He looks as cold as I feel. The engine's still dead so we're without heating and both shivering like mad.

'Any joy?' I ask uselessly.

'Let's see, shall we?' Pulling a face, he tries the engine for what feels like the twentieth time. We both wait anxiously as it clicks over and then splutters to a stop.

'We could always get the AA out again,' I prompt hopefully, desperate to be rescued from this miserable situation. I've even thought of hitching a lift the next time we see anyone. But this road, off the tourist trail, is extremely quiet. I've only seen one tractor in the last hour.

'I don't understand why I can't get it to turn over. It's always worked before.' Jim ponders helplessly, staring at the iron bar in his hand, looking more like a young boy than a grown man.

'What's it doing differently this time?' I'm keen to help. But I know my boundaries and want to avoid Jim getting annoyed with me. He knows I don't have a clue about cars. But then again, nor does he — or so it would seem.

'If I didn't know better, I'd think it had run out of petrol.'

'Jim. You did . . . I mean, you couldn't have forgotten to . . .'

Jim's eyes bulge in one of those comedic light bulb moments when the penny finally drops, and after glaring at the dashboard for a few seconds, is out of the door in a shot. Baffled, I watch him go around to the boot of the camper-van and take something out. He then appears at my door, knocking on the window. Reluctantly, I slide it down, teeth chattering with the cold. Jim has the tarpaulin back over his head and shakes a petrol can at me.

'I'll be back as soon as I can. The sign over there says it's three miles to Burford.'

* * *

It's dark by the time Jim gets back swinging a full petrol can and limping on one foot due to his fancy new trainers not being designed for actual walking. He's sodden to the skin but hasn't lost his sense of humour because, when he shows me his rucksack is full of food and drink, saying 'The hunter returns,' there's a soppy grin on his face. The Jim of old who knows he's done a respectable job and is waiting to be praised stands in front of me.

'Oh, well done, you!' I exclaim excitedly, managing to claw the rucksack out of his hands, saving it from the elements. It's still chucking it down and shows no sign of letting up.

'I thought we might as well spend the night here now it's dark?' Jim suggests. 'The weather is only supposed to get worse and soon I won't be able to see at all to drive.'

Obviously, I'm disappointed because I hadn't antici-pated the delay. It's crucial that I find Marcus's mother as soon as humanly possible so I can find out if she knows any-thing about her son rising from the dead, but I can't really argue with Jim's logic, so—

'It's okay, Jim. I wouldn't want to drive in this weather either.' I concede, albeit not as graciously as I could have done.

'At least we've got food and drink and a dry place to sleep.' After shaking off the worst of the rain, Jim climbs back inside and starts to go through the bag. 'Look, hot — well, warm — coffee, some sausage rolls, crisps, bottled water, packets of sweets *and* chocolate bars.'

'I'm starving. Can't wait.' And I really can't, but there's one thing I must do first. 'I have to pee.' I tell him half-laughing, not fancying my chances of having to go out in that weather. The one thing the campervan lacks is a toilet of any kind. Not even a bucket.

'Rather you than me.' Jim shrugs off his wet coat and gallantly hands it to me along with the piece of wet tarpaulin.

I make a dash for it, holding the tarpaulin over my head and flinching at the wetness of Jim's jacket. Finding shelter under an old tree that looks as if it regularly gets hit by lightning, I pull down my damp jeans, squat, do the business, careful not to get urine on my ankle boots and hastily pull everything back up.

'Drip-drying is something I haven't done in years,' I grumble to Jim on climbing back into the campervan only for my eyes to light up when I see what he's accomplished in the fleeting time I've been away.

The leather seats in the back have been turned around, facing each other and the table has been pulled out in front of them. The curtains are drawn, and the lights dimmed, giving the interior a cosy feel. Set out on the table is an array of treats that I can't wait to get stuck into.

'At your service, ma'am,' Jim jokes, a tea-towel balanced on his arm as if he were a waiter in a high-end establishment.

'Let me dry my hair first.' I laugh, shivering madly. The tarpaulin had proven next to useless. Worse than a chocolate fireguard as my mother, and Jim's, would have said.

'Come here, I'll do it.' Jim says and before I can argue he's spun me around and is pounding my hair none-too-gently with a scratchy towel. I grumble but it does the trick.

I stand with my back to him and relish the feeling of being looked after. It's so long since somebody cared for me that I want to cry, and when a single tear falls onto my cheek I bat it away, so Jim doesn't notice. That would be too humiliating. It upsets me that this man who once worshipped and adored me and who respected me for being strong and wise, *mostly*, might have changed his opinion of me. Others can think what they like, but Jim and I go so far back, I couldn't bear it if he pitied me.

'A feast for a king,' I say, later, when we're tucking into flaky sausage rolls with pastry crumbs spilling down our fronts. Radio 4 is quietly on in the background to hide the rolls of thunder that Jim knows I'm terrified of. God forbid there should be lightning.

'And a queen.' Jim jokes, raising his bottle of lukewarm beer as if it were a chilled glass of champagne. I wouldn't swap the god-awful cheap beer for any fancy wine. Even with everything going wrong I don't regret this time spent with Jim. Just like old times. Earlier we'd brushed our teeth together, spitting mouthwash out of the windows, using baby wipes as a method of washing and modestly changing into our PJs, each of us taking it in turns to hide under a towel. It's been a long day and, having polished off all the food, our full bellies lead to eventual tiredness. So, when I eye up the bed, Jim is quick to notice.

'I'll sleep on the floor,' he offers, like a gentleman.

'Don't be daft, Jim. We can share.'

'You sure?'

'It wouldn't be the first time we've shared a bed, and nothing happened between us.' I snort, but then stop myself from laughing when I see his horrified face. 'Oh God, Jim, sorry. I was joking. I didn't mean anything by it.'

'Well, just for that, you get to sleep on the right-hand side.' He grumbles playfully and I'm relieved I haven't offended him. Jim is being kinder to me than I deserve as he knows I always sleep on the right.

CHAPTER 13

It's the next morning and we're back on the road. So far, the campervan is behaving itself and has only come to a stop once. The same could be said for our conversation. Things are tense between us, if not plain awkward.

Last night, things had been easy and relaxed. That changed the moment we woke up, with Jim in a foul mood and me walking on eggshells around him. Again, like old times, except not in an enjoyable way. The change of mood coincided with a phone call that Jim went outside to answer, despite the rain. He was ages on the phone, pacing up and down the country lane we'd parked in, and when he finally got back into the van and we set off, he refused to offer up any explanation for keeping me waiting.

'Was that one of the girls on the phone?'

'No. Why do you ask?' He muttered, clearly not wishing to talk about it.

'Sorry, it's none of my business. I didn't mean to pry.' I feel myself shrinking into my seat, hurt by his abruptness.

'It was work, that's all.'

I can tell Jim isn't being honest with me and I go back to feeling depressed, certain that he must have been speaking to his woman, partner, other half or whatever else he might choose to call her. Who else would he have been on the phone to for so long?

Neither of us has mentioned last night and I'm blowed if I will if he won't. It had started with Jim loaning me a pair of his thick socks as I was so cold, even beneath the quilt, my teeth were chattering nonstop. It was only when he cuddled up next to me and put an arm casually around my waist that I warmed up. After that we'd talked long into the night about when the girls had been born, the hours of excruciating labour and Jim almost passing out when he saw all the blood, reminiscing how much each baby weighed, when they first talked and first walked. Once we'd exhausted that subject, we'd discussed in detail each of the three houses we'd owned together and the hard graft we'd put into each one. Especially what was meant to be our forever home in Victoria Road, the four-bedroom villa style family house with the big kitchen table. That's when I'd grown emotional and started to cry, and Jim, unable to cope with this, had gently suggested we go to sleep. And so, we had, but we did so holding hands. And now this morning, we are back to where we once were. Not exactly enemies but not friends either. A formality has crept between us that wasn't there yesterday.

Leaning back in my seat, I close my eyes and daydream about being in Marcus's arms. If I try hard enough, I can remember the way his smooth hands felt on my body, not rough or prickly like Jim's working man's hands. The smell of Marcus was something I could never get enough of. The whiskey voice and smoky breath. I used to think I might melt into the wholeness of his embrace, until he absorbed every inch of me into his own body. That's the effect he had on people, women in particular. When Jim and I were married, we were together every day but not in the sense that I wanted to be. For a while, I had that with Marcus, until his fascination for other women returned and began to drive a wedge between us.

I should have known, even then, that a man like Marcus, who'd loved many women, would never stop desiring them.

Never be able to commit to just one. I never set out to change him in the way I would have liked to have done with Jim, but I did want, no, *expect* him to be faithful. It's not that I suspected him of sleeping with anybody else, not really, but I did have my doubts. Marcus was a sensual being who lived completely in the present, never worrying about the future or the past. Or so I'd thought, until now.

'Not long now. Nearly there.'

Jim's voice, back to normal now that he's had a chance to self-reflect, has me sitting upright in my seat. Yawning, I realise I must have dropped off and that I'd been in the middle of a dream where Marcus and I were together again on a beautiful white beach with the sun on our faces and sand in our toes. As the image of us fades, I concentrate on the road ahead and the signs flashing by that announce, 'Clovelly 40 miles.'

CHAPTER 14

The house, with its thatched roof, wooden shuttered windows, and picturesque cottage garden on the edge of a cliff could have been straight out of a postcard. If I were to imagine moving to a seaside cottage in Devon, this is exactly what I would have pictured. It must be even more beautiful during the summer months with colourful flowers springing up everywhere. Multiple garden pathways lead to secretive corners, each with its own glimpse of the shiny blue sea in the distance. An attractive dry-stone wall runs around the property, encompassing a herb garden, a small greenhouse, and well-maintained lawn.

A sleepy black and white cat spawls on the path leading up to the seagrass-painted front door. It refuses to move out of our way, so we edge around it, wary of the twitching tail which is the only clue that it knows we're there. The sun is as high as it can be for November and the sky is a perfect winter blue. We pass a neat little potting shed that has plastic pots filled with compost inside. Marcus's mother is evidently greener fingered than her son ever was. Everywhere I look there are different coloured watering cans of every shape, colour, and design. This makes Mrs Bouchard something of a collector and again I'm struck by how different mother and son are, because Marcus wasn't one for hoarding anything — other than women's telephone numbers — and deemed unnecessary or excessive belongings as superficial.

Jim walks a few steps behind me on the narrow path, and I suspect he's as nervous as I am and wants me to take the lead. I can't blame him. This was my idea after all. As I tap on the door with the ornate doorknocker, I glance through the bay window to see flowery curtains, fringed lampshades, soft pastel furniture and gilt-edged country landscapes on the walls. I gulp and take a deep breath, wondering if the lady I can hear calling out musically from behind the door, *my mother-in-law*, will invite us inside or promptly shoo us away.

A waft of baking hits us as soon as the door is thrown open and I'm immediately assailed by memories of my childhood and my mother's attempts at making cakes. Smells of ginger, vanilla and lemon always remind me of her. The woman standing in front of us is small and compact though, and very unlike my mother. Tidy, well-presented, and not much more than five foot two, I wonder how someone the size of Marcus could have come out of her and try to imagine the baby that was once my husband clinging to this woman's tiny bosom, being rocked in her arms and comforted. Somehow, I can't picture it. She doesn't look the mothering sort to me but then again, who am I to judge having abandoned my own daughters.

'Yes?' She waits expectantly, her blue eyes flitting between Jim and me as she takes stock of us, wondering what it is we want.

There's no trace of a Devon accent and for a minute this throws me until I remember that this woman was born in British Columbia, before moving to South Africa. Marcus boasted that his travel-hungry parents lived on three continents at various stages of their married life.

'Mrs Bouchard, my name is Linda.' I pause before saying, 'Linda Delamere,' because I don't want to alarm her straightaway by announcing that we share the same surname.

Ignoring Jim's sidelong glance, I hold out my hand and she guardedly takes it.

'I was hoping we might speak to you about your son.'

'My son?'

Despite my intention of trying to prepare her gradually for the news I'm about to deliver, I can tell her back is up already.

'Yes, Marcus.' Now it's my turn to glance at Jim, hoping to gain a bit of encouragement, but his eyes have hit the floor and his hands are twiddling in his pockets. I could kill him for that. But instead, I put on my best smile, the one I used to save for this woman's son and say, 'Please can we come in? I need to speak to you in private.'

* * *

Mrs Bouchard, who insists on being called Tilly, has served us a pot of tea, made with proper tea leaves and a slice of homemade cake each. Jim tucks into his. I'm too nervous to take a bite out of mine, but I thank her politely for all the trouble she has gone to. While she fetches us a fork each and more sugar cubes, I study the room. Its furnishings are soft and elegant, like its owner. The bookcase is stocked with well-thumbed favourites and the piano lid is open, with sheet music in front of it, suggesting it's played regularly.

When Marcus's mother comes back into the room and finally stops fussing to sit in the armchair facing us, I get the impression nobody would dare ask her for her age. Her eyes are lively and youthful even though she must be pushing eighty-five. She is what my mum would have called a proper lady. Well-spoken, educated and no doubt artistic, judging by her long, elegant fingers whose nails are painted a subtle pink. Her white hair, framed around her face in a no-nonsense bob, looks like it gets taken to the hairdresser once a week and her clothes are inexpensively middle class. Most likely from Marks and Spencer.

'So, you're Matilda then, Tilly for short?' I break the silence, aware that she is appraising me, but not in an intimidating way. It must be unsettling for her to have two strangers rock up wanting to quiz her about her dead son.

'Yes, that's right. Matilda Bouchard. Married for more than fifty years to Caspian Bouchard. Widowed for ten. He had an aggressive brain tumour, you see, and I'm afraid it took him within six months of being diagnosed. We didn't have long to get used to the idea.'

'I'm deeply sorry for your loss,' I say, knowing exactly how she feels but at the same time realising my words won't bring any comfort. They never do.

'Thank you, dear. Now, if you don't mind, what is it you wanted to tell me about my son?'

'Well, I was wondering, could you tell me when you last heard from him?'

'Is this a joke?'

Her eyes are boring into mine and I watch her wring her hands in her lap. 'No, not at all. I'm sorry, I shouldn't have sprung it on you like that.'

'It might be best to start from the beginning, Linda.' Jim comes out of his teacup to offer some productive advice for once.

'I don't know how to tell you this, you see I don't know if Marcus ever mentioned it to you . . .'

'Mentioned what?' Mrs Bouchard is rattled.

'I'm sorry. I seem to be making a pig's ear of this so, please forgive me if I come straight to the point.'

'I wish you would,' Marcus's mother barks.

'Two-and-a-half years ago I married your son, Marcus. He told me he wrote home to tell you, but I never knew for certain that he had. I didn't see the letter, you see, but we always planned to visit you in person when we returned to England for good. That's how I got your address and knew your name.'

'Let me get this right, you're saying you married my son two-and-a-half years ago?'

'He didn't tell you then?' My heart sinks as I realise that Marcus lied to me. What else don't I know about him? How many more lies are there?

'He most certainly did not because there's nothing to tell. I can assure you, Miss Delamere, or whatever it is you call yourself, that you did not marry my son.'

'I have the marriage certificate in my bag. I can show you . . .'

'No need,' Mrs Bouchard gets to her feet and glares at me. 'Because no such certificate exists.'

'How can you be so sure of that?' Jim cuts in.

'Because my son died in a boating accident forty-two years ago, when he was eighteen.'

'That's not possible,' I gasp, jerkily getting to my feet, yet I'm unable to shake off the disturbing memory of the Greek police confirming the same thing even though both Gail and I had refused to believe it. 'Marcus Bouchard was born in South Africa on 13th July 1962, moved to British Columbia at the age of eight, married me two-and-a-half years ago on a beach in Bali and died in Corfu eight months ago.'

'Well, I'm deeply sorry for your loss, obviously, Linda.' Mrs Bouchard visibly softens on hearing that I'm a widow too, but she remains firm on her stand. 'But I can assure you it wasn't my Marcus you married. Whoever he was, he wasn't my son.'

'But he gave me your name, your details and I have his passport.'

'Perhaps there are two Marcus Bouchards.' Jim steps in obligingly, greedily helping himself to my slice of cake, knowing I won't have the stomach for it.

'Please, could I see a picture of your son, Mrs Bouchard, Tilly, I mean? I have to know if there's been some sort of mistake.'

'A case of mistaken identity, you mean. Well, I suppose it could happen, although I'm not sure why your husband would have my address.' She narrows her eyes at me but nevertheless leaves the room, coming back a moment later with a framed photograph.

'This was taken on the day Marcus died. That's him, there,' she points a finger at a tall youth, strikingly thin with a shock of red hair and pale white skin, 'with his best friend. Just before they took off for their fishing trip.'

Her voice wavers and her eyes fill with tears as she reminisces, but my attention is not on the boy she calls her son but on the best friend whose proud jutted chin and bold blue eyes deliberately torment me. He too is bare-chested, but unlike his friend he is deeply tanned. His hands rest on the steering wheel of the boat, suggesting he is the one in charge.

'What is it, Linda?' Jim gets to his feet, a concerned look on his face and cake crumbs evident on his jumper. He can tell how upset I am. My legs are so wobbly I'm struggling to stay upright, and my hands visibly shake.

'What was the best friend's name?' I ask, barely able to get my words out. I feel the blackness closing in on me. It's impossible. It can't be. But it is. It really is.

'Tony, Tony Fortin, if I remember rightly,' Mrs Bouchard confirms the worst.

After that, I don't remember anything because the floor comes up to meet me and I black out.

CHAPTER 15

Back at the flat, I make myself a cup of tea. Strong, with three teaspoons of sugar. The kind of drink my mum would have made as a cure for all the upsets in the world. On the drive back from Devon, Jim and I remained quiet and reflective, stopping only once for a comfort break, a coffee, and a Cornish pasty. Even the campervan understood the urgency to return home because it didn't break down once.

Jim floored the pedal, keeping to eighty miles per hour and I didn't murmur a single protest, which is unlike me as I'm a terrible passenger. We only spoke about what happened once. And that was enough for both of us.

'It's true, then.' Jim had muttered sheepishly, not taking his eyes off the road. 'You were right all along. About Marcus.'

I immediately thought back to the moment in Mrs Bouchard's house when my eyes had shot from the picture of her lovely son with the pale eyes and cheeky smile to fasten onto the younger version of my husband whose eyes were clouded with mystery, and a darkness that I'd never noticed before. Before I blacked out, I turned to Jim and saw the same mixture of shock and disbelief that must have been mirrored in my eyes.

In response to Jim's question, I'd nodded and pretended at a casualness that didn't exist because I hadn't been able to think about anything else since Mrs Bouchard dropped the bombshell about Tony Fortin, who my not-so-dead husband had been masquerading as. I'm finding the whole thing embarrassing. Especially around Jim who must think me a fool for being taken in by my lying, smooth-talking, worthless charmer of a husband.

'You know, it's almost funny that Marcus, having taken on his dead best friend's identity when he was alive, is back to assuming his own identity now, he's dead. Or meant to be.' Tears had rolled down my face as I said this. Jim couldn't or wouldn't look at me. Not that I blamed him. Just like our daughter Abby, I was not at my best when I cried. Blotchy skin, red nose, shrunken eyes, and a snotty nose were not viewed as attractive features by the opposite sex. 'Why would he do this, Jim? I mean how could he hurt me in this way?'

'Perhaps it's not about you. He might have other things going on. Things he doesn't want anybody else to know about, not even you.'

'You mean like a scam? Something illegal?' I'd been impressed by Jim's insight. For once he could be spot on. It sounded exactly like something Marcus might do.

'I was thinking maybe an insurance claim. Something like that. It's been done before,' Jim had suggested.

I mulled this over, thinking Jim could be right. Marcus could have lost a load of money in a game of cards that I knew nothing about. His luck at winning couldn't last forever. Perhaps he needed a big sum of money to repay someone or risk getting hurt or even losing his life in the process if he failed to pay up on time.

'Does that put me in danger too, do you think?'

'I'm not sure. Maybe. Maybe not.' Jim frowned.

'That's not exactly helpful, Jim.' I pointed out huffily as if he were to blame for my pitiful circumstances.

'I know, sorry.' He shrugged apologetically and I forgave him instantly.

'Can you think of any other reason why he'd fake his own death and come back without letting you in on the secret?'

'No.' I lied, feeling myself go red all over. Marcus had every reason to want to get his own back on me after what happened. But I can't tell Jim about the vague memories I have of pushing Marcus into the water when I don't know if they're real or not. What would he think of me?

Knocking back the last of my tea and wincing at the overdose of sweetness, I stare out of the window at the chip shop opposite. I'm due to clock on at six, but don't know how I'm going to face it. I have no choice though, I'm broke and desperately need the cash. There are only two pounds of emergency credit in the electric meter and all that's left in the cupboard is a tin of potatoes, spaghetti hoops and a pot noodle, all of which I inherited on moving in. Worse still, they're out of date. I don't even have any milk, hence the black tea.

Jim dropped me off just after three o'clock, about half an hour ago, and it's already starting to get dark, but I can't afford to turn the lights on yet in case the meter runs out of electric and I end up coming home to a blacked-out flat when my shift ends at ten. After the break-in the other night, that's not something I want to contemplate. As my stomach rumbles with hunger, I'm reminded of last night's feast in the campervan and wish I were anywhere but here in this grey, depressing flat that is always cold and dark, no matter what I do to it. I cheer myself up with the thought that George will let me bring home a free bag of chips later, scraps too. He might even sub me a tenner if I ask nicely. My circumstances are humiliating, and I'd die of embarrassment if Jim or the girls found out how I live hand-to-mouth from one day to the next. So much for the freedom and adventure I once craved, which had only been made possible in the first place because of a handout from Jim.

Sighing loudly, because I can't see my situation improving anytime soon, I'm about to give in to the urge to feel sorry for myself and have a good cry when I hear a swishing noise followed by a thump coming from the kitchen. My skin prickles as I make my way towards my most basic of kitchens which is no bigger than a prison cell, not that I'd know what one looks like, but I guess that could change in the future if Marcus has come back to seek his revenge.

Edging the door open, I gaze into the dark windowless space and establish that the sound is coming from the washing machine. I can feel the vibration of the drum as it ends its spin cycle all the way across the floor until it reaches my toes. Although there's nothing to be frightened of, I can't shake off a feeling of dread. A sense that something bad is about to happen. And that's when the penny drops. I haven't been anywhere near the washing machine since arriving home. I haven't even unpacked my holdall.

I flick the light switch on the wall, but nothing happens, confirming my suspicions that there is something strange going on here. If I didn't put the washing machine on, who did? No one else has been in the flat but me. Jim didn't accompany me inside when he dropped me off, despite being invited in for a coffee. It occurs to me that he would never have let me come in here alone if he knew about the break-in and part of me regrets not confiding in him, but I had good reason not to at the time and I can't undo that now, much as I'd like to.

I jump with fright when the washing machine beeps loudly, and the door clicks open. A light on the control panel flickers an ominous warning, reminding me of a partially closed eye.

My heart bangs against my chest as I approach the washing machine, half expecting a hand to appear out of a shadowy corner to grab me. Instinctively reaching out for the knife block that I know is no more than two feet away, the feel of the cool metal handle reassures me. Once armed, I feel less afraid. Yet, I pause, and ask myself, *do I really want to find out what's in the washing machine?* It has to be another clue. Now I'm certain somebody has been in my flat again, I want to turn and flee. But I don't because I must know if this has anything to do with Marcus. *What is he trying to tell me?*

One hand grasping the knife, I use the other to fully open the door, not liking the way it bounces back on its hinges to snatch at my hand. Crouching down by the door, the smell of lavender and jasmine washing powder assails my senses as I snake a hand inside, recoiling as it encounters a piece of damp, flimsy material that isn't mine.

CHAPTER 16

Jim has changed the locks, promising that the door is now burglar-proof, with the caveat of 'if there is such a thing.' I bite down hard on my fingernail and squash any unhelpful retorts, no matter how tempting that might be, as I watch him tidy up the mess he's made, sweeping curled bits of shaved wood, old door handles and rusty, bent screws into a bin liner.

'I can't believe you didn't tell me about the first break-in.'

Jim isn't looking at me as he doles out this well-meaning advice because he knows perfectly well, as I do, that us no longer being husband and wife means we can't continue to boss each other about, however tempting it might be to fall back into our old ways.

'I didn't want to worry you.'

'And this is me not worrying?' Jim is looking at me now and I can tell he is genuinely concerned and also a bit stunned. What's more, he's frustrated at not being able to help. By trade, he's a fixer-upper. And that trait extends to the women in his life. Even me it seems.

'Jim.' I sigh. 'I'm not your problem anymore.' I'm nobody's problem these days. No one has my back. Facing up to the fact that I'm truly alone in the world is not pleasant.

The sheer reality of it is sometimes enough to drive better people than me to jump off bridges and high-storey buildings.

'Since when?' he grumbles, wiping his dirty fingerprints from the door frame and around the shiny new lock that still looks incredibly flimsy to me.

'Since we got divorced.' I find myself grinning at him and he responds in kind. Nobody, not even me, can argue that Jim is as good-natured as they come. I wish I could be more like him but, since he'd arrived at the flat having received my damsel in distress phone call, I've been as scratchy as a stray cat. And perhaps that's exactly what I am. A homeless, angry feline fighting her way out of trouble, wanting one minute to be left alone to lick her wounds and the next to be fussed and stroked.

While Jim busies himself doing what he does best, I glance around the hallway and peer into the kitchen, which is now flooded with light. Jim put five pounds worth of pound coins into the electric meter after bullying George at the chippy into swapping a note for some change. George was not best pleased to find out I wouldn't be turning up to work again, but how can I be expected to keep my mind on the job after what's happened?

I shudder at the thought of someone being inside the flat again. This time it's much worse because it's obvious the message they left behind was intended for me. As yet, I don't know exactly what it means but I do believe Marcus — or should I say Tony? — is behind it.

Tiredness, anxiety and fear, the worst of trios, finally get to me and I find myself trembling from head to toe and feeling nauseous. A sudden wave of dizziness causes me to stumble and put a hand against a wall to steady myself. Luckily, Jim catches me before I fall, and manhandles me into the kitchen where he forcefully plonks me down onto a chair.

'I thought you were going to pass out again,' he mutters, scrambling to fill a glass of water from the tap, which he hands me. Dutifully, I take a huge gulp before bursting into tears.

'I'm scared, Jim,' I manage between sobs, 'and I don't know what to do. I have no idea what all this means. What Marcus even wants from me.'

'Whatever happened here tonight, Linda,' Jim grimaces, 'Marcus wouldn't hurt you. He loved you.'

'Did he though?' I demand angrily, picking up the cream linen shirt between my thumb and forefinger, holding it at arm's length as if it might try and bite me. It's still damp from having gone through a full 30-degree, delicate setting wash cycle. 'Does this sound or look like love to you?' I fume, angry with myself and Marcus. Jim is the only person I'm not furious with, yet he's the one I'm taking my temper out on. Old habits die hard. 'This shirt is the same as the one Marcus wore on the night he went into the sea. The same brand and everything. It even has a lipstick stain, a similar colour to the one I wear, on the collar.'

'I don't know what to say, Linda.' Jim pats my hand. It's a gesture I know well, used for any sad or difficult occasion that distresses his female folk. He's always been protective.

'Oh, God, Jim,' I say, inhaling on the piece of familiar material. 'It's been through the wash but I swear it smells of Marcus.' I resist the urge to tear it into pieces. It's there to taunt me, to remind me that I may or may not have pushed my husband into the sea that night and caused him to drown. I was drunk and in a jealous rage. There's no telling what I might have done. But I can't admit my fears to Jim. He'd be horrified and would never look at me in the same way again. Like our daughter Abby, Jim's a stickler for the law and a follower of rules. He might even turn me in to the authorities.

'It's Eau Sauvage by Christian Dior,' I howl, before turning away, not wanting Jim to see the pained expression on my face. Even now when my world has collapsed and it feels like I've lost Marcus all over again, I don't want to hurt Jim's feelings.

'Look, why don't you come back to the house with me? I don't like to think of you here on your own, even with the locks changed.'

'I couldn't do that,' I sob, though right now I've never wanted anything more.

'Why not?' He appears so innocent standing there, not understanding the complexity of it all. He never was one to dig too deep into feelings and always avoided heated discussions.

'Abby.' I state the obvious, as a way of avoiding mentioning the other woman.

'Never mind Abby,' Jim growls, which is unusual for him as he would normally never confront Abby with anything she might not want to hear.

'No,' I wave him away, staging a herculean effort to smile bravely. 'I'll go and stay at Gail's. She won't mind.'

'On the boat?' Jim chuckles, instantly making me cross with him.

'Yes, on the boat,' I grit my teeth. 'Why not?'

'You hate boats,' Jim points out reasonably.

'What's the alternative?' I snap. 'I don't feel safe here, Jim. I'm grateful to you for coming out and changing the locks though. And I will pay you for it. For your time and everything.'

Jim stares at me as if he's not listening. As if he doesn't even see me. 'You could just go to the police and tell them everything. It's an option,' he insists.

'No.' I bark louder than I intended and collect myself quickly. 'Not until I know what Marcus is up to and what he wants. I don't want to put him in any danger or get him into trouble. Obviously, he wants me to know he's back, that he's alive, but doesn't feel it's safe to confide in me yet.'

To prove my point, I get unsteadily to my feet. 'I need to be strong, for Marcus's sake and I shouldn't have involved . . .' but I stagger into the wall before I can finish what I intended to say. What is wrong with me? It's not like me to react so badly to shock. I'm usually as tough as old boots. But that was before I lost my husband to the sea. Or realised how horribly I'd been betrayed by him. I'm not sure how, if ever, I'll get over the deceit and lies. The fact that I've been over-medicating as a way of coping doesn't help. I wonder what my doctor would say if she found out.

'That settles it. You're coming home with me.' Jim puts an arm around me and marches me towards the door, helping me into my anorak and handing me my bag.

'But I can't, Jim. I don't want to be in the way.' Tiredness wraps itself around me, like a welcome embrace, and I long to melt into it and let somebody take responsibility for me.

'You're family, Linda. You'll never be in the way.'

I feel as if I'm sleepwalking. But it's nice having someone tell me what to do. To know they've got my back.

There's nothing else for it. I must be straight with Jim and say the words that I know will pain me to have confirmed. 'Gail told me about your girlfriend.' I slur my words as if I'm drunk or more likely, over-medicated. *What is wrong with me? Is it the delayed shock of discovering Marcus is alive and well after all this time?* 'I don't want to cause any trouble between you.' I point a finger vaguely in Jim's direction as he's become quite blurry.

'Gail said I had a new woman?' Jim stares at me with a comically shocked expression.

'*Yes*, but I don't think she thought it was meant to be a secret,' I say, backtracking. I don't want to get Gail in trouble. Judging by the surprise on Jim's face, he never meant for this to get out. It dawns on me then that the girls might not even know. The next thing I know, Jim is laughing and zipping up my jacket with scratchy working man's hands.

'Why are you laughing? It's not funny.'

'Oh, but it is.' Jim marches me to the door and guides me through it, afterwards carefully locking it behind us and slipping the key into his pocket. Not mine, nor my handbag which he's thrown over my arm, which I think is a bit weird. But what do I know?

'Because she's played you.' Jim's tone is more serious than it was a moment ago. When did he get so difficult to read? I always thought he was as straight as they come.

'Played me? What do you mean?'

'I mean she lied, Linda,' Jim shakes his head ruefully. 'Because there is no girlfriend.'

CHAPTER 17

The table I have missed so much, as if it were another family member, is finally in front of me. My shaking hands, so grateful to be there, rest on its reliably solid, pine surface, instantly soothing me while Jim busies himself in the background pouring coffee and finding biscuits. I would have done everything much quicker than my hapless ex, but I remind myself I am now a guest in the house that was once my home.

The table holds many precious memories of happy family times. Birthdays, celebrations, homework sessions, baking with the children and dinners with relatives who are sadly long gone. For now, I forget the past rows with Jim and the children and the irritations of family life. Of wanting to break free from the relentless boredom of marriage. And of being a mother. All the things that got me into the mess I'm in.

'Why would Gail lie though, about you having a girlfriend?' I ask, picking our conversation back up. 'I just don't get it.' To say I'm upset with my best friend is putting it mildly. I'm bloody furious.

'I don't know. But I'm sure, knowing you, you'll get to the bottom of it.'

Jim joins me at the table and takes a noisy slurp of his coffee. I check once again, inwardly, of course, to find out if my former intolerance of his slurping has returned and find I'm still good with it. That's how much I've chilled over the years.

Jim has showered, changed into jogging pants, kicked off his trainers and is in his slippers. I'd like to do the same or take a long hot bath and get some rest, but it's Jim's house and Jim's rules, so I'll wait to be asked.

'Too bloody right I will,' I respond, finding a cheeky grin for him because he's earned it.

Secretly, I'm relieved to find Jim is single still, but I can't wait to give Gail a piece of my mind. What right does she have to interfere with my family? It's not as if she has a monopoly on Jim and the girls, even if she does think she's protecting them from me.

'Look,' Jim reaches out a hand to rest on mine, 'we don't have to do this now. It can wait.'

'Do what?' I gulp my coffee down, terrified of what he's going to say. I'm not sure I'm ready for the proposition of a reconciliation. It's still early days.

'Talk about what's happened and what we're going to do about it,' Jim continues in earnest, his eyes never leaving mine.

'I'm not sure, Jim, I mean . . .' I gently retract my hand from his, not wanting to hurt his feelings but sensing this is too soon for both of us.

'Why don't you take a long, hot bath and get some rest first?' Jim sighs, as if guessing my thoughts, 'we can talk about what we're going to do about Marcus later.'

My cheeks burn as I realise Jim was not about to propose us getting back together but wanting instead to talk about my not-so-dead husband, which is understandable given the circumstances. Feeling like I've come close to making a fool of myself *again*, I wonder how many more times I can get things wrong when it comes to men?

I'm saved from having to make any response when the back door opens, and an angry-looking Abby comes in.

'What's going on here?' Abby's eyes flit accusingly between Jim and me. He maintains a calm kind of eye contact with her, but I look down, wanting the ground to swallow me up.

'Well?' Abby demands of her father when he doesn't answer quickly enough for her. 'What's she doing here?'

'Now, Abby. That's not how we treat guests, is it?' Jim counters.

'Is that what she is now?' Abby narrows her eyes at me and pulls a spiteful face. I've seen it used many times as a weapon against those who get in her way.

'Abby, I—' I begin pathetically, not having a clue where I'm going with this conversation.

'Your mum is staying with us for a few days,' Jim interrupts, calmly yet authoritatively.

'*You're not serious*?' Abby, thank goodness, now has eyes only for her father, letting me off the hook.

'I'm deadly serious.'

Coward that I am, I continue to keep my head down, not willing to witness her response.

'Have you lost your mind?' Abby demands, slamming her bag onto the table and not noticing when her purse and lip balm tumble out of it. Dior all the way for my daughter.

'Apparently so, to another woman by all accounts.' Jim yawns and casually folds his arms, as if nothing were amiss and he were settling in for the night.

Now, Abby's eyes flicker to me and I catch the panic in her gaze. 'What is he talking about?' she demands to know.

'I take it you weren't in on Gail's plot then, to convince me your dad has a girlfriend.'

'Do you?' Abby, darting a furious look Jim's way, appears mortified and I can tell by the way she asks her father this question that she's more horrified by the idea of her dad having another woman than finding me with my feet under the kitchen table.

'No. Absolutely not.'

I glance at him. Jim is clearly enjoying himself. Having his women argue over him is like old times. In his world, this is nothing to get uncomfortable about.

'So why would Aunty Gail lie?'

Having long been jealous of the close relationship my daughter shares with my best friend, I decide to ignore the wounded expression on Abby's face. In her eyes, Gail is the only grown-up who has never let her down.

'Let's find out, shall we?' I take charge by hitting the most often dialled contact in my phone's history, making sure it's on speakerphone so we can all hear. 'No time like the present,' I continue, as we wait for Gail to pick up.

'Hi, babe,' she answers after a couple of rings. 'How're things?'

'I'm at Jim's house.' I don't waste time with small talk.

Her groan is audible to us all. 'What are you doing there?' she complains. 'I thought you were in Devon.'

'I was but now I'm back.' *Back in so many ways*, I want to tell her, but of course, I don't.

'The confusion can't be good for Jim and the girls.'

I feel mean letting her continue when she's unaware she has an audience, but she's stepped on my toes one too many times. 'There's no confusion,' I snap. 'And by girls do you mean my two adult daughters who are perfectly capable of making their own decisions in life?' I can't resist adding that last bit.

'Is something up?' she asks slowly. 'You sound all mardy.'

Gail can read me like an open book. We go back a long way. But that doesn't give her the right to interfere in my life.

'Yes, well I think I've got a right to be put out after the lie you told.'

'Lie? I don't know what you're talking about?' She sounds unfazed by my accusation and audibly inhales. The fact that she's continuing to smoke during our conversation lets me know she has no idea she's been found out.

'The lie about Jim having a girlfriend. What was that all about?'

A longer pause this time. *Bingo, she's sussed it out at last.*

'Is Jim there with you now?' she asks.

'Yes, and Abby too.' I take pleasure in telling her. 'Why?'

'Then give the phone to one of them and let me talk to them.'

'Absolutely not. Why would you even ask me to do that?'

'Because you've clearly been taking too many pills again. That's why. No offence, Linda, but you know how you tend to invent things when that happens.'

'No offence,' I'm deliberately sarcastic, feeling she deserves it. 'But are you trying to tell me that you never lied about Jim having a girlfriend?' I'm incensed at this point. How bloody *dare* she?

'Obviously, I never said that because as far as I know, it isn't true. And I wouldn't lie to you, or Abby and Jim, you know that. Unlike . . .'

'Unlike what, Gail? Are you trying to infer that I'm the one lying?'

The phone goes dead and when I look down, I see that Jim has his finger over the end call button.

'Don't put yourself through any more of her bullshit. It's not worth it.' Jim says kindly.

'I can't believe Gail would lie like that. After everything you've been through.' Abby swipes away a tear from her eye. I can't tell if the waterworks are for me or due to her disappointment in Gail but she places a hand on my shoulder, patting it awkwardly. Who'd have thought twenty-four hours ago I'd be back in my old house with Abby comforting me!

'You believe me then? Abby? Jim?'

'You might be many things, Mum, but you're not a liar.'

'Hear, hear,' Jim agrees, 'I can second that and Gail has always been a bitch to you. You've just never opened your eyes to how she really is before.'

'Oh, thank God,' I say welling up. 'I thought you'd take her side and that I was going to get my marching orders and be shown the door.'

'You can stay as long as you want, Linda.' Jim takes my hand again as if to emphasise this. 'You've had a rough time with everything, what with losing Marcus, the break-ins and . . .' he pauses, not wanting to let Abby in on our secret. *The Marcus thing.*

'Break-ins! What break-ins? Oh my God, Dad, are you telling me Mum's been burgled?' Horrified and concerned all at once, Abby plonks herself down in the chair next to me, and taking my other hand, the one Jim isn't holding, she looks close to tears.

Being fussed over by Abby helps me see what I never could before, that family is all that matters. Men come and go in life. Friends too, *as I'm learning.* But your children are with you forever. It's true what they say — you can choose your friends but not your family, yet I think it should be the other way around. We should always choose our family first. It's a shame it has taken me all this time to realise it. An even bigger shame is that Jim and Abby clearly don't know me at all. Because I *am* a liar.

CHAPTER 18

It's been three weeks since our ill-fated trip to Devon and life has returned to some sort of normality, although Marcus's presence is, of course, still deeply felt, even if he has gone deadly silent. There have been no more text messages. No new clues. I'm not sure what this implies or whether it's a good thing or a bad thing but I do know that the dread of his returning to punish me haunts me every second of the day. Yet I've also grown accustomed to a new sort of contentment I've not experienced before, in that nobody has suggested I go back to the miserable, grey flat I'm meant to call home. In many ways, it feels like I've already moved back into the house on Victoria Road but I'm conscious that nothing has been made official. All I can do is keep my fingers crossed and be on my best behaviour.

Most nights are spent around the big kitchen table with my family and, more recently, the addition of Abby's fiancé, Josh who is back on the scene now that the couple has worked things out between them. Or, in other words, Josh has backtracked and agreed to Abby's demands. Sensing that Abby wanted to wait a while before officially introducing me as his future mother-in-law, I never pushed her on the subject, understanding her need to ensure I was serious about being a part of this family again before trusting me. Not as she used to, that goes without saying, but the breadcrumbs she's offering will do fine for now. Nor do I blame her for being cautious after the way I behaved. I'm simply grateful to be on good terms with my daughters again. Rosie, being the softest of the Delameres, turned out to be a pushover once her sister's approval was gained.

I'm still working at the chippy three nights a week, but Jim pays me to clean and look after the house too. It felt humiliating at first to accept money from him, but he insisted this arrangement suited him better than employing someone he didn't know. I understood where Jim was coming from, he'd never liked opening the house up to strangers. He's the quiet, homely type. As a family man, he's never been one for the pub, gym, or golf course, unlike so many of the husbands we used to know. A real catch, I've come to realise. One who many a divorcee would count herself lucky to have landed.

Although I used to hate cleaning, finding the monotony and repetitiveness of it tedious, I'm now in my element hoovering, polishing, washing, ironing, and cooking. Having a beautiful home to take care of has brought out the natural homemaker in me, even though I used to complain it was demeaning for women to have to do the bulk of the domestic work and not be recognised for it. Anything's better than living in the flat and not having money, but I never imagined, in my wildest dreams, that I would once again get to spend time taking care of my family's every need. Some days I pinch myself and jokingly liken myself to Cinderella, convinced I must have a fairy Godmother looking out for me, as I dust and mop floors without a care in the world. Then Marcus springs ominously to mind and I feel more akin to the evil, wicked stepmother because of what I did, or *may* have done. *Did I really try to kill the man I loved?* I still can't believe I could do anything like that, no matter how angry I might have been. Yet I can't get the horrible image of me pushing him into the water out of my head. I'd give anything to know whether or not that memory is real. I may never know how

Marcus survived that night and lived to tell the tale, but it's no surprise the Greek authorities were unable to find his body.

Life has changed dramatically from a year ago when Marcus was all I wanted in life. Unable to recognise myself, I wonder, *was it madness? Was I going through a mid-life crisis? Was any of it real? And did it take Marcus to die for me to realise this?* Because it's 'nice, salt-of-the-earth Linda' who sits down to dinner every night with Jim, Abby, and Rosie, serving up their favourite delicious, winter-warming dishes.

I'm testing out the fancy new Shark cordless vacuum cleaner that Jim went out and bought after seeing me struggle with the heavier Henry when my phone vibrates in my pocket. It's rare for anyone to call as Jim and the girls prefer to text rather than talk. I wonder if it could be Gail, and my stomach turns over. *Was* I always frightened of her, as Jim implied? I still haven't made up with her, even though she texts me most days demanding that I stop being childish and talk to her. But, when I look at the screen, it's a number I don't recognise, so I cautiously pick up, deciding I can always hang up if it's someone trying to sell me something.

'Hello.' Switching off the almost-silent Shark, I sit down on Jim's double bed, automatically smoothing out a crease in the tropical bird-print bedspread that matches the curtains. Jim always hated the design and I'm surprised he never changed the dark blue and pink colour scheme when I moved out four years ago. I try not to glance at the right-hand side of the bed where my head laid for over twenty-eight years.

'Is that Linda Bouchard?'

Inhaling on what feels like fear rather than air, my body physically recoils, shrinks even, at the mention of my married name, which I dropped sooner than any widow should on my return to the UK. So many memories assail me at once. The morning of our wedding timed for when the sun rose as we exchanged vows that at least one of us didn't mean. 'I Marcus Bouchard, take Linda Delamere . . .' The sound of the sea — angry and insistent in the background, a threat of what was to come. The sand beneath our feet, getting in between our toes. The smiley-faced Abba speciality band, who played 'I do, I do, I do,' on repeat.

'Yes,' my voice is tight, strangulated. Nobody ever calls me by this name. 'Who is this?'

'Tilly Bouchard, from Devon. We met a few weeks ago.'

I want to tell her that no explanation is necessary. 'Yes, of course, how could I forget. How are you?' I hate resorting to small talk but I've gone into panic mode at the sound of her voice.

'I thought you might have been in touch after I left you that message,' she sniffs, sounding offended.

'What message? When was this?' I bark.

'It was over a week ago. On the landline number I was given by your friend.'

'You mean Jim?'

'Yes, Jim, that's it!' She sounds delighted at having remembered. 'I've been trying desperately to remember his name. But you know how it is when you get old.'

'Jim gave you *his* number?' *What the fuck.* 'And you left him a message?' I ask shakily, struggling to take this news in.

'Yes. That's what I said, dear. Only it was intended for you. And when I didn't hear back, I sent you a letter with the details instead, thinking you might be interested. When I still didn't hear anything, I was about to give up, until I remembered you also gave me a mobile number. I was wary of ringing it at first. You can't trust these modern devices, can you?'

'Mrs Bouchard,' I tremble harder at having to speak the name aloud, 'what exactly did you send me in the post?'

'You mean you haven't received it! Honestly, Royal Mail has gone downhill over the years. Back in my day . . .'

'I haven't been staying at my flat if that's where you sent it.' I interrupt rudely. 'I've been at a friend's house since we came back from yours.'

'Ah, that makes sense, I suppose,' she suggests weakly, as if afraid I'll rip into her.

It dawns on me that she sounds a lot vaguer than when we last spoke and I put this down to the shock of our visit when she discovered a stranger, aka *me*, had married a man who they, *I*, believed was her son. All of that must have had a profound effect on someone her age, causing her to grieve for her son all over again. Deciding to go gently on her, I remind myself to be patient, even though I'm dying to find out what those details are.

'What is it you wanted me to know? Can you tell me now, over the phone? Was it something to do with Marcus? I mean *my* Marcus.'

'Tony Fortin, yes. I was talking to one of the village committee members who volunteer at the library, and she remembered a man coming in a few months ago, to ask questions about Tony Fortin and my son. She said he came across as odd and when she asked for some ID he left in a hurry, but not before reading all about the accident in old newspaper records.'

'Did she, your friend, did she get a name?'

'Yes. Although I kept forgetting it. That's why I wrote it down in the end and decided with Alice Pope's help, to post it and copies of the newspaper clippings he'd searched for, out to you. Quite the detective, is Alice. Miss Marple, they call her in the village, although one could argue she's nothing but a busybody who eats more than her share of digestives at our Women's Institute meetings.' Mrs Bouchard's laughter fills the phone, making her sound young again, and beautiful somehow. 'Anyway,' she sighs despondently, coming back to earth, as I imagine she must do every time her dead son's name is spoken. 'I thought you'd like to know, dear, and that it might help with your troubles. I'm sorry I can't be more helpful over the phone but my memory is not what it used to be.'

After thanking Mrs Bouchard profusely and loudly because she's quite deaf on the phone, I hang up and immediately beat myself up with the knowledge that Jim kept this from me. *But why? Why would he not pass on Mrs Bouchard's message? It doesn't make sense.* I decide to visit the flat to find out what was in that envelope. With a bit of luck, I'll also uncover the identity of the mystery man who has shown such an interest in Marcus's history. Only then will I tackle Jim.

Abandoning the hoovering, ironing and window cleaning, all tasks on my to-do list for today, I stomp to the cloakroom instead. Tugging on my trusty charity-shop anorak, I throw my tired bag over my tense-as-hell shoulder, ignoring Abby and Rosie's various designer ones hanging from the same hook and promptly leave the house.

CHAPTER 19

As soon as I throw open the communal door which is accessed from Broad Street and situated immediately opposite the chippy, I know something's wrong. I felt it in my bones on the walk here. Every step conjured up a rising fear of the unknown and a desire to be safe at home, even though I'm not exactly sure where home is these days or if anywhere is safe.

It doesn't help that the shared entrance to the two flats is in a busy pedestrianised area of town, visible to shoppers, who are now on their way home as the shops are closing. Marcus could be hiding among the stragglers, a grey shadow standing taller than everyone else, watching me. He could have followed me, waiting to see if I go into the flat alone. And there's no Jim, no Abby to protect me now.

It's usually a good fifteen-minute walk from Victoria Road to here, but in my rush to find out what the hell is going on it took only ten. That's not the only reason my heart is racing. Something is amiss. I can feel it.

It's market day, and contractors are clearing away the market stalls. The smell of the fish stall, long gone, still hangs heavy in the air. Marcus used to catch and cook his own fish and I haven't been able to touch it since, even though I work in a fish shop. Fighting back a feeling of nausea, I glance around to see if anybody is paying me more attention than usual. Everything appears normal. Litter already streaks the cobbled streets. It's almost dark and the last busker of the day is packing away his guitar. Even the Big Issue seller has stopped calling out to shoppers and is ferreted away in a shop corner counting her pile of coins. I wonder if she'll hand in every penny or keep a few quid back for herself. Good on her if she does is my verdict.

As the external door closes behind me, hissing snake-like on its hinges, the comforting daylight is shut out — I reach for the light switch, but the main light does not come on. 'Typical,' I grumble softly, sensing things are only going to get worse. Rummaging around in the dusty greyness of the communal entrance hall, I reach into the mailbox that I know is mine, the one labelled Flat Thirteen, and my hand lands on a bulky envelope. *This must be it. The information Mrs Bouchard sent me.* I can't wait to rip it open, yet at the same time, the feeling of dread consumes me. What will I find out?

Above me, a large fly, one of those horrible bluebottles that feast on dead flesh, rattles around in the dirty glass shade of the light fitting. Angrily, it flings itself from side to side, determined not to succumb to its fate. Wishing I were as brave, I tiptoe up the stone steps to my flat, praying that the fly will soon die, because the sound, following me up the stairs, gives me goosebumps. It feels like every hair on my body is standing on end.

The door to my flat is in one piece. Not kicked in or left wide open as I'd feverishly imagined, so I insert the key into the shiny new lock that Jim installed and push open the door. Silence. A stale, dusty smell, not entirely unexpected after being shut up for so long, creeps into my nostrils. Before entering the too-small-to-swing-a-cat entrance hall, I fumble for the light switch but like downstairs, nothing happens when I hit it. Guessing that there is no credit left in the meter, I scrabble in my bag for my purse, certain that I have a few pound coins knocking around. *Ta-dah, yes, I do.* More confident now, I head for the electric meter in the kitchen, careful not to bounce off an item of furniture in the gloom.

I'm forced to stand on a kitchen chair so I can reach the meter cupboard as it's been put up impossibly high on the wall. I balance unsteadily before I find my feet in the dark, worried I might fall and break a leg, and then, inserting one pound, two, three . . . hey presto, we have light. That's when I notice the kitchen drawers have been pulled open and the contents are spilt on the floor. Heart racing, I scramble down from my perch, careful not to make a sound. *This can't be happening again, can it? Surely to God, nobody's that unlucky to get a break-in three times in a row.*

Swearing under my breath and holding my bag to my chest as if it were going to protect me, I cautiously move out of the kitchen, then silently dart across the hall into the living room, coming to an abrupt stop when I see the ugly, hard-backed marigold sofa has been toppled on its side. As if it were a slaughtered beast, yellow foam spills out of it, like animal organs. Worse still, my old laptop has been smashed to pieces. Shards of plastic and metal are sprinkled across the floor. I'm torn between wanting to escape the flat, feeling like I might be in danger, and wanting suddenly to see if Marcus's profile still exists on the Welcome Back website. My thirst for knowledge wins and I pick it up, immediately switching it on. I haven't felt able to do any investigating at Victoria Road in case Jim or the girls were to look over my shoulder. I also hadn't wanted to ask to borrow one of their laptops or iPads, only for them to ask me why I wanted it. I'm fairly sure the website has an app that I could have downloaded to my phone but I haven't quite mastered modern day technology yet and I'm too embarrassed to ask for help in case I'm labelled a dinosaur.

Eyes darting from one end of the room to the other, I gaze at the damaged screen hoping for a reassuring beep or the whir of a programme starting up, but it appears broken beyond repair. Sweeping a hand nervously through my hair, wondering what to do next, I watch in horror as a shadow, which is not mine, falls across the screen. Someone is standing right behind me. I should have run when I had the chance.

Comparing myself to the fly downstairs desperately trying to escape its fate I spin around to confront the intruder, ready to fight if necessary, but there's no one there. Logically, I know that nobody, certainly not anyone living, could have escaped that quickly or silently, so I have no choice but to put this down as an illusion. *A result of heightened nerves and extreme anxiety caused by grief,* that's how my doctor would describe it.

Damn Gail for sometimes being right. Suddenly I doubt myself. Perhaps I did make up the lie about Jim having a girlfriend just to get attention . . . Who knows for sure? Not me. Some days I feel like I'm losing my mind. Gail was spot on when she warned me that I need to come off those pills. Although serotonin syndrome is rare, the resulting confusion and, in my case, overactive reflexes caused by taking sertraline can be crippling.

Deciding it might be time to talk to my friend and equally wise to get out of the flat in case whoever did this damage comes back, but first I feel compelled to check out the one room I haven't been in, so I slip the envelope Mrs Bouchard sent me inside my anorak and creep into the bedroom. This room seems untouched at first. Then I freeze. There's a large indentation, a shape, on the quilt cover. It looks like someone has been lying on the bed. A shudder rips through my body and I fight back tears of anger. Is this Marcus's work, I wonder, or has he hired somebody, a paid thug, to terrify me? If so, it's working. If Marcus were here right now, I'd claw his eyes out. How could he do this to me? What does he want? And how long does he intend to string out this form of torture?

I might be grasping at straws but I'm hoping the information Mrs Bouchard sent me will help make sense of all of this, but I dare not risk opening it or reading it here. It's not safe. And I can't take it home either. Not until I figure out why Jim didn't tell me about the voicemail. All I can conclude is that he was trying to protect me. But he must know me well enough by now to realise that doing something like that was bound to alienate me as well as put my back up . . . As for Rosie and Abby, I can't risk involving them. Not when it could endanger them too. Right now, like it or not, there's only one person to whom I can talk. Gail.

CHAPTER 20

As I descend the steps to the communal entrance hall, I notice that the door to flat twelve is slightly ajar. I can't be sure if it was like that when I arrived, due to the dark. A streak of warm yellow light leaks through from the other side of my neighbour's door.

Feeling as irritated as I am frightened, I steal a furtive glance down the darkened staircase, terrified in case anything should be waiting for me at the bottom of it. My skin crawls and I get the sense that today's horrors are not yet over. All I want is to get the hell out of here to safety, but "nice Linda" who takes her social responsibilities seriously, is not going to do a runner without first checking to see if my nameless neighbour, who I've never even met, is okay. It's strange that their door is open. Anything could have happened to them. You hear about people dying alone all the time. Some end up getting eaten by their pets who would otherwise starve after being locked inside with their deceased owners. Jim and I have always prided ourselves on being decent people, the type who would help anyone if they needed it, at least that's how things were before the divorce. We're each more scepti-cal now. Yet, having recently received the gift of forgiveness from my family, I owe it to myself, to Jim and our girls to do the right thing. Even if the thought makes me squirm.

Tapping on the door, my throat tightens. It's as if I'm about to step into a trap that I know will be hard to extricate myself from. 'Hello, is anyone there?' I call hesitantly. Then after knocking again, louder this time, I nervously push the door half open. I'm not sure what I dread most, coming across a dead body or a living, breathing one. 'I'm the tenant from upstairs, just coming in to see if you're okay. Is that all right?' I announce.

There is no answering murmur from within, so I dare to push the door wide open and peer inside. I'm familiar with the floor plan as it's almost identical to my flat, apart from it's back to front to mine, so it's hard to get my bearings. Where my kitchen would have been, this one is positioned in the opposite direction. Leaving the door open behind me, allowing me the chance to flee if I so desire, I tiptoe through the entrance hall, which I find just as claustrophobic as my own, before walking into the living room.

The place doesn't look lived-in. Furniture is sparse. Soft furnishings or decorative ornaments even more so. This is about ten times worse than my flat. Whoever lives here has my sympathy. I thought I was hard up. There's no sofa, just a plastic chair. No sign of a TV either. The windows are dressed in old, stained more-grey-than-white net, to prevent anyone from looking in, I imagine, rather than allowing for privacy. And not a single light shade in place. All the bulbs are exposed, casting gloomy yellow circles on the mildewed ceilings. At least they have money for electricity.

Whoever exists in these conditions must live a frugal, tramp-like existence. The atmosphere is tight and oppressive. The air, which feels hard to breathe, is as still as a pond. The windows look as if they haven't been opened in months, never mind cleaned. Going into the kitchen, I open the fridge and the light pops on to startle me, revealing cans of cheap beer, a tub of old margarine and an opened packet of curling-at-the-corners ham well past its sell-by date. An old-fashioned bottle of milk, the kind that gets delivered to your door, contains what is no longer milk but more like something resembling cottage cheese.

As I explore further, going into the bedroom, my glance is drawn to the discarded cans of beer scattered across the bed, which is bare of any bedding. The stained mattress lies upturned on bare floorboards. A copy of *The Guardian* newspaper, dated four days ago has been left behind. All this smacks of a sad, wasted life. I wonder what sort of person has to live in such a state of poverty and neglect which is as bad, if not worse, as anything I've seen on my travels with Marcus. The copy of the analytical newspaper is out of place, however. *The Sun* newspaper, open on page three, would be more appropriate to these surroundings. But that could just be me, being snobbish.

Feeling sure this is where the bluebottle fly escaped from, as the place reeks of death and decay, I close the door gently behind me on my way out and exit the communal door. Back out on the street, I sit cross-legged on the step outside and punch in a call to George.

'George, it's me, Linda.'

'You're not going to let me down tonight as well, are you? Steph's already called in sick, so I need you more than ever.'

Pulling a face, because I had hoped to get the night off, but realising pulling a sicky is out of the question now, I inject normality into my voice although that's far from how I'm feeling.

'No, George, it's fine. I'll be there. I've just been back to the flat and I thought you'd want to know that I've been burgled again. I also noticed that the downstairs tenant had left their door open, so I went inside and . . .'

'You shouldn't have done that. You'll be the one accused of breaking and entering now.' George admonishes fiercely, wearing his landlord hat.

'I had no choice. I thought something might have happened to them.'

'What do you mean that something might have happened to them? Are they all right?'

'I don't know, George, they weren't there.'

I hear George sigh heavily. I know he thinks I'm trouble. Although I don't agree with him, I can see his point. I've let him down on numerous occasions.

'So, we're back to you breaking and entering. You'll have the police over if you're not careful, and no one wants that, Linda.'

George, once a small-time criminal himself, having spent three months in jail for petty theft, is phobic about the police, resenting them for unfairly pursuing him — as he puts it. Out of fear of being arrested and consequently banged up, he has kept straight ever since. I get where he's coming from, more than most.

'My flat has been ransacked three times in a row in the last month. And you won't believe this, but it looks like someone has been sleeping in my bed while I've been away. Judging by the state of their flat, I'd say your other tenant has disappeared off the face of the earth and bailed, owing you money. All of that happened right under your nose, George. If none of that is of interest to the police, I'll eat my hat.'

'*Jesus Christ*.' George manages between clenched teeth. 'What do you want me to do? Shall I come over?'

'That's up to you. I gave you a spare key to mine after Jim changed the locks, so you should have access to both flats. It might be worth taking a look and getting some photographic evidence. I know I should have done the same but I couldn't face being in there any longer. I had to get out. I'm on my way home now, George, and I won't be coming back.' The very thought of stepping inside flat thirteen again makes me shudder. 'I can't go back there. Not after . . .'

'I can't say I blame you. You may not be the best fish shop assistant in the world, but you've been a good tenant on the whole. Put it in writing, will you? So, it's official, like. I'll give you another month to clear your stuff out if it helps. Don't worry about paying any more rent either, not after all that's happened. I'm sorry for the way things have worked out.'

'George, if you're really sorry and want to help, do me one thing.'

There's a pause on the other end of the phone.

'What's that, Linda?'

He sounds cagey: I wonder if he imagines I'm about to ask him to find a hired assassin to take somebody out for me or something of that nature. The thought is absurd, but — George does have dodgy friends, most of whom have done time in prison. They play late-night games of cards in the back of the chippy while tucking into Pukka pies and chips. Marcus would have fitted in well in George's circle, although he would have ended up rubbing them up the wrong way by lording it over them with his superiority. Marcus wouldn't have been able to help himself.

'What's the tenant's name? At number twelve?'

'That's GDPR, private and confidential,' George stammers, as if he were a pillar of society, 'I could get in a lot of trouble for sharing information like that.'

It's my turn to sigh. He'll spill the beans in the end but likes to play games. So, I go along with it. Best to let him think he's pulling the shots. Isn't that how it is with most men?

'Is it a woman or a man? Your tenant? You must be able to tell me that,' I insist.

'A bloke,' George snorts as if it would be ridiculous to assume a woman would live in such a pigsty as one of his flats even though that's exactly what I'd done.

'What does he look like?'

'Look like? How am I supposed to know? I haven't got time for all that. He came about through a friend of a friend. Someone wanting to crash for a while, the usual.'

I wonder if I was insane agreeing to take on the flat, knowing how George operates. There's no telling who's been living below me all this time. They could have been a drug baron or a paedophile. 'Name, George, you must have it for legal reasons if nothing else.'

'Just a minute,' he grumbles, and the phone goes quiet. I hear rustling in the background and the sound of hot fat bubbling over in the fryers, a reminder that my shift starts in just over an hour. The thought makes me feel physically ill. 'Wayne,' George returns breathlessly to the phone. He has asthma, is diabetic and is morbidly obese, poor man. You wouldn't know it to look at him but when his wife, Helen, was alive, he used to run marathons for Cancer Research in memory of his late mother. But when he lost his wife to the same disease when she was only forty-five, he gave up. Only the fish shop keeps him going. That, and his Friday night game of cards with Stamford's mafia.

'Do you have a surname?' I ask despondently, realising this is quickly going nowhere. I don't know anybody called Wayne.

'That *is* the surname,' George says in a way that makes it clear he thinks I'm being thick.

'A *first* name then,' I say impatiently, more than a little frustrated now and wanting to give him a piece of my mind. A little more sympathy wouldn't go amiss after what I've been through in one of his properties.

More rustling from George as he goes through his paper-work again. He keeps a desk out back with all his accounts, surprisingly up to date, stored on a yellowing PC that smells of chip fat. 'Bruce.' George whoops as if he'd won something, impressed by his own stealth.

The street falls away. Everything slows. The heavy-booted council workers, the busker and the Big Issue seller freeze in time, as if the bad queen from Narnia had cast a spell on them. My head spins from this latest revelation.

'What is it, Linda? You've gone all quiet on me?' George, insistent in my ear, brings me back to earth like a shot of adrenalin.

'You let Batman move in, George. The bloody caped crusader has been living in the flat below me for months without my knowing.'

'Huh?'

'Bruce Wayne, George. Your tenant called himself after Batman's real persona. You've been had. We both have.'

As I pretend to listen to George's unintelligent observations down the line, all I can think about is how none of this is a coincidence, not when Marcus, *my own dark knight*, was a self-confessed super fan of the comic book era. A man who admired, above all others, the philanthropist, playboy, *they were alike in many ways*, and superhero that was Batman.

CHAPTER 21

The Batman theme has been running through my mind all evening, ever since opening time, obliterating all the customers' requests for extra pickled onions, mushy peas, curry sauce on the side or scraps with their chips. Lord knows what I served them! Having found me in the street earlier sobbing my eyes out, George, sympathetic for ten whole minutes now, keeps scowling at me, willing me not to screw up. But screw up I do, all the time while Del Boy and Rodney acting out the famous Christmas episode of *Only Fools and Horses*, the one where they were dressed as Batman and Robin, plays on repeat in my head.

As a result, I feel dangerously close to collapsing into hysterical laughter, the kind they lock you up for. But I must keep it together for George's sake. He's already rescued me from serving a vegetarian customer a meat burger instead of one of those distinctive-looking Quorn patties. All I can obsess over is how Marcus confessed to watching every episode or movie ever made about Batman and how, when he was a kid, he'd collected all the comics, wanting to become just like his hero. *Impressive job, Marcus. You got your wish in the end. How's that working out for you?* I want to yell.

'You're making a mess,' I shriek at a wide-eyed kid cuddling a bag of chips while backing towards the door. He's poured too much vinegar onto his chips and it's leaking all over the tiled floor that muggins here will have to get down on her hands and knees to clean.

'Don't worry about it,' George says kindly to the kid, looking up from the fish fryer with startled eyes, but only because the kids' parents are regulars, and he doesn't want to offend a good customer. If it were anybody else's child he'd be whining about the mess too.

Thirty seconds later, I'm down on my hands and knees, where I'd predicted I'd be, fighting back tears of humiliation as I sop up the acidic vinegar with a soapy yellow sponge. My thoughts remain firmly on Marcus and the situation I find myself in. *Has my husband been living under the same roof as me all this time in the flat below mine? Is he the tenant that goes by the name of Bruce Wayne? Has he been breathing in the same air as me, when all this time I thought he was dead? Is he the one who's been sleeping in my bed?*

When I think about what I may or may not have done to Marcus that night on the beach, *and I'd give anything to remember everything properly*, it's no wonder he's mad at me. But the behaviour I've just described doesn't feel like love anymore. I ask myself if I ever really knew Marcus. I mean *really* knew him. He has many secrets, one of which is not being the person (i.e. Marcus Bouchard) he's meant to be. Now that I'm out of the relationship I'm beginning to believe he may have been toxic all along. *Was Marcus, aka Tony Fortin, a bad person masquerading as an everyday hero? The dark knight I'd described him as earlier.* Is he dangerous? Should I be concerned for my family? Or is it just me he's after? What punishment am I to expect from him? How long will it be before his thirst for revenge lures him out of the shadows?

Such questions flood my mind until I start to feel physically unwell. White stars flash across my forehead, like small rockets taking off, and a wave of nausea has me bent over double. The stench of the vinegar is not helping, as I fight against throwing up last night's homemade lasagne. George would never forgive me if that were to happen in his shop.

'Leave it till later, Linda. It's not that bad.' George shakes his head at the mess on the floor and the bigger mess that is me, before rolling his eyes.

Avoiding his eyes, I stare out of the shop window instead. It's dark, cold, and wet outside. Only those desperate for fish and chips are brave enough to venture out. Several customers waiting for special orders like scampi or haddock are in no hurry to leave. To avoid the rain, they'll drag their order out, making an uncooperative George chat to them while they wait. This is meant to be my job, and putting myself out of their reach will have made George, who hates having to make small talk with customers, even more resentful.

A sudden movement catches my eye, forcing me to straighten up as I zoom in on the shadow outside. A man is lingering outside the communal door to mine and Batman's flat. I watch him shake himself like a wet dog before crossing the road towards the chippy, taking unhurried strides despite the downpour. I wonder what he was doing outside numbers twelve and thirteen. Could *he* be the one, and not Marcus, who has been dossing at my flat? Correction, breaking into my flat! Has he got a key? On that thought, I realise how nuts I sound. Talk about being paranoid. *Get a grip, Linda,* I tell myself. He was probably just strolling past my door like any other normal person would.

I watch him pause a few feet from the shop door, dig into his pocket to fish out a cigarette, and bend his head to light it. Immediately I think of Marcus. But, then again, many people smoke. The spark of a lighter ignites and dies several times before he's able to get his cigarette going, but when smoke billows from his mouth, his shoulders visibly relax. He has his back to me, so I can't see his face, but there's something familiar about his stance. When the door flies open and three customers pile in back-to-back, blocking my view, I scowl as they approach the counter.

'Hurry up, Linda. It's getting a bit lively back here,' George complains, scooping a freshly cooked batch of chips into a wire basket.

Ignoring the bedraggled, carb-starved customers who are all insistent on having curry sauce with their main meal, I take in the height of the man outside and feel a lump catch in my throat when he smooths back his wet hair. It's a gesture I'm familiar with. Marcus always was fussy over his appearance; some would say vain. This man may have silvery white hair too, but it's difficult to tell in this light. When he turns ever so slightly, however, as if to stare into the chippy, I catch sight of his angular cheekbone and my heart stops.

It's him. Marcus.

I gasp, staggering to my feet, waiting for my heart to start pumping again and for my lungs to fill with air. Every customer turns to stare in my direction as I will my uncooperative legs to move. They must wonder what on earth's wrong with me as I continue to stand there, immobile, fixated on a door that feels impossibly out of reach.

At last, the man's glance turns towards me, and I swear I can see his eyes are blue even though it's pitch-black outside. 'Oh, God.' I drop to my knees again with a nasty bone-crunching scrape. My gaze swings back to the door as I watch it slowly opening, inch by inch, and my body bends over like a broken branch as I realise that he's coming inside. Marcus has returned to punish me, as I always feared he would. I just see part of his hand at first, a familiar flash of gold on his ring finger. Next, I catch sight of a stubbled face. And then, finally, the man appears in front of me, half in and half out of the shop doorway, as alive as I am, if you can call this living. His coat is damp with rain and his shoe-polish brown eyes are locked on mine, not with anger but in compassion. There's a frown on his forehead I don't know. Lines on his skin that shouldn't be there . . .

When I realise the man standing in front of me is not my meant-to-be dead husband I'm sick over George's tiled floor, leaving behind a trail of garden peas and minced lamb that's much more unpleasant than a few drops of vinegar. I don't know what's worse, George's anger at me for making a fool of myself — and therefore *him* — in his shop, or the realisation that the stranger only shares a passing resemblance to my husband.

CHAPTER 22

'How could I be so bloody stupid, Gail?' I whine, knocking back a shot of something black that tastes of liquorice, which makes my toes curl. 'I really thought it was Marcus!' I don't remember much of the car journey here, only that I was thrown into the passenger seat by a grim-faced George and that I sobbed all the way. But I do recall being surrounded by Gail's reassuring bossiness as she expertly threw her sportscar around the unlit country lanes, until we reached her boat, moored illegally on an ugly, out-of-the-way stretch of the River Nene in Nassington, within walking distance of the Queen's Head Inn but too far from Stamford (eight miles as the crow flies) for a car-less me to visit regularly.

'You always were a dozy mare,' Gail cackles, knocking back a matching shot. I don't take her words to heart, knowing she means well.

'Point taken,' I observe dryly, marvelling at how easy it is to slip back into a close friendship with her. To her credit, she was never one to hold a grudge. But what about me? I'm still pissed at her for lying about Jim having a girlfriend, but, if I'm honest, not enough to want to have it out with her. I always come off worse when we quarrel. And it would seem bloody ungrateful of me given how she has just rescued me.

Knowing Gail won't thank me for bringing up *the lie* and that she'd prefer we just forget about it, I wimp out, telling myself it can wait until another time.

Besides, the whirlwind that is Gail usually has a good, if screwed-up, reason for the trail of chaos she creates. She would only have done something like that to protect me. Never to hurt me. She has always had my best interest at heart. Since arriving at the boat, she's wrapped me in a warm blanket, lent me a pair of her pyjamas, too fancy for my taste, and given me several bear hugs that I couldn't fight off, dissolving into her arms instead and counting myself lucky to have her as a friend.

'So, you ready to tell me all about it, babe?' Gail throws firewood onto the log burner and parks herself at the other end of the L-framed wooden sofa so she is facing me. With a sense of doom enveloping me, I watch her tuck her size five feet up under her, settling in for, what seems to her, like a gossipy, cosy girls' night in.

'Do I have any choice?' I laugh. I'm desperate to confide in my best friend. Not just to talk, but to share everything. Back in the day, in our golden years, we were inseparable. At school, and then as adults. We always swore things would never change between us but life, boys, men, and then husbands got in the way. Children too, at least for me, as poor Gail was unable to have them. It's not something she likes to talk about, so I've never pressed her on the subject. I wonder now if that was the right thing to do? Should I have been more insistent on knowing what was going on with her, the way she does with me?

'Are you happy, Gail?' I blurt out without thinking. I can tell by the way she sits up in her seat and blinks several times that the question has surprised her.

Noticing how her fake nails, painted sky blue, are digging into the bare flesh of her arm, I know I've made her uncomfortable. Should I persist anyway? Is that what loyal friends do? Have I let her down in some way by not doing so in the past? I couldn't bear to think I've been less of a friend to her than she has me. She's got me out of all sorts of trouble over the years, not least when she flew to Greece to rescue me after Marcus was lost in the water. I no longer use the word "died". It doesn't seem relevant to Marcus anymore.

There's something very cat-like about Gail, always has been. Her attractive green eyes light up during the day but turn almost black at night. Her personality, often scatty, sometimes serious, even outright bitchy, is as changeable as her hair colour. Although a natural redhead, tonight it's tinged with purple, but she's been known to dye it all the colours of the rainbow. Sassy and confident, especially with men and her sexuality, I've always admired her for her courage. She comes across as someone who couldn't give a flying fuck what anybody thinks of her. But I know different.

Losing her husband to another woman and not being able to have children could have turned her bitter. But instead of checking in more regularly to see how she is, I've been consumed with my own selfish needs. It occurs to me, like a sudden lifting of menopausal brain fog, that she only ever wanted what I had, and what I later rejected — a husband, kids, and a happy home, in that order. God, that must have rubbed her up the wrong way and yet, despite it all, she's remained a true friend, never judging me or ostracising me like my other so-called friends, Sadie and Rachel, had done. They were no great loss anyway.

'You're the sister I never had,' I tell her, my eyes welling up once again. The alcohol content in my drink must be high because my muscles are already unwinding and I'm experiencing a warm, life's-not-so-bad feeling.

'Oh, no, you bloody don't,' Gail throws a pug-faced cushion at me, harder than is warranted, taking me by surprise, but her eyes have gone watery too. Gail rarely cries but deep down she has a big heart. Why else would I let her be an auntie to my girls?

'You don't get out of it that easily,' Gail snorts, pouring us both another shot — Black Sambuca the bottle says, 'so don't make this about me.'

I make up my mind to tell her everything. Not just about recent events: the envelope for instance which remains unopened on a pile of the clothes I'd shrugged off earlier, but *everything*, including what I fear may have happened the night Marcus disappeared. She deserves the truth. I love Jim and the girls, I would die for the latter, because they are my family, even though Jim doesn't fall under that umbrella anymore. But it's only possible to be one hundred per cent yourself with another woman who has your back.

Even when I was with Marcus, the so-called love of my life, I had to watch what I said and did so as not to annoy him. It's the way of the world we live in, where some men, without thinking, expect women to mother them while also acting like goddesses. They don't want to see our flaws, and expect us to hide them. None of us are perfect. We all have defects. As grown women, Gail and I understand each other in ways men cannot. Even when they're your twin flame or soulmate, *or you think they are*. Gail and I have walked in each other's footsteps, shared the same thoughts, pain and feelings and laughed at life in ways only women can fathom. That makes our friendship priceless.

CHAPTER 23

My head spins and throbs simultaneously. I'm not sure which symptom is worse. My throat too, is painfully dry as if it has never known water. On that thought, I open one eye, desperate for a drink. I'm so dehydrated I think I might die. Anything will do. I'd drink from the toilet bowl if I had to. But first I must figure out where I am and if I have any legs.

The room is in almost-darkness. Curtains high up on the walls have been drawn, yet beams of light penetrate through, searing into my brain like daggers. Putting a hand up to shield my eyes, I take in the carnage around me. Empty bottles on a small fixed-to-the-floor table, two of wine, one of sambuca and half a bottle of vodka with the lid left off. The smell makes me retch and I throw off the blanket that's pinning me down as I don't want to vomit into it. Once I'm sitting up, it's a different story, and I'm no longer concerned with being sick, more worried about how to keep my head on my shoulders. It feels big and heavy compared to the rest of my body, which doesn't work in the way I expect it to.

'Oh, God, Oh God,' I moan, trying to remember what happened last night. This isn't the first time I've experienced a blackout as a result of drinking too much, and that night on the beach immediately springs to mind as a reminder. I'm sensible enough to realise I haven't been abducted or raped and that I'm alive, but that's as good as it gets. When my right calf spasms and goes into cramp mode I cry out and fall off what I now realise is the L-framed sofa bed onto a wooden floor that feels damp to the touch.

'Jesus Christ, get a grip,' I tell myself, feeling increasingly panicked. *What exactly happened last night? What did I do?* Trying to put the missing pieces together, I stagger to my feet, gripping onto what looks like part of a kitchen unit. Then, ripping open one of the curtains, I peer out of the small gap to discover I'm surrounded by green reeds and water. Gail's boat. *The Grand Dame.* It's starting to come back to me. The drive here, with me crying my eyes out. What happened in the fish shop when I thought I saw Marcus, and prior to that discovering a stranger had been sleeping in my flat. Fucking hell, excuse my language, but I'm still having a tough time getting my head around that. Next, George's call to Gail to come and pick me up because I didn't want Jim to see me in the state I was in. Then back here with Gail and the drinks flowing. The rest, as they say, is history.

'Gail,' I call sharply, wanting to feel reassured by another human's presence that everything is okay, no boundaries were broken, and we are still friends. And more importantly wanting to find out what the hell I confided in my drunken state. *Did I spill all the beans?*

I fling open the door to Gail's bedroom, finding the bed unmade and the room as messy as a teenager's den. Gail's underwear is scattered across the floor and baby wipes have been disposed of next to a mascara-stained pillow. Spotting a glass of water next to the bed, I grab it, knocking the liquid back in one go and grimacing at how painful that feels. The water is tepid, and the glass has a lipstick stain on it, but I don't care.

I must pee before I wet my knickers, something that isn't entirely uncommon at my age although deeply embarrassing when it does. I swing open the folding door to the shower room and cram my tall frame into it. Pulling a face at how uncomfortable it is to empty my swollen bladder, I pee for England, and while I wait to finish, I run the tap and somehow edge my face under it until I'm lapping like a dog.

Coming out of the bedroom feeling slightly better, I ignite the gas stove in the galley kitchen and place an old-fashioned whistling kettle on top, sighing at how long it's likely to take to boil. The stench of oil is heavy in this area of the boat because this is where the engine room is situated. Searching for milk and hoping it's fresh as Gail's housekeeping skills are not one of her strengths, I notice a note stuck to the fridge with a "Prosecco warning" magnet. Grimacing, because Prosecco is not something I want to be reminded of this morning, I recognise Gail's handwriting, surprisingly neat for her, and see the note is meant for me.

Morning, sleepyhead. Had to be at work by eight. Tried to wake you but wasn't happening so thought it best to leave you. Hope the hangover isn't too bad. Worth it though. Lol. Stay as long as you like and catch up with you later. XXX

Feeling calmer for reading that, I almost smile as I vaguely remember someone, Gail obviously, trying and failing to shake me awake at silly o'clock when it was still dark. She'd even left a black coffee next to the bed, I realise now, so she must still be speaking to me. She wouldn't leave three kisses if she were pissed off. Gail is as straight as they come. She's more likely to hurt you by speaking the ugly truth than playing games. *Can I assume by this that I didn't reveal my worst fears to her, about Marcus and my role in what happened? Or, if the worst did happen and I drunkenly revealed my shameful secret, then perhaps she's okay with it, and understands? Otherwise, wouldn't she be refusing to have anything to do with me rather than leaving me coffee and notes? If she meant to dob me in, she'd have done it by now and I'd be waking up in a prison cell instead of her boat.* I feel incredibly lucky to have gotten off so lightly.

I decide against bringing the topic of our drunken conversation up unless Gail does, even if I do manage to remember everything, which I'm seriously doubtful of. Nope, I'm more than happy to bury my head in the sand about this, just as I had with her lying about Jim having a girlfriend. If Gail is willing to let bygones be bygones, then so am I. If anything, she did me a favour as the lie brought me, Jim, and my daughters closer together. A feeling of unease persists though. What else might Gail have lied about?

Spying my pile of crumpled clothes with the large brown envelope on top, I feel every hair on my body stand on end. I can't believe I still haven't opened Mrs Bouchard's letter. I'm surprised Gail didn't make me last night. Normally, it would be the first thing she'd bully me into. Picking it up, I turn it over in my hand and examine it. The seal is unbroken. Nobody but me will know its contents, unless I choose otherwise. Deciding there's no time like the present to find out what's inside, I slip my anorak on over Gail's silky pyjamas, feeling for the weight of my phone in the front pocket, reassured to find it's still there. Then I poke my size sevens into a tiny pair of Gail's crocs until my toes are pinched together, and my heels are hanging off the back of the soles. Finally, after rummaging in a kitchen drawer where Gail keeps cigarettes and a collection of brightly coloured plastic lighters, I thrust open the door, gasping as the icy air hits me and climb the steps up to the bow of the boat.

The air is damp and chilly enough to seep into my bones. The sun, low in the sky, is a pale yellow and does nothing to brighten the landscape, which on a good day swarms with wildlife. A few small dullish brown birds skip from reed to reed as they hunt for unsuspecting insects. The boat is hidden from dog walkers and bird spotters by tall reeds. I never understood Gail's decision to live on a boat, other than it being a cheap rent-free alternative to living, as she's not into wildlife or nature.

It dawns on me that the boat is more Jim's style, as he enjoys bird watching and has been known to cast a fishing rod. He'd be able to tell me what kind of fish were causing the circles of bubbles to pop up below the water's surface. But the Linda of old isn't so far removed from the Linda of today, because like Gail, I find that kind of thing boring as hell.

I haven't smoked in ages and never would around Jim who is anti-smoking. Unlike Gail, who is a proper fag-ash-Lil, as the saying goes, I've only ever been a social smoker and can take them or leave them. I used to like sitting beside Marcus while he puffed away at a cigar, enjoying the way the smoke settled around us casting its aromatic spell of coffee, cedar, and wood. I'll never inhale those scents again without thinking of him. But I don't let memories of him spoil the moment for me as I inhale on one of Gail's John Player Specials.

Because they relax me like nothing else can, not even the sleeping tablets and anti-depressant tablets I've been prescribed, I smoke three back-to-back until my lungs feel like they are on fire. Deciding I've polluted the countryside, and myself, enough, I stub out the last one before taking out my phone. I'm surprised to see six missed calls and three new voicemails, a combination of Abby, Rosie and Jim trying to get hold of me. Before getting too drunk last night, I texted Jim to let him know I was staying over at Gail's for a "girls' night in" so quite why there are so many urgent messages is beyond me.

Filled with renewed panic, I wonder if I've fucked everything up with my family just as everything was coming nicely together. Will they see this unexpected and unexplained night out as a sign of abandonment and conclude that I still can't be trusted? I resolve to go home straight away, rather than attacking the envelope, so I can make amends for my poor behaviour, if necessary, although I dread the thought of walking into a frosty, silent, atmosphere where nobody is speaking to me. *Please, God, anything but that.*

I text Gail; *Are we okay? Is everything all right or did I make a fool of myself last night?* She could secretly be seething or outright disgusted at what I may or may not have told her. She replies instantly, thank God. *All fine. No worries. How's the head? Loving this new ballsy Linda BTW.*

Shrugging off that last bit, which would suggest that I said more than was good for me, I thank my lucky stars that she and I are okay. All that's left for me to do now is worry about Jim and the girls. It's them I'm terrified of facing. *Please don't let me have fucked up with them again.* I go back inside the boat, call the taxi firm I have on speed dial and ask them to pick me up ASAP. Ali, dependable as ever, tells me he'll be with me in ten minutes.

Next, I steal twenty quid out of Gail's secret money jar, knowing she'll understand, and I leave her an I Owe You on the back of the note she wrote me. Adding three big kisses, as she did me, to make up for whatever cringeworthy crap I might have come out with last night and resisting the urge to go down the *whatever does she think of me?* route, I stop for a minute and wonder if Gail can truly be trusted. Until recently, I'd have taken a swipe at anyone who dared to suggest my best friend was anything other than fiercely loyal, but since finding out she'd lied to me about Jim having a girlfriend, even if it did work in my favour, an element of doubt has crept into my mind. The thought instantly fills me with guilt. How could I doubt her after everything she's done for me? She's my oldest friend so of course, I can trust her. With my life, if I had to and I know she feels the same. That's what friends are for.

CHAPTER 24

In the taxi, once I've exchanged pleasantries with Ali, who fondly tells me, as he always does, that I'm his favourite customer, I get to do what I should have done yesterday: rip open the bulky brown envelope from Mrs Bouchard. A bunch of photocopied documents fall into my lap, neatly cut to the same size. These must be the news cuttings she told me the mystery man asked to see in the library. Alice whatever her name was, the one Mrs Bouchard nicknamed Miss Marple, has done a competent job, making notes on each slip of paper. There are four in all, plus a handwritten note from Mrs Bouchard.

Dear Linda, her writing flows in artistic loops with just a hint of arthritic unsteadiness. I note the use of my first name and realise calling me "Mrs Bouchard" would hurt, her son being dead and never having married. *As I didn't hear back from you, I thought I'd send you these articles in case they're useful.*

Personally, I'm unable to see any connection between your circumstances and mine, except for the obvious — in that Tony Fortin and your husband are one and the same, but it does seem odd that a stranger should turn up in our village prior to your visit, to research my son's accident and the Fortin boy's mysterious disappearance which, as far as I can recall, happened a few months after Marcus died. Anyway, I wish

133

you all the best in your search and pray that you will find the answers you are looking for.

My face suddenly feels flushed, and I steady my ragged breathing as I read her note again, memorising the words that matter most — *the Fortin boy's mysterious disappearance, which as far as I can recall, happened a few months after Marcus died.* Why didn't she tell us this when we visited her? Perhaps she was so overcome with shock at the time that she didn't think to mention her son's best friend had taken off shortly after the funeral? Back then, she might not have been able to look eighteen-year-old Tony Fortin in the eye knowing he had survived the accident when her son had not. She might not have been able to bring herself to even mention his name. Nobody would blame her if that were the case, *certainly not me.* I know how I'd have felt, God forbid, if it had been Rosie or Abby. On a less sinister note, Mrs Bouchard could have been completely unaware of Fortin's vanishing act until much later. Her mind would have been otherwise occupied. A grieving mother surely wouldn't have paid much attention to idle gossip at such a time.

My shoulders curl forward with grief and a dull ache pulses in my chest as I wipe away fresh tears from my already puffy eyes, still red from yesterday's disaster when I thought I'd come face to face with my meant-to-be-dead husband. I can't decide if these tears are for Mrs Bouchard, her late son Marcus, or me, so I turn my attention to the other documents, avoiding gazing in the rear-view mirror in case Ali's sympathetic eyes, piqued with interest, should meet mine. If that should happen, I'm bound to properly break down.

The news cutting shows a picture of Marcus Bouchard and Tony Fortin preparing for their fishing trip. It's identical to the one Mrs Bouchard showed me, but this time it's accompanied by the newspaper report announcing the young man's death.

Clovelly man, Marcus Bouchard, (aged eighteen, seen on the left), died in a tragic accident after he and best friend, Tony

Fortin (pictured on the right) set out on a fishing trip on Saturday. Both went to the same school in the village and were keen fishermen, but the boat got into trouble when it hit an unexpected squall near Lundy Island, during which Marcus, a non-swimmer, went into the water. Despite various attempts to save him, Tony (also eighteen) was unable to locate his friend and had to be rescued by a passing boat. Marcus's body was pulled out of the sea three days later. He was the only son of Caspian and Matilda Bouchard, of Bay View Cottage, who moved to the UK from South Africa and settled in Clovelly when Marcus was eight years old. A funeral service will be held at All Saints Church.

Can it be a coincidence that Tony Fortin, who I know for certain is my husband, and his best friend, Marcus Bouchard, both died at sea? Except in my husband's case, his body was never found and, as far as I'm concerned, is still very much alive. Did he plan it this way? On purpose? Deliberately making us think he'd drowned? But why? What can he hope to gain from pretending to be dead? Now that I know he disappeared from Clovelly shortly after Marcus died, my mind boggles at the mystery of it all. Did he leave because he couldn't bear living there once his friend died?

The loss of a close friend would have been difficult for him to accept, particularly when they were as close as brothers, according to Mrs Bouchard. Or did Tony have an ulterior motive? Had he intended to steal Marcus's identity all along?

Squeezing my eyes shut, my throat contracts as I will myself not to go down the road that signposts the possibility that Marcus Bouchard's death was no accident.

And what of Fortin's parents? The article doesn't mention them. Are they still alive, I wonder? Did they remain in Clovelly, or did they flee with their son? I suppose that would make more sense, but how can I find out?

Still hungover from last night, my head hurts from all the unanswered questions, so I switch my attention to the next article, just as the car lurches to a stop. I'm surprised to find we're outside Victoria Road already. The large charcoal driveway makes the house stand out from the others on the tree-lined street as does the trio of vehicles which reflect my family's personalities. The diesel-guzzling pickup truck is Jim's, whereas the yellow smart car belongs to an eco-conscious, carbon-footprint-aware Rosie. Abby's shiny, impressive black Audi takes centre stage in the walled and gated driveway which also houses a brick-built separate double garage. The campervan is tucked away in a corner and is covered in a shroud of black material as if it too were a widow in mourning.

Swallowing nervously, I hand Ali the borrowed twenty-pound note, embarrassed at not having a tip for him. Then, getting out of the car I stuff everything back in the envelope, hiding it once again in my anorak as I walk up the path. I used to hate the feeling of arriving home. The boredom of what was behind the glossy, red-painted door — a life of drudgery, a loveless marriage, *on my side at least*, and two selfish, squabbling grown-up daughters who made me want to turn around and run. And run I had. Only to regret it. *Is that what Marcus is doing? Running from me, from our life?* Knowing I'll never be able to think of him as Tony, I curse him anyway for the way my life has turned out even though I have only myself to blame.

Having crawled home with my tail between my legs once before, nine months ago to be precise, after Marcus disappeared, to test the waters with my children, only to be shunned, it feels as if I'm about to undergo the same ordeal after staying out last night. Certain that Abby and Rosie will be furious with me, I imagine they'll accuse me of letting them down, claiming I can't be trusted. Jim won't be *as* bothered, although he'll have whittled and worried. He's chilled about most things and has always been easy-going. Look how good he was when I decided to up and leave him, taking everything in his stride. Even when I met Marcus and asked for a divorce, Jim never stood in my way, although, being a family man through and through, I knew it wasn't what he wanted. Jim is a bloody good man, and I never deserved him. Strange how you don't appreciate what you've got until it's gone. It's true what people say, you always want what you can't have in life. And I'm no exception.

CHAPTER 25

When I crept apologetically through the back door, like a criminal, to find everyone staring wide-eyed at me, I was too scared to say anything. But then my family sprang into action and fell on me as if I were the best thing since sliced bread, everyone fussing around me at once. It was as if I'd stepped into some strange Stepford family experiment, with Rosie stroking my hair as if I were a pet cat, and Abby helping me out of my anorak and ushering me over to the table with a gentle command to 'sit down and take the weight off your feet.' Jim, on the other hand, kept his distance and observed me with secretive eyes. The defensively crossed arms didn't fool me for one minute. For once, he seemed just as concerned over my absence as the girls.

It was as if they were actually grateful to have me back, a fact that blindsided me at first. Shame continues to grip me though, causing beads of sweat to break out on my forehead and upper lip, as it dawns on me that they're terrified I might abandon them again.

What I did to my family four years ago was unpardonable. My heart shatters into a thousand pieces when I think of how they must have suffered. I've said it before and I'll say it again, I don't deserve their forgiveness and acceptance, but I'll take their hand off for it, all the same. And now, a few hours later, I'm guest of honour at the lunch they're preparing for me.

'I'll have to stay out more often,' I joke as I watch my family perform their kitchen duties. Each has a job and they do it well, never getting in each other's way. Rosie dutifully fills the dishwasher. Abby lays the table with the second-best dinner service, not the sage green John Lewis set, but the blue and white Spode one off the dresser, while Jim grapples with simmering saucepans and checks regularly on the lamb dish in the oven. It smells delicious and my mouth waters at the thought of tucking in. After all that alcohol last night, my body needs carbs. Moving my arms out of the way, so Abby can fill my place setting with a plate and some cutlery, I notice she's using the silver-plated Viner King's box set that was gifted to me and Jim on our wedding day. On my nomadic travels abroad with Marcus, I secretly missed the material things I'd left behind. Especially the things I'd treasured, like the John Lewis dinner service and this special edition cutlery set. Marcus would have labelled me superficial had he known this, so I kept that side of me hidden from him.

There had been so many things I couldn't take with me into my new life and my children, the most precious asset of all, were one of them. Only me being Linda, I didn't appreciate the loss of them at the time. God, what is a man or property compared to one's children? Looking back, I believe I must have gone through some sort of mid-life, menopausal crisis to behave the way I did. It was so unlike me. Everybody said so. Only Gail understood my restlessness. And she was the only one among my friends who encouraged me to be true to myself.

Guilt nags me, like a terrier at one's heels, as I listen to Abby and Rosie sharing stories about their day, inviting me into their world in a way I never imagined would be possible again. For once, Abby doesn't boss her sister around. Instead, she throws warm glances at us all, like butter wouldn't melt in her mouth. Jim is too busy finishing dinner to take notice of what they're saying, but I hang on to every word.

'I was thinking, Mum, that maybe you could come with me and Rosie to look at wedding dresses next Saturday if you're not busy.'

'Oh yes, that would be lovely,' Rosie pipes up, 'we could grab some lunch too. Just us girls. How does that sound?'

A sob almost escapes my throat, but I beat it into submission before the girls notice. 'I'd love to, thank you, Abby. Count me in for lunch too.'

Abby flashes me a grateful smile while Rosie nods, no doubt making a mental note in her well-organised school-teacher's diary not to forget that date.

'Everyone in their places. We're good to go,' Jim suddenly announces.

'Want any help?' I dutifully get to my feet, but Jim flaps a tea towel in my direction, so I collapse into my chair again, feeling suddenly exhausted. Staying up late last night with Gail and drinking more than I should, plus the accumulating stress after all that has happened, has finally caught up with me. I give a wide yawn at the table, something I'd usually be the first one to grumble about, but luckily, nobody notices as Jim chooses that moment to slide the sizzling dish of roast lamb, decorated with sprigs of rosemary and cloves of garlic, onto the table. Lemon roasted potatoes arrive next, browned to perfection, causing my stomach to rumble hungrily.

'Wow, Jim. You've done an amazing job.' I can't disguise how impressed I am.

'He's become quite the cook, hasn't he, Mum?' Rosie's voice swells with pride.

'And to think he couldn't even boil an egg before . . .'

I see the warning glance Jim flashes Abby, and she falls silent at once, as if fearful she has put her foot in it. Everyone knows she was about to say *before you left*.

'Well, I'm enormously proud of him.' I say giving everyone the thumbs up. It works, the elephant in the room vanishes, leaving behind an easier, more comfortable mood.

But threads of anxiety continue to pull at my insides as I tuck into my meal, Jim heaping steamed broccoli and carrots high on our plates. Everyone but me has a glass of wine with their Sunday lunch.

'I'll settle for water after last night,' I grin through my nausea.

Despite the happy, family atmosphere that everyone's tried so hard to create, Jim isn't fooling me. There's something off about him. *What's he acting all shifty for?* I try to convince myself that it's all in my head but every time our eyes meet, he looks away and when he does manage a smile, it doesn't quite reach his eyes.

I suspect him of hiding something. But what? Everyone knows Jim's as straight as they come. At least that's what I thought before I found out he hadn't relayed Mrs Bouchard's message. I'm still trying to work out whether this was intentional or not. He may even have accidentally deleted it before listening to it, although knowing Jim, that's not likely. He obviously doesn't have a clue about the information she sent me in the post or the revelation I discovered among Mrs Bouchard's friend's notes, news so shocking it hasn't registered in my own mind yet — the fact that the mystery man in the library had, when pressured to do so, identified himself as Brian James. Not Tony Fortin, or Marcus Bouchard.

A less dramatic name couldn't have been chosen if you tried, which suggested to me that it was made up, just as the fake tenant's identity of Bruce Wayne had been. And I would have been happy to have gone on thinking so, until it hit me, like a bolt of lightning, on entering the kitchen earlier how much Jim reminds me of his dad and granddad. Jim's father was called Brian, while his paternal grandfather was christened James. Of course, all of this could be just another of those strange flukes I keep coming up against in my search to find Marcus and solve the mystery of his reappearance, but these so-called chance occurrences are beginning to stack up to disproportionate levels. And that can mean only one thing.

None of what is happening is a coincidence.

CHAPTER 26

I've never been a fan of Sundays, believing them endlessly dull, no more than a depressing reminder that tomorrow is Monday and a back-to-work day, and tonight is no exception. Yet here we are cosied up together in the living room watching — of all things — my, or should I say *our*, wedding video. I desperately want to question Jim about the Brian James connection but instead, we must munch popcorn and stare at a grainy, jittery screen, while he points out all the best bits of our "special" day. By now, I'm certain he's guilty of something. Whereas yesterday I might have given him the benefit of the doubt, now that the cat is out of the bag, so to speak with the whole Brian James blunder, I can't wait to get him on his own so I can accuse him and see if he crumbles under my scrutiny.

Now I've had time to think about it, I'm convinced he must have produced the first name he could think of when questioned by Mrs Bouchard's fearless friend. He's hiding something and I'm determined to find out what that is, but Abby and Rosie are equally determined to keep us all together as one happy family. Hence, this forced, never-ending evening.

One minute we were talking about Abby's wedding dress and the next she was demanding to see her parents' wedding video, claiming she didn't know it existed.

'Oh, not now, Abby,' my words had come out stilted and sharp, so I immediately retracted and softened my tone, caving in to her request. Feeling as I did, the last thing I wanted was to watch a video of me and Jim, but I couldn't let on to Abby.

We're halfway through the old, ninety-minute-long VHS video, which Jim had converted to DVD years ago, and so far, most of it has been boring church stuff, but I must admit it's lovely to see moving images of my mum and dad again, Jim's parents too. The Delameres and the Butchers were such close-knit families, having grown up together in the same street, two doors apart. When I steal a glance at Jim to see if this trip down memory lane is having a similar effect on him, he avoids eye contact with me. From his armchair position, the one nearest the white marble fireplace, known as "Dad's chair", his eyes are glued to the TV, but his slipper-clad feet jiggle up and down in a way that's uncomfortable to watch. It gives him away.

This makes me even more suspicious, and anger churns inside me as I focus on the faces of my father-in-law and grandfather-in-law. Jim, who is now around the same age as they are in the video, is the spitting image of his father and grandfather, Brian and James Delamere, just as I had thought earlier. Nothing can prevent me from shooting daggers at my ex-husband now that I've decided he has to be the same man Mrs Bouchard's friend ran into at the library. I'm convinced there's no other explanation. When he refuses to look me in the eye, my gut instinct, and his uneasiness seem to back up this theory. Suddenly, I'm steaming mad, but I'm having to hide it for the sake of the girls. How bloody dare he meddle in my life. *What on earth was he thinking? Why? Just why?*

'Oh, Mum, you looked so beautiful.' Abby pauses on her popcorn, her eyes bright with unshed tears. 'Didn't she, Rosie?'

'Less of the past tense,' I quip in a bid to redeem myself with Abby, who has been an emotional wreck since news of her wedding date was announced. 'I've still got it.'

'You definitely do,' Rosie laughs good-naturedly, 'everyone says you look far too young to be our mum.'

'Aw, thank you, Rosie. That's sweet of you.'

I study myself on screen and hardly know myself. This young woman who knew nothing of life. But was full of it anyway. It was bursting out of her. Anyone can see that. Was she the woman who eventually ran away to start a new life abroad? Is she the real me? Hiding dormant for years, behind babies, nappies, and armfuls of washing, dreaming of escape and adventure. As I watch her walk down the aisle, accompanied by her proud-as-punch dad, smiling confidently as if the world were hers for the taking, I wish I could revisit this moment and give her the advice every girl needs. *Find yourself before you go looking for anyone else.*

For the first time I find myself believing that I did look beautiful on my wedding day. But what bride doesn't? My naturally blonde hair was half up, half down with spirals of loose curls falling around my face. I was twenty pounds lighter back then and could get away with wearing minimal make-up because, apart from a few light freckles dotted around my nose, I had a flawless complexion.

'I do look young, don't I?' I say in surprise. 'Twenty-six was a ridiculous age to get married and to think four years later I was a stay-at-home mum of two.' The words fall out of my mouth before I can stop them. Luckily, Abby and Rosie are entranced by what is happening on screen, so don't pay too much attention otherwise they would pull me up on not considering marriage to their dad and being mother to two beautiful children enough for me. And they'd be right of course, otherwise, we wouldn't be in the situation we find ourselves in now.

I go back to watching the video. By now, my dad has stepped back and I'm joining Jim at the altar, where the vicar is waiting, a rehearsed smile on his face because we weren't regular churchgoers and therefore, he didn't know us, only pretended to. The camera, operated by one of Jim's workmates, pans in on my soon-to-be husband's face to catch him glancing over his shoulder at his bride-to-be for the first time. The look on his face is priceless. It's as if he's won the lottery. He might have been hungover from the night before but that doesn't prevent him from acting as if he's the luckiest man alive.

Abby and Rosie see it too and glance sideways at their dad in something like awe, each no doubt hoping that their future husbands will look at them in the same way. I know what they'll also be thinking, *how could Mum ever have left someone like him?*

'Did you always know Mum was the one for you, Dad?' Abby wants to know, seeming to have forgotten for the moment that Jim and I are no longer married.

I suspect my daughter is desperate to know that fairy tales and happy endings *do* exist but with my track record, I've hardly set the right example. Unable to bear it any longer — the nostalgia, smiles, and happy expectant faces of our parents and friends, I jump to my feet and fight down the bile rising in my throat.

'I'm so sorry but I need to lie down. I've got a terrible headache,' I lie, hoping for understanding from my daughters and not caring what Jim thinks.

'You never could take your drink,' Abby says disapprovingly as if she were a teetotaller, while Rosie throws me an understanding smile.

I catch Jim scanning my face, looking for clues, but avert my eyes. He knows there's something up. Neither of us has forgotten what the other is like in the four years we've been apart. Acid curdles my stomach and I'm forced to swallow down a mouthful of sick, as well as the fact Abby is right about my drinking, before leaving the room.

CHAPTER 27

Tears prickle my eyelids as I lie, snuggled up on my bed in a foetal position, staring at the magnolia wall of the guest bedroom. The plan was to redecorate it in blue when our future baby boy was born but after having two girls back-to-back, I'd told Jim I was done and didn't want any more children. He was disappointed but, as always, conceded to my wishes. I used to find myself wishing he would fight back, make a stand, or demand something of me for a change, but he never did. Jim was always the stoic pragmatist. It used to drive me crazy.

Yet it was the opposite with Marcus and me. I was the one who prioritised our relationship, who gave more and would have kept on doing so until eventually I lost myself. A sense of doom had lain heavy on my heart even in those passion-filled early days when we couldn't get enough of each other. Gut instinct is never wrong, and I've since learned that if you avoid red flags in the beginning of a relationship, they come back to haunt you in the end. This was true of Marcus's womanising. He was a huge flirt, but if I ever challenged him on this, he'd grow sullen and snap at me, claiming I didn't genuinely love him if he couldn't be himself around me. 'It's essential to me,' he once told me, 'That I'm allowed to be an authentic version of myself, or else what's the point?'

In hindsight, what Marcus was asking for was permission to flirt. I'd never been the jealous type before, certainly not with Jim who was as trustworthy as they come, so seeing Marcus enamoured with another woman was like having a knife plunged into my chest. At times, I feared I shouldn't have married him. That we weren't the soulmates we proclaimed ourselves to be. Just an old couple in lust who would have ended up going our separate ways eventually had he not disappeared into the sea that night.

When I hear the click of the door opening and the soft tread of footsteps on the deep pile carpet, I close my eyes and pretend to be asleep. I can tell it's Jim as the aroma of his coconut shampoo gives him away. I also sense that he knows I'm faking it. *Nothing new there, then.* There's a rattle of crockery at my side, confirming my suspicions as only Jim would go to the trouble of making me tea in a china cup and saucer, and then pressure on the bed as he sits down on the edge of it. I groan inwardly, realising he's not going to go away. Earlier, I'd wanted nothing more than a confrontation with him but now I feel ridiculously sad and heartbroken, craving only to be left alone. I get like this when I think about Marcus.

'I was thinking, Linda,' Jim's words come out strained, 'if you wanted to move back into your old room, I could move in here. The main room was always more to your taste than mine anyway.'

If he'd said this to me any other day, I'd have been deliriously happy as it's true, I'd decorated that room, quite selfishly, with myself in mind. It was my dream bedroom. Jim called it a showroom and claimed to feel uncomfortable in the tropical bird surroundings.

I open my eyes and feel my heart twist when I see the thinning crown of Jim's lowered head. Soon he will have a bald spot like his dad. It hits me then that we're both ageing, and our time is running out. Suddenly, fighting with the man who used to be my husband but is still the father of my two girls, and a brilliant one at that, seems unimportant. Whatever Jim has done he would have had a good reason for it. I still need to get to the bottom of the mystery surrounding Marcus, but I'm not angry with Jim anymore. He's a good man, and there are few of those around.

'I'd like that, Jim.' I clear my throat and try again, 'But it wouldn't be fair or right.'

Jim wrings his hands in his lap. His mouth is drawn into a thin line. It's not like him to be so serious. I feel another tug on my heartstrings.

'No matter what happens in the future, Linda, this will always be your home so you might as well take me up on my offer. This is where your family is. And that's where you belong. Right here.'

'I don't deserve it, not after . . .'

'Give me an hour to move my things out and then you can move back in,' Jim cuts me off with a steely determination in his voice and eyes that's new. Or it was always there, and I simply never saw it before. Never looked hard enough more like it. *Selfish, spoiled, Linda.*

I pull myself into a sitting position with my feet curled under me, a pillow in my lap to lend some support for what I'm about to say. It occurs to me that I might be ruining something special by bringing this up now, but I can't put it off any longer.

'Jim. There's something I need to ask you and I want the truth, mind,' The words come tumbling out of my mouth so fast that I trip over them.

Suspicion flashes in Jim's eyes and I feel his body tense next to me. The poor man appears terrified, so I know I must put him out of his misery fast.

'I know that you went to Devon, and to Clovelly library, to find out about Marcus months before we went there, so don't bother denying it. I also know that Mrs Bouchard left a telephone message that you never told me about. I want to know why you would keep something like that from me. And why go to Devon and not tell me?'

Jim's face softens in an instant. I can almost hear the collapse of his shoulders as the tension leaves his body. He doesn't seem all that bothered to have been found out. Strange that, when a moment ago he looked like he might shit his pants, pardon the language.

'I didn't tell you in case I came across something that would hurt you, and because I knew you'd be mad at me, but yes, I did go to Devon to see if I could find out who Marcus really was. Gail told me that the Greek police had their suspicions about him, that they didn't think he was who he said he was. And I never trusted him. So, I thought if I could prove to you that he was a liar who didn't deserve you, you'd stop pining for him and go back to being happy.'

'Oh Jim,' I sigh. 'I wish it were as easy as that.'

'I first came across the name Tony Fortin in the library in Devon, but I never saw the photograph of him and Marcus, so I didn't make the connection until the day you told me you'd received a message from someone with the same name. After that, I was even more worried. I know I shouldn't have interfered, Linda, but I swear I was just looking out for you,'

'And what about Mrs Bouchard's voicemail?' I draw my mouth into a thin line to show him I'm still cross.

'Guilty as charged.' Jim throws up his hands in an inappropriately playful gesture.

His casual attitude surprises me. 'You're not taking this seriously enough! Make no mistake, I'm really pissed off at you, Jim, and the least you could do is show you're sorry.'

Jim's eyes bulge with alarm, his smile drops instantly from his face. 'I really am sorry, Linda. Honestly, I am, but I was only trying to help, or thought I was. It was nothing more sinister than that so please don't be mad at me. I know I should have told you, but the longer I left it . . .'

'It's my business, Jim,' I say firmly. 'Nobody else's.'

'I know. I know.' Jim flinches at my words and bows his head again.

Part of me is riddled with guilt and I wonder if I'm making too much of it. He was only trying to help. In the only way Jim knows how, by being active and getting stuff done. Other men woo with words and romantic gestures, Jim simply gets up and fixes things and if he can't mend people, then he goes all inward and feels helpless. He's not one to stand idly by in a crisis, whereas I go to pieces. Even *I* have to admit that my emotions are all over the place at the moment. I might have wanted to throttle Jim two seconds ago, but now I see him for the good man he is. *You won't find a better, Linda Butcher*, my mother used to tell me. I hadn't believed her back then, but I'm starting to. What a bloody fool I've been, I realise, because that bald patch on Jim's head has made me appreciate how much I love, respect, and want to look after him. In moments like this, I crave nothing more than to grow old with this man and the idea of holidays in the caravan at Hunstanton suddenly seem so much more appealing. What I wouldn't give for a weekend away by the sea right now.

'It's okay, Jim. Just promise me you won't keep anything like that from me again.'

As I smile at him, I'm unable to shake off an uneasy thought that I know will nag at me for days. *What if there's something he isn't telling me?* He seems relieved to have gotten off so lightly because he's now smiling and the colour of his skin has gone from a dirty grey to a healthy salmon, but the way he acted before when I first accused him . . . It makes me suspect he thought he'd been caught out for something much bigger than this and that's why he wasn't so concerned just now. *Is this another of my so-called red flags that will come back to haunt me?* But then it's all forgotten about when I hear Jim say—

'I made you a promise once over thirty years ago remember, and I kept my word then, didn't I? It's like the girls said downstairs. I always knew you were the one.'

Willing my heart to stop racing, I tell myself that Jim doesn't mean what I think he's implying. He couldn't because, well, he just wouldn't. And yet . . . No, don't be an idiot. Your days of making a fool of yourself are over. *Snap out of it, Linda.*

'And I will take you up on your offer,' I change the subject, my cheeks flushing with heat.

'Offer?' A look of confusion tinted with hope dawns on Jim's face.

'Of the bedroom.' I laugh. 'How could you have forgotten so quickly. You owe me now, so I'm not going to feel guilty about it. Not one bit,' I joke.

'Good because I don't want you to,' Jim gets to his feet and hops from toe to toe. I can tell he's already restless, keen to get on with the job of moving himself out of the bedroom so I can move back in. But suddenly he goes still and his chin jerks upwards in a defiant motion.

'You'll always be my girl, Linda, and I'm yours forever, like it or not. I'm not asking for anything, I'm just speaking plain, so we both know where we are.'

Jim turns away from me then, his Adam's apple nervously bobbing up and down. I suspect he feels vulnerable now he's played all his cards. It takes a brave man to do that. A good man. The marrying kind. The faithful, loyal type. Everything my Marcus wasn't, *isn't*.

'Jim,' my body temperature rages at what I'm going to say. *Am I about to do something completely crazy, or will it be the making of me?* I'm not sure if this feeling of panic is caused by excitement or nerves, or a combination of the two, as I've only been widowed nine months and my heart and mind are all over the place, but the truth is that I desperately want to feel safe and protected. Which means I need Jim like I've never needed anyone before. He is not only the gatekeeper to my children, but he is as much my home as the house we're in.

'I don't want you to move out of the bedroom, but I do want to move back in.' I blink several times as I say this, watching shock and then understanding register on Jim's face.

With a twitch of a smile, I add, 'I'm just speaking plain, so we both know where we are.'

CHAPTER 28

Last night in bed, Jim cuddled up to me and I responded by laying my head against his shoulder. He might as well have been fully clothed in his T-shirt and pyjama bottoms, but I was as bad, having slipped on a full-length nightdress over my bra and matching big girl pants. Things were awkward at first, but I felt comforted by the familiar scent of Jim's no-nonsense, cheap, minty toothpaste breath. He relaxed too when I took his hand and folded it around my stomach where our girls started their lives, a reminder of our shared history. The surface of his skin was scratchy and worn, unlike Marcus's much softer flesh, but I knew those working man's hands as well as my own. They were honest.

The ring finger on his left hand was as bare as mine, having decided before bed to remove the plain gold band I'd worn to my most recent wedding. My muscles stiffened involuntarily when I slipped it off as it felt like another betrayal, *if Marcus is alive, doesn't that mean I'm cheating on him with another man?* but I refused to allow Marcus to linger on my mind. Tomorrow, I would allow the remorse and regret to creep back in. Tonight, was about Jim and me and there was no room for ghosts. The last time Jim and I had shared a bed, not counting the night in the campervan, we were still

152

husband and wife. Although it had never bothered us before, we were both conscious of the fact our two grown-up daughters were sleeping only feet away from us in their respective bedrooms.

'We can take this as slow as you like. There's no need to rush on my part,' Jim had whispered in my ear.

In response, I'd craned my neck and kissed him on the lips, allowing my mouth to linger on his. I hadn't expected Jim's reaction to be so enthusiastic. It surprised us both. When his cold hands found their way under my almost-virtuous nighty, I didn't tense as much as I thought I would. There was a need in me to feel loved and wanted. And alive. I had lived with death for long enough. And with Jim, I could be myself. I would never have to compete with other women for his attention and that brought immense peace of mind. I was enough as I was. There was no desire to wish myself thinner, younger, or more beautiful. I was all those things and more to Jim. Knowing Jim considers himself lucky to have me is incredibly sexy and I wouldn't swap that feeling for anything. For too long it had been the other way around when I assumed the role of the "lucky one", even though Marcus had been the one to pursue me. It was all about the chase for him.

Jim had shrugged off his pyjamas by this point and was about to remove my knickers when he paused, smiling shyly at me in the dimly lit room. I felt almost embarrassed to look down at his erection, even though I could feel it against my leg. Oddly, it was as if I were a young girl again. Not exactly a virgin bride, but like we'd gone back in time to when we were first married and were getting to know each other's bodies.

'I can't believe I used to go around telling you that I didn't need to change as there was nothing wrong with me.' He reminisces seriously, the tone of his voice implying self-criticism and regret.

I nod silently, not wanting to spoil the moment.

'What a load of tosh. No wonder you couldn't put up with me.' He continues in the same vein, but by now he's waving my pants triumphantly above his head, as if deserving of a prize. Tickled by this, I laugh along with him.

'That was the boy in me talking. Do you remember how I used to tell you that you deserved better?'

'Always,' I agree, enjoying the memory.

'Well from now on, I'm going to be the man who deserves you.'

'Is that another of your once-in-a-lifetime promises?' I pant, feeling aroused in a way I'd never felt before with him. I couldn't begin to explain why it felt so different. It just did. And we both felt it.

'Tell me what you want, Linda. Show me.'

The boy was still there, in Jim's voice and his eyes but the man that I loved like an old friend was in charge for once. So, I didn't hesitate to do exactly that, not regretting for one moment that I was showing him what Marcus had taught me about my body's desires.

* * *

Jim brings me a cup of tea and even stirs it for me before placing it in my hand. He's fully dressed and ready for work whereas I'm still in bed, sleepy-eyed and smelling of sex. Much as I'm grateful to have Jim back in my life I can't wait for him to leave so I can have the house to myself and think about all that's happened. The girls have already left for work and Jim has lingered behind so he can have a few private moments with me.

'When should we tell them? The girls, I mean?'

Jim is like an exuberant puppy this morning, bouncing around with enough energy for both of us. His mood is infectious, and I find myself grinning back at him though I'm more cautious.

'Maybe we should wait a while. What do you think?'

'That would be the sensible thing to do.'

'I thought that was your preferred choice in all things of the heart,' I tease.

'Not where you're concerned, young lady.'

'Young!' I laugh. 'I feel at least a hundred today and I must look it too.' As soon as the words are out of my mouth I fret about the bags under my eyes, my sagging boobs and wrinkled skin until I remind myself that this is Jim I'm talking to. My Jim. He's nothing like Marcus who would sometimes compare me to younger women who hadn't had babies. Jim doesn't care what I look like or what I wear. Being together is what matters. He has a simple outlook on life, putting his family first. Before anything else. Sighing happily, I sink back onto the pillows and let him smother me with noisy kisses. They are not the enthusiastic ones of last night, but they still feel good, like coming home to a hot meal on a cold day.

'We'll tell them tonight,' I announce bravely and am immediately rewarded with yet more pecks on the cheek. But then, my body runs cold, and I sit up straight, pushing Jim away. 'What if they hate the idea? They might worry about me hurting you again.'

'It will be fine. You'll see. They love us, so they're bound to be pleased. Knowing our daughters, I don't even think it will come as much of a surprise.'

'Especially to Abby.'

'Especially to Abby,' Jim agrees.

'Oh my God! What about Gail?' My nerves spike at the thought of her hostile reaction.

'What about Gail?' Jim is indifferent.

He never was her biggest admirer, yet I somehow never picked up on this before. It just shows you that you never one hundred per cent know anyone. People are full of surprises. Even good, old, reliable ones like Jim.

'Gail's been so protective of you and the girls. She's not going to like it. Not after what I did.'

'Who cares what Gail thinks?' he says, shrugging. 'She's nothing to us. She's not even family.'

155

Jim's words and tone surprise me. I used to think he valued her as an unofficial part of our family and enjoyed the fact she played the role of aunt to our girls.

I watch as he takes a deep breath. 'The truth is, Linda, and you won't like what I'm going to say, but she came on to me.'

I can do nothing more than stare at him for second. 'What?' I finally manage. 'You're not serious? You can't be, I mean . . .' My voice trails off as I try to picture this never before thought of scenario in my head. My husband, *conveniently forgetting for the moment that he's my ex*, and my best friend. The idea is unthinkable. Absurd.

'She invited me to the boat, said an afternoon's fishing would do me good.' Jim picks up my suddenly cold hand and tries to rub some life back into it.

'You went to Gail's boat! But she never mentioned it.' Jealousy surges within me and it jolts me back to the times spent with Marcus when I worried about losing him to another woman or being replaced by a younger model. Those fears, real or otherwise, wore me down over time until I no longer knew myself anymore. With Marcus, I became someone completely new. A stranger that I wouldn't want to shake hands with.

'She took the hump when I turned her down and even tried to make out she was only messing around, but she was dead serious. I could tell.' Jim gives it to me straight. It hurts.

'How? I mean what did she do to make you think that?'

'Linda,' Jim sighs, his face darkening, because he doesn't want to hurt me, 'Gail doesn't have your best interests at heart. For a long time now she's been trying to get her feet under the table. Always popping around on the pretext she wants to see Abby or Rosie, when she knows full well they're not here. She's made herself clear, if you get what I mean.'

'So she lied about you having a girlfriend to keep me away from you because she wanted you for herself?' As it dawns on me that my friend has betrayed me, I feel my heart break. If ever there was anybody I thought I could count on, it was Gail. We've been through so much together.

'I've been such a fool. A complete idiot.' I tell Jim, allowing the tears to fall. 'How could she do that to me? Why would she?'

'She wanted what you had, but you were too blind to see it,' he replies sadly. 'Ever since school, when you were first friends, she had to beat you at everything. First, the expensive wedding, which had to be bigger and better than ours, and then the six bridesmaids to top your three. But when she couldn't have children and Adam left, it all went tits-up for her. It's no surprise really that she tried to pick up with me where you left off. A ready-made family and a proper home are what she was after. I'm not daft, Linda.'

What Jim says makes sense now, even if I'm annoyed with myself for not having the insight to see what he had, but I'll need more time to think about this when he's not around. Right now, unfairly, I'm mad at him for never mentioning this before. *Gail and Jim.* The thought had never crossed my mind. Not once. *How dumb can I be?* First Marcus. Now Gail.

'Thank God, I've got you, Jim. That's all I can say. You're the only one I can trust.'

'You can always count on me, Linda. You know that.' Jim gets to his feet as he says this, and I'm reminded of how uncomfortable he is around tearful displays of emotion. I no longer consider it the worst personality trait in the world, because he's got so much more to offer, but back when we were young it used to irritate me. There were times when I felt alone in our marriage, especially when I was down or suffering and he couldn't give me the emotional support I craved.

But I'm a girl no more and capable of standing on my own two feet. I dutifully wave Jim off to work, keen for him to think I'm okay so I can get back to self-destruct mode and tear myself to pieces for not having the sense to see beyond my nose. First, the lie about Jim having another woman, told to put my nose out of joint, and now this! Bloody Gail.

The sense of betrayal is huge, especially after yesterday when I confided my darkest fear to her that I might have been responsible for what happened on the beach that night, *did I push Marcus?*, or at least I may have done because I can't remember what was actually said because she got me drunk on purpose to find out more about Jim and my family.

As I stomp around, picking up Jim's pyjamas from the floor, I know I can't let this go.

CHAPTER 29

Jim doesn't know I've borrowed the campervan, but I've made up my mind that what he doesn't know won't hurt him. It's been several years since I last drove, and I can't pretend to be anything other than terrified. So far, the roads have been clear and at least it's not raining so the gods are on my side for once. As I pull up — stall more like — outside the pub where Gail keeps her car, the coward in me hopes she won't be in, but her bright red sports car stands out a mile, acting as a reminder of her single, sexy lifestyle.

Slut is the first word that comes to mind as I scowl at the car. *Bitch* and *liar* pile up in my brain next as I climb down from the campervan, remembering to lock it and stowing the key in my pocket. Jim would kill me if anything were to happen to it. Hugging my anorak around me, because out here by the river it's even colder than in the town, I shove my gloveless hands into my pockets and resist the urge to key the shiny exterior of Gail's car.

It's only a two-minute stroll to her narrow boat and as I walk the plankway, which trembles beneath my feet, I toy with the idea of pushing Gail in the dirty water. *The Grand Dame*, my eye. Who the hell is she trying to kid?

'Gail! You in there?' I pound on the wooden doors, decorated with colourful spiritual symbols I don't understand, nor want to, barely giving her a chance to reply before calling again. 'Come on, open up. I know you're there.'

'Jesus Christ.' The doors fly open to reveal a sleepy-eyed, messy-haired Gail, still in her barely-there silk pyjamas which does nothing to improve my impression of her. *Slut.*

'Fuck's sake. What time do you call this?' Gail yawns casually, exposing even more of her plunge bra and crinkly, faked-tanned cleavage as if there's nothing unusual about my visiting at what is for her the unearthly hour of 9 a.m. 'What's up?' She slurs as if hungover, which wouldn't surprise me one bit. Everything to excess. That's our Gail.

I don't wait to be invited in and push by her, not caring if I'm interrupting one of her regular one-night stands. Once inside, I stand my ground waiting for her to close the doors and come back in. Luckily, there's no evidence to suggest she has a man over.

'What's up with you?' She demands, lighting a cigarette. 'Something's got your knickers in a twist.'

'Jim told me,' I spit it out, unable to hold it in any longer, 'that you tried it on with him. You've been chasing after him ever since I went away.'

'Jim said that?' Gail smirks and turns her back on me to put the kettle on. The devil in me wants to grab hold of a handful of her dyed hair and yank it.

'Well?!' I yell, spit flying from my mouth onto one of her ugly pug cushions which are arranged messily on the sofa. I've never liked them, only pretended to for her sake. Childishly, I want to tell her so but decide it's beneath me.

'Well, what?' Gail inhales her cigarette while putting teabags into mugs. One for her and one for me. If she thinks I'm staying to have a cuppa she's got another think coming.

'You were meant to be my friend, Gail. I *trusted* you.'

'Of course, I'm your friend, but I don't get what the big deal is. You didn't want him, so why not?'

'Why not?' I scream, even more incensed now than I was earlier. 'This is my family we're talking about, Gail. Mine. And you don't get to mess with them. Lying about Jim having a girlfriend to put my nose out of joint is one thing but making a pass at him . . .'

'I never had Jim down as a snitch,' Gail grimaces but I can tell there's a smile hiding somewhere on her once-beautiful, now jaded face.

'So, you admit it then? All of it?' I can't believe how casually she's taking all of this. Like she's done nothing wrong.

'Look,' she sighs. 'If you must know, Jim came on to me, not the other way around.'

'You're a liar.'

'I admit I lied about Jim having a girlfriend, but I did that for your own good. I knew you'd go crawling back to him in the end, and let's face it, he never made you happy. But I guessed you wouldn't be able to help yourself. You never could stand being on your own, could you, Linda?'

'That's not fair. How can you stand there and say that after everything I've been through?'

'After everything *you've* been through? Don't make me laugh. Everything you got was your own doing, but what about me, Linda?' Gail is in my face, looking like she wants to punch me. If we got into a fight, she'd win. 'Three miscarriages and a fucking lying cheating scumbag of a husband who left me for a much younger woman, who *was* able to carry a baby full term, when I did nothing wrong. Nothing. And you expect me to feel sorry for you when you left Jim on a whim to go "find yourself" and to become truly independent, or so you said, only to five minutes later find another man to rely on. God, you make me *sick*.'

She pauses for breath, but our eyes remain locked on each other. I can't tell for sure which one of us is angrier, but I'd like to bet it's me.

'It's good to know at last what you honestly think of me,' I spit, grinding my teeth.

'Oh, hell, Linda! You fucked up but nobody really cares. Just don't go around preaching to other people about their behaviour. So what if Jim got a bit lonely and tried his hand? The only reason I said no that day was because I wanted him to take me seriously. I thought with you out of the way, we might have made a proper go of it. But he was only trying to get me in bed to make you jealous and I wasn't prepared to play second best anymore.'

'I can't believe you're still lying. To my face as well. Jim would never do that.'

'Why not? He's a man, isn't he?'

I think about her words for a second but shake them off just as quickly. Yes, Jim is a man, but he's never run around after other women, and he doesn't even like Gail. She has given me no reason to trust her whereas Jim has always had mine and the girls' best interest at heart.

'I'll never forgive you for this, Gail. Never. So, don't try to come between my family again. *Is that understood*?' I shout the last three words, making Gail visibly jump and drop her cigarette, which she quickly retrieves from the wooden floor.

'Deal. Jesus. When did you grow a pair?' and then smirking, she says 'I like this new Linda.'

'I mean it, Gail. I don't think we can be friends again after this, so don't come around no more, okay, not until I make up my mind one way or another. I don't want to hear from you at all. No phone calls. Texts. Nothing.'

Having said what I've come to say, I turn away and am about to head towards the doors when her next words cause my heart to flip over.

'Well, just you remember, Linda, that friends keep each other's secrets, but when you're no longer friends those rules change.'

'What's that supposed to mean?' I demand, barely able to breathe because I know exactly what she's referring to but can't yet face the thought of it. *Is she threatening me?*

'Just that I was practically taking notes, shorthand in my head if you like,' she laughs cruelly, 'when you were telling me all about that last night on the beach with Marcus. And to think, I never knew you had it in you.'

'I was drunk. I didn't know what I was saying.'

'I've seen you in worse states,' Gail shakes her head dismissively, 'and, unlike you,' she stabs a finger at my chest and blows cigarette smoke on my face, 'I know when a friend is lying and when they're telling the truth.'

CHAPTER 30

Oh my God. What have I done? I can't believe I've been so bloody stupid. Risking everything I've worked for, and by that, I mean getting my family back, Jim and the girls, who mean everything to me, just to get even with a friend. *Former friend and first-class bitch*, I fume inwardly, resisting the urge to smash something, like the mug of coffee in my hand. The truth is I'm angrier with myself more than Gail, who is notorious for hitting below the belt when under attack. Who can blame her when she has nothing to lose?

The campervan is safely back where Jim parked it, so he'll be none the wiser when he comes home. I can't tell him about this latest row with Gail because he'll want to know what it was about. Of course, I could just make out it was about him, and Gail hitting on him, but knowing Jim, he'd interrogate me further and the way I'm feeling right now, I might easily weaken and end up confessing my secret. But if I told Jim what I suspected happened that night on the beach, *me angrily pushing Marcus into the water and drunkenly doing nothing to help when he got into trouble*, he'd throw me out on the street. Worse still, I could find myself behind bars, just as I feared would happen in Greece during the investigation into Marcus's disappearance. The girls are bound to abandon me too. I can imagine how Abby would react if she found out her mother had attempted murder. Even if they believed I didn't mean to hurt Marcus, and I have no idea if that's true or not because I don't remember, they'd be horrified and wouldn't want any more to do with me.

The uncertainty of whether or not I am to blame for what happened to my husband is slowly killing me. What *actually* happened to Marcus? He came back. Only to disappear again. Why has he gone silent on me? And how can he go missing twice in one lifetime, three times if you count when he was eighteen and took on his best friend's identity? He's like a bloody tomcat with nine lives. The mystery of what happened to him gnaws away at me, festering inside, like a deadly cancer that has gone undetected.

Jim accuses me of overcomplicating things, but that's because he doesn't know everything. He'd rather focus on moving forwards; conveniently forgetting about the mysterious appearance and subsequent vanishing of Tony Fortin. I wish I could do the same, but Marcus was my husband and I loved him once. God forgive me, but I believe it would have been better for all concerned if Marcus had stayed dead. I wouldn't have wished it on him back then, of course, at least not in my normal, sober state, but now I know him to be a liar and a fake, my feelings for him have changed. Now that he's back, most likely to punish me for what I may or may not have done, *if only I could remember*, I fear his real mission is to publicly expose me and then my world really will come crashing down. Knowing this makes me want to kill him again, regardless of whether I was responsible the first time. Not a thought most fifty-something housewives have, I'm sure.

Or do they?

A memory from deep within me stirs as I go back in time to visualise . . . a setting sun, the sound of angry, white-tipped waves, sand between my toes, ice and lemon on my tongue, salt in the air, wet cheeks, warm skin, and a cold heart.

A feeling of indignation.

Of being drunk.

In a jealous rage.

CHAPTER 31

Then

My eyes were swollen from crying and my nose red from too much drink. After our row, Marcus had come looking for me, and found me, where he knew he would — on the beach. But he wasn't in the mood for talking. He was still angry with me. I stood watching him, thinking what a fine-looking man he was, but that it was a superficial beauty. On the inside, he was dark and secretive. Sometimes even outright cruel. His eyes, though, were as blue as the water and his hair as white as the froth on the incoming tide. The setting sun created a soft golden halo around his handsome, movie-star face.

Except he was no angel. Not with that devilish, teasing smile and those sharklike teeth. He was dressed in his trademark middle-aged, middle-class, linen shirt and trousers, and his bare feet, pedicured to perfection, paused on the wet sand when he recognised the shadow of his wife approaching, except he seemed to look through me as if I weren't there. Had our marriage deteriorated so much that he could no longer bear to look at me? He had every right to be annoyed with me after I had shown him up at the bar, accusing him of flirting with another woman, but I was equally as entitled to be mad. He seemed to forget at times that he was married.

Behind us, the calming hum of insects could be heard and further away in the distance loved-up holidaymakers clinked glasses of iced ouzo while rolling pitted olives around in their mouths while their red faces recovered from a day in the sun. Greek God-like waiters took care of their every whim and pocketed tips and room numbers, for later.

The smell of tobacco and marijuana overpowered the other night-time scents of sulphur and seaweed and stuck to my clothes. Marcus pulled a crumpled packet of cigars out of a back pocket and put one in his mouth, lighting it. Closing his lazily suggestive eyes, he inhaled, savouring the smoke as if it were a woman's scent. This made me hate him all over again. Marcus the lover. Marcus the womaniser. Marcus the liar.

His eyes were cloudy with drink, and he was unsteady on his feet — swaying as if to a slow dance, only this time there was no woman in his arms. I'd also drunk too much and in an act of rebellion had even smoked a spliff, given to me by one of the Greek waiters who liked to practice his English on me. I was staggering as much as Marcus was. He tried to say something to me as I stood there watching him, but the sound of the ocean roared in my ears, and I couldn't make out what it was.

When I put one foot in front of the other, a surge of nausea rose up inside me. I tried to shake off the dizziness and focus on my husband as he gazed distractedly across at the Albanian coastline. Something about his expression suggested he wanted to be there, although not with me. Life was an adventure to Marcus. I don't think he had any intention of settling down and returning to the UK with me as he'd promised.

When he lost his footing and tried to stop himself from falling into the water swirling around his feet, I saw panic in his eyes. As he lunged forward, intent on saving himself, I stumbled towards him, reaching out a hand to save him or push him, I can't say for sure, but the water rose quickly until it was above his chest. The seafloor then disappeared from under him. Arms flailing, he fought back but in his drunken state, he was too slow. Fear flickered in his eyes as he went down.

Watching open-mouthed, unsure if what I was seeing was a drink and drug-induced hallucination, I saw him come up only once, eyes bulging, hair covering one eye, sucking in deep breaths but choking and spluttering on the water at the same time.

CHAPTER 32

Now

I find myself standing in a circle of broken enamel where the coffee mug must have slipped out of my hand as memories of that night, when Marcus went into the water and never resurfaced, flood through my mind like a murmur of starlings captured on film. It hits me then, like a spade in hallowed ground, that the Marcus I've been seeing in my head, the one who sent the text messages and the one who signed up to the Welcome Back website are the same — a ghost of my imagination.

There is no Marcus Bouchard. Eighteen-year-old Tony Fortin had stolen his dead friend's identity all those years ago, but he met the same fate in the end and died in the water. I know that because I watched him drown. That terrifying flashback to the night on the beach proves it. Only moments earlier I'd wished for my memory to return and now that it has, I can no longer deceive myself into thinking I'm the innocent, grieving widow. I'm a hateful, jealous, crazy person. A killer. Worse still, I'd involved Jim in my warped fantasy, leading him down such a fanciful path until even he believed that Marcus was back.

Gail's words ring in my head, growing ever louder until I think it will explode. 'I never knew you had it in you,' and then, 'Unlike you, I know when a friend is lying.' Worst of all, I'd lied to myself as well as my friends and family. Angry waves crash against my skull. All I can think about is what I saw. *Oh God, what I saw.* The bulging eyes. The hair covering one eye.

I killed my husband. I may not have meant to, but I'm still guilty. How could I have not known? Has my grief and fear finally pushed me over the edge? I wonder if the pills are to blame. If so, Gail was right and I should have listened to her. Even the doctor warned me of the side effects, but I was desperate for the unbearable pain, which felt more physical as time wore on, to go away, so I kept on taking them. I should go back to the doctor and tell her how mentally ill I've become. But I'm afraid to. If she knew the sertraline was causing me to hallucinate, she'd make me come off them. What if they're the only thing keeping me from completely losing it? Without them, where would I be then? *In a psychiatric ward, Linda.* On the other hand, the medication is clearly responsible for my confusion. If my mum were here now, she'd say I was as mad as a box of frogs and she'd be right because I must also have sent those text messages to myself and made up a fake profile for Marcus on the dating website. Who else could have done it?

Although my body is spent, I go to fetch a dustpan and brush and begin sweeping up the pieces of broken mug. My heart beats so loud I expect it to burst. As I inhale slowly to prevent the onset of a panic attack, a sickening sense of guilt consumes me.

'I'm so sorry, Marcus,' I find myself mumbling. 'Please forgive me. I didn't mean to . . . I just . . .'

Deep down I must have known all along that I pushed my husband to his death. That he drowned because of me, and I failed to do anything to save him. Shame has a hold of my heart, wrapping it in pure terror, like a giant fist.

Blood rushes in my ears as I tell myself that I'll never forgive myself for what I did, and from now on I will have to live my life as if Marcus had never been a part of it. It's the only way I'll be able to deal with it. It doesn't seem right that I have everything when his body is lying undiscovered at the bottom of the ocean. But even if I turned myself in to the police, it wouldn't bring Marcus back. Nor yet secure him the funeral he deserves.

The person stood here now is not the Linda I know. I don't have flashbacks or make things up in my head. Nor do I believe in ghosts. I certainly don't hide from the truth and, as a rule, I never lie unless it's absolutely essential. I'm not even prone to exaggeration. I'm known as no-nonsense Linda and that's how I see myself. What happened to her, is what I want to know. The answer is obvious — Marcus.

CHAPTER 33

Time has crept up on me, taking me by surprise like an unexpected gift from a stranger, because it's Christmas Eve already and I'm out shopping for last-minute presents for the girls. Since Jim sat down three weeks ago to tell Abby and Rosie about our plans to re-marry, our family has come together as if it had never been torn apart.

To say life has completely gone back to normal would be a lie, as things between Jim and I are better than ever, in every way . . . including the bedroom. I put this down to the fact we're both now aware there are no guarantees when it comes to love and each of us must water the grass in our relationship to keep it green. We are doing a lot of watering behind closed doors at night. I never knew Jim had it in him!

As always, Stamford looks so pretty in the fading afternoon light, lit up as it is with fairy lights. Christmas songs, "Do They Know It's Christmas?" by *Band Aid* and "Merry Christmas Everybody" by *Slade* boom out of shop doorways making many shoppers smile. Others, sick to death of the overplaying of such tunes, pull grumpy faces. I secretly fall into the latter category, thinking that Christmas is too commercial these days.

I have so much to be thankful for, yet anxiety holds me back from being genuinely happy. All I can hope for, at best, is contentment, considering I've been widowed less than a year. Marcus is frequently on my mind and there are times when I'm heartbroken that he's no longer around. These days I try not to think about my part in his death, preferring to focus on the happier memories we shared. There was a good deal of those too, despite how things turned out. I can't talk to Jim about those times because, as good as he is, he shuts down whenever I bring "Marcus back into our lives", as he refers to it. Which is more than understandable.

Because of this, it feels as if Marcus was never real, like he was a ghost all along, and that suits me. Following in their father's footsteps, Abby and Rosie don't mention my former husband either. Only the other day, Abby referred to my time away from them as simply a "mid-life crisis". They refer to my upcoming wedding to their father, planned for January 31st, to coincide with Jim's 60th birthday, as a renewal of our vows rather than a second time around thing. My family shelter me from harm and that's why those missing years are never mentioned. I'm Mum and that's all that matters. The same person as when I went away, except I'm not, but I put on a good show for their sakes. Every day I lose another part of myself. My independence. My free spirit. My desire for life and adventure. I sometimes worry that going back to being the old Linda is a mistake. Am I rushing into marrying Jim? My grief recovery coach advised me not to do anything drastic or make major life-changing decisions for at least a year, but I'm guilty of doing exactly that, because I want to feel safe in my comfortable old life. Is it any wonder I'm in denial as much as my family is?

The other niggle dragging my mood down is Gail. My feelings for her softened when I realised that she'd be spending Christmas alone. Usually she'd be at our house, joining in as if she were one of the family. So, I rang her, expecting her to be as keen as I was to repair our friendship. But oh no, not Gail, who liked to be difficult for the sake of it. It wasn't that she was cold or distant, she sounded like her old self, acting as if she didn't hold a grudge, but it's what she said that troubled me. Gail is an open book, without too many filters holding her back, so I was thrown by how mysterious she was being about her plans.

'I haven't even thought about Christmas, Linda,' she told me, which I knew was a lie as Gail loved the magic of it even more than the girls. She'd arrive at our house on Christmas Eve, piled up with presents for everybody, dressed in a cute elf outfit; making us play festive games like Charades and Scrabble, which Jim hated. The next day she'd insist we watched the King's speech and would sulk if we didn't take turns pulling crackers to see who could find the worst joke. She also provided the best pavlovas our family ever tasted. Every year we looked forward to them.

I'll miss Gail more than I care to admit. Apart from when I was travelling, I'd spent every Christmas with her since we were kids. It won't be the same without her. But according to her, she's doing some travelling of her own this year, if she's to be believed because, to be honest, I have my doubts. Gail never goes on holiday alone, always choosing to drag along a friends-with-benefits guy or someone she knows at work, only to fall out with them over a minor incident, never to speak again. That's partly why the conversation we had keeps coming back to me. None of what she said made sense.

'I'm working on something important. A secret.' She informed me.

'What are you, a spy all of a sudden?' I'd been scathing, annoyed that I'd gone to the effort of trying to make up with her only to be rejected. I didn't want to be without my best friend, and I suppose I thought she should have been grateful that I still wanted to have anything to do with her. Our relationship needed to change as we could never be as close as we once were, but I never got the chance to tell her that and it still bugs me.

'I can't tell you what I'm up to. Not yet anyway. But, when I do, you'll thank me for it.'

She'd hung up at that point. Since then, I've tried ringing her countless times, but each time her phone had gone straight to voicemail, which is infuriating. I haven't heard from her in weeks. A drive out to the boat one day last week confirmed my worst fears — it was boarded up, yet her sportscar, dusty from non-use, remained in the pub car park. There's something very wrong about all of this, and without wanting to sound overly dramatic, or self-obsessed, I suspect that whatever Gail is up to is somehow connected to me. I've decided to pop into the Cosy Club in the hope of bumping into Ray, who works there as a barman, and who also happens to have an on-off relationship with Gail. According to Gail, when she's drunk, he has a bit of a soft spot for me, and I intend to use this to my advantage. I need to find out what my best friend is up to.

CHAPTER 34

Ray helps me out of my coat, which is new, an early Christmas present to myself. I watch him as he hangs it up on the coat rack nearest the bar before proceeding to make our drinks — a coffee for him as he's on duty but can afford to take a cheeky fifteen-minute break for me, and a large glass of Pinot Grigio for his *favourite lady*. As expected, the place is packed with shoppers pausing for a skinny latte, while groups of party-going girls in glittery clothes and high heels crowd around their porn star martinis and plant-based food. Their girlish conversations remind me of the days when Gail and I would meet up for a bottomless brunch.

It's loud in here, what with the background music and constant chatter, yet it's a pleasant hum that doesn't set my nerves on edge. Ray has seated me on one of the comfortable leather sofas near the bar so he can keep an eye on things. He's already explained that he's been promoted to head barman so is currently taking his new responsibilities seriously which doesn't sound like the Ray I know.

As I catch sight of my reflection in the mirror behind me, I use the opportunity to touch up my lip gloss and admire my new hair and clothes. Since news of our wedding was announced, Jim has deposited three thousand pounds into my account to fund Christmas, encouraging me to spend some of it on myself, so I returned my anorak to the charity shop I bought it from when I returned to England, broke and homeless. The coat Jim's money replaced it with cost over £200 and is a gorgeous plum, woollen, three-quarter length affair with a hood trimmed in faux fur. It makes me feel like Little Red Riding Hood when I wear it. My long wavy beach hair was left on the floor of a trendy hairdressers in town and in its place is the shiny, neat bob Jim claims suits me better — I'm sure that's because I wore it that way for most of our married life. I'm also back to wearing my old perfume which I haven't touched in years, Poison by Dior — another early Christmas gift, this time from the girls.

Looking as I do, comfortably off with a middle-class, middle-aged taste in clothes, sitting here in my fancy, yet comfortable, M&S knickers, I suspect that if my old friends Sadie and Rachel were to walk in now they'd be all over me, rather than ignore me as they had that day in the park. If that were to happen, would I really tell them to go to hell, as I'd like to think I would, or might I embrace their fake kisses and hugs because part of me is desperate to claw back every last missing part of my old life? It's as if I'm trying to convince myself that surrounding myself with my past will eradicate those missing years and what I did to Marcus. He haunts me wherever I go. Even here, in the Cosy Club, where he's never set foot.

Every time I glimpse a white-haired gent my heart bangs against my ribs until I break into a sweat. *When will it end?* With my death, I suspect. And not a day before. I deserve no less. My mind is quite made up on that score. But I've promised myself that I owe it to everyone to live my best life, and that's what I intend to do. If I'm allowed. And by that, I mean providing my secret remains just that. A terrible, dark secret that no one must uncover. Ever.

I might look like my old self more every day, judging by my reflection in the mirror, but I no longer know who I am. It's a feeling I've come to know well. As if I'm drowning. But on that thought, I switch my attention to Ray who's heading back with our drinks. Although incredibly good-looking, in a six-foot tall, slim, golden-tanned way, everything about Ray is effeminate. The way he walks with a little skip to his step and how he expresses himself, with dramatic body language. He couldn't be camper if he tried. But he's every bit as heterosexual as Jim or Marcus. I know that from the exploits Gail tells me they get up to in bed. By all accounts, he's good, which is why she's prone to repeating the experience even though they don't get on so well out of the sheets.

'What brings you to the Cosy Club, Linda? We don't often see you in here, more's the pity.' Ray places the drinks down on a table and takes a seat next to me, uncomfortably close.

Rather than edge away from him, I maintain eye contact and smile as if it's going out of fashion. 'Oh well, thought I'd pop in and say hello. It's been a while.'

'Forever, in fact. I hope you like it, it's from our cellar selection.' Ray gestures to my drink.

Dutifully, I take a sip and then another, smiling to show him how appreciative I am. I'd forgotten how high-maintenance Ray can be. He and Gail would be a nightmare as a full-time couple. I'm about to broach the subject of my absent friend when—

'So, what do you think about what Gail's gone and done? I couldn't believe it when she told me. I mean Greece of all places!'

Ray almost chokes on his coffee when he sees the shocked expression on my face. No longer able to keep my smile up, I take a huge mouthful of wine and knock it back.

'I think I'm going to need a bottle,' I attempt a joke, but it falls flat. 'Are you telling me she's in Greece? All by herself?'

'You didn't know? Oh my God, I can't believe she didn't tell you. She always was a sly one. Didn't think to ask me to go with her,' Ray sulks. He has just as much to get off his chest as I do where Gail's concerned. She owes him money too, apparently. As his voice drones on in the background,

I check out of the room, ignoring the toned thigh pressed against mine. *Greece?* What the fuck. Why the hell would she go there alone? What is she up to?

Now I'm convinced her trip has something to do with me and nothing at all to do with her wanting a holiday in the sun. Why I confided in Gail that drunken night on her boat, *and I now know I must have done, for her to have gone back to Greece where it all started*, I'll never know. But what can she do? *Nothing*, I tell myself. If she were going to report me to the police, she'd have done it by now. Besides, who would believe her? There's no proof. If a whole police investigation failed to find anything suspicious, then what chance has Gail got?

'Unfinished business, she said. Something about a lost love.'

On hearing this, the glass falls from my hand and shatters on the floor, causing heads to turn in our direction. Ray is on the broken glass immediately, going into health and safety mode, ordering it to be cleared away. I'm on my feet not seeing him, reaching for my coat, and shakily slipping it on. Everything is a blur. I can't breathe.

Finally, my brain jerks into action and I garble an apology to Ray, my voice pulsating with fear, before fleeing the place.

Heat rushes through me as I crash into the door on the way out and collide with a tall, white-haired man who could easily be mistaken for Marcus. I gasp when I see him and openly recoil, causing him to give me a wide berth. He must think me crazy, and perhaps I am. A sickness worse than insanity has invaded my home and my life, and it feels as if I'm living in a nightmare. Gail wants to punish me for coming back. For ruining her chances with Jim. It's happening again. First, there was the imagined threat of Marcus returning to take his revenge and now Gail.

CHAPTER 35

I got through Christmas by muddling along in a vague, detached way that Jim found off-putting. Being young and self-centred, the girls were less affected by my mood swings. When provoked into a response by Jim I would angrily insist there was nothing wrong, despite spending hours each day crying. Jim couldn't cope with these open displays of emotion so he left me alone after that, I felt bad for him, but couldn't help it.

My life was in tatters. I was meant to be planning a wedding and looking forward to my big day — despite it being my third attempt — but all I could think about was Gail. Not knowing what she was up to was torture. How long did I have before I was sent back to Greece and put on trial for murder?

I've tried ringing Gail hundreds of times, but her phone goes straight to voicemail every time. Ray rang me on Boxing Day to ask if I'd heard anything, and I could hardly bring myself to talk to him. I stayed on the phone just long enough to figure out he hadn't heard from her either and to gather he was still mad at her. *You and me both*, I wanted to say, but of course, I didn't. There's so much I can't say to anyone. It's driving me insane.

No matter how I might feel on the inside, New Year's Eve isn't going to go away and right now I'm preparing a buffet for tonight's get-together. This year we're seeing the New Year in as a family. Even Josh is coming. It's another of Jim's ways of seeing out the old and bringing in the new. Meaning there's to be no more talk of Marcus and the old days. I suspect Jim of being jealous, but I'm sure he's just being protective and looking out for me, as he's always done.

I'm glad to be busy and so far, I've baked sausage rolls, *not homemade but nobody will ever know*, made brie and cranberry canapés and a massive, caramelised onion and goat's cheese quiche. I've lost so much weight over the last week, I'm surprised nobody's noticed, but then again, they'd put this down to pre-wedding nerves. I can hardly believe I'll be married again in thirty days' time. The girls have helped me pick out an outfit from Phase Eight. It's a simple, ivory belted mid-length dress with short sleeves, and to go with it, navy court shoes, and a matching bag. Very age-appropriate, I'm told, nothing like the flowing, lace, bohemian one I wore at my barefoot-on-the-beach wedding to Marcus. Jim being Jim didn't want to buy anything new for himself and was insistent on wearing his only grey suit which he's had for years and wears to all events, including funerals. Abby wasn't having any of it and whipped him off shopping for the day. Now, he parades around in his smart navy blazer and cream chinos whenever he gets the chance to show off.

Unlike our first wedding, this one will be a small, private affair at the registrar's office with only the girls and Josh present. To celebrate afterwards we're having a posh meal at the George Hotel, no expense spared. The thought of it makes my chest tighten.

So, I focus on tonight instead when I'll be wearing my new cobalt blue velvet maxi dress that Jim says matches my eyes, but he's just being kind, and the silver Swarovski matching necklace and earrings that he bought me as a surprise Christmas gift. It's lovely to be spoiled but I don't feel worthy of receiving anything nice, so it's hard to show genuine gratitude. If Jim knew what I'd done he wouldn't buy me fancy jewellery, he'd throw me out of the house and get the locks changed.

Once I've washed the pastry off my hands, I pick up my phone and tap in Gail's number. Again, no answer, just her flipping annoying voicemail. *'Hi peeps, it's me, the one and only Gail Somersby. Can't chat now, loser, as I'm busy living my best life. Ciao and speak soon.'*

'Except you're not living *your* best life. You're living *mine*.' I fume to an empty room, stuffing a still-warm sausage roll in my mouth. I don't want to be back in Greece but, for obvious reasons, I also don't want Gail prying into what happened there. Then, deciding that I *will* text Gail, even though I've been too frightened to do so until now, I punch out the following words:

'This shouldn't come as any great surprise but me and Jim are getting re-married on the 31st. I'd like you to be there if you can, but I'll understand if you can't. Didn't want you finding out from anyone else. Hope you're okay. PS I really need to speak to you. Why won't you answer your phone?'

* * *

The evening is going better than I hoped. Everyone's in a good mood and getting along. Josh and Jim are like two peas in a pod. They're both easy-going and calm, placid even up to a point, so rub along nicely. Rosie, being the only one without a partner, appears in awe of Josh in a way that Abby isn't, hanging on his every word, and this makes me nervous, thinking she might have a soft spot for him. Realistically, she's a much better match for him than her younger, spoiled, high-maintenance sister, not that I would say so in a million years. But I'm sure it will all sort itself out in the wash, as my mum used to say.

Hopefully, Rosie will find someone soon. A nice boy who deserves her. The girls are always saying that the guys they meet don't compare to their dad and that he's set the bar too high, but obviously, Abby got lucky because she found one just like Jim. While I would prefer Abby to stay single for a while longer and focus on finding herself first, so that she doesn't make the same mistake I did by settling down too young — if marriage to Josh is what she wants, I for one will encourage her with every breath in my body, to hang on to him for all she's worth as men like Jim and Josh don't come around very often.

The canapés have gone down a storm and everyone's on their third glass of Prosecco, apart from Jim who only drinks ginger beer. I've received compliments tonight from everyone over my appearance and I'm pleased with how the new dress flatters my body shape, cleverly disguising my pear-shaped bottom half. The only downside is I miss my long hair. A soft curl added to it would have made me look younger. The bob I've resurrected for Jim makes me feel matronly due to the fact so many middle-aged women like myself settle for the same look.

Feeling like this stirs up unease in me, and I remind myself *settling isn't a bad thing*. This is how I got before when I left my family and ran away to a new life abroad and look where that got me. Mature and matronly is a better fit for someone my age.

The living room is very Christmassy. This year Jim let us have a real tree for the first time, a blue spruce that doesn't shed needles. Abby and Rosie decorated it in white and gold to match the living room décor and my contribution was to hang our family collection of personalised stockings on the fireplace. This year, 'mum' is back in its rightful place. Rosie has put a New Year's playlist on and because we still have three hours left before we can wish the New Year in, and I already feel a bit tipsy, I decide to top my glass up with water.

As I walk into the kitchen to do just that, my phone goes off and I pick it up without wondering who it could be. It has rung several times tonight already, well wishes from old friends who are happy to include me now that I'm back with Jim. Word gets around quickly. We've even had a Christmas card from Rachel and John, but nothing from Sadie and Charles. Sadie was the alpha female of our group, so I know it will take more time for her to come around.

'Hello,' I answer distractedly while adding ice to my glass.

'It's me.' A clipped voice, one I know well, cuts through my ear.

'Gail? Oh my God, Gail. How are you? Are you okay?' I might be mad at her but concern for my best friend takes precedence.

'Don't worry about me. I'm fine. I got your message . . .'

'I hope it wasn't too much of a shock.' I have the grace to blush, knowing how Gail was counting on making a go of it with Jim. 'I'm really sorry, Gail, that things didn't work out the way you wanted.'

'Oh, I'm so over that. I guess I should congratulate you.'

Is it me or does she still sound pissed off? I can't tell for sure. 'That would be nice,' I say tentatively.

'I'll be back in time for the wedding,' she concedes bluntly as if doing me a favour.

'That's fantastic,' I gush. 'Honestly, it wouldn't be the same without you.'

'That didn't stop you when you married husband number two,' she's quick to sarcasm, which is so like her that I begin to hope nothing is wrong and that she's simply gone away on holiday to escape the embarrassment of what happened between me, her, and Jim.

'That was a bit different, Gail. You know that.' I bite down on my defensiveness, not wanting to annoy her. Gail has all the cards currently, while I wait to be put out of my misery.

'Don't you want to know where I am?' Gail's smoky voice breaks into a cackle. I'm not sure I like the sound of it.

'I saw Ray. He told me you'd gone to Greece . . . on holiday,' I add as an afterthought hoping it's the truth. 'Whereabouts in Greece did you go?' The words tumble out of my mouth too fast, giving away how desperate I am for an answer, even though I don't want her to know that. *Surely not Corfu where Marcus died? Please don't let it be there.*

I hear her huff down the phone. 'He never could keep a secret. Just wait till I get hold of him.'

'But why was it a secret? Why couldn't you have told me? I'm still your best friend even if we did have a row.'

'Because, *Lindy,* I don't think you'd have approved of what I've been doing.'

Why is she suddenly calling me Lindy? She's never done that before. Only Marcus called me that. No one else. Is she tormenting me? Like a cat with a mouse. Is this part of her game?

'What *have* you been doing?' I clear my throat and come to the point.

'You'll never guess where I am now?' Gail sniggers, changing tack.

'Aren't you still in Greece?' I play it cool, wise now to the fact that she's playing me, and I remind myself to choose my battles carefully. Whatever Gail's up to she clearly wants me to find out, but at the same time, she's having fun with it, wanting me to tease it out of her. But I won't do that. I'll play her at her own game instead.

'Not anymore. I'm in Albania, of all fucking places.' Gail can't help herself. Her big mouth is always getting her into trouble. She never could keep it zipped.

'Albania?' I'm truly gobsmacked. Gail's exploits have taken a change of direction that I wasn't expecting. 'What on earth are you doing there? I take it you're not there for the sun and the men?'

'Don't be so sure of that,' Gail is deliberately secretive, 'you see, I did meet *someone.*'

'Well, I'm very pleased for you.' I grit my teeth, determined not to give myself away.

Inside, I'm a quivering wreck, terrified of what she might say next. I keep stealing glances at the door, worried someone is going to come in and overhear this conversation or that Gail might demand to speak to Jim or the girls and tell them she knows what I did to Marcus. Not that I'd let her. But I can't prevent her from calling them directly. If that happens, I'll deny everything. They won't believe Gail anyway, not after the lies she made up about Jim.

'You're the one who always gets the guy,' Gail quips bitterly. 'It's never me, is it?'

'I'm not sure what you're getting at . . .'

'I thought you might have guessed by now. Never mind, it will be a massive surprise for you, but you'll have to wait till I'm back to hear all about it. Just like you, I've been on the lookout for a husband but I'm not sure I'm the marrying kind these days. Do you really not have any idea who I might have come across on my travels?'

Gail has lost the plot, I decide. Her failed marriage and the multiple miscarriages she suffered have brought her hurtling towards a breakdown. All those lies about Jim and making a play for him too. I should have seen this coming but as usual, I've been so wrapped up in my own world I hadn't paid attention to my best friend's mental health. Marcus is dead, I remind myself because that's clearly who she's referring to. A fool could work that out. Whatever Gail thinks she's discovered is not real. She's delusional. But, unlike her, I know for sure Marcus is never coming back and that she won't find him in Greece or anywhere else because I watched him drown.

'Marcus is dead, Gail.' I tell her firmly, for her sake more than my own. I want to encourage her to come home and get help, but I know she won't listen, not in the dark mood she's in. I've seen her like this before, firstly when Adam walked out on her for a younger woman, and then when she found out they were expecting twins. Healthy baby boys were born exactly six months later, to add insult to injury.

'Are you sure about that, *Lindy*?' Gail hisses, before hanging up the phone.

CHAPTER 36

Nothing is going to plan. The buttonholes and handheld wedding posy arrived crushed, and my sleek bob has a kink in it that even Abby couldn't iron out with the straighteners. My tights have a ladder in them that keeps getting longer. Worse still, the girls have fallen out over something that they're keeping me in the dark about. Josh has lost the capacity to voice an opinion and Abby keeps giving him furious looks that he chooses to ignore. This is so unlike my first wedding to Jim it's almost laughable. I can't shake off the feeling that our wedding day is doomed. That it was never meant to be. But there's no point trying to convince Jim of that. He's as happy as I've ever seen him and hasn't yet noticed the tense atmosphere.

I wish my mum and dad were here, as they had been the first time I married Jim all those years ago. I wonder what they'd think of the mess I've made of my life. They loved Jim as a son and would have been horrified by what I did to my family. Thank God they weren't around at the time of my so-called mid-life crisis. Coming from a different part of the world and not what they were used to, they wouldn't have taken to Marcus. Them having no prior knowledge of his parents or background meant they would have viewed him as a dangerous stranger. Heaven knows they'd have been wrong — at least in the sense that he wasn't physically dangerous. Marcus had his faults, but he was a pacifist — *cowardly* might be a better choice of word. Me, on the other hand, well I'm a different matter.

As a mother I've always known that I would be capable of harming another person if it meant saving my family. When the girls were little, I turned into a ferocious creature for a while. A personality transplant, my family called it. Until giving birth, I'd gone out of my way to avoid conflict and had never been involved in a fight in my life. But as a new mum, guarding first Rosie then Abby in my arms — not that my second daughter ever needed protecting — instinct took over and I became a considerable force, picking fights with receptionists at the doctor's surgery and arguing with the midwife, convinced I knew better. There were times I'd rage at Jim for getting one of them to stop crying when I couldn't. I was like a bad-tempered lioness.

A tiger to my lioness, Abby's helping me to get ready for my big day, but she's in a foul mood. This was meant to be Rosie's job, as the eldest, but it was my second-born who turned up red-eyed at my bedroom door holding my freshly ironed dress in her hands.

'It wasn't real.' She eyeballed me as I sat, head tilted upwards, while she applied vanilla eyeshadow to my crepey eyelids.

'What wasn't real?' I asked absently, pursing my lips so as not to smudge my lipstick.

'You and Marcus. What you had. It was a lie.'

I'd looked into my daughter's eyes then and saw something like scorn and hatred there. The look on her face made me want to recoil.

'Of course it was real, Abby.' I retaliated gently, not wanting to upset her, even though today was meant to be about me. 'We were married for three and a half years.'

My love for Marcus had been very real. Of that I'm in no doubt. And because of that I can't, won't, completely regret our marriage. How it ended is a different story. But had Marcus loved me in the way I wanted to be loved? Probably not. Even on the day we met he'd been waiting for another woman, but he'd stood her up and gone off with me instead, just like that. *Lucky her, she got off lightly*.

The free spirit that was Marcus adored *all women*, not just young, beautiful ones either — but it was something he'd always been up front about. At first anyway. I thought his marrying me would change him and make him more loyal and faithful. That's why I'd been so angry the night I caught him flirting with that other woman. *Is this what I gave up my comfortable life for?* I'd fumed internally, conveniently forgetting that there had been no Marcus on the scene when I left Jim and the girls to travel abroad and start a new life. This was not the kind of adventure I'd imagined for myself when I left my home and England for foreign shores.

My last words to Marcus, when I said I wished I'd never married him and regretted ever meeting him, cause me to suffer to this very day. But I didn't stop there. I went on to tell him that Jim was a better man. Called him a womaniser and a cheat. I can't take back those words, but I hope he knew I didn't mean them. That they were said out of anger and jealousy. An unheard-of emotion when I was married to Jim.

'I know you find it hard to believe that an old woman like me can inspire love in two men, but it did happen.' I pull a jokey face to soften my words, not wanting to cause offence to my daughter, then take a sip from my glass of way-too-early Prosecco, the bubbles reminding me once again of my barefoot-wedding on the beach to Marcus. From thousands of miles away, I can almost smell the ocean, feel the golden rays of a breaking sun on my face and the fine white sand in my toes. Memories of gazing into the bluest of eyes cause a wave of panic to flood through me, making me flinch as I'm reminded of the cold tidal wave that took Marcus away.

Of course, today I'm marrying Jim and it's him I should be thinking about, not Marcus. *It's all Abby's fault*, I think unfairly, wanting to change the subject.

'Is everything alright between you and Rosie?' I probe. 'You both seemed a little off with each other earlier, at breakfast?'

'I think you've already got enough to worry about today, don't you?' Abby warns darkly, causing my stomach to flip.

'So, there is something wrong?' Dread won't let go of me. It clings to me like the satin underwear I'm wearing. 'Nothing that can't be fixed, I hope.'

Abby slides her eyes away from mine and gets on with the task of applying my make-up, none too gently I have to say. I know I won't get anywhere by trying to force it out of her and that my best bet is to have a word with Rosie on the quiet. Knowing her, she'll spill the beans immediately. It can't be anything that bad, I kid myself. Although they're sisters, they're quite different but they rarely fight. Rosie is easy-going and, like me, keen to avoid conflict. Knowing that's a red flag right there, I nevertheless choose to ignore the warning.

* * *

'You look beautiful, Mum.' Rosie takes the first picture of the day with her mobile phone. I'm leaning against the white fireplace in the living room, one arm by my side the other on my ivory polyester-clad hip, the ornate mirror behind me reflecting the back of my hair and revealing the kink in it that won't go away. Like a bad omen.

Rosie's sun-averse face is paler than usual and her eyes, which are usually bright, are hiding something. Until now, I haven't managed to get her on her own even for one minute. There's always been someone else around. Jim usually, who has a presence larger than anyone else today. I'm about to open my mouth and ask her what's wrong when who should stumble in, but you name it — Jim.

'You're not meant to see Mum's outfit.' Rosie complains.

'It's fine, Rosie. Honestly.' I dismiss her concerns although I can't help thinking it was a little insensitive of him to come in here knowing I'm fully dressed. What happened to the groom not seeing the bride's wedding outfit until they're at the church? Or in our case, registry office.

'But it's bad luck.' Rosie grumbles, and once again a heavy feeling settles on my chest. *Could my wedding day be any less blessed?*

'Your father and I have no secrets from each other,' I insist, taking a deep breath, all the while thinking nothing could be further than the truth. *Liar, liar, pants on fire.*

CHAPTER 37

We're on our way to the registry office in Abby's Audi and the atmosphere couldn't be any more tense. My youngest daughter purses her lips and remains silent, but you can tell she's mad as hell because her driving is jerky and erratic. Her hands, white at the knuckles, clench the steering wheel while her shoulders are erect with suppressed rage. Rosie, quiet as a mouse next to her hangs onto the door handle as if that will stop us from crashing.

Jim was meant to go with Josh, who has taken it upon himself to act as unofficial best man, but as my soon-to-be husband has already seen my outfit, he decided to join "us girls" for the journey. Like my daughters, and unlike his happy mood of the morning, Jim is not himself. He's jumpy and restless, eyes darting everywhere, and he won't stop talking. Rubbish mostly. Even his voice has taken on an unnaturally excitable air. I want to ask him what's up because he wasn't nervous like this the first time we got married. It occurs to me that he might, like me, be having second thoughts which makes me wonder if I should suggest putting this off for another time. But one glance at Abby and Rosie's frosty faces makes me think better of it, or else things could kick off.

What makes things worse is I still haven't been able to have a word with Rosie to find out what's wrong. Back at the house, there was always someone hovering. Jim mostly. Even though he's finally cottoned on to the fact the girls are not speaking, his response was to shrug his shoulders and pretend everything was hunky dory. In a house of women, Jim knows not to involve himself in female arguments, predicting — as I'd mistakenly done — that things would sort themselves out. Thankfully, Jim hasn't antagonised the girls as he usually does, by putting any friction between them down to the "wrong time of the month". For someone who claims to be sensitive to the needs of his womenfolk Jim is oblivious to our feelings at times and it surprises me that I've not noticed this about him before.

He has my hand in a vice-like grip as if afraid I might run away at any minute, or jilt him at the registry office, anything rather than marry him a second time. *Is that why his palm is sweaty in mine?* Pins and needles shoot up and down the length of my arm due to the possessive way he's holding on to me. I want to yank my hand away and tell him to calm down, but I fear saying anything in case it causes a row. What with the girls not talking to each other and Jim acting shifty, my anxiety is all over the place.

Because my nerves are shredded, I keep wishing Gail were here. She'd been chief bridesmaid at my first wedding to Jim and predictably bossed everyone around on the day, including me. If she were here, she'd pour me a large glass of Prosecco and tell me not to get my knickers in a twist, making me see the funny side of things. I have no way of knowing if she's going to turn up for the wedding as I haven't been able to get hold of her. No surprise there! She promised she'd be here, but I can't be certain she's even in the country. She could still be gallivanting around Greece and Albania for all I know, looking for a man who doesn't exist, except as bones at the bottom of the sea . . .

On that thought, I glance out of the car window, squinting against the light of the low winter sun as I force back the threat of tears. My stomach hardens as a sickening sense of guilt consumes me once again, and I jump hard at the sound of my phone bleeping from inside my bag. Using this as an excuse to pull my hand away from Jim's, I take it out of my bag.

'It might be Gail.' I say by way of explanation, but Jim simply rolls his eyes, very Abby-like, and stares out of the window.

Bowing my head, I scroll through my phone to see I have a new message from a number I don't recognise. When I open it the hair on my arms stands to attention and my jaw clenches. As the words sink in, I'm hit by a wave of dizziness so strong it feels as if I've been kicked by a horse. Adrenalin courses through my veins and black spots, like miniature crows, dance in front of my eyes.

Jim, hearing my sharp intake of breath, trains his eyes back on me. As he takes in my pinched expression, I see a vein bulge across his forehead, but he doesn't ask me what's wrong. Averting his eyes, he shuffles uncomfortably in his seat, leaving me to focus on the message. It's not that I want to see those words again, but I must check they're real. That I haven't imagined them as I've done so many other things.

What are you doing, Lindy? How could you do this to me?

The words are like a weight around my heart, heavy enough to drag me to the bottom of the ocean where my former husband is meant to lie. Questions swirl around my brain, like waves, making my head swim. The ghost of Marcus sits heavily on my chest like a demon, the kind people with night terrors wake up to. I remind myself all over again that Marcus is dead. I watched him go into the sea where he drowned. *But they never did find a body.* Even if it were from him, Tony Fortin, and I know that to be impossible, then how could he know that today is my wedding day? It can't be him. This must be Gail's doing. It's the only other explanation I can think of. She called me Lindy once before, I remember.

She means to frighten me and make me lose my nerve, in the hope that I'll refuse to marry Jim and leave the door open for her. She's wanted him for herself all along. But does she seriously think she'd be in with a chance even if that were to happen? My best friend is many things, but she's not stupid.

Making up my mind that I won't be intimidated, I delete the message and impulsively reach across to reclaim Jim's hand. I won't let anyone come between us or my family again. If Gail wants war, then she's got one because I'm done with her and her mind games. When Jim throws me a comforting smile my heart settles and I instinctively know I'm doing the right thing in marrying him. Jim is one in a million and he would do anything for his family. I return his smile, forcing any feelings of doubt out of my head.

CHAPTER 38

We've spilt out of the car onto the pavement in an untidy little huddle to gaze up at the town hall on St Mary's Hill in Stamford, where the registry office is situated, while we wait for Abby to find a parking space. It's an impressive Georgian Grade II listed municipal building adorned with a blue and gold chequer coat of arms and it also has a number of steep steps leading up to it which makes me glad I opted for sensible heels.

Disappointment in my matronly attire would have dripped off Marcus had I worn this outfit to our wedding. Marcus loved to see me in high heels, claiming he found them sexy, even though I'd been barefoot at our wedding. Marcus said they made him horny as hell, but Jim would never have used such language with me. If Jim wanted sex, he asked for it and didn't take offence if the answer was no. Unlike Marcus, who sulked like a toddler at not getting his way. Years ago, I'd get angry with Jim, accusing him of not being passionate or romantic enough. But rather than respond in anger he'd turn over in bed and would be snoring within minutes.

My cheeks burn as I become conscious of the fact that I'm comparing one husband's lovemaking to another's on what is meant to be my wedding day. Stealing a sideways glance at my husband-to-be, I'm relieved to see he has finally settled down. Josh, who greeted us at the kerbside having arrived first, must have a calming effect on Jim because he's no longer jittery and loud. Rather, he's gone back to the stoic man I know. Abby joins us, eyes narrowed to mere slits and looking as if she'd like to murder every single one of us, and storms up the steps ahead of us, our submissive little group trailing behind her.

* * *

Inside, we're told to wait in the corridor while the ceremony room is prepared. We stand around awkwardly, no one speaking. We were told the room has the capacity for fifty guests but today there are only five of us. Six if you count Gail, but as there's no sign of her yet I'm inclined to think it will be a no-show from her. Just as well with the way I'm feeling after receiving that text message which can only be from her. With the girls acting as our two witnesses, it looks like Josh will be our only guest.

At last, a tired-looking woman brandishing a clipboard and wearing a tight, official smile ushers us into the room, waving her arms to hurry us along. As if there's no time to lose, she instructs Abby, Rosie, and Josh to take a seat but tells Jim and me to—

'Stay standing, please. The registrars will be with you in just a moment.'

When she's gone Jim takes hold of my hand, gently this time, and grins encouragingly at me but I look past him to where Abby and Rosie are sitting. My heart somersaults when I notice they have the same angry look on their faces, making them appear alike for the first time. They stand further apart than can be considered normal, worse than if they were strangers. What's also odd is that Abby and Josh aren't touching or holding hands, let alone looking at each other. Although Abby is not the demonstrative type, Josh is very tactile, so none of this makes any sense. My fingers clench as I realise something seriously wrong is going on with my family but how am I meant to fix things when right now the two registrars are walking through the door with smiles plastered on their faces?

'Good morning, everybody, and on behalf of Jim and Linda, I'd like to extend a warm welcome to Stamford registrar's office.'

The woman doing the talking is tall, elegant, and extremely attractive with a smoky voice that I imagine men find sexy. She's swathed in an unusual avocado shade, a match for her eyes, and has impeccable peaches-and-cream skin. Marcus wouldn't have been able to keep his eyes off her. Sneakily I check out Jim's profile, but he looks like he barely notices her. Good old Jim. And to think Gail accused him of being the one to come onto her. The cheek!

'My name is Elinor Lacey, I will conduct the ceremony, and' she gestures toward the woman standing next to her, who is plain in comparison but whose smile appears more genuine, 'Claire Fraser will complete the schedule, which is the legal record of the marriage.'

Jim and I nod as if we know all about registry office weddings, which we don't. There's still no sound from behind us. Not one cough or scraping of a chair. I wonder if the registrars will notice and think us a sad, odd little group. I'm inclined to agree.

'This ceremony will be in accordance with the civil law of this country. This requires Jim and Linda to declare their freedom to marry one another. They will then go on to make their marriage vows in which they promise to take each other as partners for life.' Elinor adds.

And there it is. Subtle, yet obvious enough to me. A sarcastic little cough from Abby. Is this a dig at me for having broken my vows to her father four years ago, I wonder, or is it something to do with whatever is going on in hers and Josh's relationship?

'These vows are a formal and public pledge of their love and a promise of a lifelong commitment to each other.'

Elinor pauses and brings her beautiful green gaze to rest on Abby, Rosie, and Josh as if wanting to engage with them. Fat chance of that happening. Swivelling around, I see that nothing has changed. Each wears the same tight, defensive expression they've had on all morning, and my cheeks burn with embarrassment.

A look of confusion passes between the two registrars, but Elinor is a consummate professional and doesn't let my family's rudeness phase her. Having married countless couples from all walks of life, I'm sure she's used to dealing with all sorts.

'The place in which we are now met, has been duly sanctioned, according to law, for the celebration of marriages, and we are here today to witness the joining in matrimony of this couple and to share in their happiness, so please can everyone be upstanding for this part.'

I hear movement behind me. The scraping of chairs and clearing of throats. A heavy sigh escapes someone as if being required to stand up is too much of an ask. Abby, probably. When I glance at Jim, I see that his forehead is shiny with sweat. He appears uncomfortable in his shirt and tie and tugs at the collar as if it has been buttoned too tight. Nerves must have got to him again. Maybe he's worried I might change my mind at the last moment. I suspect we'll both be glad when the official side of things is over.

'If there is any person here present who knows of any lawful impediment to this marriage, then they should declare it now.' Elinor states authoritatively.

This statement is met with an ominous if predictable silence that seems to go on forever. I'd forgotten that these words formed part of the ceremony and therefore foolishly hadn't anticipated them. The message I received in the car *'What are you doing, Lindy? How could you do this to me?'* acts as a grim reminder that someone out there doesn't want me to marry Jim. I still think Gail sent it, but the what ifs keep coming. What if Marcus miraculously survived that night and is alive? If that were true, then I would be committing bigamy by marrying Jim. But then it occurs to me that my marriage to Marcus, AKA Tony Fortin, wouldn't have been legal anyway, not if he'd stolen someone else's identity. Talk about complicated . . .

Gritting my teeth, I will this service to be over. *What's taking them so long? What are they waiting for? Do they suspect something?* It's as if the registrar is expecting an interruption. I consider telling her to hurry up, but that would be plain rude. Plus, Jim would kill me if I did that. And if Jim drags this ceremony out, I'll kill *him*. Then, remembering that this particular bride is already responsible for the death of one of her husbands, I take it back and hope God will forgive me for having such thoughts.

Just as the registrar is about to speak again, the door behind us opens. Holding my breath, I cling on to the hope that somebody has entered the room by mistake, but then I hear muffled footsteps. Blood rushes in my ears and my first thought is that Marcus has come back to take his revenge, even though I know that this is just my mind playing tricks on me again. But they never found a body, did they? The urge to check over my shoulder is overwhelming, but I resist and remain still, terrified that the slightest movement from me will be my undoing. I watch Jim and both registrars' eyes follow the movement of the person who has walked in, but I cannot bring myself to do the same. I think I'll faint if I do. My legs already feel as if they are about to disappear from under me while I wait for this person to come into my line of vision. As I steal myself for the inevitable, I know that if it *is* Marcus then my life, as I know it, is over.

CHAPTER 39

As Gail slides stealthily into the seat next to Abby, I press my palm to my chest to stop my heart from thumping. It's beating so fast it feels as if it will burst through my ribcage. The registrars are the only ones to acknowledge Gail's presence, with a faint smile. The rest of us, even Abby and Rosie, ignore her. While I glare at Gail, she keeps her eyes pinned to the floor. Obviously, she cannot bring herself to face me.

Having slunk in late, almost causing me to have a heart attack, I can't help noticing that Gail looks suntanned and healthy, hot actually, in a navy jumpsuit and red, enviously high-heeled shoes. Now that all eyes are on her, and not on the bride, she'll be satisfied.

'Before you are joined in matrimony, it's my duty to remind you of the solemn and binding character of the vows you are about to make,' Elinor picks up where she left off before Gail's untimely interruption. 'Marriage in this country means the union of two people, voluntarily entered into for life, to the exclusion of all others.'

At this point, the smaller registrar beams at Jim as if she knows for certain that he's the dependable type but has some reservations about me. I may be imagining this of course, but that's how it comes across. And she wouldn't be wrong, would she?

'Before we continue, may I ask if you have your rings? You will need them shortly.'

'I have them.' Josh says too loudly for the large, echoing room before joining us in the centre of it, clutching a small red box in his hand. When the second registrar relieves him of it, he looks delighted to be free of the responsibility. As he re-takes his place behind us, the second registrar places the box on a small ornate table and opens it to reveal two matching platinum and yellow gold rings.

I was amazed when Jim confessed that he'd kept our old wedding rings out of sentimental value, even after four years apart. I imagined he would have sold them or given them to the girls, although they wouldn't have wanted any reminders of their parents' failed marriage. Not only had he kept them, in their original H. Samuel's jewellers' box, he wanted us to reuse them. I'd been unsure at first, thinking it might jinx us but after a while it made sense as we were continuing our lives, bringing the past, present, and future together.

'I am now going to ask each of you if you are free lawfully to marry,' Elinor explains turning towards Jim, 'Are you, Jim, free lawfully to marry Linda?'

'I am.' Jim's face stretches into a clownish grin as he gazes around the room, seeking out our daughters' faces, wanting approval. Only Rosie responds with a weak smile. Abby remains stony-faced and Josh, mirroring Gail, stares at the floor. *What is going on?*

'And are you, Linda, free lawfully to marry Jim?'

A dull pulse in the base of my skull has my heart thundering in my ears, causing me to zone out until I am on a beach, with the sun on my skin, sand in my toes and a band playing Abba songs, *I do, I do, I do,* in the background. My hands shake violently as I feel Jim scan my face. Our eyes lock and I see real fear and something else in his eyes that both surprises me and makes me afraid — the determination to get what he wants at any cost. Under such scrutiny and unconcealed irritation, I clear my throat and croak out a reply.

'I am.' My voice sounds shrill, as if it belongs to someone else. Even Elinor stares at me in concern, as if she thinks I might be here under duress, but when I nod my head at her as if to say everything's okay her eyes dip back to the script she's reading from.

'I am now going to ask each of you, in turn, to declare that you know of no legal reason why you may not be married to each other.'

Jesus. Not again. Bloody hell. Do they need to keep asking the same question? My nerves can't stand much more of this. Glancing over my shoulder, back at the door, wanting to escape from this suffocating environment, I catch Gail's eye without meaning to and I stiffen. I've never seen her look quite so smug. My skin prickles. At this rate I'm likely to pass out before Jim gets the chance to put a ring on my finger. Gail would love that. Knowing she's baiting me and looking for a reaction, I purse my lips in annoyance.

'Jim Delamere, do you solemnly declare that you know not of any lawful impediment why you may not be joined in matrimony to Linda Susan Bouchard?' Elinor's voice pulls me out of my thoughts, and I train my eyes back on her, not wanting to witness that intimidating look in Jim's eyes again which made me recoil before.

'I do.' Jim responds firmly.

'And do you, Linda Susan Bouchard, solemnly declare that you know not of any lawful impediment why you may not be joined in matrimony to Jim Delamere?'

This time there's no hesitation from me. 'I do,' I declare, my words sounding stilted and sharp, but at least they soften Jim's profile slightly. Thank goodness. For a moment there, I hardly knew him. Elinor rewards me with a smile too.

'Now that you have both declared that you are free to marry, we have come to the part of the ceremony where you take each other as husband and wife. Please repeat after me: I, Jim.'

'I, Jim.' Jim pulls at his tie again.

'Take you, Linda.' Elinor smiles encouragingly.

'Take you, Linda.'

'To be my wedded wife.'

'To be my wedded wife.' Jim sneaks a glance at me and grins as if he'd never looked at me so darkly a moment ago, adding 'Again,' which earns him a laugh from one of our guests at least. Josh.

My cheeks burn in embarrassment. The registrars are looking at us in confusion, sensing there is more of a story between us than they had been led to believe. A flame of anger rears up inside me, and my voice pulsates with rage as I turn to Elinor and say, 'I, Linda.'

My taking the lead throws her off her stride but she quickly resumes control, 'take you, Jim.'

'Take you, Jim.' I'm furious with him for breaking his promise, but there's no point kicking off now. That would only make things worse. To think all these weeks, he'd gone along with my decision not to mention that we'd been married before, agreeing that nobody but us needed to know. Jim knew how mortified I'd be if it were made part of the ceremony. And now he's done just that, knowing how much it would upset me.

'To be my wedded husband,' Elinor waits expectantly for my response, for me to repeat those words back to her, but my mind, having the capacity to drift off on its own like an injured animal, is on the rings. He'd spent a whole month's wages on my ring alone, I recall, all those years ago. His was of lesser quality, being only 9ct and therefore, cheaper — not that anybody could ever tell the difference. Jim has no idea that the money he paid to me in my divorce settlement paid for mine and Marcus's rings.

Or that the ones we picked out together in Denpasar City in Bali were much nicer than those in front of us. Yet all I can think about is that night on the beach when Marcus's hand had pushed up through the water, palm splayed open, fingers clawing in a last cry for help. Then, seeing the glimpse of gold on his finger before it disappeared beneath the waves.

'To be my wedded husband . . .' Elinor prompts me again.

As I'm jerked back to the present, my mouth opens to speak but right at that moment the door violently crashes open. A loud, echoing voice booms out across the room.

'You can't marry him. You're already married to me.'

CHAPTER 40

He casually strolls towards me as if he'd never been away, an amused, twisted expression on his handsome face. Hadn't I always known he would return one day to seek revenge and punish me? Still, I pinch myself to check what I'm seeing is real. But one look at everybody else's stunned expressions confirms that Marcus is very much alive; that I haven't conjured him up from my imagination.

The message *was* from him then, not Gail. Instinct tells me she's involved though. That she's to blame. She deliberately planned Marcus's return to coincide with my wedding. When I seek her out, among the other horrified faces in the room, her feline eyes are watching me. Smug and triumphant. His being here is no shock to her. Bitch.

Fingers clenched, I'm a trembling mess, incapable of speech or movement. I keep stealing glances at Marcus until I can bear it no longer and tear my eyes away to study Jim's reaction, but he appears even more shocked than me. Although I'm paralysed trying to make sense of what I'm seeing, part of me feels as if my life has, so far, existed purely for this moment.

All those months spent mourning Marcus. I'd have given anything to magic him back from the dead. But if I could conjure up that power now, I'd send him straight back to Satan before he brings my world toppling down. Why else would he be here if not to make me pay? Gail may get her man after all, once Jim is made aware of what I did to the ghost in front of us, whose familiar blue eyes are staring right at me.

He looks just the same. Hair a shade whiter perhaps and a handful more wrinkles around the corners of the eyes that I used to trace lovingly with my fingers. But on closer inspection, I notice that the blue of his eyes, once the colour of the Ionian Sea that he went into, and somehow survived, sparkle less. I guess this is expected of someone who has returned from the dead.

'Excuse me but can somebody please tell me what's going on?' Elinor, on her high horse, wants to know.

'A wedding, I believe,' Marcus chuckles.

Stunned into helplessness by his well-remembered laughter, tears sting my eyes, blurring my vision. Against my wishes, I want to reach out and stroke his face, feel his lips on mine, fall into his arms.

'I didn't think you had it in you, Jim.' Marcus winks lewdly at Jim, patting him on the arm in a congratulatory manner as if they were best mates. This is Marcus at his finest. He used to love nothing more than winding Jim up and trying to make him jealous.

'I suppose my invite got lost in the post.' he sniggers, glancing between Jim and me.

I wonder why Jim doesn't say something. He seems to have lost the power of speech. The poor man looks as if he's about to have a heart attack. I guess he's thinking I won't marry him now and that I'll go off with Marcus instead. He's right to be worried. Everything depends, as it's always done, on what Marcus wants to happen. He's known for getting his way.

'Marcus, you're really here. Alive. You're not . . . But where have you been all this time? What happened to you? I mean, I know what happened . . . I can explain.' I garble

207

tearfully, clutching at my heart to stop it from racing. Torn as I am between wanting Marcus to disappear and feeling relieved that I'm not a murderer, my mouth searches for the right words but finds none.

'I know you can, sweetheart.' Marcus's focus is back on me, and his reaction is just as confusing as Jim's silence. There's no malice in his expression. Yet I tried to kill him. Thought *I had* killed him. My body runs cold with fear as it occurs to me that I could still go to prison for attempted murder. Once Marcus has finished playing with us, he's bound to reveal what really happened that night. There's no way of stopping him.

Looking beyond Marcus, wanting to see Abby and Rosie's alarmed faces one last time before the police arrive to arrest me as I'm sure Gail will have already told them everything, I see they each have a hand clasped to their mouths as if they can't believe what they're seeing and hearing. *Join the club.* Josh however looks tortured with embarrassment. That's when I see him reach out for Rosie's hand.

But wait, that can't be right, can it? He must have reached out to the wrong sister by mistake, due to the shock. But Rosie doesn't immediately drop his hand. There's a definite pause and an exchange of glances between them before she breaks contact. I'm not the only one to notice. Abby, eyes flashing with rage, has seen it too. Hands scrunched into fists at her sides, she glowers at them.

'Lindy, my Lindy.' Marcus is saying in my ear. But when his hand gently caresses my cheek, I recoil out of shame for what I did to him. *What sort of monster am I?* He staggers backwards in shock.

'I really must insist on an explanation.' Elinor cuts in, looking at Jim and me. But whereas I don't know where to start, Jim doesn't seem to be even listening.

'I think he's in shock,' I stammer by way of an explanation.

At that, Marcus switches his attention back to Jim. 'Is that what you are, Jim? In shock? Not half as much as I was when I found myself being attacked and left for dead in the sea.'

'I thought his drowning was an accident.' Abby pipes up, coming to stand beside her father and placing a supporting hand on his unresponsive arm. She can't bring herself to look at Marcus, but her hatred for him doesn't go unnoticed.

'What does he mean by *attacked*, Mum?' Abby demands, her eyes narrowing in suspicion, and I know then that I've lost her already.

'Marcus, I'm so sorry. I never meant for it to happen.'

'Finally, we're getting somewhere. The truth at last.' Gail says from behind us, finally finding her voice, earning looks of disapproval from Rosie and Josh who are sitting next to her.

'Keep out of this, Gail,' I warn. To think I once trusted her.

'Hah. No chance.' She throws back. 'I told you I was going husband searching in Greece, but you didn't believe me, did you?'

Putting a hand on Marcus's arm, as if that will make up for what I did to him, I gaze into his eyes and pray he sees nothing but honesty in mine. The familiar smell of him causes my heart to melt and I close my eyes. That's all it takes for the words to pour out.

'I didn't mean to hurt you. I wouldn't. Couldn't. You know how much you meant to me, but I was drunk and jealous after catching you talking to that woman. I know that's no excuse, but I swear I didn't know what I was doing . . .' my words trail off as my bravery runs out. I don't know how much to reveal. So far, Marcus hasn't mentioned my part in this. Nor is he acting towards me in the way I'd expect him to after having tried to kill him. You'd think he'd be in my face, screaming "murdering bitch".

'Mum, what are you saying? That you tried to . . . ?' Abby, visibly shocked and trembling at my part confession, can't bring herself to say the word that's on everybody's lips.

CHAPTER 41

'Tried to kill me,' Marcus steals the word right out of Abby's mouth, like the heart thief he is. 'Do you honestly think your mother, who wouldn't hurt a fly, would do something like that?' His face twists with anger as he turns to confront Abby, whose hands are covering her mouth.

'Linda,' Marcus demands my attention in a loud, insistent voice. 'I know I've got a lot of explaining to do, about where I've been and why I haven't tried to find you before now, but there was a very good reason for that. One of them being that I lost my memory.'

'That sounds convenient,' Abby snaps.

'If it weren't for your mum's gutsy friend over there, I may never have made it back at all.' Marcus waves a hand vaguely in Gail's direction.

'She's no friend of mine.' I say sharply, causing a crack in Marcus's confident demeanour.

'If it weren't for me, he'd still be living like a tramp on a fishing boat in Albania not knowing what happened to him,' Gail screeches unpleasantly. 'It was a fisherman who saved him from the water and took him back to shore. I heard about it from a guy I met in Greece, except he thought it was just a rumour, but knowing they never found Marcus's body,

I took a boat over there to find out for myself if it was him, and it was me who helped fill his memory in. So, you want to think yourself lucky your husband didn't drown that night, Linda, otherwise you'd be doing time for murder.'

'Stop that, Aunty Gail. I won't let you talk to Mum like that. You've already heard Marcus say Mum wouldn't do something like that.' Rosie surprises the hell out of me, and Gail too it would seem, by abruptly cutting her off. It's so unlike Rosie, I want to applaud.

'But that isn't true,' Gail persists now, in a whiny tone, 'she told me herself what she did to Marcus. She admitted it the night she got drunk on my boat.' Gail's cat-like eyes rest on me then dart accusingly to Marcus. 'I told you all this, remember?'

'Of course, I remember, that's what happens when you get your memory back.' Marcus dismisses Gail's concerns with a toss of his head and a sarcastic smile.

I watch confusion flash across Gail's face as she tries to make sense of the situation. I'm equally perplexed. *Why would Marcus lie about what happened or bother trying to cover it up?* Unless he still has feelings for me and wants to protect me. But surely, knowing I tried to kill him once is enough to put any man off. No, he's more likely playing games and toying with me. I can't allow that, so I decide it's time to speak the truth at last.

'But, Marcus, I did push you into the water. I might not have meant to but—'

'Memory, as I've learned is a very complex thing, and one is quite capable of believing one did something one did not, as happened in your case.' Marcus recites.

'I saw you. I watched you go into the sea.' I maintain, running out of thumbnails to bite.

'Indeed, you did. That part is correct. But your recollection of what you saw is wrong. Not surprising when you consider how much you'd had to drink that night. And then there was the fight on the beach. I take it you remember that too?'

'That's when I pushed you,' I insist, tears running down my cheeks and onto my ivory wedding outfit, spoiling it for good.

'That's when *somebody* pushed me, Linda. But it wasn't you. You'd passed out on the beach by this time. But you must have come around at some point because you witnessed the whole thing without realising it. Once morning came and you found out I was missing, presumed dead, you would have been racked with guilt after the hurtful things you said to me, so you put two and two together, making five. You blamed yourself for what happened when you kept getting flashbacks of me going into the water.'

Can there be any truth in this? Or is Marcus lying? I don't know who my husband really is, only that his name isn't Marcus Bouchard. There had always been doubt in my mind as to what actually happened that night but, as Marcus implied, it was easy to assume I was the attacker. I had seen him go into the water, hadn't I? Even if I wasn't the one who pushed him, I'd witnessed him drowning — or thought I had — without doing anything to help him.

'If Mum didn't try to kill you, then who did?' Abby asks the question everybody is dying to know the answer to.

CHAPTER 42

'I would do anything for my family. Anything,' Jim garbles suddenly, surprising us all as he stumbles forward, seeming to come out of his shocked state. A stream of snot escapes his nostrils as he bends over, hands clutching his stomach, vomiting. Groaning, he straightens up and stares directly at me, his mouth moving but no words coming out of it.

'What is it, Jim? Are you okay?' I ask, wondering why he doesn't wipe the trail of snot dangling from his nose. Should someone call an ambulance? Shock can do funny things to a person.

'I did it for you, Linda. Everything I ever did was for you and the girls.'

A chill run downs my back. A sense of foreboding creeps over me, like a long, dark, menacing shadow. I cannot breathe properly, so I inhale slowly through my mouth, trying to make sense of what Jim is saying, all the while conscious of the fact that Abby is moving away from her father and stepping closer to me.

'What are you talking about, Jim? What are you saying?' I manage to ask.

'I never set out to kill anyone. It was an accident,' Jim blurts out, spittle flying from his lip. Pulling a sad face, he portrays himself as a victim, no more than an innocent bystander.

'You!' I screw up my face in disbelief, not sure what to think. 'But it couldn't have been . . .' The look on Jim's face is something else, though. It's a picture of guilt and misery. I know then that he's telling the truth and I collapse shakily onto a chair before I fall.

'Oh my God. It was you. All this time. You pushed Marcus into the water.' The words are dragged out of the darkest, saddest part of my soul as my eyes bore into the man I thought I knew and loved.

'No, Mum, that can't be true. He wouldn't, couldn't. Would you, Dad?' Abby interjects desperately, hanging onto my arm as if to stop herself from crashing to the floor.

'How could you, Jim? Why?' I plead, not understanding any of this.

Jim hangs his head, unable to meet mine or his daughter's gaze but his head bounces on his shoulders when Marcus gets in his face, shoving an index finger in his chest.

'The why is the easy part,' Marcus interrupts mockingly, 'to get his ex-wife back.'

'I only went to convince you that you had made a terrible mistake.' Jim cries, maintaining eye contact with me while shrinking back from Marcus, 'and to beg you to return home, if not for me, then for the girls. Nothing else was meant to happen.'

'So, you flew out to Corfu without telling anyone?' I gasp, squeezing the bridge of my nose which feels as if it is filled with bad blood.

'But when he turned up on the beach that night, you were already out for the count, Linda, and I was very much awake, drunk and in the mood for a fight.' Marcus states dramatically as if enjoying himself. 'Except it didn't quite go my way, did it, Jim?'

I blink, unable to believe what I'm hearing. But rather than worry about justice for Marcus at this stage, all I'm concerned with is what Jim has done to me. Something about being lied to by him hits a nerve in my body I didn't know existed.

'So, you lied to me all this time and let me think I was mad to imagine Marcus was still alive.' It hits me then, hard, what else Jim is guilty of, and I feel a fresh surge of rage tear through me. Shrugging off a tearful, red-faced Abby, I stagger over to Jim. As Marcus moves aside, I poke Jim hard in the chest.

'You were the one who put Marcus's profile on the website and sent those messages pretending to be him. For fuck's sake, Jim, you broke into my flat several times knowing it would scare the shit out of me, and rented the downstairs flat so you could keep an eye on me. Don't you dare deny it.' I state simply, not wanting it to be true but deep down I know it is.

A long silence stretches between Jim and me, eventually broken by him burying his head in his hands. 'I would have done anything to get my family back,' he sobs pitifully.

'Including murder,' I hiss. I've never been so angry in my entire life.

'I'm sorry. I never meant for it to happen.'

Jim utters the same words I've been repeating over to myself this past year as a way of easing my conscience over what I believed I'd done to Marcus. But knowing what Jim did to me, the woman he was meant to love, means I'm unable to feel sorry for him.

'It was an accident. You've got to believe me, Linda,' Jim begs. As I would have done if our roles were reversed.

'An accident that you snuck off to Greece on the sly and then hightailed it back to the UK before anyone realised you were missing?' Marcus points out stoically. 'And when I got into trouble in the water you didn't exactly try to help me out, nor report what happened.'

'You never deserved her!' Jim cries angrily, aiming a sly and unexpected punch at Marcus.

'That makes two of us.' Marcus ducks out of the way to expertly get Jim in a headlock.

'Stop it,' Abby roars. Jim and Marcus freeze, and we all stare at her in stunned silence.

'Men are nothing but *liars* and *cheats*,' she screams. 'And I hate you all.'

CHAPTER 43

My eyes track the constant blur of movement outside the window as uniformed police officers come and go. Jim has been handcuffed and sits obediently at the back of the room under a police guard.

I watch him from a distance, feeling overwhelmed by all that has happened. After she screamed at us, Abby stormed out of the building and nobody knows where she is, and the police are keen to find her as she is classed as a missing witness. I want to know if Jim will get a custodial sentence for what he's done, but I can't bring myself to enquire after him. The numerous cups of sweet tea the rest of us have been given do nothing to numb the shock, contrary to what everybody else seems to think. Noticing that nobody has thought to take a cup to Jim, I remind myself he doesn't deserve any tea and sympathy, least of all from me. But it's hard to instantly switch off your feelings for another person, even when they've done you wrong. Take Marcus, for instance. I still don't know how I feel about him. All I know is that his presence is large and that his voice booms louder than anyone else's in the room, even the detective's assigned to this case.

Now I know that you can never really know what is going on inside someone's head, no matter how honest and dependable they seem. I worry about what Marcus's return means for me and my family. Do I owe it to him, after what Jim has done, to give him another chance? Is that even what he wants? We'll have to talk about this. The thing that bothers me most is I don't know if I'm pleased that he's back. On the one hand, I'm delighted that he's alive and that I'm not responsible for his disappearance, but to imagine myself living with him again is hard to get my head around. As for Abby and Rosie, they've got enough going on with the possibility of their father going to prison, to endure any more change. But however much I might not relish the idea, I do still have a husband to consider.

But then as I observe Josh comforting Rosie, a hand wrapped protectively around her shoulders, I think of Abby and wonder if I have a family at all. A sickness, which has developed slowly over time, starting with me abandoning my family, has obviously invaded our home. My suspicion that something seriously wrong was going on with my daughters has proven true. It looks like Josh has fallen out of love with my youngest daughter and in love with my eldest. I'm not sure how any of us will be able to come to terms with this betrayal, least of all Abby, who isn't the forgiving kind.

When I spoke to Rosie earlier, to make sure she was okay, and to confirm that she understood what was going on, I was thrown by the immediate change in her. It was as if she had finally morphed into the eldest child she was meant to be. There was defiance in her eyes and a confidence in her step that I've never seen before. I wonder how shy, people-pleasing, empathetic Rosie could do something like this to her own sister without seeming to bat an eye. But then again, I remind myself cynically, she is Jim's daughter.

Marcus is in deep discussion with the detective, DI Angelina Rossi, and I can tell by the way she flicks back her long, black hair and chews on the gold chunky "A" for Angelina pendant around her neck that she finds him charming. *That's Marcus for you*, I remind myself, except it no longer hurts to see. Their voices, meant to be hushed, nevertheless carry across the room and Elinor and the other registrar hang on to every word. Curiosity follows the pair everywhere, even into the toilets where they go to gossip and dissect what is happening. Four other couples have been turned away because of what's happened and they, like Jim and I, won't be getting married today.

My feelings for Jim are conflicted. I'm still angry, shocked, and bewildered but the more I go over in my mind what happened the closer I am to understanding his motivation. Indeed, Jim has always been fond of saying he would do anything for his family, but I'd had no idea how far he would go to make sure nobody broke up his home. As we'd drifted back together it would never have occurred to me to think he was behind Marcus's fake profile, the text messages, and the break-ins. I would never have imagined him capable of such deceit; didn't think it was in his nature or that he had it in him. He'd always proved himself to be a loyal and devoted friend, or so I thought. Instead, he'd manipulated me into believing I needed him, if only to protect me from Tony Fortin. His mission all along had been to get me to fall out of love with Marcus and back in love with him. I do believe Jim when he says he didn't set out to kill Marcus that night, but what happened played into his hands.

Groaning inwardly, my body cringes with disgust when I spy Gail making her way over to me, her heels clip-clopping on the floor, causing everyone to glance up. I don't want to talk to her. The only person I'd like to see right now, oddly enough, is tough, abrasive Abby, sensing that she needs me more than anybody else in the room. Her sister doesn't appear to need anyone's assistance but Josh's and, though Marcus is already back to playing the returned adoring husband, he'd rather be the centre of attention than remain by my side. I asked the police officers if I could go and look for Abby but both Marcus and DI Rossi, as if they were already partners in crime, advised against it.

'Happy now, Gail?' I demand, glaring up at her, not liking the way she towers above me when I haven't the strength to crawl across the room let alone get up out of my chair. In contrast to her earlier smugness, she looks as shocked as the rest of us — and also guilty as hell and desperate to be forgiven. It looks like she's realised that our friendship is more important than ever now that Jim is out of the picture.

'Linda, I would never have done any of this had I known it was Jim! He deserves everything he gets for what he did.'

When her eyes, hooded and downcast for once rather than blazing with certainty, glance at the chair beside me I can tell she's itching to sit down next to me, so I deliberately push it away with my foot, not caring if I'm being childish.

'You would have seen me go to prison,' I state, looking out of the window again where a small spider, waiting at the edge of a perfectly formed web, prepares to pounce on an unsuspecting fly. No matter how much I pretend Gail's betrayal doesn't hurt it does. She's the spider. I'm the fly. That's how our friendship dynamic has evolved.

'Not if you were innocent! But you told me, admitted it to me that night on the boat, that you'd killed Marcus. What was I supposed to do?'

'Not take the word of a drunk, grieving, depressed widow on hallucinatory medication, maybe?' I quip.

'You think I should have kept a murder a secret, lied for you because you're my friend and pretend it didn't happen?' Gail asks, shocked.

'But it didn't happen, did it, Gail?' I shrug and then my voice rising I say, 'I'd have had some respect for you if you'd actually told me how you felt and what you were planning to do. We could even have gone to the police station together so I could confess. But oh no, you had to go one better and disappear off on a crazy adventure, determined to prove me wrong. Anything so you could get your hands on Jim.'

Looking uncomfortable, Gail shoves her hands in the pockets of her nice jumpsuit. 'Fair point but your intentions were hardly honourable either. You thought you *had* killed Marcus and were keeping it a secret.'

'What else was I supposed to do? And what would you have done, Gail? Huh? I'll tell you, shall I? You'd have done the same in my position if you could get away with it. There's no way you'd have thrown your life away for the sake of telling the truth.'

'But you'd already thrown your life away, hadn't you? Deciding that it wasn't good enough anymore. You did that when you left Jim and the girls, and me, without a care in the world.' Gail stamps her foot and glances shiftily around to make sure nobody is listening in on our row. 'You had everything a woman could want. A lovely home. Two beautiful children. A faithful husband who adored you. I would have killed for what you had.'

'And it would have been convenient for you if I'd done the same, wouldn't it? Because if I were a murderer who had killed her own husband, I'd be behind bars by now and the door would be open for you to move in on my husband and my family.'

'I never could get over how selfish you were to do that to them,' Gail admits, ignoring me.

'You wanted Jim for yourself,' I scoff. 'And that's why you encouraged me to be true to myself and live the life I thought I wanted even if that meant breaking up my family. Don't bother denying it.'

'Well, turns out he wasn't worth fighting over anyway.' Gail shrugs as if it's no big thing, and I almost want to laugh.

'Answer me one thing honestly, Gail, did you try it on with Jim or was that another of his lies?'

'He fooled us all, Linda.' Gail's eyes flash with something like regret. 'But I didn't sleep with him, if that's what you're getting at. I could tell he was only trying to use me to get to you. He wanted to make you jealous, that's all.'

'Otherwise, you would have?'

Gail nods bluntly. 'Otherwise, I would have.'

I dip my head by way of acknowledgement and then say, 'We can never be friends again, Gail, not after you betrayed me, and my family, and then tried to get me sent to prison for something I didn't do. But I appreciate your honesty.'

'Message received and understood. Have a good life, Linda, and try not to do anything I wouldn't do.' Gail attempts a laugh but instead her eyes well up. As she turns her face away and tries unsuccessfully to bat the tears away without my noticing, her glance falls on Marcus who is laughing inappropriately at something DI Rossi is saying. I watch her eyes narrow to slits before coming to rest on me. Her pupils swirl like wine in a glass.

'Maybe it would have been better for everyone if he'd stayed dead.'

CHAPTER 44

Every time I see Marcus enter or leave by a door, brandish a tool before fixing something or get behind the wheel of what is now considered *his* pickup truck, I struggle to come to terms with the fact that this was all Jim's. Yet Marcus feels no shame in taking what isn't his. I wonder if he sees me as another possession that he's inherited now that Jim is serving an eight-year prison sentence for attempted murder. I suppose when you consider Marcus lost over a year of his life due to Jim's attempt to kill him, I can understand his sense of entitlement, but it's a hard win.

Living with Marcus in England is vastly different to the life we shared travelling the globe. Here, Marcus acts like he's more of a prisoner than Jim, and is keen for us to start travelling again. I, on the other hand, have grown tired of adventure and want nothing more than a quiet life without drama. Long-haul flights and exotic destinations have lost their appeal. And who can blame me? It's only been six months since Marcus showed up at the registry office like an angry grenade and everyone's still trying to adjust.

It's not easy. Marcus is like a bear with a sore head and is difficult to be around. Prone to flying into rages and then grovelling with an apology five minutes later, he shows no resemblance to the chilled-out, generous lover of old and instead drives us both crazy, leaving me feeling emotionally exhausted. I try not to give in to the thought that being around Marcus is like having to mind a spoiled toddler. It's worse than when I was a mum with two babies to look after. Although his memory has almost returned to normal, the doctors say his brain went through severe trauma and as a result, any changes in personality and behaviour could be permanent. Sometimes he mixes up his words and then acts as if it's everyone else's fault for not understanding. Remembering him as he was means I feel so sorry for him that I'm reduced to tears at times. But the weeping stops when he accuses me of things I haven't done or criticises and puts me down.

Last week, without Marcus's knowledge, I went to see Jim in prison for the first time. He's only up the road in HMP Peterborough so I pretended I was going shopping in Queensgate for the day, knowing Marcus would be furious if he found out, which again is something new because he never used to be controlling, possessive or jealous but now he's the opposite, especially where Jim's concerned.

But Jim had been extremely specific about his request. I wasn't to tell Marcus under any circumstance and so I'd agreed. My attitude towards my ex-husband has softened since his shocking confession at the registry office and I've finally found it in my heart to forgive him, for all our sakes. Who am I to judge anyway? It could so easily have been me behind bars and not Jim.

He'd appeared gaunt and grey on my visit but seemed grateful that I'd agreed to see him. As soon as I saw him sitting there, a lesser version of himself in every conceivable way — humble and broken, I'd burst into tears, leaving Jim to comfort me instead of the other way around. *He* was the one in need of friendship, love, and support. Not me.

Eager to appease his guilty conscience, Jim told me he wanted to do the right thing and make it up to everyone, so he'd made plans to sign the house over to me with immediate effect. There was one condition. He wanted me to sell it and hand over half of the sale value to Marcus as penance, claiming that pleading guilty to his crime wasn't enough. The other half I was meant to give to the girls. I'd almost asked, *What about me?* but thought it inappropriate. I didn't have any right to Jim's money. He'd paid me off once before and look where that got him. Besides, he refused to listen to any of my objections.

I've not communicated any of this to Marcus as yet and I have no intention of doing so until I know for sure if his name change from Tony Fortin to Marcus Bouchard was ever formalised. A lot depends on this factor, because if Marcus's new identity is a fake, then our marriage is also fake and invalid in the eyes of the law — which leaves me a divorced woman and free if I want to be. But do I want to abandon Marcus after everything that has happened to him? Don't I owe him somehow? I might not have been the one who pushed him into the water, but Jim had, which makes me partly responsible. Guilt is like a stray dog — hard to walk away from.

Every time I try to bring up the subject of the name change with Marcus, he uses his memory loss to deflect my questions. But there's so much I need to know, like *who actually is he*, if I'm to believe in him again. It scares me that I don't trust him. Neither do Rosie and Abby. They'd see him evicted from the family home if it were up to them. Josh too, although he did try to give Marcus the benefit of the doubt in the beginning. But Marcus turned on Josh the same way he does everyone these days. With arrogance and uncontrollable rage. He blames his mood swings and nasty temper on memory loss, but I wonder if we're starting to glimpse the real Marcus. Had I overlooked this cruel streak when we were first together when I was still lovestruck?

My heart breaks afresh every day when I think of my daughters and the hopeless situation they're in. Abby refuses to come to the house while I continue to allow Rosie and Josh to visit, but how can I turn either of my daughters away, especially after what we've been through? As for her dad,

Abby won't even acknowledge she has a father, let alone mention his name. A tremor of anxiety causes my bones to shake as I realise she would have dealt with me in the same cold, ruthless way if I'd been found guilty of attempted murder. If I had pushed Marcus into the water that night, as I once feared I had, then I'd be as dead to her now as Jim is. Abby has thrown off her old life, moved into a shared flat with two other young women and resigned from her job at the unemployment office. Nowadays, she can be found at the foodbank where she volunteers. I'm not sure what she's doing for money, but I suspect she's living off the savings that had been intended towards a deposit on a house for her and Josh.

I should hate Josh, but I don't. He's keen to make amends and is apologetic for breaking Abby's heart, unlike Rosie. He reminds me so much of Jim that I worry for Rosie, but she appears completely in charge of him which is a battle even Abby didn't win. I don't understand my eldest daughter in the slightest, but she's firm in her stance. I either accept her and Josh as a couple or I don't. It's up to me. Otherwise, they'll get on with life without me. They too are planning to marry and have children which is another dagger to poor Abby's heart. Who'd have thought I'd ever refer to her as "poor"? Not me, that's for sure. Unlike her sister, Rosie is pragmatic about her dad and happy to forgive and forget. She and Josh visit him whenever they can and have told him he'll always have a home with them when he's eventually released, which could be in as little as five years with good behaviour.

When Abby asked me where Josh and Rosie are living as she planned to go around there and give them a piece of her mind, again, I had to lie and tell her I didn't know their exact address — only that they were renting a house in Grantham while waiting to buy. Abby being as astute as they come, didn't believe me and accused me of taking sides. When it comes to revenge, six months to Abby is like six days.

'You can't expect me to choose one daughter over another,' I told her primly.

'Yet you chose yourself over all of us five years ago,' was Abby's cutting response.

Her reminder has haunted me since. When I look back on that period of my life, I hardly recognise myself, yet I have to accept that everything Abby accused me of is true. It was selfish of me to walk out on my family when I had everything I wanted right here. My therapist insists that doing the right thing, rather than the easy thing, is the way to move forward, especially when it comes to following your dreams. For me, the easiest thing would have been to remain in an unhappy marriage and not seek the adventures I craved. But, then again, following my dream never did me any good either. I can testify to that.

And what of Marcus's dream? I wonder what his intentions will be towards me if I refuse to do as he wishes and go travelling with him. Only time will tell, I suppose. As it does with everything else, like Marcus's gradual transition into a stranger. Having settled back into the role of adoring husband, at least outwardly, behind closed doors Marcus changes for the worse as soon as we are alone together. I've come to learn that he has many faces, one for the neighbours, one for the petrol pump attendant and one for the corner shop owner, all of whom shower him with the adoration and validation he so desperately needs. The face he reserves for me is dark, empty, and guarded.

Sometimes I catch him looking at me oddly, like I'm the enemy — judging by the appalled, disgusted faces he pulls. I suppose this is understandable given that I almost married another man only months after his being pronounced dead, so I try to make allowances for his increasingly unhealthy behaviour. He's impossible to love yet it's also impossible not to, because I occasionally glimpse the vulnerable man that I fell head over heels in love with when I first met him. He remains hidden most of the time but every so often the mask slips and there he is, melting my heart all over again.

The red flags I ignored in the early days of our courtship have come back to haunt me as I predicted they would. Now

I'm able to look back with fresh eyes, I could kick myself for not seeing clearly then what I can now. First, there was the love bombing stage and a real desire to progress the relationship at an unhealthy pace which should have made me run the other way. Next, the claims that all his exes were crazy but that he'd finally met 'the one' in me. Stupidly, I fell for it, thinking I was something special but grew to envy the so-called psycho girlfriends who got away because they were the smart ones. Had Gail known any of this she would have bluntly asked me why I didn't just leave. Simple enough, right? Except it's not. Ask anyone who has ever been trauma bonded to a narcissistic person and they'll tell you that the more they hurt you, the more attached you become.

What I hadn't realised back then was that Marcus had idealised me in the honeymoon stage of our relationship, but once he understood I wasn't perfect and had flaws the same as everyone else he took it personally and began to devalue me. Hate me, even. He did this by flirting openly with other women, spending my money, and lying over trivial things, as well as making out I was the crazy one whenever I called him out on his behaviour.

Hearing a loud sneeze from the garden, I put down the steam iron, realising I've been holding it so long in mid-air that it's switched itself off, and walk across to the window. It's practically summer and the garden needs attention. Jim would be heartbroken if he could see the state it's in. But Marcus is not the green-fingered type. Cleaning windows, taking out the bins, mowing lawns and doing odd jobs around the house all form part of the suburban nightmare he despises. Despite this, Marcus is out there, attempting to cut down the long edges of grass that have sprung up around the lawn with a pair of rusty shears. His hair has grown rebelliously long, reaching his shoulders, and he wears it in a ponytail that swings back and forth as he works. He likes to boast that he'll never grow old gracefully and that's evident in the skinny jeans, espadrilles, and faded college sweater he's wearing.

He doesn't know I'm watching him and I'm about to knock on the glass and ask him if he wants a cup of tea when I see him toss the shears to the ground, take a mobile phone out of his pocket, and put it to his ear. There's something suspicious about the hunch of Marcus's shoulders and the way he disappears behind the summerhouse, out of sight, to take the call, as if he doesn't want anyone, anyone being me, to know what he's up to.

Then something occurs to me. Frowning, I head back to the kitchen. There, lying on top of the microwave, is Marcus's phone. *How long has he had another phone?* Picking up the phone I *am* allowed to know about, I turn it around in my hand. Marcus is fond of telling me that unlike Jim he keeps no secrets from me and that I'm free to look at his phone whenever I like. He even gave me the password for it. Something tells me I won't find anything of interest going through this particular phone, but that I need to get my hands on the other one.

CHAPTER 45

Outside, the darkened sky is leaden with rain, and lightning intermittently throws a blade of yellow light across the bedroom making it glow. Summer storms like this put Marcus in an unfathomable mood, nostalgic for warmer climates and Mediterranean food. 'It's June but it's barely twelve degrees,' I heard him complain earlier, all the while shaking his head like a dog with an ear infection.

I'm meant to be in bed. At least that's what I told Marcus, claiming I needed to bury my head under the covers to escape the storm. He knows that thunder and lightning terrify me so he had no reason to suspect me of lying. But a few moments ago, I crept onto the landing to try to locate his whereabouts downstairs. If I'm to go through his personal possessions without him knowing, then I need to know where he is. The last thing my nerves could stand is him creeping up on me unannounced. When I heard his voice just now rumbling in the dark, arguing with the television like a madman, only Jeremy Clarkson on *Top Gear* has that effect on him, the sound vibrated through me, making my bones shake.

I knew what I had to do, having already made up my mind there was no time to lose in the search for Marcus's secret phone: not since I'd discovered that money has also gone missing from mine and Jim's joint account. The first thing Jim had done while he was awaiting trial was to transfer funds across to our old account in case money was needed for bail, but we soon learned that pleading guilty to a serious crime meant he would remain in custody right up to his court case.

Jim, having returned at least outwardly to his good, old, dependable, self, decided that I should keep the money anyway in case I, or the girls, needed it. And now Jim's £50,000 bank balance has somehow been slashed to £35,000, and I haven't touched a penny of it. Wherever that money has disappeared to, I'm certain Marcus is to blame. I also suspect he's using his secret phone, which I now know is likely to be a "burner" phone thanks to the Google search engine, to organise some of his dodgy deals. Old habits die hard, as they say, and it wouldn't surprise me if he were up to his old gambling tricks again.

Opting first for Marcus's bedside drawer, I kneel down and very gently ease it open. Inside, I discover a stash of low-value foreign coins, an old lottery ticket, a crumpled packet of ibuprofen and a chewed-at-one-end pen. When I hear the creak of a floorboard, I shoot up, knocking my face against the table lamp. My heart rolls into my mouth and my neck cricks as I twist around to check Marcus isn't standing behind me, waiting to catch me out. Relief floods through me when I realise there's no one there. Must just be the sound of the house groaning in sympathy with my misery and turmoil.

Sighing, I pull myself to my feet and agitatedly run my hands down my long night dress, the dirtiness of what I'm doing getting to me. Having benefited from a decent upbringing, I know it's wrong to go through other people's belongings, but *needs must*, I tell myself. I'm mulling over where to search next when my glance falls on the top of Marcus's wardrobe where his suitcase is stored. *Bingo.* A perfect hiding place for a man who likes to travel.

Being tall, I'm able to reach the suitcase without having to stand on anything other than my toes, but it's heavier than I anticipated. Rather than ease it down as was my intention, I have to yank it across first. I feel my heart stop as the case falls through my hands, painfully clipping my wrist, and crashing to the floor. The thud of Marcus's footsteps bounding up the stairs roars in my ears as I steady myself against the wardrobe.

'What happened? Are you okay?' Marcus, taking in my startled appearance, the fact I'm holding one injured hand in the other, and the case on the floor which has spat out a multitude of toiletries, swimming trunks and beach shoes, looks concerned.

'I knocked into the wardrobe in the dark and, well the case fell and hurt my hand,' I stammer, having to react quickly. Relief rushes through me as I realise he doesn't suspect me of anything.

'Come here, you, and let me kiss it better.'

Marcus slides a snug arm around my middle and rests his chin on my shoulder. My eyelids flutter closed, his touch stirring up the wrong kind of feelings, like fear, disgust, and shame.

'You don't think it's broken, do you?' he asks, trying to keep the worried tone out of his voice while attempting to examine my hand. I snatch it away more quickly than he'd like and try to laugh it off.

'You're too rough. You'll hurt me.'

'I would never hurt you, Linda. You know that.' Pursing his lips as if he were the injured party, *as if he hadn't stolen Jim's money*, Marcus pulls off his shirt revealing a deep tan that never fades and throws off his slippers. 'Going to jump in the shower before bed.'

I can tell I've hurt his feelings and that he's sulking. There'll be no more concerns over my wrist tonight. Marcus and boundaries don't go together, I've found. He hates not having access to my body whenever he wants. It's as if he views me as an object. I don't ask myself why I don't simply ask him about the phone or demand to know where all that money has gone because, having lived with him these last six months, I've come to understand that this new version of my husband is a danger to himself and others. His impulsive nature, reckless behaviour and increasing arrogance and sense of entitlement keep me on eggshells and, as a result, my anxiety is spiralling out of control.

As he stomps over to the ensuite bathroom he passes close enough for me to smell whiskey on his breath and, now that he's shirtless, I notice that both of his trouser pockets bulge with items that are distinctively phone shaped. With a sinking feeling, I realise that getting hold of that phone is going to be harder than I imagined if he always keeps it on his person. This means the only chance I've got is when he's asleep. And Marcus is not a heavy sleeper. *When someone's made an attempt on your life once, you make sure to keep one eye open after that, even when you're asleep,* he'd told me.

Feeling disheartened, I go back to bed, propping myself up on the pillows so that I can massage my wrist which really does hurt. Knowing I'm bound to wake up with bad bruising in the morning, I reach into my bedside drawer for a tube of Arnica cream, kept there for this very reason. I'm about to apply a generous blob or two when I change my mind and put it back in the drawer. *So, what if it bruises.* I'll leave it there for all to see, like the broken heart I wear on my sleeve.

When Marcus eventually comes back into the room, he's naked and aroused so I pin my eyes to the bird-print duvet that both Jim and Marcus have an aversion to and pretend not to notice. But when a body sinks onto the bed next to mine and he lifts my chin with his fingers, I can't ignore him any longer.

'Sorry, Marcus, I'm not in the mood.'

'When *are* you in the mood?' he complains, snatching his fingers away so hard that they graze my skin.

'When I'm in the mood.' My mouth curls into a grimace.

'Why are you wearing that old woman's nightdress anyway?' He demands to know, grabbing a handful of white broderie anglaise.

'Because I *am* an old woman,' I tell him, primly rearranging my nightdress.

'You're okay with old, are you?' he sneers.

'I'm happy in my skin, Marcus. Isn't that what you taught me to be?'

'You never used to be like this.'

'Like what?'

'Frigid. You've changed, Linda. You're not the woman you used to be.'

'Pot calling kettle,' I snap, twisting away from him to switch on my sidelight. If we're going to have a row, I want to see his lying face. His brain must be crammed full of untruths. When I turn to face him, I see that my remark has hit home, because his face has reddened.

'Marcus,' I inhale deeply, readying myself, 'please don't bite my head off but I want to know if you've remembered any more about taking on your friend's identity. Do you know yet if the name change was legal or not? Have you remembered anything at all?'

'I've told you a hundred times I can't remember,' he snaps sulkily and gets up from the bed, attempting to hide his erection with his discarded shirt. Yet only moments ago, he'd delighted in showing off his manhood. The self-satisfied gleam in his eye had been quite disturbing and I'm sure he would have beat his chest with pride had it occurred to him.

'But isn't there a way we can find out?' I persist, for once not backing down.

He sighs as if about to concede something. 'Why is it so important to you?'

'Because I want to find out if I'm legally married to you,' I smile to soften my words in the hope I can win him over, but I realise my mistake almost immediately. I should have said I wanted to find out if *we* were legally married. He's bound to take offence now.

'Why? So, you can walk away, abandon me when you feel like it?'

'That didn't stop me from leaving Jim and I *was* legally married to him,' I point out logically forgetting that Marcus no longer does logic.

'We couldn't be more married if we tried,' he puffs out his chest in anger. 'What with you in that old woman's nightdress and us hardly ever having sex. Besides, married or not, what's mine is yours, and always has been if that's what you're worried about.'

'Except there's not much of yours is there?' I choke on my words, beyond shocked with myself, firstly for daring to speak my mind and secondly for using the tone of voice I'd normally reserve for a spoiled toddler.

'I can't believe you'd say such a thing. I have money—'

'You do?' I screw up my face in surprise. Is he about to give himself away as a thief by admitting to suddenly being cash-rich?

'Investments, trust funds, the kind of income that isn't easily accessible,' he says being deliberately evasive and not meeting my eye. 'Talk about hitting a man when he's down.'

I bow my head in shame because it was a pretty shitty thing for me to say when he's broke but is pretending not to be, because it makes him feel less of a man. If only I could be sure he hadn't stolen Jim's money I'd give him the benefit of the doubt, but as it is, I can't.

'You've turned into a cruel woman, Linda. It must be said. And, quite frankly, I don't want to be around you when you're being toxic like this.'

'And what about you, Marcus?' I rage at his words and scramble out of bed to stand directly in front of him, so I'm in his face. How bloody dare he project his faults onto me. 'Have you ever hit a man when he's down?'

'What's that supposed to mean?'

'I'm talking about the real Marcus Bouchard.'

'What about him?'

As I watch Marcus's eyes come alive with fear I know then, in that moment, that if I push him on this, I'm going to hear something that I'll never be able to unhear. Something bad. Worse than bad. I dive in anyway, God help me.

'I've always found it strange that both you and your best friend went into the water and were presumed dead, only he drowned for real, whereas you survived.'

'No thanks to your husband who tried to drown me.'

'Jim isn't my husband as you well know. And I don't even know if you are because you won't tell me if Bouchard is your real name or not.'

'I've told you I can't remember. It's hardly my fault if you choose not to believe me.'

'So explain to me why you wanted to take on your best friend's identity in the first place. Even if you did do it legally, it doesn't make sense. What was wrong with being Tony Fortin?'

'Everything was wrong with being Tony Fortin,' Marcus says in a voice I don't recognise. Cold. Quiet. Threatening.

CHAPTER 46

I've never seen Marcus like this before, seemingly close to imploding from anger. The veins on his neck stand out as if they'd been hard wired on to him and his face is as white as his bunched-up knuckles. He looks like a pumped-up fighter in need of a punching bag to take out his temper on and I'm determined it's not going to be me so I take a step back from him, regretting my decision to pressure him into a confession.

'You want to know what happened to Marcus Bouchard?' Marcus finally snaps.

I shake my head, afraid of the way he's looking at me, and glance over his motionless shoulder at the door beyond, hoping for a chance to escape.

'He had everything I did not, for one thing. A proper home. Money. Parents who doted on him. On top of that, he was super intelligent which meant he had a chance to make something of his life. Be somebody. That day on the boat when we went fishing, he told me he'd been accepted at his first-choice university, Bristol, whereas I couldn't scrape together the grades needed to be a beach bum.'

I'm all eyes and ears. Nothing can stop me from wanting to hear the whole story now that I'm finally close to finding out who my secretive second husband is.

'What did you do, Marcus?' I ask warily.

'I was four when my father walked out on me and my mum, who was disabled and couldn't work, so we lived on benefits. I grew up poor, Linda. I mean really, really poor. The most expensive thing we owned was mum's wheelchair.'

'You should have told me this.'

'You wouldn't have understood.'

I open my mouth to argue and then change my mind because he's probably right. I might have grown up on a council estate, but we owned the house outright and we had everything we needed. Unlike Marcus, I was loved by both of my parents, whose relationship was solid as a rock.

'What was she like, your mum?' I ask instead.

'She never got over my father leaving us. But I was her golden boy and I became the man of the house from a very early age.'

'Is she still alive?'

'Sadly, no. She died of a broken heart three years after I left Clovelly.'

'You never went back?' I gasp.

'I was on a cruise ship at the time working as a casino dealer but even if I wasn't, do you really think I would have gone back to Clovelly, where I was known as a charity case, to visit my dying, disabled mother after publicly abandoning her?'

'I don't know what to say.' The truth falls out of my mouth before I can stop it.

'If you're that easily shocked, you'd better prepare yourself for the rest,' Marcus sneers contemptuously.

I begin to think that he secretly hates me. No, not secretly, openly.

'So, none of what you told me was true. You never lived in British Columbia or South Africa.

'I always planned to visit one day,' Marcus says, shaking his head. 'After going to all the trouble of learning the language it would have made sense.'

'Why did you even bother learning to speak Afrikaans?'

'It was Marcus who got me started on it. He'd teach me the odd word or two after school when we did our homework together. His mum would bake cake every day and liked to feed me up with hot dinners, so I used to love going to their house. The house on the cliff became like a second home to me.'

'I've been there. I've met Tilly Bouchard.'

'So, you have. You know, I always planned on being rich enough one day to buy that house.'

'What else of Marcus's did you covet, besides his house and his name?'

'The one thing I had that Marcus did not was good looks and a certain charm, but I'd have traded that any day of the week for his popularity. He might have been a skinny ginger with white skin but he was well-liked, whereas I wasn't. I think he only made friends with me because his mother felt sorry for me. She used to give my mum all his hand-me-downs and I was made to wear them until I grew too big for them. I was glad when that happened because it was deeply humiliating for me.'

Knowing how he appreciates the good things in life, like classic designer clothing, hand-made shoes, fine dining, expensive cigars and that he used to crave the first-class lifestyle, I almost feel sorry for him as it must have been hard for him growing up. But when I remember that he did get to grow up whereas Marcus Bouchard did not, I toughen up.

'What did you do to make people not like you?'

'What did I do?' Marcus rolls his eyes. 'You mean apart from being the only poor kid at school who got bullied for having free meals.'

'Lots of schoolkids get free meals. It's not that big a deal.'

'That's so like you to say so,' Marcus snaps. 'And funnily enough my mum would have agreed with you. She didn't see any shame in us living on benefits, but I hated it. And I hated her, because it was all her fault.'

'She was in a wheelchair, Marcus. How could it have been her fault?'

'I wanted a different life. A nice house to come home to. Proper home-cooked meals, not tinned soup day after day. I wanted a packed lunch to take to school like all the other kids. And a dad who worked and came home every night. But most of all I wanted a decent education and a mum who wasn't in a wheelchair, because I hated her being in it.'

That's a lot of wants, my mum would have said, but I don't repeat her words now, realising how foolish that would be. I feel weary and want to sink back down on the bed, but I'm scared that if I move, I'll break a spell of sorts and Marcus will stop talking. That mustn't happen. Not before I find out what happened between the two best friends and why one of them is dead.

'When I was little, she'd keep me at home with her all the time and wouldn't let me play outside with the other kids. I didn't see a park till I was nearly ten years old. And if I so much as sneezed she'd refuse to send me to school.'

'Oh, God, Marcus, that sounds awful,' I say, genuinely moved.

'It was,' he concedes. 'And Marcus knew all this and still wanted to be my friend. I was grateful for that and I looked up to him. Admired him, even.'

'You wanted to be like him.' I interrupt, trying to understand. The desire to dig deeper intensifies.

'Yes. He was all I had. I wasn't anything without Marcus. So, when he told me he was going away to Brighton, and would be leaving me behind, alone, with my rotten life, something inside me snapped and I saw red.'

'What did you do, Marcus?' I whisper, my heart in my mouth.

'He couldn't swim,' Marcus's eyes fill with regretful tears as he says this. 'So, I held him down, under the water. I held him down until he eventually stopped moving.'

Marcus sinks onto the bed and his body goes limp. When he reaches for my hand and holds it to his heart, as if trying to gain comfort from my touch, it feels as if Marcus Bouchard's ghost had reached out to me. For that reason alone, I don't tug my hand away even though I'd like to.

'And then I became him,' Marcus states simply.

CHAPTER 47

Raspberry jam oozes out of my sponge cake like blood as I carry it and a chocolate-dusted cappuccino over to the only available table in the outside courtyard area. I've never been to Cakes + Co in Cheyne Lane before, but it's extremely popular with Stamford's done-well-for-themselves crowd. By that I mean the Barbour and Range Rover gaggle of tall, blonde, skinnier-than-skinny-jeans women. The kind who talk openly about orgasms and insist on firm boundaries, because they know they're high-value women. All of them are young, of course, and filled with confidence and no cake whatsoever, just calorie-free green tea.

Much as I admire the way they toss their beach-waved hair at each other and wear Coast crossover bags across their laps as if they were badges of honour, I've never fitted in with sophisticated groups like these. I think that's mostly due to my council house upbringing. Gail and I used to take the mickey out of these groups on the quiet, which wasn't nice of us, but we secretly longed to be included, especially when we were younger.

My hand trembles as I stir my coffee and I deliberately keep my eyes lowered so as not to attract any attention, in case I'm recognised by a passing customer, although that's not likely in here, as they're not my kind of people. Instead, I watch the chocolate in my drink melt into a gooey lump and feel my stomach churn. I know I'm not going to be able to drink it all, nor take more than one small bite out of the slice of cake. I'm too nervous for that, and convinced I'll vomit it straight back up if I do. It's just for show. Like my straightened-to-a-blunt-edge hair, Boden knee-length suede boots and Joules "Burghley House" print scarf.

My husband, the cold-blooded murderer, was right when he said it was cold for June. Most of the customers sitting outside are wearing coats and boots as if it were mid-winter. I shiver in my flowery tea dress and zip my gilet up to my chin but after Marcus's drunken confession a few nights ago, when he admitted to killing the real Marcus Bouchard, I don't believe I'll ever warm up again. I've not fully processed this information yet. It just won't sink in that I married a killer. Or that I'm living with one. Sharing a bed with one, even.

Even more concerning is the fact that he's going around acting as if everything is normal between us, as if he'd never told me any of this, which makes me wonder, was his confession true or did he make it up? But I only have to remember the way he looked when he told me how he killed his best friend, *details I can't get out of my head*, to know he was speaking the truth. Judging by his erratic and inconsistent behaviour, I have to assume that his memory recall is still not dependable, and that he's forgotten the whole conversation, which could go in my favour because if he thinks his secret remains safe then he has no reason to see me as a threat. But if he suddenly remembers that he told me how he murdered his best friend and then tried to make it look like an accident, I could be in danger. *Once a killer, always a killer*, my mum would have said. For all my size, Marcus could snap my neck in two with one hand.

How did I get here? Married. Divorced. Married. Widowed. Almost married. Living with a killer. Honestly, I feel like one of Henry VIII's wives. But will I survive being married to Marcus?

Sighing heavily, I focus my attention back on my surroundings as a way of taking my mind off what happened to Marcus's poor friend and my current abysmal situation. The place is packed and through the window, I can see a queue forming behind the counter, the hungry-eyed customers eagerly waiting for us to leave so they can grab a table.

When I catch a glimpse of flame-red hair and dark denim jacket, I sigh into my drink, worrying for the hundredth time if I'm doing the right thing. But it's too late to change my mind because Gail is already filling the doorway, her cat-like eyes searching for me among the tables. I help her out by holding up a hand as if I were a regular person meeting a friend for coffee and she squints in recognition before heading over.

'Well, well, well, if it isn't you know who,' she snips, placing a black coffee on the table in front of her. Like the other female customers, Gail doesn't get a cake. She's always watching her weight. I begin to wonder how the café makes any money.

My heart beats erratically as I watch her ease off her jacket, run a hand through her hair and sit down, folding one long leg over another.

'How have you been?' I ask nervously.

'Oh, you know, friendless, nieceless.' Gail stirs her coffee as if she's angry with it when we both know who she's really mad at—herself for ruining our friendship for a man. My man. Gail might think that my reaching out to her is a first step towards my forgiveness but she'd be mistaken. I intend to keep that knowledge to myself though. At least for the time being.

'You're not going to make this easy, are you?'

Gail grins and gives me a one-shouldered shrug that is so her. 'Hell, no.'

'It's good to see you,' I say, hiding a smile behind my coffee cup. That earns me a raise of an eyebrow, so I try again. 'I mean it. I've missed you. How could I not?'

'Easy when you've got a hot, sexy back-from-the-dead lover to fall back on,' she cackles rudely. I shift in my seat, worried in case anybody overheard.

'How are things with Marcus?' Gail asks in a more serious tone, appearing surprised by my lack of enthusiasm for the subject.

'We're fine, thank you.'

Having anticipated her question, I had my reply ready, but I never could get one over on Gail and I see nothing has changed. She can see right through me and is doing so now; hunting me down with a stare that's intended to bully any lies out of me.

'I bet you're still in the honeymoon stage when you can't get enough of each other,' she says, whispering behind a ring-laden hand.

'As I said, things are just fine.' I attempt a laugh, pretending to be embarrassed.

'Fine?' she repeats pointedly, arching her eyebrows.

'It's you I want to talk about,' I stammer, 'and to find out what you've been up to.'

'Sure, you do,' she snaps, reddening.

'Is something wrong, Gail? I mean something other than you and me. You seem a bit down.'

'Oh, the usual man trouble,' she grimaces, 'you know how it is, except you don't, not now you've got Marcus back.'

I wince at that, but if Gail thinks she's going to get me to elaborate then she's mistaken. When I don't comment, she pulls a sad face and bites her lip.

'It was horrible not having you around to talk to. I missed you too, babe, loads in fact,' she finally concedes, reaching over to pat me on the back of my hand. But when I flinch and pull away, she frowns and throws me a questioning look.

'Bit jumpy, aren't you?'

'Sorry, I hurt my wrist, that's all.' I hold my palm outwards so she can see the nasty purple bruise that has spread across my wrist like the worst kind of bracelet.

'Ouch.' Gail purses her lips in sympathy. 'How'd you do that?'

'It was an accident,' I blurt out, forcing myself to swallow a mouthful of coffee.

Gail eyes me again, suspiciously this time. 'I never said it wasn't.'

'Anyway, I'm pleased you agreed to meet me today. I wasn't sure if you would.'

'You've got to be kidding. I've been waiting for you to call these last six months.'

'You have?'

Gail nods and squeezes her eyes shut as if to fend off tears.

'Don't you dare start blubbing out here, Gail Somersby,' I warn her forcefully, causing her eyes to pop open again. She seems surprised to see me grinning.

'Gawd. I'm turning into such a baby the older I get. I never used to get emotional.'

'You're human, Gail. You're allowed.'

Impulsively, Gail leans across the table and grabs hold of my left hand this time, the one that isn't bruised.

'Your skin feels cold and prickly, like the Gail I used to know.' I laugh. 'What have you done with my best friend?'

'Am I still your best friend though? Will you ever be able to forgive me, do you think, for what I did?' Gail asks in earnest, her eyes and mouth downcast.

'You'll always be my best friend no matter what,' I tell her, not meaning it, but wanting her to believe it, as it's all part of my plan. 'And if I can forgive Jim for what *he* did, then I can do the same for you.'

Gail sighs in admiration. 'You always were the bigger person.'

'Thanks, and there I was thinking I'd lost weight.'

'You know what I mean.' Gail dismisses me with a wave of her hand. Then leaning back in her seat, she appraises me.

'You look tired.'

'Thanks.' I pull a mock-stern face. 'You on the other hand look amazing. As you always do.'

'Shame about the black eye.'

'What, oh, this,' I put a hand to my eye, realising my half-hearted attempt to cover the bruising with concealer and foundation has failed, as it was meant to. 'It's nothing, just another—'

'Accident?'

The way she's looking at me now, with challenging eyes, is enough to make me tremble. I can feel the walls of the courtyard pushing in on me until there's no air left to breathe. On the verge of welling up myself, I cradle my head in my hands and squeeze my eyes shut.

'So, when are you going to tell me what's really going on?' Gail demands in a no-nonsense, clipped, business-like tone.

CHAPTER 48

A sudden gust of wind whips my hair around my face as I let myself into the house, grateful to find the pickup truck has gone from the drive, which means I'll get another opportunity to search for Marcus's secret phone before he arrives back from wherever he's gone. I don't hold out much hope of finding it as I'm sure he has it with him, but it's worth a shot. Even though Gail has agreed to help me find out what he's up to, I can't let a chance like this slip by.

No sooner have I stepped inside the kitchen, which is warm and welcoming, I feel my phone vibrating in my handbag. I pull it out and scroll hurriedly through Gail's text message, worried she's changed her mind. But no, she remains fully committed to our plan.

'*What a bastard. I could kill him for what he's done to you. I really could. Anyway, you've got me now and I'm on the case. XXX.*'

'*Thanks, Gail,*' my thumbs stab out a response, remembering to add a suitably expressive emoji. '*If anyone can help me, you can. You found Marcus when no one else could. XX.*' I can't resist the jibe, nor the gesture of adding one fewer kiss than she did.

'*Worst mistake of my life. But I promise never to let you down again. No need for thanks. Least I can do. Besides, that's what friends are for. XXX.*'

'*Exactly,*' I type back, pondering on Gail's words and promises of friendship. She betrayed me once before, so I'd be an idiot to trust her. Allowing her to play detective by digging up whatever she can on my untrustworthy husband could prove risky, but it's too late now to let doubts set in even though Marcus would be furious if he found out. It crosses my mind that I might be putting us both in danger. I know what he's capable of. But Gail's my secret weapon. Besides, it wasn't like I forced her. She volunteered to help. In her own words, she's willing to do anything to make things up to me. Just as Jim has tried to do with Marcus. The fool.

Admittedly, I shouldn't have allowed her to think Marcus was responsible for the black eye and bruised wrist, but it added weight to my argument, so I don't regret it. Without evidence, Gail might not have been quite so enthusiastic about getting involved. Besides, now I know what he did to his best friend, I'm convinced that Marcus is more than capable of hurting me — physically as well as mentally — so the idea isn't as outrageous as it sounds. Guilt continues to nag at me though because a lie is a lie at the end of the day. And I hate liars. It turns out that I'm a better actor than I thought, because I was flinching in that café as if I feared my own shadow and Gail being Gail made a big fuss out of everything, calling Marcus every name under the sun and threatening to cut his balls off. 'Men, huh,' she'd spat, before going back to the counter to buy the biggest, most indulgent slice of cake ever, which she scoffed in four large mouthfuls.

Placing my bag on the kitchen table that has known the assorted sizes of my children's handprints over the years, I slip off my gilet and hang it on the back of a chair, rubbing my hands together to warm them. Like Marcus, I'm longing for warmer days. I feel the cold more as I get older, just as my mother warned me I would. Not that I believed her! Mother and daughter relationships are never simple, are they? Although I'm tempted to put on the kettle, sit at the table with a cup of tea and mope, even have a stress-busting cry, I force myself into action. *Now, where's that bloody phone?*

As my gaze roams the room, and then the ceiling, I try to picture where Marcus might have hidden it. That's when I spot the redundant Amazon Echo on the dresser and huff in annoyance. It's a leftover of Jim's, who loved his technology. The same can't be said of me. I haven't a clue when it comes to that sort of thing and Marcus is only slightly better. Alexa must be lonely now that Jim's gone. I am too, sometimes. His absence is felt by us all. Everyone except Abby that is, but then again, she's probably just pretending not to miss her dad as she's not in a good place herself.

'Alexa, who is my husband?' I bark out a challenge.

'I'm a little concerned you don't know that,' Alexa preaches.

'Alexa, where would Marcus hide his phone.'

'Calling Jim,' Alexa announces, only picking up on the word "phone".

'Good luck with that,' I mutter, resisting the urge to waste the afternoon interrogating Alexa with questions like, *is my husband cheating on me?* and *is my husband actually my husband?* Slipping off shoes I pad upstairs, convinced it's where Marcus would choose to hide something. My hunch is still on it being among his personal possessions. That's what I used to do with receipts if I spent more than I should on clothing for me or the girls. I'd hide them in the bottom of a shoe box beneath the tissue paper so Jim wouldn't find them. Otherwise, I'm stumped, having ruled out the garage and summer house because, not being into DIY or mechanics, Marcus rarely goes into the outdoor buildings, unless nagged.

I'm halfway up the stairs when my words slap me in the face, *I'd hide them in the bottom of a shoe box*. My God, could it be that simple? Taking the steps two at a time, I break into a run. In the bedroom, I finally tear open the door to Marcus's wardrobe, making it snap back on itself. Moving aside hanger after hanger of linen shirts, jackets, and trousers, noticing for the first time that Marcus owns little in the way of winter clothing, I find four shoe boxes partially hidden at the bottom of the wardrobe. From memory, I know he has four good pairs for dining out, dancing, that sort of thing. One black pair for funerals, two brown and the white Russell & Bromley snaffle bar loafers that he wore when we got married. Because he thinks the white ones make him look trendy, they're his favourites, so I choose this box first. He's lucky to have any personal possessions at all, but out of sentimentality I brought everything back to England with me and put them in storage, thinking I might want to see them again one day. Marcus had been touched when he found this out and had insisted on collecting everything the same day. But it was me that paid the extortionate storage fee. Not him.

My fingers dip into the crisp white paper and immediately land on something hard and glossy. Squeezing my eyes shut, I hold my breath, not daring to believe I could be this lucky, this soon. *Please be it.* And when my eyes slide open, and the shiny surface of a slightly older Android phone is revealed, I punch a hand in the air. *Yes.*

Only then does it occur to me that whatever is stored on this phone is likely to be unpleasant and hurtful for me to see. But no amount of preparing for that will make it any easier, so I pick up the phone and it comes to life in my hand, lighting up with orange and red colours, reminding me of foreign sunsets, which is why Marcus would have chosen it as a background.

It's locked. *Of course it is, dumbo.* Marcus isn't stupid. Well, he is stupid enough to leave the phone behind but not stupid enough, surely, to have used the date of our wedding anniversary for a PIN. I tap it in anyway, 0106 . . . Bingo. A screenful of apps is revealed.

Friends With Benefits, Only Flirts, Sex Finder, Mashable. Fuck Buddy, Porn Dude, Hook-Up-Date, I click on them all. One by one. Until I feel sick to my stomach. These hook-up apps might have different names but they're identical in content, showing gross overblown images of giant-breasted women and erect penises, one of which is ejaculating sperm onto an expectant woman's face. I'm too much of a prude, even at the ripe old age of fifty-eight to think, let alone say aloud, the word *cock*. Just when I imagine it can't get any worse, I click on the phone's photo gallery and my eyes bulge when I see there are hundreds of images of real-life women stored in it. These women are unlike the ones from the hook-up sites in that they appear, mostly, to have had their pictures taken without their consent.

There are blurry shots of bums in tight jeans, a flash of panties as one woman climbs a metal staircase at Peterborough Railway Station and a close-up of cleavage captured from over a woman's shoulder. So, this is what Marcus gets up to when he's out — stalking women around the streets of Stamford and Peterborough while they're going about their everyday lives. Shopping. Visiting the dentist. Attending an interview. Picking the kids up from school. *My God, I'm married to a pervert. A predator. A monster. A killer.*

Feeling like I need to sit down before I crash to the floor, I collapse onto the bed, careful not to intrude on Marcus's side because the thought of even the memory of that man being anywhere near me is enough to make me cringe. The impact of what Marcus has done, and what he's capable of doing knocks the wind out of me. A word erupts from the very core of me: *liar*. And then another: *cheat*. My mind takes me back to that night on the beach when I caught Marcus flirting with that woman, who I unfairly labelled Lilo Lil as if she were a cheap, middle-aged whore. I was right to be upset and angry, yet he insisted I was kicking up a fuss over nothing, accusing me of being a crazy, jealous woman like all his other exes. It doesn't hurt any less to finally have my feelings and insecurities validated.

'Bastard.' My whole body is rigid with righteous anger. So much so that it feels as if my muscles will never unclench.

Behind me, the voice of a monster slices through the silence like a knife.

'What are you doing, Lindy?'

CHAPTER 49

'Don't you Lindy me, Marcus Bouchard, or should I say Tony Fortin,' I snap, before I have time to think, lobbing the phone at his face without warning. My aim though is off, and it soars past his shoulder instead, bouncing off the wall before sliding, intact, onto the carpet. Shoulders slumped and eyes wide in fearful realisation, Marcus does not attempt to retrieve it from the floor. He knows the damage has been done and that I've already seen everything. Anger surges inside me, turning my mouth into a snarl and my hands into fists.

'You disgust me. How could you?'

I expect him to reel off a list of pathetic excuses or explode with fury at finding me going through his stuff, but he does neither of these things. He just appears embarrassed, judging by the redness of his face and rabbit-caught-in-the-headlights expression.

'Linda, I can explain,' he edges closer, eyes lowered, and arms extended as if I'm about to fall into them, *as if*, so I back up a foot and stop him with a forceful palm.

'Don't you dare come anywhere near me,' I hiss, sounding snakelike. 'I can't bear to look at you right now, let alone have you touch me.'

When he cocks his head to one side, a gesture he knows I usually find endearing, I make a disgusted sound in the back of my throat that does nothing to match how angry I feel.

'It's not what you think,' he stammers, finally, gazing down at his shoes, unable to look me in the eye now that I've unmasked his dirty little secret.

'Tell that to those poor unsuspecting women. And as for those sex hook-up sites!' I scream. 'Quite why I'm not scratching your eyes out right now is beyond me.'

Irritation surges up my chest when his brow crumples with disapproval at my choice of words. He inhales sharply but doesn't say anything. Then, catching me off guard, he whips around and slinks off without another word, leaving the phone where it landed.

'That's it, walk away like the bloody coward you are.' I stalk him along the hallway, resisting the very strong urge to punch him in the back of the head. 'What, you're not going to take your precious phone with you,' I scoff sarcastically.

Marcus says nothing and slams into the family bathroom, firmly closing the door in my face, still without looking at me.

'I wish you'd never come back and that you really were lying dead at the bottom of the sea,' I yell. A string of vengeful thoughts goes off in my head like fireworks as I shout that last bit. None of which bring me any joy.

Feeling suddenly exhausted, I stumble unsteadily back to the bedroom, using the wall as a guide, and sink onto the bed, curling myself into a ball. But not before flinging Marcus's pillows across the room. I don't want his familiar stench anywhere near me. Then, pressing both hands to my mouth to stifle the sound, I sob until I'm a crumpled, snotty mess. Anger rises inside me all over again when I realise with a sickening thump in the chest that Marcus only pretends to like women but secretly despises and resents us.

I find myself thinking that it's almost a shame he didn't hit me because I could have called the police then and had him thrown out on the street, maybe even got a restraining order. Either way, tomorrow I'm going to ask him to leave. It's not going to be easy. Marcus has effectively come back from the dead to be with me and has nowhere else to go, so he'll fight this decision tooth and nail. Without me he is homeless, jobless, and broke. As far as I can tell he doesn't even have an identity to call his own. Legally, he doesn't exist. God knows how Gail managed to get him on a plane back to the UK without a passport or any ID. I'm guessing Marcus made some corrupt friends in Albania. As I roll that thought around in my head, I realise a change of tactic is called for. If I'm going to get rid of Marcus for good, then I need to think as he does and stay one step ahead. One of my mother's sayings springs to mind, *there's more than one way to skin a cat*. Or a rat, in Marcus's case.

CHAPTER 50

'Fucking hell, babe.' Gail's voice trails off in astonishment as she automatically refills my glass with red wine. We're both already quite tipsy and I'm reminded of that night on the boat all those months ago when I drunkenly confessed to having killed my husband. I almost wish now this had been the case. After two days of being on the receiving end of Marcus's deliberately cruel silent treatment, during which he has refused to discuss our situation, a spell in prison would have seemed a breeze in comparison.

Gail jumped out of her skin in fright when she arrived home from work to find me hiding on the boat, waiting for her. It had only been two days since we met up at the cake shop and I was the last person she was expecting to see. But, like the faithful friend she is, one look at my tearful face and she ushered me inside; offering me a bed for the night, hell, for as long as I liked. I've so far regaled her with all that's happened, and she's sat through the entire conversation with bugged-out eyes until now.

Gail, chewing gum, wearing a fake black leather jacket and giant hoop earrings that bash against her neck, seems to want to hang on to her thirty-year-old younger self. I, on the other hand, in elasticated-waist-for-comfort mum jeans, striped top and unobtrusive stud earrings look what I am: someone's invisible, middle-aged, unloved wife.

'But if he's taken your phone and purse and is keeping you locked inside the house, how did you manage to get out tonight?' Gail stops chewing her gum for one second to ask.

'I sneaked out the window,' I lie, but with a gleam in my eye.

'Oh my God. You'll do yourself a mischief at your age.' Gail laughs inappropriately and then slaps a hand across her mouth, spilling her drink down her top in the process.

'I flagged Ali down outside the taxi office in town and he agreed to bring me here, even though I didn't have any money on me.'

'That man is a saint,' Gail smacks her glossy lips in approval, then purses them, deep in thought. 'But what about the devil you've got at home? He's bound to come looking for you when he realises you've gone AWOL.'

Shaking my head, I grab a tea towel from a hook on the kitchen cupboard and dab at the wine stain on Gail's top but all I end up doing is spreading it around, making it worse. 'I've left him a note threatening him with the police if he tries to find me.'

'So, why don't you?' Gail asks, puzzled.

'Why don't I what?'

'Go to the police.'

'Gail,' I say tearfully, 'You know what happens to women in cases like these, when the husband is,' I swallow, struggling to get the unspeakable word out, 'abusive . . .'

'No,' she admits, lighting up another cigarette, having only just put one out.

'They'll take his side. Nobody will believe my version of events. Marcus can be so convincing, you know that. Besides he . . .'

'He what?' Gail is on her feet, eyes swimming wildly like piranhas in a lake.

'He's threatened to change his story. He says if I leave him or tell anyone about what he's done, he'll go to the police himself and say he got it wrong before and that Jim is innocent. Gail, he's going to tell them I'm the one who tried to kill him.'

Gail sucks in her breath and throws me a confused look. 'But they won't believe him. Nobody would, least of all the police. Not without evidence. And Jim would never change his story and go along with it.'

'Marcus swears his doctor can supply them with proof that his full memory has only just returned. They'll blame his mistake on the trauma, claiming they now want to put the record straight so that justice is done and the real criminal, *as in me*,' my voice rises in desperation, 'is banged up behind bars. And it wouldn't matter what Jim said, because the police would assume he was just trying to protect me.'

'Shit.' Gail chokes on her cigarette smoke and runs a hand across her face in distress, smudging the mascara around her eyes.

'I don't know what to do, Gail. I can't leave Marcus in case he follows through on his threat and goes to the police, but how am I meant to stay with a man like that? After everything he's done. He won't leave of his own free will because he's got nowhere else to go, nor will he divorce me. I'm stuck.' My voice cracks as I sit back down, pulling Gail alongside me. Curling my hand around my glass, I watch my tears drip into it.

'What a cunt.' Gail's eyes blaze with anger as she passes the cigarette to me. I take a pull on it but it's hot and burns my lip, so I pass it back.

'Well, two can play at that game.' Gail lurches to her feet again, flicking ash everywhere. 'I've got it,' she cries jubilantly. 'We'll get our own proof.'

'What sort of proof? His phone with the apps and pictures has conveniently disappeared. I told you that already,' I say quietly, wondering where she's going with this.

'Proof of his affair.'

'What affair?' I demand, fighting off a surge of jealousy that I have no right to feel.

'With me,' Gail declares smugly. It's a look that suits her.

'What are you talking about?' My back goes ramrod straight. 'I know you fancied my first husband but surely you wouldn't steal a second from me.'

'Don't be daft,' Gail wrinkles her nose, out of fun or from disgust, I can't tell. 'We'll set a honey trap for him. Stitch him up. You'll have all the evidence you need then to divorce him for adultery. And he wouldn't be able to go to the police with a change of story then. It would look too suspicious, like he was trying to get his own back on you.'

Gail's suggestion slams into me like a runaway train. 'You know something, that could work. But how? I mean what would we have to do?'

'You wouldn't have to do anything.' Gail's face spreads into a grin. 'I'd lure him here, get him drunk and then when he's out cold, I'd remove his clothes before slipping into bed next to him wearing something sexy. All I'd have to do then is post a selection of revealing selfies online and overnight he'd become known as the man who shagged his wife's best friend.'

'And you'd be known around town as a homewrecker,' I point out, thinking it's not far from the truth. She'd have wrecked my home and stolen my family months ago given the chance.

'Who gives a flying fuck,' Gail shrugs as if to suggest she couldn't care less. 'We both know I owe you big time and this will be my way of making it up to you.'

'You think he'd go for it?' I worry at a thumbnail, feeling a sense of unease.

'What red-blooded male wouldn't want a piece of this ass?' Gail shakes her booty.

'I love your low morals,' I tell her, throwing an apologetic smile her way for having doubted her, 'they're so . . .'

'Immoral,' she chuckles dirtily into her drink.

'I don't know, though. I mean, we'd be breaking the law, wouldn't we? And it feels so dishonest and wrong. Surely, there must be another way.'

'No, there isn't. You said so yourself, remember? He's got you well and truly screwed, and you need to beat him at his own game if you're ever going to be free of him. Besides, he deserves everything he gets for what he's done to you and those other women. He's scum, Linda. So, you mustn't start feeling sorry for him. Unless—'

'Unless what?' My head bounces up to find Gail's concerned gaze waiting for me.

'Unless you still have feelings for him.'

CHAPTER 51

Truth slams me in the gut as I realise that Gail is spot on. I *do* still have feelings for Marcus, despite everything. I think a part of me always will. But I'm wise enough to know that love isn't enough. By now, I'm back home, catching up on Eastenders and Corrie, but ironically my life is more dramatic than both soaps put together. Having taken in my inebriated state as I walked in the door, Marcus legged it up the stairs straight away, no doubt fearing another fight. It's still only ten o'clock but the night is taking forever to end. Too much to mull over, that's my problem. There's no chance I'll get any sleep, even though I've drunk the equivalent of three-quarters of a bottle of wine. I'm perfectly lucid though and I suspect that's because there's more adrenalin than alcohol flowing through my body.

I've made myself a milky coffee, just as my mum used to do when she was anxious and couldn't sleep, and I've also nibbled on custard creams to sop up the booze. When I hear the groan of a floorboard above my head, I pause the screen with the remote control and listen. The flush of the loo, and another creak of a floorboard, inform me that Marcus has nipped to the toilet and is on his way back to bed, in Jim's study where he's taken up occupancy. No longer interested in what's going on in Albert Square, I switch off the TV and curl my legs under me, tugging the belt of my dressing gown tighter around me in a hug.

Gail had begged me to stay the night with her, claiming she was worried about what Marcus might to do me. 'Did you know that eighty per cent of murder victims are killed by someone they know?' she'd quoted as if she owned shares in Netflix. I'd laughed her concerns off, telling her she watched too many murder mystery documentaries but it wasn't as easy to shake off the disturbing images that came to mind when I thought about what happened to the real Marcus Bouchard.

After reminding Gail that it was important for me to act normal, whatever that meant, around Marcus, for our plan to work, she'd backed down, but then remembering he had possession of my phone, she'd whittled over how we would stay in touch. In the end, we came up with the idea of using the landline. Every so often, I would ring Gail's mobile, so she'd know I was okay. It was too risky to talk when Marcus was around, so we agreed on three rings for *I'm okay*, and two for *help*. After that, I insisted on going home, adding 'There's no telling what he'll do if I stay over.'

Poor Gail. Her eyes almost popped out of her head when I said that. She always did like a good crisis to liven things up. I can't believe she fell for it, hook, line, and sinker and that I didn't even have to prompt her very much before she stumbled upon the idea of setting Marcus up. Honestly, it was like taking candy from a baby. I was telling the truth when I told Gail I admired her low morals. It's the one thing I'd been counting on. Although she was shocked to learn about the sex apps on Marcus's phone and the sexualised images of the women, I suspect she thought this was routine stuff for most men, but she'd seemed genuinely horrified to discover Marcus was keeping me locked in the house and refusing to let me have access to my phone. That offended her strong female, independent spirit.

Except that's not exactly how things are. My phone is on silent in my bag, next to my purse and the key to my front door, which I can enter and exit as I like. The only danger I was at risk of coming home to tonight was more love bombing from Marcus, which commenced in earnest this morning when the silent treatment failed to get my attention. Since then, he's tried to win me over with offers of presents, cooking meals, running scented baths, and foot rubs without expecting sex in return. It was fun while it lasted but I can already sense an imminent change, noticeable by the empty, dark look in Marcus's eyes. I'm wise to his MO by now and can expect the devalue and discard stages any time soon. People like Marcus, who I now know, after scrolling endlessly through Quora, suffer from narcissistic personality disorder are predictable if nothing else in their cruel and sadistic treatment of others.

I can't tell Gail that this form of manipulative abuse is worse than any physical threat. She wouldn't be able to comprehend that I was suffering from a trauma bond so deep it had become who I was and that the push, pull techniques Marcus used to control me, alongside the cold silent treatments, attempts at isolating me, gaslighting and projecting his faults onto me, were making me question my own sanity as well as keeping me in a prison of my own anxiety. Or that when I described how I'd been locked inside my own house I was really talking about how it felt to be locked inside myself. Marcus might not have taken my phone away or given me a black eye, but he could have done any of those things in one of his unreasonable rages and that makes my smear campaign against him fair.

Abby was right when she said all men were liars, but women can be just as bad, as I'm finding out. Gail didn't doubt me for one second. Who'd have thought I could tell such outrageous lies? Jim. Marcus. Gail. We've all done things this past year that none of us could have imagined the other doing. Men tell lies because they can, and because they like the power it gives them over women. Women lie because they don't have a choice and because men make them. That's my take on it anyway.

Another thing I'm only now learning is that life can change in a second. A heartbeat even. And that good people can become bad, but can bad people become good? I used to think I was a good person, but was I really? I'd left my husband and abandoned my children to start a new life elsewhere. And for what? So, I could travel. So, I could be free. Yet here I am in a prison of my own making. They might as well have locked me up with Jim.

Questions never leave me alone but I'm no closer to finding out what happened to Jim's money and Marcus could be screwing around on Fuckbuddy.com for all I know. Abby and Rosie are irreversibly estranged and family life as I once knew it is over. What's not over is the lie I'm living with a man who, I now know, never loved me, because narcissists are incapable of love. A bubble of excitement rises in my chest when I think of Gail's plan to take revenge on my husband so I can finally be free of him. It can't come soon enough.

CHAPTER 52

It's a warm day, finally, and Marcus, in a short-sleeved shirt and shorts, is mowing the lawn. His hair, untied for once, reminds me of an albino lion's mane. It suits him, I grudgingly admit, still hating the fact I'd had my lovely long locks cut off. As I hang the washing on the line, the smell of freshly cut grass takes me back to my childhood, of barbecues and inflatable swimming pools, mum's homemade potato salad and dad's finest steak burgers.

Funny that, how human beings can become philosophers, psychiatrists and scientists who can build robots that look just like us, but we have no control over our memories. When they come, like now, they take us by surprise and can even bring us to our knees. My eyes fill with tears as I think back to those precious days with my parents who I still miss very much.

'Are you alright?' Marcus asks, having turned off the lawnmower to empty the grass box.

He's noticed the waterworks and is pretending to be concerned so I don't bother wiping away my tears. Nor do I reply. I simply twitch my lips and look away.

'How long are you going to keep this up, Linda?' He sighs, running a hand through his mane.

I want to retaliate by asking him how long he is going to continue helping himself to Jim's money, having discovered only this morning that another five thousand has disappeared. I dread to think what Jim will say when he finds out. But if he thinks I'm going to hand over half of the proceeds from the sale of the house to Marcus now, he's got another think coming. Over my dead body. Little does my ex-husband know that I haven't so much as contacted an estate agent, never mind put the house on the market.

Treating Marcus to an Abby eye roll, I viciously stab a pair of his underpants to the line with a peg, causing him to drop his shoulders into a despondent shrug, before sloping off to start the lawnmower up again. The sound of its whiny engine fills the silence between us.

If Gail were here, she'd want to know why I'm still washing his clothes and I've asked myself the same question but I'm no wiser, except that I've been a wife for longer than I haven't. So, like the Stepford wife I am, I take the empty laundry basket back into the house, put on some more of my husband's washing and go into the kitchen to check on the fish pie that he likes me to cook for him. Deciding it's not brown enough and could do with another ten minutes, I close the oven door and switch on the timer.

Reassured by the ongoing whir of the lawnmower outside, I pick up the landline phone, scroll through the saved numbers, and dial Gail, making sure Marcus is in plain sight through the window.

'How're things?' Gail picks up on the fourth ring having recognised my number.

'The same,' I reply despondently. 'He's mowing the lawn.'

'I wondered why you didn't hang up after three rings. By the way, I've got that sorted.'

'Got what sorted?' I furrow my brow, not understanding.

'Your very own burner phone.'

'Oh wow. Thank you, Gail,' I say, touched.

'How shall I get it to you?'

'Hmm, how about you drop it in the plastic box where the postman leaves parcels? The one on the front porch. Marcus never looks in there.'

'Okay. I'll wait till it's dark and the front curtains are closed before I come round. How's that for a plan?'

'Yep, sounds good. Have you given any thought to our other plan?'

'You still want to go ahead with it, then?'

I feel a prickle of unease as I realise Gail is having doubts. Last night the drink had made her brave but now she's sobered up she's seeing things differently.

'Don't you? I mean, I'll understand if you've changed your mind and no longer want to help. It's a big ask.'

'Of course, I do,' Gail reacts defensively, as I knew she would. 'I told you that. Besides, you didn't ask, I volunteered. I thought *you* might be having second thoughts, that's all.'

I don't believe Gail but that doesn't matter. So long as she's still on board that's the main thing. It's also important for her to think she's calling the shots, and that it's all her idea.

'When will you do it?' I say, deliberately avoiding the word *we*.

'Your call, babe, I'm ready whenever.'

I suddenly picture Gail failing epically at this without me there to hold her hand. Any number of things could happen. Marcus could become suspicious; in which case he'd refuse the drink and the offer of free sex. I'm not even sure he finds Gail attractive. As for Gail, she could easily chicken out or get drunk herself and forget to take any pictures. Marcus is a great lover when he wants to be and knowing Gail as I do, she could end up enjoying the sex too much to give a toss about saving my arse.

'You know, Gail, I'm worried in case something goes wrong. I couldn't live with myself if he caught on to what you were up to and hurt you.'

'Hurt *me*? As if?' she snorts. 'I can take care of myself, you know that, so don't worry about me.'

'You've never seen him in one of his rages though. He could beat you up, or worse.' I pause, waiting for Gail to catch on.

'Do you mean murder? You think he'd kill me?'

'I don't know, Gail. I just . . . I mean . . . all I'm saying is it wouldn't be the first time.'

'Oh my God, the bastard. Who? How? When?'

'He killed the real Marcus Bouchard eighteen years ago. I wasn't going to tell you in case . . . I didn't want to scare you . . .

'Fucking hell, Linda. Did he tell you this or did you find out?'

'He told me.' I nod and avert my eyes, still very much shaken by Marcus's drunken confession. 'I'll spare you the gruesome details. To be honest, I can't think about it without feeling sick.'

'You're married to a killer.'

'And if he killed once, he could do it again.' I warn, ignoring the thread of awe that has crept into Gail's voice. 'That's why I can't let you do this on your own. I'd never forgive myself if anything happened.'

'But how else could it work?'

'What if I hid somewhere on the boat, just in case?'

'Too dangerous,' Gail shoots back. 'Besides, you're not allowed out, remember?'

'Okay then,' I gulp at the close call, realising how difficult it is to lie well when under pressure. I'm also very conscious that my story has holes. 'How about you ring me on my burner phone just before he arrives, and I listen in? That way I could call for help if it were needed.'

'Not a bad idea,' Gail concedes, 'but why not go one better and film the whole thing.'

'A sex tape?' I screw up my nose in disgust.

'You'd have all the evidence you need then.'

'But he could use it as proof against you, that you set him up.'

'I hadn't thought of that,' Gail admits.

'Uploading the photos online is still the best bet. You were so clever to think of it.'

'But if we filmed it as well, we could use it as backup. For safety reasons.'

'Exactly,' I agree, then drop in as casually as I can, 'it's a shame we don't know anyone techy who could set up a camera in your bedroom and feed it back to the burner phone so I could watch what was going on from here. That way I could really have your back.'

'And my boobs and my bum,' Gail laughs, and a chill runs up my spine as I picture her stripping off her trademark red, lacy underwear in front of my husband.

'OMG!' Gail squeals excitedly as if she'd just had an epiphany.

'What?'

'It's your lucky day, babe.'

I can hear the swagger in Gail's voice as she relays this to me. 'How come?'

'Because I know exactly the right techy. One who knows how to keep his mouth shut.'

'Who?' I gasp.

'Ray from the Cosy Club of course.'

'Ray from the Cosy Club,' I repeat back to her as if the answer hadn't been obvious all along, which it had, it just took Gail longer than anticipated to work it out.

'I'll have to blow job him into it but that's no hardship, as he's circumcised.'

'You're a bloody genius,' I tell Gail, while keeping one eye on my smirking predator of a husband, who has stopped mowing and is now deep in conversation over the fence with the young mum from next door whose husband is frequently away.

'I know. Proper sleuth, aren't I?' Gail chirrups in my ear, like an annoying budgie.

When the timer for the fish pie goes off, I can't believe ten minutes have passed already. Now that I've got what I wanted from the conversation it's time to end it.

'Got to go, Gail, he's on his way back inside,' I fake panic, and abruptly cut her off.

Slipping my hands into oven gloves, I wrestle the pie out of the oven, pleased to see that the top is now browned to perfection. And then I do something very unwifelike. I slip two laxatives out of my apron pocket and sprinkle them over the pie's mashed potato peaks.

CHAPTER 53

'I'm off out,' Marcus informs me curtly, his eyes flitting back and forth like a bird of prey, anywhere except resting on me. He's made more of an effort than I'd anticipated, and I'm surprised to find that this hurts more than it should. His freshly washed hair has been neatly tied back in a black velvet ribbon and he smells of Eau Sauvage, an alluring mix of wood and citrus that has the power to give me butterflies still. I notice that he's wearing the linen shirt and trousers I ironed yesterday. Parading would be a better word to describe his movements as he can't stop fidgeting or checking out his reflection. His gaze lands on the large white Laura Ashley mirror on the wall as we speak.

'Anywhere nice?' I ask, glancing up from the romance novel I'm only pretending to read. I know exactly where he's going, of course, but I'm curious as to what explanation he'll give.

'Surprised you care,' he mutters, shoving restless hands in his pockets. When I don't respond, he coughs into his hand, as guilty a gesture as I've ever seen him make. 'Game of cards actually. Going to be a late one.'

'Well, I won't wait up, obviously,' I say testily.

'Obviously.'

My invasive stare catches him out, and he looks momentarily confused. It's as if he'd never caught the expression on my face before. It baffles him, I can tell. He thinks he knows me. That I can't surprise him anymore. But, as he's about to find out, he's very much mistaken.

It wouldn't occur to him that the two-day bout of illness he's just experienced was down to me, having slipped enough laxatives into his food to make him not want to leave the house. Thinking he'd caught a bug, Marcus insisted on staying within a reasonable distance of the toilet in case he got caught short. And that's where he was, trousers around his ankles, air freshener at the ready, when the young mum from next door, who I've since learned is called Becky, came knocking to find out why Marcus hadn't been around as promised to help her move a heavy piece of furniture. I'd explained apologetically that he had a bad case of diarrhoea. Gazing at her loose, shiny breasts which were clearly visible under her tiny vest top, I went on to tell her he'd even shit his pants by accident. 'But that's what happens when you get old,' I'd added as if ageing were a transmittable disease, like an STI. She'd responded by screwing her freckled nose up in disgust and I surmised that she wouldn't be chasing around after my husband again after that.

When I hear the front door slam, I creep over to the window and peer out, just in time to see Marcus dive into the front seat of a taxi. I've seen him do this before, so I know what he's up to. He intends to impress the driver by proving he's not stuck-up like those customers who remain on the back seat, not saying a dicky bird. He'll talk all the way there too, pretend he's interested in what kind of day the driver's had, how many fares, that sort of thing, when really, he couldn't care less. It's all for show. It's sad really, that he needs other people's validation so much. *Fuck them*, is what I say. But that's the new Linda talking.

Grief wells up in me when I think about where he's heading. To the boat. To Gail. Suddenly, it's real. The thought of Marcus being intimate with another woman temporarily overshadows everything and a fierce wave of nausea causes me to gag. Swallowing the bile, I straighten up, reminding myself that I need to be tough as old boots to get through this. I'm determined to stay strong and in control of my emotions. I just hope Gail can do the same.

Taking the burner phone out of my pocket, that Gail dropped off at the house a couple of days ago, I double-tap the only app on the screen and enter the password, GailPLAN@69. Almost immediately a blurry image appears. While I wait for the loading circle to disappear, I tilt the phone on its side and maximise the screen. I'm in and staring straight at a crumpled bed with a wine-coloured quilt cover, which I recognise immediately as Gail's.

'Hey, Gail. Are you there? Marcus is on his way,' I inject a fake singsong tone into my voice because if I exhibit nervousness Gail will mirror me. And that's the last thing I want.

'I'm here.'

Gail comes into shot, perching on the end of the bed so she's facing me. She feels so close. As if I could physically reach out and touch her.

'The footage is really good. Better than I expected.'

'Who knew you could buy a spy camera online for less than fifty quid which looks like a digital clock?'

'Marcus will never know it's there.'

'How long ago did he leave?' Gail asks, running an agitated hand through her hair.

I can tell she's nervous, but it's best I don't mention it. She'll only get defensive, so I say instead, 'About three minutes ago. You've got fifteen minutes till he arrives.'

'Shit. It's really happening. I can't believe he fell for it.'

'I take it you told him you wanted to meet up to talk about my mental health issues.'

Gail nods vigorously. 'Yep at first, then I got a bit flirty, like you said I should.'

'And what did he say in his last text before he came over?'

Gail slides her phone open and reads aloud, 'How about I bring a bottle of red with me to go with that sexy underwear you mentioned.'

'You were meant to be subtle, Gail.' I groan, putting my head in my hands.

'That is subtle for me. Anyway, chill out. It did the trick.'

'Have you got everything prepared as we discussed?' I sigh, biting back a surge of irritation. 'Did you manage to get his favourite whiskey?'

'Of course,' Gail holds up a bottle of Macallan that she's obviously been dying to show me. 'He has good taste.'

'What about the pills? Have you got them somewhere safe?'

Gail rattles an envelope at the camera to prove she has them. 'Good,' I tell her. 'But remember what I said. They're harmless when taken orally but you mustn't let your skin come into contact with them otherwise you could have a bad reaction.'

Once again, Gail dangles something in front of me. This time it's a pair of blue surgical gloves.

'Are you sure about the pills though? I mean, what if he falls asleep on me?'

'He won't. They're antidepressants not sleeping tablets. I take them all the time and they never do me any harm. What they will do is get him to chill out and relax.'

'What if he notices them in his drink?'

'He won't. I've tested them. There's no taste and no sediment.'

Gail sighs and drops her shoulders as if most of her worries have disappeared. When she smiles for the first time this evening, I realise how lovely she looks, and experience a familiar stirring of jealousy that I can't shrug off. Gail has a great body. Not a stretch mark in sight. Her boobs, though small, remain pert and she has the arse of a twenty-year-old. Underneath her skinny jeans and green satin blouse, I'm fairly sure she'll be wearing the red sexy underwear she told Marcus about. But I can't bring myself to ask.

'You sure about this, babe? I mean I know he's a prize twat and a bastard to boot who doesn't deserve any pity, but he's still your husband.'

She asks this as if she were able to read my mind, and I swallow hard and glance away for a second. The concern in her green eyes is too much and I'm reduced to blinking away tears.

'You know when this is over, I'm going to be there for you.' Gail throws me a kiss. 'And we can go travelling together, just you and me, like we said. Like the old days.'

'Just you and me,' I repeat, thinking there's something very childlike about Gail tonight and for the briefest moment I almost feel sorry for her, but then I remind myself that she can be cold and heartless when it suits her. I won't let emotions get in the way of what must be done. *No softening now, Linda.* My escape from this marriage is more important than doing the right thing. As Gail reminded me, Marcus doesn't deserve my pity and neither does she. Not after what she did. All those years pretending to be my friend and encouraging me to follow my dream when secretly she was plotting on getting her hands on Jim. And then stitching me up over Marcus. The bitch. She'd have seen me thrown into prison without blinking an eye. No. Contrary to what she might think, I'll never forgive her for that. Never.

'I thought New York, then Las Vegas. We could find ourselves some rich cowboys . . .'

Gail is on a roll, going on about places I have no intention of ever visiting. I have to stop her.

'I am sure, Gail,' I interrupt bluntly, 'about Marcus, I mean. He's not the person I married. I don't know if he's changed because of the accident or if he was always going to end up the way he is now. All I know is that man is not my husband.'

CHAPTER 54

As soon as we heard the knock at the door, Gail threw back the last of her wine and let out a stream of fucks under her breath. I, meanwhile, mouthed what was meant to be a reassuring 'I'm not far away,' while gesturing to her, with a cutthroat action that I've killed my microphone so neither she nor Marcus will hear me. Then, rearranging her boobs in her plunge bra for maximum effect, she took several deep, steadying breaths and winked lewdly at me before exiting the bedroom.

. That was an hour ago. Now, all I can do is imagine what is going on in Gail's living area, internally berating Roy from the Cosy Club for not installing a camera in there as well. I'm keeping my fingers and everything else crossed in the hope that Gail hasn't wasted any time getting those pills into Marcus. Although his flirting with Gail is a good sign that he *is* into her, the big question remains will he try to get her into bed? It's one thing to sign up for online dating apps but quite another to cheat on your wife, especially with her best friend. He also knows where his bread is buttered as he relies on me for everything including money so would he risk it?

My fingers are like raw stumps where I've nibbled them. The pressure is building. My nerves are shattered. I'm tempted to go and pour myself a large glass of wine as Gail had done for her nerves, but I keep my eyes glued to the screen, not wanting to miss a single second. Then, desperate to pee, I'm about to get up from my seat and nip to the cloakroom when Gail's bedroom door opens and Marcus strolls casually into the room, hand wrapped around a large glass of whiskey. When he stares straight at me as if aware I'm watching him, my heart thumps so loud I think he must be able to hear it.

Gail stumbles into the bedroom after him and her wide, heavily made-up eyes land straight on the camera, but she tears them away again before Marcus notices or becomes suspicious. I swear several more of the buttons on her blouse have been undone since I last saw her.

When Marcus slams his over-full glass down on the bedside table, next to the camera, and his face looms inches from mine, I panic because his eyes are dark, empty, and vacant like a vampire's, making me recoil. As I clasp a palm over my mouth, the burner phone falls out of my other hand onto the fireplace hearth, landing with a crash. Reminding myself that I can hear them, but they can't hear me, I scramble to pick it up, relieved to find it undamaged. My hands and knees continue to shake though, making the film and the characters in it wobble as if the boat had become unmoored and was sailing down the river.

Marcus checks out the room, paying close attention to the bed, before disappearing with a grunt into the small ensuite shower room. I catch him unzipping his fly before he's even closed the door. He's looking queasy, but I can't decide if that's down to alcohol or the medication. *I wish I could be sure she's given it to him.* As if she can read my mind, Gail approaches the camera and gives me a thumbs-up sign. Turning her back, she unfolds the envelope in her hand, letting me know that the drugs have been administered. For the first time tonight, my breath leaves my body without threatening to choke me. As I watch her slide the envelope into her knicker drawer, I thank God for Gail. She's done brilliantly so far.

A faint thud comes from the ensuite, and Gail's brows climb as she stands deerlike, with alarmed eyes, waiting for Marcus to come back out.

'You all right in there, babe?' she calls in a butter-wouldn't-melt voice.

But Marcus doesn't reply and a few more minutes of intolerable silence pass by, leaving Gail and me frozen in place, fearful that something unexpected may have happened. *But what?* At last, we hear Marcus clearing his throat, then the flush of the toilet and suddenly he's filling the doorway. It becomes apparent that this is a quite different Marcus from the one who went into the ensuite. This version's eyes are glassy and unfocused and sweat glistens on his forehead. Looking as if he's going to throw up, he staggers to the bed and sinks onto it, arms hanging limply by his side.

'I like your style. You're a quick mover, I'll say that for you,' Gail says seductively in his ear, winding herself around him like one of those snakes that squeeze their prey to death.

Thanks to the fast-acting drugs, Marcus is stoned. His movements are slow and sluggish, and he's obviously finding it hard to keep up with what is going on. Now that Gail has him where she wants him, she intends to have fun. But he resists all her efforts to tug off his polo shirt.

'What have you done to me?' Marcus grumbles, putting his head in his hands.

'It's what I'm *going* to do that matters,' Gail leers sexily, batting off his big paws.

This time Gail manages to pull off Marcus's top and his once firm, toned stomach, now turned to flab, is released. Cheeks pink with excitement, Gail attacks his belt next and, even without his help, has his trousers off in less than a minute. The fact that he's wearing his favourite navy designer boxers is like a sharp claw down my back. Although I have the power to prevent his humiliation from worsening, I do nothing except remember the pain and suffering he's put me through and what he did to his best friend.

Ignoring his resistant hands and illegible moans, Gail straddles Marcus's waist and peels away her blouse, revealing a Christmas wrapper-coloured bra. When Marcus whips his head away to the side, Gail grabs his chin and forces it back again, so she's looking into his eyes.

'I thought this was what you wanted. Why else would you ask to see a picture of me in my red lacy underwear?'

I stare at my lap and fight back the feeling of betrayal. I don't know why this news should surprise me, Gail has already told me that she'd told him about her underwear. But I still can't seem to stop myself from feeling shocked by his adulterous behaviour. Knowing this makes my heart ice over and when I next look up, I try to pretend I'm watching a porn movie and that the two people in it are not known to me. Easier to stomach that way. Except it's not. Not really. There's something entirely surreal about watching the man you love, *loved*, make out with another woman, who happens to be your best friend. Although to be fair, in Marcus's case, he's so dazed he can hardly be described as participating. It's better this way, I decide, as I won't have to suffer flashbacks of him trying to get his lecherous hands on Gail's body.

By now, Gail has forcibly pushed Marcus's hands above his head. He doesn't fight her even when she lands a cheeky kiss on his belly. Whipping her phone out of her jeans pocket, she selfishly takes wet-mouthed, pouting selfies instead of concentrating on what she's meant to be doing. Typical Gail! By the time she dismounts Marcus's body he's unconscious. Gail, barely noticing or caring, stretches out on the bed next to him, casually throwing one leg across his crotch before taking pictures of them together. As she snaps away, moving Marcus's body this way and that as if he were a male doll, putting him in comical poses, I think back to when he and I last lay like that together.

It's been at least six weeks since Marcus and I made love. Could that be the reason for him joining dating apps and photographing strangers' body parts? *Am I to blame?* I roll the question around in my brain only to arrive at a firm *no*. Only cheaters are responsible for their actions and behaviour.

Nobody else. For all I know Marcus could be fucking any number of women. This thought makes me gag and I'm reminded of what Abby went through when she found out Josh was sleeping with her sister.

'Just going to upload this one to Facebook. You don't mind, do you, babe?' Gail giggles as her thumbs tear up the phone. Then, 'Babe? BABE.' Her voice suddenly rises, high and wild, as she stares down at Marcus. Whatever she's seen has spooked her. She looks like death warmed up.

'What is it?' I bark, forgetting that Gail can't hear me.

Lurching upright, Gail swivels onto her knees, her mouth dropping open in horror as she gazes down at Marcus.

'Marcus. Marcus. Wake up. Can you hear me?' Gail shakes him, then picks up his lifeless hand only to drop it again. Her wide horrified eyes swing to the camera, her gaze finding mine, as her jaw sets with the gravity of the situation. 'This isn't funny,' she sobs hysterically, her face tightening into a scowl.

My finger lingers on her stricken face. 'Check his breathing,' I urge, but I'm talking to air.

Gail has turned her attention back to Marcus and is angrily pounding his body with a fist. When that doesn't get a response, she slaps his face hard, twice, but he still doesn't stir. Shrugging hard as if unsure what to do next she finally thinks to check out his heartbeat, by pressing her ear to his heart. She stays there for what seems like forever, while I teeter on the edge of terror. When it comes, the long, drawn-out shake of her head causes my hair to stand on end. As Gail curls into a ball on the other side of the bed, away from Marcus, and buries her head in her hands, I snatch a ragged breath of air and zoom in on my husband's face.

Marcus's normally healthy, glowing skin is the colour of ash with a marble-like vein of blue running through it. His eyes, once likened to the shade of the ocean, have shrunken to black pinpricks. And I realise my husband is, once again, dead.

CHAPTER 55

I arrived on the scene just over an hour ago, making sure to cover my tracks by parking Jim's pickup truck a mile from the boat and walking the rest of the way. In those sixty minutes, Gail's emotions have spiralled out of control. This I anticipated. Her mood has gone full circle, from rage to weeping, to hysterical laughter and back to feeling sorry for herself. She's desperate for me to rescue her, and I will, but first I require her to suffer. It's payback time.

'How can you remain calm at a time like this?' Gail screeches, throwing back the last of her whiskey.

'One of us has to,' I point out curtly, helping myself to a tumbler of the Macallan whiskey.

'Oh, my God,' Gail bounces to her feet, limbs jangling as much as her nerves. Mascara streaks her pale face. 'When am I going to wake up and discover this is all a bad dream?'

Knowing that the real nightmare is about to begin, I bite back any reply, but keep a close eye on her as she grabs one of the pug cushions from the sofa and hugs it to her as if it will bring her comfort. It won't. How can it when my husband's dead body is just through there, on the other side of the door? Laid out on the bed as if it were already in the morgue.

'I don't know what to do, Linda. I can't go to prison for this. It isn't my fault.'

It's on the tip of my tongue to remind the bitch that she would have sent me to jail in a heartbeat if it meant getting her dirty paws on Jim, but that had all gone horribly wrong for her too. *When will she ever learn?* Instead, I say, 'You said something interesting to me when Marcus turned up at the registrar's office. Do you remember?'

She shakes her head angrily as if she doesn't have time for reminiscing.

'You said that it would have been better for everyone if Marcus had stayed dead.'

Surprise flashes across Gail's face. 'For fuck's sake, kick a girl when she's down, why don't you? I didn't mean it, obviously.'

'I know you didn't. But that's not what the police will think when they find out he died on your boat.'

'The police?' Gail collapses onto the sofa, dumbstruck. 'Who said anything about the police?' She clutches at her face as if that will help her, as if anything can. Poor Gail.

'We can't put off calling them forever,' I say matter-of-factly.

'Shit, Linda.' Gail's eyes ice over with fear.

I land a reassuring hand on her shoulder. 'And then there are the text messages.'

Her gaze explores my face as if trying to read my mind, a reminder that I need to rein myself in if I don't want her to become suspicious of my intentions. There's no way I'm going down for this. I have two daughters. A life. Gail has no one.

'What messages?' she squirms.

'The ones you sent to my phone saying you wanted to kill Marcus.'

'You kept them?' she snaps in disbelief.

'Of course not,' I lie. 'I deleted them as we agreed but the police will find them anyway. Nothing ever truly disappears, does it?' I add coyly, thinking the same could be applied to husbands. 'They're bound to go to town for a murder investigation.'

'Murder? Gail's jaw drops open. 'But it was an accident.'

'You and I know that, but they won't believe it when they find out you drugged him.'

Gail stares at me. 'You said they were safe. If this is anybody's fault it's yours.' She's unable to conceal her anger now.

I had wondered how long it would be before my best friend turned on me and tried to put the blame on me. Turns out sooner than I thought. I'm tempted to throw back my head and laugh sarcastically, but of course, I don't.

'They usually are safe. I've been taking them for months and they never did me any harm. He must have had an allergic reaction, which we couldn't have anticipated.'

'Well, we should have! And we should never have given them to him in the first place. If you hadn't made me, none of this would have happened and Marcus would still be alive.'

Made her! I decide to let that go too. Now is not the time to pick a fight. 'It doesn't matter now, does it? What's done is done. What's important is that we think on our feet.'

Gail does the opposite and reacts with hysterical tears. 'Are you sure he's definitely dead?' She sniffs pitifully in a childlike voice that's intended to make me want to protect her.

I fold my arms and purse my lips. 'Of course he's fucking dead.'

As soon as I arrived at the boat, bleary-eyed and numb with fear, I'd gone into the bedroom, alone, leaving Gail sobbing in the other room, consoling herself with alcohol. When I bent over Marcus's body, to check for myself that his breathing had stopped, I was terrified he'd lurch upwards lightning-quick to grab me by my throat, accusing me of setting him up. Of being responsible for his death. But rigor mortis of the face had already set in, making it appear as if he were grimacing. There was no way he was going to get up again.

His skin was cold and clammy, and his mouth was propped open with a trail of saliva leaking out of it. Both lips curled downwards as if he were pulling a playful, sad face. But it was the eyes that really got to me. No matter how many times I tell myself Marcus was already dead behind the eyes when he was alive, seeing his unseeing eyes now, hard evidence that he really was dead, I wanted to curl into a ball and weep as Gail had done. But I've grieved for this man twice already, once when he disappeared into the sea and again after he came back when I realised the man I married no longer existed. *How many times can a man die?* Knowing I'll never have to tense at the sound of his cruel, bullying voice again or tolerate his narcissistic rages doesn't however give me the peace I thought it would.

'They'll throw the book at both of us for this, Gail. But you're the one they'll go after for his murder.'

'Why me?' She frowns.

Her whiny, self-serving voice is beginning to chip away at my patience, so I take a deep breath and push my anger down. She couldn't care less that my husband is dead. All she's concerned with is herself and staying out of trouble.

'Because eighty per cent of murder victims are killed by someone they know, usually by the last person they saw. And in this case, that's you.' I reel off a couple of damaging statistics. 'He died on your boat after you lured him here with false promises, drugging him so you could pretend he'd had sex with you. Christ, Gail, you even uploaded pictures of him to Facebook when he was unconscious. He might even have been dead at the time and that's not something the police are going to overlook even if you were to delete the photos. Have you thought about that?'

Looking wild-eyed and shaken, Gail bolts out of the door onto the boat deck, where she can be heard vomiting. She comes back in wiping her mouth with the back of her hand. I notice that her skin is near to the colour of the corpse in the other room. Plonking herself down on the sofa, she beats a fist on the table. 'So, that's me screwed.'

As her gaze warily slides over me, like a prey animal's might, a niggle of guilt sneaks up on me and my expression softens. We're both trapped in a hellhole of our own making.

'There's only one thing we can do.'

'What?' Gail's voice is thick with sarcasm. She's given up already, like the quitter she is.

'Put him back in the water.'

There's nothing to fill the silence between us. Not the sound of our breathing nor the reassuring tick of a clock to remind us that life goes on regardless, for us at least. I swish around the last of my whiskey as I watch Gail's frown deepen.

'You're fucking kidding me, right.'

'Do I look like I'm kidding?' I hiss, not batting an eyelid.

'That's insane. You're insane.' She's on her feet again, stomping up and down the room, running both hands through her hair and down her face.

'Think about it, Gail. Technically, Marcus doesn't exist. He has fake ID which means there's nothing traceable about him. He couldn't get his death certificate reversed because the real Marcus Bouchard died over forty years ago. I can count on one hand the number of people who actually know he came back from the dead. You. Me. Jim. The girls. Josh.'

'You're forgetting the detective who put Jim away and the celebrants at the registry office, and . . .' Gail is hot on my heels.

'If the police or anyone else come looking for him, I'll tell them I caught you and him at it and that he packed his bag afterwards and left.' I interrupt before she can further ruin my plan. 'We have the photos to prove it. We'll say he ran off with a wealthy widow after fucking us both over.'

Gail's shoulders slump into a more relaxed position and she stops gnawing at her lip.

'Only you and I know what really happened. And it can stay that way as far as I'm concerned.' I make it sound like I'm doing her a favour.

'You'd do that for me?' Gail's eyes well up and I have to glance away before I become emotional. Being exhausted doesn't help. I feel as if I'm teetering on the edge of sleep.

'The more I think about it, the more I'm convinced it'll work. After we've,' I pause, not wanting my words to sound as cold and detached as they're going to, 'disposed of the body, we'll get rid of everything else that links Marcus to the boat and you.'

'I don't know what I'd do without you,' Gail envelops me in a fog of body odour and cigarette smoke. I can even detect a faint whiff of Marcus's aftershave on her top which causes my heart to jumpstart.

Shrugging her off, I gesture to the bottle of whiskey on the table. 'I'll take that and the envelope that the pills were in so I can dispose of them.'

'I'd have lost my shit if it weren't for you.' Gail admits, appearing genuinely grateful for once. But then, in an instant, she reverts to her normal inconsiderate, selfish self by saying, 'I'll never be able to sleep in that bed again, let alone have sex in it. Ew. Gross.'

CHAPTER 56

'Lindy. How could you do this to me? Lindy.' His voice, desperate and wild, causes grief to well up inside me like a sudden tide. My chest rises and falls in the darkness as I become aware of his shadow sliding across the room. I want to scream loud enough to burn the back of my throat, yet no sound escapes my mouth. As my eyes suddenly snap open, I realise I'm having another nightmare. These night terrors occur almost every night. I don't think they'll stop while I remain under this roof, or in the bed we once shared.

In my dreams, I'm flailing around in dirty, brown river water searching for Marcus's body. I'm cold and exhausted but I keep moving otherwise I'm in danger of disappearing forever. Gail's boat is nowhere to be seen. I'm alone. I swim to the other side of the river where I pause to rest. As I inhale deep gulps of the wintry night air, I glimpse Marcus's hand pushing up through the water, palm splayed open, fingers clawing. My heart is in my mouth as I watch. *Should I try to rescue someone who can't be saved?* But when I see the glint of gold on his finger, mocking me in the moonlight, something inside me dies. He comes up only once, eyes bulging, wet hair covering one eye, sucking in deep breaths but choking and spluttering on the water at the same time. 'I won't stay dead.

I'll come back for you,' he warns before sinking beneath the water again, his face twisting with rage as if he wants to take me down with him.

Now that I've jolted awake, I notice that the sheets are damp with sweat yet I'm as cold as ice. I've been like this ever since Marcus . . . left. I don't allow myself to use the D word. It's no longer in my vocabulary. For others to believe my story, I've had to recreate the truth in my head. As far as I'm concerned, Marcus is living the good life in sunny Spain with a rich widow, known only as Lilian who wears cold shoulder tops. Abby and Rosie took the news of Marcus's sudden departure from our lives as I'd anticipated they would. They were relieved, although they didn't say so to my face as they wanted to spare my feelings. To them, he was a waste of space, a loser. Abby, I know, couldn't understand what I ever saw in Marcus. I wonder the same thing too at times, but I try not to think badly of him now. He's paid for what he's done and is finally at peace — hopefully. The same can't be said of me because Marcus haunts me still as I knew he would.

Running my hands through my hair, I groan at the tight knots in my shoulders that refuse to unwind. I need a long holiday, to feel the sun on my back, to heal properly. I wonder how Gail's coping. She never was one to keep a secret, but she has no choice. She knows what will happen to her if she so much as breathes a word about what happened on the boat that night.

It's been three months since I spoke to her, and our last conversation wasn't pleasant. She was losing it big time and I had to threaten her to keep silent. I also ended up revealing a couple of secrets I'd have sooner kept to myself. But she kept banging on about going to the police, even after we'd agreed on a plan of action. The body was long gone by that time, weighted down and lying at the bottom of the river, eyes no doubt sucked out by fish.

'If we explain to the police what happened and why we did what we did, I mean about Marcus being a killer and hitting you and keeping you prisoner in your own home, that's bound to go in our favour. Then, when we've helped them find the body, the post-mortem report will reveal we only gave him two mild antidepressants which somehow caused a massive reaction, leading to what we think was a sudden heart attack. I read up on sertraline, and you were right about it being safe for most people to take, but what I did find out is that it's traceable in body fluids long after death. Once they have all the facts, they'll know we're telling the truth.'

'It's you who don't have all the facts, I'm afraid, Gail,' I snapped, annoyed by the investigative work she'd been doing without telling me.

'What do you mean?' I could feel her tense over the phone.

We'd agreed not to meet in person in case we needed to rely on the story of me catching her and Marcus at it. If that were true, it would look highly suspicious if we remained friends.

'Have you ever heard of grey death?'

'Sounds like a heavy metal band.' Gail's ammunition of inappropriate humour is never exhausted.

'It's an illegal, lethal opioid, more potent than heroin, which can cause death within minutes of being taken.' This news is met with a long pause.

'Why are you telling me this?' She asks eventually.

'You're not daft, Gail. Figure it out.'

'Oh, my God. Tell me you didn't. You wouldn't.'

'I didn't. You did.'

'There's no fucking way I would've given them to him if I'd known that.'

'But can you prove you didn't know?'

'I'll tell them it was you.' She pauses, shocked. 'I can't believe you murdered your own husband.'

'Why not? You did before.'

'That was different. Not like now. And you've involved me in it this time.'

'Then, it should come as no surprise to know you're more involved than you think, because I used your name and email address to buy those black-market drugs.'

'You bitch! How could you do that to me? We're meant to be friends.'

'Friends don't go around stealing each other's husbands,' I remind her spikily, 'or trying to get you thrown in prison for something you didn't do.'

'You do realise I could go to prison for life for what you've done?' Gail is beside herself now, intermittently sobbing and shouting. I know if she could climb down the phone, she'd beat me black and blue and pull all my hair out. I wouldn't blame her.

'As I said, Gail, friends don't try to get each other thrown into jail. You should be thanking me for saving your arse, so you don't end up doing time.'

'You used me. Lied to me all along. You didn't even want to be friends again, did you?'

'I'm pleased the penny has finally dropped.' I was enjoying myself too much, but it had been a long time coming, so I forgave myself for the indulgence.

'And to think I felt sorry for you, Linda. But no amount of abuse you suffered at Marcus's hands can justify what you've done. It makes you as bad as him. Worse.'

When I don't reply immediately, she catches on quickly. 'Or was that a lie as well about him hitting you? Please tell me you didn't make that up.'

'Have a nice life, Gail, and try to stay out of prison,' I'd said, hanging up the phone.

One thing I didn't let on to Gail was *how* the real Marcus Bouchard had died. Ever since Marcus had described to me what he'd done, it has haunted me. As a mother, I'm appalled by it. Without that knowledge, I may never have gone through with my plan to kill my husband, who was a monster.

But the more Mrs Bouchard's suffering played on my mind, my desire to punish Marcus grew stronger. It pained me to think of the long empty years she had spent without her only child. If anybody had taken one of my children's lives in such a brutal way, I'd want them dead too. That secret will have to accompany me to the grave because I can't let the poor woman find out Tony Fortin had held her son's head under water until he stopped crying, shouting, pleading, choking and his limbs eventually stopped flailing. He was only eighteen and had his whole life ahead of him. A bright future. He could have been a doctor, a pilot, a solicitor, led a charmed life blessed with children and grandchildren, and Tony stole that from him out of nothing more than jealousy.

Stealing his best friend's identity wasn't enough for my husband though. He wanted to *be* him. Anything was better than being Tony Fortin who grew up in poverty. With his history of emotional abuse and childhood trauma, it's no wonder he developed a personality disorder he'd never be able to fix. If anything, I felt I'd done him a favour by putting him out of his misery. I couldn't allow him to ruin any more lives. Mine included.

CHAPTER 57

Tipping my head back, I use the palm of my hand to shield my eyes from the sun so I can follow the path of the jet as it heads for the clouds, leaving a plume of white behind it. I picture the passengers on board: excited about where they're heading, tucking into bland-tasting food, and knocking back warm alcoholic drinks while others watch movie after movie, hating the idea of returning home. I imagine there are also one or two anxiety-ridden passengers on board who'll catastrophise about the plane crashing out of the sky.

I was one of those nervous flyers once, but having faced the worst possible thing that could happen and lived to survive it, I've nothing left to fear. Now that I'm into my sixtieth year, I've finally become self-reliant and I've even found a true best friend, one who will never let me down — *me*. I have this woman's back and will see she lives her best life always. Not a single second of my life is to be wasted again. The journey I've been on has taught me that I'm stronger and more resilient than I ever imagined and super excited about what the future holds because I know whatever life throws at me, I can handle it.

I've also learned, the hard way, that life as a mature, single woman two years on doesn't have an expiry date.

More people than ever want to talk to me these days. It's the chilled-out vibe I give off. As for men, well what can I say, other than I could go on a date every night of the week if I wanted to? I don't, by the way. And I know that might sound boastful but it's the plain truth. My daughters would be horrified if they found out I'd taken half a dozen hot lovers to bed over the last eighteen months. Younger men mostly, by quite a number of years. They're unlike their older rivals; eager to please rather than be pleased. And fun, too.

These modern young men find all kinds of women attractive, not just young, slim, beautiful ones. For them, it's all about the experience. I'm sure most people would think I should be ashamed of myself, at my age, taking advantage of boys young enough to be my sons, but I'm not. Nobody cares when it's the other way around. You see older men with young girls all the time. Besides, it's them who do the chasing. I like that there's no danger of my falling in love with a twenty-five-year-old no matter how cute he might be. They're not shy about propositioning you either. It happens often. Honestly, I think most middle-aged married-for-donkey's-years women would be shocked but delighted to find this out.

Most mature couples I come across feel sorry for me at first travelling alone as an older, single woman, but I sense that the wives come to secretly envy me. I can tell when they're glancing at their inattentive, loose-bellied, grey-haired *better halves,* they wish they could follow in my footsteps. This makes me smile inwardly and hope for their sakes that they one day can also enjoy some fun and freedom. We mothers and wives find it difficult to put ourselves first but only by doing so do we get to live the life that all women deserve. That doesn't make me a man-hater. Far from it. I enjoy spending time with gentlemen my age, for the interesting conversations though, not for sex.

I've taken to lugging my laptop around with me wherever I go and that's proven to be something of a conversation starter. People are curious and want to know if I'm writing a novel, but the truth is not as exciting. I'm studying for an online law degree. I don't know where it will take me, nowhere probably, but it's more about proving to myself that I can learn new things at any age. My first-class level marks so far prove it. This thirst for adventure continues to grow inside me too, meaning I hardly recognise myself. I've accomplished things I never thought I was capable of, such as diving off a cliff, learning how to surf, climbing a mountain at sunrise, and having Abby's and Rosie's names tattooed across my shoulders. No longer limiting myself has given me the freedom I've always craved.

Before settling in Sri Lanka, I visited other countries including Vietnam, India, Egypt, and Thailand, avoiding anywhere I'd been with Marcus. Especially Corfu! It's so much easier to travel when you have money. You see the world differently. Luckily, I have lots of it thanks to good, old, reliable Jim. When I told him that Marcus had done a runner with his life savings, leaving me on my own again, Jim insisted I keep half of the cash from the sale of the house that had originally been intended for Marcus. Selling the family home hadn't hurt anywhere near as much as I thought it would. It didn't seem to affect the girls that much either. When you consider all that had gone wrong for us under its roof, it felt right to say goodbye.

When I told Jim that Marcus had stolen all his life savings that wasn't strictly true. But nor was anything else. Marcus had taken some of the money, but not all. Knowing I'd need funds if I were to go travelling again, I was inventive with the truth. It was no use to Jim in jail and the girls would each inherit a generous amount from their shared half of the house sale, so I ended up pocketing the remaining thirty thousand in cash. Together with my half of the house sale, I'm a quarter of a million pounds richer than I've ever been. I don't intend to spend it all as I'm determined to keep some back for when Jim gets out of prison. I know he says he doesn't want or need anything, but fair's fair. He owed me and now I owe him. That makes us equal.

Having decided to remain in Sri Lanka until my visa runs out, I've rented a treehouse on Ahungalla beach in the southern province, close to Galle where the Boxing Day tsunami of 2004 struck, killing thousands of people, and demolishing many homes. When I drive into the village in my rented tuk-tuk I come across sad gaps in the neighbourhood, which appear like missing teeth where those houses once stood. Despite the obvious poverty, the island people welcome tourists. The locals on my stretch of the beach go out of their way to include me, especially the younger generation, who all speak English. I'm on first-name terms with most of them yet they insist on greeting me as Mrs Linda even though I tell them it's just Linda.

The treehouse floods when it rains so there are rusty, metal buckets in the raised living and bedroom areas to catch the water. It might be small, but I don't complain because I'm living in luxury compared to most Sri Lankans. The Airbnb owner described it as a jungle boutique residence one moment, an ocean treehouse the next, and then, to appeal to my English origins, a colonial-style villa. I knew I'd take it as soon as I saw it, despite being overcharged thousands of rupees for it.

My new home comes with a small private cove where I swim every day. Unlike the angry ocean surrounding it, where only the strongest, bravest local boys swim, the water there is calm. My favourite feature of all though about my rental is the hanging bed made of thick rope, which is suspended over palm trees and sand and has a glorious view of the Indian Ocean. Here I read books and self-reflect.

I've also inherited a large tropical garden but thankfully this is tended by my landlord's son. We have a deal where we share whatever is grown. I cook my vegetable curries and coconut rice on an open wood fire in the outdoor cooking area and eat with my fingers, the same as everyone else. Thanks to the locals, who've taught me how to cook their native dishes, I've adopted a much stronger palate which means I can stomach spicier food. My westernised tastes are gone for good.

I've come to love these Sinhala people and their way of life. Every day I thank my lucky stars that I'm accepted and no longer considered an oddity among them. Living in a Buddhist community, I've learned more about the religion, and receive blessings in the temple alongside my neighbours. It's one of the few places in the world where you're not judged by your race, religion, or wealth. Family and friendship are what count here.

This reminds me that Abby is flying out in just over a week and is intending to stay a whole month. I'm not sure what she'll think of the tree house and the way I exist, barefoot in the sand with my long, sun-bleached, wavy hair hanging down my back, but I hope she embraces life here as I have done. Like mother, like daughter is bound to take effect one day. There's nothing I'd like more than to laugh and joke with my serious girl whose sense of humour is yet to return. Poor, darling Abby. I love her so much, but I know better than anyone that I can't fix her. She must do the work herself and for that to happen she'll need to forgive her sister and Josh. Otherwise, she'll never move on.

Conveniently, I don't ask myself if I've forgiven the ones who've hurt me the most. As for forgiving myself, I've come to accept that this is simply not possible. How can you be forgiven for murder? Cold-blooded, premeditated murder at that! Add to that all the lies I've told and the money I've stolen from loved ones and it's obvious I'm destined for hell. Until then, I intend to love myself anyway. I'm proud of who I am, not of what I've done.

I'm a strong woman, who was vastly underestimated by those who believed me weak. That makes me a survivor. As Jim would say, I'd do anything for my family, and there was no way I was going to let Marcus spoil things by taking the girls' inheritance or isolating me from them, as was his intention, of which I'm convinced he would have succeeded in the end by wearing me down. The way I see it, Tony Fortin was lucky to be given a second chance after the attempt on his life, and what he did to his friend, but what did he do with it? Nothing except abuse others. How many chances does a man deserve?

I'm living my best life as a result of the choices I made. Nothing was left to chance. That puts me in charge of my own destiny. Being in Sri Lanka feels like coming home. I'd go as far as to say I love this country more than I ever loved Marcus, even during those passionate honeymoon days when I quite literally would have done anything for him. But, as I've told myself countless times, love is not always enough. That's not to say I've given up on the idea of finding true love again, because as luck would have it, I have met someone who I think really could be *the one* this time, but he's not how you might imagine him to be.

We met six weeks ago at a fish market in Negombo. Our first encounter was not a particularly touching or romantic one because the place stunk to high heaven and the floor was covered in blood and fishbones. Over the hustle and bustle, our eyes met at first light, when the sky was still tinged with violet and the night not yet a memory. It was love at first sight for both of us. We've been inseparable ever since, joined at the hip. He doesn't care about my wrinkly skin, loose upper arms and crepey thighs. To him, I am flawless.

Here he is now, coming to find me, as he so often does, but not in an intrusive, controlling way. He worries about me, that's all, and the feeling is mutual. I'd hate for anything bad to happen to him. He is my world, and I am his. As I watch him walk towards me, his gaze rests adoringly on me, convincing me once again that there's no danger of him straying or abandoning me. Although I've been fooled before, I passionately believe he's incapable of hurting me. He doesn't have mood swings, nor yet grow angry with me. Rather, he would die protecting me if he had to. There's nothing he wouldn't do for me. One thing I know for certain is that we won't be separated. When I return to England, he's coming with me.

The most noticeable thing about him is the missing left eye and the butchered skin around it. I could have done a better job of the stitching myself, but when I tell him this, he simply wags his tail. This too is broken and bent, causing it to curl in places where it shouldn't, making him easy to pick out among the millions of other stray dogs that live on the island. These semi-wild canines are called Sinhala hounds, landrace dogs known for their friendly temperament. You can't help but bump into them at every street corner. When this one took to following me around, even accompanying me in my tuk-tuk, I took him to the local vet for a check-up who assured me that apart from the obvious signs he'd been hit by a car, he was in reasonably good health. Luckily, he didn't show any sign of the mange that a sizeable proportion of the stray dogs here suffer from. I'm told he's only around two years old so he could live for another fifteen years.

His coat is the colour of orange sand, with a darker muzzle and white socks, which remind me of Jim who always insisted on wearing socks with everything, even sandals. At three feet tall, he's bigger than most of his kind and his large, erect ears make him appear dingo-like, causing locals to keep their distance. But, though he sometimes bares his incredibly long canines at strangers, he's never once shown them to me.

'Come on, Match,' I put my thumb and forefinger to my mouth and whistle loudly, a new skill I've learned, thanks to an Australian guy with a surfer's body, straw-like hair, and an insatiable sexual appetite. I smile whenever I think of him, yet I can't recall his name.

Falling into position by my right hip, like a keen foot soldier, Match doesn't let me out of his sight for long if he can help it. In companiable silence, we stroll along the beach heading towards home. Match sniffs seaweed and shells, while paddling in and out of the seashore, but I keep to the sand even though I no longer think of Marcus every time I catch sight of water. The white belly of the jet is long gone, and the sky is as blue as the sapphires Sri Lanka is famous for mining, including the iconic gemstone Lady Diana wore on her engagement finger. Hot white sand collects in my toes and the air tastes of coconut. These are the sights; smells and sounds I've come to associate with my new home.

Along the way, we come across the tenacious fisherman who peddles boat trips to tourists, who in turn do their best to avoid him, and he throws me a friendly high five. He once told me that he is from one of the lowest castes in Sri Lanka, known as the Sinhalese Bathgama, but I consider it an honour to know him. Match though, refuses to have anything to do with him, but when we come across the lady who sells saris to hotel guests, he licks her hand in greeting. Kishini spends all day on the beach selling her wares. She isn't allowed to enter the hotel grounds but gestures to the rich women to come onto the beach to buy from her. It's demanding work as the temperature is rarely lower than thirty degrees all year round.

When Match's ears prick and he emits a low growl, I glance ahead to see what's caught his attention. When I realise it's a pack of stray dogs playing in the sand, my heart doesn't go into a panic, because I know Match will never leave my side, no matter the temptation. He's going nowhere. How do I know this? Because out of all the millions of creatures on this island, natives, and tourists among them, he chose me. I'm his perfect match.

THE END

ACKNOWLEDGEMENTS

Her Second Husband was written during a difficult time of my life when I was going through a painful divorce. I couldn't have known when I started writing it that my sixteen-year marriage to *my second husband* would end abruptly before I made it to Chapter Three, leaving me to finish a book about a woman losing her husband when I was going through a similar experience, although in my case my husband didn't die, but ran off to start a new life in a new town with guess what, a new woman. Imagine the fun I had with the disloyal husband in my story after that!

A big shout out must go to my amazing family who wrapped their arms around me and made me believe in myself again. I cannot thank them enough for helping me through those first dark months of separation. Special mention goes to my sister Karen, big brother John and my two beautiful daughters, Natasha, and Siobhan, who have finally got their real mum back. The lesson I've learned from this episode is to cherish those who love you and who want to be in your life and to not waste time on those who don't.

I also want to say a massive thank you to everyone at Joffe Books for all their hard work in getting this story ready for publication. They have been an absolute pleasure to work with and I'm both proud and pleased that they took home the prize of Trade Publisher of the Year in 2023. A well-deserved win. Special thanks go to Kate Lyall Grant, Joffe's publishing director, who described my protagonist, Linda, as disarmingly frank, funny, and forthright — a beacon of hope for independent minded, spirited fifty something women everywhere. I've loved working with Kate. I also want to thank editor, Alice Latchford, for her assistance in bringing this narrative to life and ironing out any inconsistencies, and proofreader, Becky Wyde, as well as everybody else involved, from jacket design through to marketing. Go Team Joffe.

One of the first countries I visited as a divorced woman was Sri Lanka, in South Asia. I chose it because I wanted to experience a real adventure. My time spent exploring the island, known as the pearl of the Indian ocean, proved life changing. Not only did I overcome my fear of flying, during the extremely turbulent long-haul flights there and back but, with the help of my guide Priyantha Thennakoon, I travelled from one end of the island to another, exploring the poorest and richest regions, visiting city, mountain, jungle, and beach locations, as well as the working tea plantations where I grew enamoured by the native population. Never have I felt so at home, away from home. The people are the most peaceful and spiritual in the world and I came to embrace their strong Buddhist and Hindu cultures.

As a result, I'm delighted to announce that *Her Second Husband* ends its days in the country I fell in love with, not least because I'm a dog lover and discovered Sri Lanka has millions of stray dogs to its name. These semi-wild canines are called Sinhala hounds, a landrace dog known for its friendly temperament. You can't help but bump into them everywhere.

Readers who are familiar with my work will know that this novel is a bit of a genre sidestep for me as it has evolved into more of a domestic, contemporary psychological thriller without the usual hint of supernatural thrown in. This wasn't intentional but the story really pulled me in from the beginning and, as it never hurts to try something new, I hope you enjoy it. As a writer, I don't always have a say in what my heart insists I focus on.

Once again, I've used my hometown of Stamford in Lincolnshire in the UK as a backdrop for this story as I've fallen in love with the place and can't imagine living anywhere else, except perhaps for the green valleys of Wales, where my late, lovely mum, Valerie James, was born and where I spent my childhood summers. Or, indeed, Sri Lanka.

If you are not from the UK, please excuse the English spelling. Oopsy daisy, it's just the way we do things across the pond. Apologies also for any swearing but this is down to the characters (Gail mostly) and nothing to do with me. Lol. The same goes for any blaspheming.

Now for the best bit where I get to thank my lovely readers for all their support, especially my ARC reading group. You know who you are!

Your loyalty and friendship mean everything. As do your reviews.

THE JOFFE BOOKS STORY

We began in 2014 when Jasper agreed to publish his mum's much-rejected romance novel and it became a bestseller.

Since then we've grown into the largest independent publisher in the UK. We're extremely proud to publish some of the very best writers in the world, including Joy Ellis, Faith Martin, Caro Ramsay, Helen Forrester, Simon Brett and Robert Goddard. Everyone at Joffe Books loves reading and we never forget that it all begins with the magic of an author telling a story.

We are proud to publish talented first-time authors, as well as established writers whose books we love introducing to a new generation of readers.

We have been shortlisted for Independent Publisher of the Year at the British Book Awards three times, in 2020, 2021 and 2022, and for the Diversity and Inclusivity Award at the Independent Publishing Awards in 2022.

We built this company with your help, and we love to hear from you, so please email us about absolutely anything bookish at feedback@joffebooks.com.

If you want to receive free books every Friday and hear about all our new releases, join our mailing list: www.joffebooks.com/contact.

And when you tell your friends about us, just remember: it's pronounced Joffe as in coffee or toffee!